King, Ship, and Sword

King, Ship, and Sword

An Alan Lewrie Naval Adventure

Dewey Lambdin

THOMAS DUNNE BOOKS

ST. MARTIN'S PRESS

NEW YORK

THOMAS DUNNE BOOKS.
An imprint of St. Martin's Press.

KING, SHIP, AND SWORD. Copyright © 2010 by Dewey Lambdin. All rights reserved. Printed in the United States of America. For information, address St. Martin's Press, 175 Fifth Avenue, New York, N.Y. 10010.

www.thomasdunnebooks.com
www.stmartins.com

Maps copyright © 2009 by Carolyn Chu

LIBRARY OF CONGRESS CATALOGING-IN-PUBLICATION DATA

Lambdin, Dewey.
  King, ship, and sword : an Alan Lewrie naval adventure / Dewey Lambdin.—1st ed.
    p. cm.
  ISBN 978-0-312-55184-1
  1. Lewrie, Alan (Fictitious character)—Fiction. 2. Ship captains—Fiction. 3. Great Britain—History, Naval—18th century—Fiction. 4. France—History, Naval—18th century— Fiction. 5. Naval battles—History—18th century—Fiction. I. Title.
  PS3562.A435K47 2010
  813'.54—dc22

                                                    2009040285

First Edition: March 2010

10   9   8   7   6   5   4   3   2   1

To

"The Immortal Memory"

Full-Rigged Ship: Starboard (right) side view

1. Mizen Topgallant
2. Mizen Topsail
3. Spanker
4. Main Royal
5. Main Topgallant
6. Mizen T'gallant Staysail
7. Main Topsail
8. Main Course
9. Main T'gallant Staysail
10. Middle Staysail

11. Main Topmast Staysail
12. Fore Royal
13. Fore Topgallant
14. Fore Topsail
15. Fore Course
16. Fore Topmast Staysail
17. Inner Jib
18. Outer Flying Jib
19. Spritsail

A. Taffrail & Lanterns
B. Stern & Quarter-galleries
C. Poop Deck/Great Cabins Under
D. Rudder & Transom Post
E. Quarterdeck
F. Mizen Chains & Stays
G. Main Chains & Stays
H. Boarding Battens/Entry Port
I. Cargo Loading Skids
J. Shrouds & Ratlines
K. Fore Chains & Stays

L. Waist
M. Gripe & Cutwater
N. Figurehead & Beakhead Rails
O. Bow Sprit
P. Jib Boom
Q. Foc's'le & Anchor Cat-heads
R. Cro'jack Yard (no sail fitted)
S. Top Platforms
T. Cross-Trees
U. Spanker Gaff

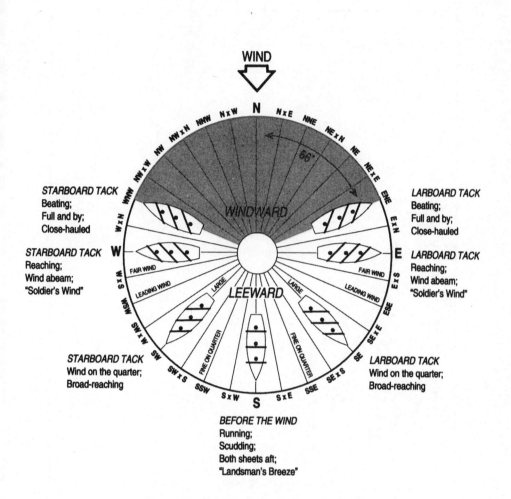

POINTS OF SAIL AND 32-POINT WIND-ROSE

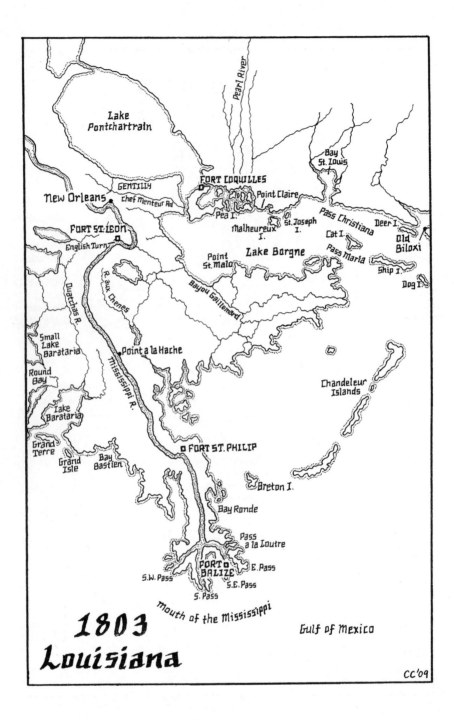

1803
Louisiana

Mouth of the Mississippi

Gulf of Mexico

CC'09

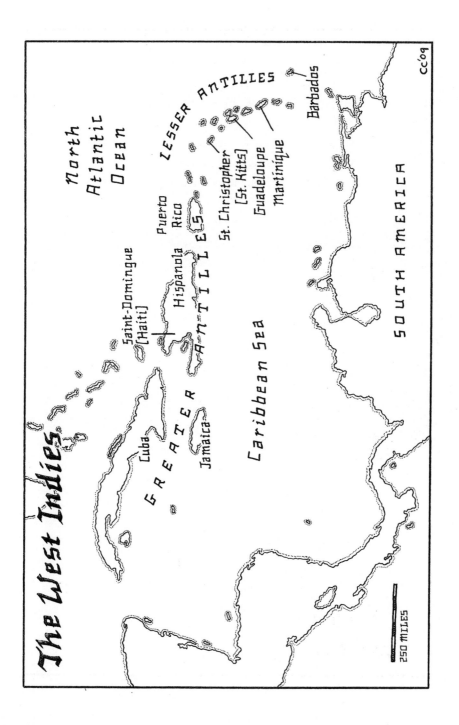

The West Indies

North Atlantic Ocean

LESSER ANTILLES

Barbados

St. Christopher [St. Kitts]
Guadeloupe
Martinique

Puerto Rico

Saint-Domingue [Haiti]

Hispaniola

GREATER ANTILLES

Cuba

Jamaica

Caribbean Sea

SOUTH AMERICA

CC'09

250 MILES

Therefore I cast mee by a little writing
To shewe at eye this conclusion,
For conscience and for mine acquiting
Against God and ageyne abusion,
And Cowardise, and to our enimies confusion.

For foure things our Noble sheweth to mee,
King, Ship, and Swerd, and power of the Sea.

HAKLUYT'S VOYAGES

PROLOGUE

At nobis, Pax alma, veni spicamque teneto,
profluat et pomis candidus ante sinus.

Then come to us, gracious Peace; grasp the
cornspike in thy hand, and from the bosom of thy
white robe let fruits pour out before thee.

TIBULLUS, AGAINST WAR,
BOOK I, X 67-68

CHAPTER ONE

*H*MS *Thermopylae,* a 38-gun Fifth Rate frigate, prowled slowly off the Texel to keep a wary eye on the Dutch coast . . . for several years a conquered "allied" power under French control, now named the Batavian Republic. It was a sullen endeavour for *Thermopylae*'s people, for the Dutch had not much of a fleet left since the Battle of Camperdown, four years before, in 1797, when Adm. Duncan had caught them, headed for the English Channel to combine with their French masters' fleet for an invasion of Great Britain, had forced them to run for home close inshore of their own coast, where Duncan had given them the choice of wrecking on their own shoals or fighting, and had taken, sunk, or burned almost all of them. By now, the few surviving Batavian warships were slowly rotting away at their moorings, their new construction rotting on the stocks, and all their vaunting plans for a larger fleet scrapped.

Sullen, too, was the general attitude aboard *Thermopylae* after months of dull blockade duty, for it could not hold a candle to the heady and daring adventures of the first of the year of 1801. As the League of Armed Neutrality had readied their navies to confront the Royal Navy, it had been *Thermopylae* that had been ordered into the Baltic—alone!—to "smoak out" the types and numbers of ships being prepared in Danish, Swedish, and Russian harbours, to determine the thickness of the ice that kept all Baltic navies penned in port, and to ascertain how long it would be before the ice would melt and free them.

Oh, there'd also been the delivery of a pair of Russian nobles to somewhere as close as possible to St. Petersburg . . . one of whom had tried to kill their new captain as they were being set ashore, an attempted murder right by the entry-port . . . all over a London whore, of all things! . . . And for certain the younger Roosky was love-sick mad, but what could be expected of *foreigners*, and wasn't their new captain a scrapper, though!

Out of the Baltic at last, and there'd been their own British Expeditionary squadrons under Vice-Admiral Sir Hyde Parker, and Vice-Admiral Horatio Nelson, and they'd been just in time to take part in the glorious Battle of Copenhagen and squash the Danes like so many roaches round the galley butter tubs!

All downhill from there, though; first cruising in the Baltic 'til midsummer, watching first Vice-Admiral Parker go home (in a bit of disgrace, the hands had heard-tell) then Nelson departing for his always fragile health, and, at last, a spell of re-victualling and repairs at Great Yarmouth, where the adventures had begun, and a spell of shore liberty. After that, *Thermopylae* had been seconded to the small North Sea Fleet to serve as a scout, doing much of a boresome much as they did this morning . . . making her presence known under reduced sail about two leagues seaward of the shoals, and counting windmills, for all the good that *Thermopylae*'s "people" knew.

In a thin and fine mist on this particular morning, a cold early-October rain was falling and dripping in great dollops from sails and rigging, over a grey and dingy-white-foamed sea that chopped and hissed and imparted to the frigate a slow and queasy wallowing roll. And the wind . . . if freed, *Thermopylae* could cup that wind and rush like a Cambridge coach, nigh on eleven knots or better . . . yet that wind was wasted on her twice-reefed or gathered sails. And it was a *nippy* wind, to boot, a raw'un out of the Nor'west, fresh from Arctic ice sheets that made nettled tars wish for their Franklin-pattern stoves to be set up on the gun-deck once again, blow warm breaths into cupped fists, and shiver under their tarred tarpaulins.

HMS *Thermopylae*'s Second Officer, Lt. James Fox, let out a pleased sigh as a ship's boy turned the half-hour glass, then slowly struck Eight Bells up by the forecastle. His watch was done, and hot tea or coffee awaited him in the gun-room below, along with his breakfast. Lt. Fox clapped gloved hands together in joy as his replacement, his old chum Lt. Dick

Farley, stepped from the lee side of the quarterdeck to amidships before the double-helm drum and the binnacle cabinet to assume command of the Forenoon Watch.

"A thouroughly miserable day, and I wish ye joy of it, Dick," Lt. Fox said with a grin and a roll of his eyes.

"Worse things happen at sea, Jemmy," Lt. Farley replied as he formally doffed his hat, a second-best and much-battered old thing with its gilt lace gone verdigris green. Fox's wasn't a whit better.

"Just thinking that, in point of fact," Lt. Fox quipped. "So, the usual . . . wind's still Nor'westerly, we're beam-reaching, as anyone can clearly *see*, course Nor'East, half East, and making six *agonisingly* slow knots. What's for breakfast?"

"Scrambled eggs, cheese, and biscuit, speaking of *usual*," Lt. Farley replied. "Has the captain determined whether we'll exercise at the great-guns this morning?"

"Hasn't said yet," Lt. Fox replied, letting a yawn escape him. "Damme, I was hoping for hot porridge. Do we drill on the artillery, I'd prefer a steadier point of sail."

"Aye, this roll'd be a bugger," Lt. Farley agreed.

"Well, I leave you to it, Dick," Fox said, cheering up.

"I relieve you, sir," Lt. Farley said with another doff of his hat, and the Second Officer, along with his Midshipmen of the Watch, and the Starboard Watch of the quarterdeck and Afterguard, were scrambling below, some to their breakfasts, some to the uncertain warmth of the gun-deck.

Right aft, and just below the quarterdeck in the great-cabins, Captain Alan Lewrie was shaving . . . or trying to. It was not a chore comfortably, or safely, done in such a wallowing, rolling sea-way, in the small mirror of his wash-hand stand with a straight razor. Lewrie had to brace himself like a runner frozen in mid-stride, his left leg behind him and his right in front, balancing from one to the other as *Thermopylae* heaved from beam to beam like a metronome, about fifteen degrees or better to each roll. He could have sat himself down in a chair, but would be without the mirror, or the small enamelled basin that held his single pint of water ration for washing daily.

"Get out of it, ye bloody little. . . !" Lewrie snapped as Chalky, the younger and spryer of his cats, leaped atop the wash-hand stand for the *third* time, fascinated in equal measure by the lapping water in the basin and his reflection in the mirror. "Shoo! Scat! Pettus!"

"Sir?" his cabin steward replied, carefully hiding his smile.

"Isn't there some amusement ye could offer him?" Lewrie griped.

"I'll take him, sir," Pettus offered, coming to scoop up the white and grey-splotched cat and bear him away, spraddled atop his forearm. An instant later, and it was Toulon, the bigger and older (and clumsier) black-and-white tom that wished to see what had taken Chalky's attention, but *his* leap was just a tad off (blame it on the roll) and he went tumbling back to the deck, with the hand towel in his paws. *Mrrf!* he carped, tail bottled up in disgrace. Then *Marr!* as he looked up plaintively at Lewrie, as if to ask if he'd seen that flub.

"I still love ye t'death, Toulon," Lewrie commiserated, bending down to retrieve the hand towel and give the embarrassed cat a "wubbie" or two. He had to grin, for there had been scraped-off shaving soap on the towel, and Toulon had gotten some of it on his whiskers, which made him go slightly cross-eyed trying to see it and swipe it off, sitting up rabbit-fashion and whacking away with both paws.

Thermopylae rose up to a rare scending wave and heaved another slow roll to starboard, timbers, masts, and windward stays groaning in concert, and Lewrie half-staggered almost to amidships before catching himself. "Mine arse on a band-box!" he hissed under his breath, using one of his favourite expressions. That stagger involved some complicated foot stamp-ing, which only drove the cat under the starboard-side settee, into relative darkness where Toulon could blink in shame and in umbrage, consulting his cat gods.

The larboard roll took Lewrie back to the wash-hand stand, where he took a firm grip with one hand and braced himself for another stab at shaving.

"Um . . . might you need me to do it for you, sir?" Pettus asked.

"No no, Pettus!" Lewrie countered with a false grin on his phyz, "Done for meself for years, in worse weather than this. Dined *out* on my dexterity!"

"If you say so, sir," Pettus replied with a dubious expression.

Once he'd scraped his whiskers as close as he dared, without cutting his own throat, Lewrie swabbed his face, tied his neck-stock, and donned his uniform coat. He made a careful way forrud to the dining-coach and his table, and his breakfast.

It was a Banyan Day, without any salt-meat issue, and after a miserable two months on blockade, a paltry and dull breakfast it was. There was oatmeal porridge, boiled up in water, not milk, and livened with a daub of rancid butter and a largish dollop of strawberry preserves. There was a slab of cheese from his own stores, not that crumbling, dry-as-sawdust Navy issue so beloved of the Victualling Board, but even that was beginning to go over, though showed no signs of red worms yet. And there was ship's biscuit. Lewrie had purchased extra-fine for himself, but it was tough going, even after being soaked in water for the better part of an hour before being served, and, did he wish to keep his remaining teeth, he'd chew it *hellish*-careful. There was coffee, at least, with sugar grated off a cone from his locking caddy, and sweet goat's milk from the nanny up forrud in the manger.

Lewrie turned his eyes towards the cats' dish at the far end of his table, where a reassured Toulon and a cocky Chalky were having their own porridge, laced with cut-up sausages and jerkied beef, and felt a trifle envious!

With his second piping-hot cup of coffee, Lewrie considered one more biscuit, and peered into the bread barge . . . just in time to see the weevils crawling out of the last piece. *No thankee!* he thought.

"I'll be on deck, Pettus," Lewrie said, shoving back from his plate and rising. "Shove me into my boat-cloak, and I'm off."

"Captain's on deck!" Midshipman Tillyard announced to one and all as Lewrie trotted up the larboard gangway ladder from the waist. "Morning, sir," Tillyard added, with a hand to his hat.

"And a dull'un, Mister Tillyard," Lewrie replied, his own right hand touching the front of his cocked hat. "Good morning to you, Mister Farley. Anything of interest to report?"

"Good morning, Captain. No, nothing of interest so far, sorry to say," the First Officer told him. Lewrie began to pace the windward side of the quarterdeck, with Farley in-board of him. "The mast-head lookouts have reported seeing some of those canal barges under sail behind the dikes, every now and then, but I can't imagine a way to get at them, not through those shoals, yonder."

"Seemed an organised sort o' thing?" Lewrie asked. "Or merely a civilian barge or two?"

"We've gathered they're singletons, sir, swanning along slowly in both directions," Lt. Farley said in answer as they reached the flag lockers and taffrail lanthorns right aft, forcing them both to turn inwards and reverse their course. "One or two with washing strung up, and women aboard, and not more than two of those could be described as being close together."

"Dull as Dutchmen," Lewrie decided aloud, with a sigh.

"Unfortunately, sir," Lt. Farley agreed.

"Dead-boresome," Lewrie said further.

"Indeed, sir," Farley said with a nod.

"*I'm* so bored," Lewrie admitted. "A *cutter* could perform this duty better. A frigate's *wasted* on close blockade."

"I fear we all are, sir. Bored, that is," Farley told him. "Ah, about drill on the great-guns, sir . . ."

"Not with this bloody rolling, Mister Farley. Not today. We'd be safer at pike and cutlass work. And musketry, aye!" Lewrie said in suddenly brighter takings. "One hour o' cut an' thrust, then an hour o' musketry at a towed keg."

"Very good, sir," Lt. Farley said with a relieved grin.

"*Deck*, there!" a lookout on the main-mast cross-trees shouted down. "Cutter off th' larboard quarter, hull up, an' makin' signal!"

No more'n eight or nine miles off, Lewrie decided to himself as he turned to peer to windward. Even from the deck, he could faintly make out a dingy white triangle of sail—a set of triangular jibs and a gaff-rigged fore-and-aft mains'l barely peeking from behind the jibs—with a tiny splotch of colour at her mast-head that presumably was a national ensign. Perhaps the lookout had better eyes to espy the even tinier signal hoist from so far away.

"Aloft with you, Mister Pannabaker," Lt. Farley ordered one of the younger Midshipmen of the Forenoon Watch, "and mind you don't drop the glass."

"Aye, sir!" young Pannabaker, *Thermopylae's* cockiest "younker," piped up in reply, scrambling for a long telescope, then hopping atop the weather bulwarks for the mizer-mast shrouds. Quick as a cat, and as agile as an ape, he was at the mizen top, then to its cross-trees in a dozen eye-blinks.

"Come to spell us, one'd hope," Lewrie said with a yawn, rocking impatiently on the balls of his booted feet.

"She's the *Osprey,* sir!" Pannabaker shouted down in his thin and high voice. "This month's private signal, and 'Have Despatches,' sir!"

"Mister Tillyard, do you hoist 'Acknowledged' to *Osprey,* and I s'pose we'll just loaf along . . . as we're already doing . . .'til she's close aboard."

"Aye aye, sir."

"Hmm, sir," Lt. Farley commented, drawing Lewrie's attention to his First Lieutenant, whose face bore a pensive, wolfish grin. It was not the done thing to speculate, but . . .

"I'd not get my hopes up, Mister Farley," Lewrie had to say to him. "The Baltic powers've had quite enough of us. . . . The Dutch can't put a rowing boat regatta to sea . . . and, are the French out, I doubt they've business in the North Sea. One'd *wish,* but . . . ," he concluded with a shrug.

"They also serve, who only stand and wait, I suppose, sir," Lt. Farley replied, seeming to slump into his tarpaulin coat.

"Indeed," Lewrie said with a very bored grimace.

CHAPTER TWO

*H*MS *Osprey* was a saucy-looking little thing, a single-masted cutter that could spread a lone tops'l yard above her gaff mainsail if the wind was right. By the number of her closed gun-ports, she mounted no more than eight 4-pounders and was a Lieutenant's command. She might have been bright-painted, tarred, and oiled at one time, but one year in the sometimes boisterous North Sea had taken the shine off her. Now, she was a dowdy scow, and even her sails had gone old-parchment brown. She drew alongside of *Thermopylae* about a cable to windward and sent her jolly-boat over with her despatches, under the command of one of her Midshipmen, and a boat crew of five.

"I will come to your larboard entry-port, sir!" the Midshipman shouted to the quarterdeck, sporting a cheeky, wind-reddened grin on his face. "No need for ceremony for the likes of me!"

Usually, officers—even the lowest sort of petty officers as Midshipmen— were greeted at the starboard entry-port, the port of honour, welcomed with a side-party and bosuns' calls. In this case, though, as soon as the oarsmen in the jolly-boat had hoisted up their dripping oars, and the bow man had hooked onto the main-chains with a gaff pole, the Midshipman was scrambling up the boarding-battens to the temporarily opened port in the larboard bulkwarks, and stayed just long enough to doff his hat to the flag, to the quarterdeck, and to Lewrie, whom he espied waiting impatiently, then handed over a single folded-over letter to Lt. Farley. A second later, and he was clomping down the battens, judging his moment, and dropping back into the row boat to return to *Osprey*, waving his hat chearly as he put its tiller over and got his oarsmen back to work.

"How odd, sir," Lt. Farley commented as he came to the quarterdeck from the larboard sail-tending gangway, and handing over the lone despatch. "I expected a weighted bag . . . fresh mail from home . . ."

What the Devil? Lewrie wondered, for the letter, though sealed with wax where the folds met, was not addressed to him, nor to *Thermopylae*, but bore a cryptic Number Eleven of Twenty-One. In smaller longhand script was the caution "Captain's Eyes Only."

"Ah, hum," Lewrie said. "I'll be below, Mister Farley. Carry on with cutlass drill."

Once seated at his desk in his day-cabin, Lewrie broke the seal and unfolded the letter.

> Sir,
>
> Admiralty has informed us that a Cessation of Hostilities between Great Britain and France, as well as all her allies, has been agreed to by all parties. The preliminary Articles were signed in London on the 1st of October, with Ratifications exchanged on the 10th, and our Sovereign, His Majesty King George III, issuing a Proclamation of peace by sea and land on the 12th of this month.
>
> From the receipt of this Letter, you are Directed and Required to commit no Aggression towards any National ships or merchant Vessels of France, or the Batavian Republic, nor any formerly hostile vessels you may encounter. Do you currently hold any Prize, such vessel or vessels must be despatched to an Admiralty Court for a swift Adjudication; should you hold any Naval or Civilian officers or sailors from said Prize or Prizes, they are to be sent in with said Prize or Prizes on Parole, or, from a vessel not made Prize but burned or sunk, they are to be landed ashore with all due honours and all their properties.
>
> (for) Adm. Viscount Duncan

"Oh, Jesus!" Lewrie dared mutter after reading that for a quick second time. "It *can't* be . . . it simply *can't*! Don't those fools in London know we're *winnin'*? A year or two more, and . . . Ch-rist! Ye can't *trust* the French t'keep it. Not for *long*!"

"Sir?" Pettus said from the wee pantry built right-aft of the chart-space. "You need something, sir?"

"Guy Fawkes, t'torch Parliament, Pettus," Lewrie growled back. "The hen-heads've gone and signed articles of peace with the Frogs."

"War's *over,* sir?" Pettus said with a gawp.

"If it ain't a sly trick . . . aye," Lewrie grumbled. "The war's over. Before Christmas, we all might be paid off and 'beached,' does it hold. Mine arse on a band-box!"

Thermopylae *paid off an' laid up in-ordinary,* Lewrie silently gloomed, still squirming with sullen anger; *me,* all *of us, paid off, too, on half-pay, with nothin' t'do but* . . . go home? *Oh, fuck* me!

Lewrie had a mental picture of the village of Anglesgreen and North Surrey in mid-winter, at Christmastide; of him sipping ale at the Olde Ploughman (for he still would be as unwelcome at the fashionable Red Swan as a whore in church, just as he would be goggled at did he attend the Divine Services at mossy, nose-high old St. George's parish church).

He fantasised just how *long* this peace might hold, and if he thought that dull blockade duty was boresome, it didn't have a patch on farming, animal husbandry . . . or even pretending to know what he was about at *civilian* pursuits. At home . . . in Anglesgreen . . . with his wife, Caroline . . . forever-bloody-more, by God?

It wasn't just the chill of a mid-October rainy day that made him shiver! He scooped up his boat-cloak and hat, and headed out for the quarterdeck once more.

"Mister Farley, . . . pipe 'All Hands,' do ye please," he ordered.

And as he waited for the ship's people off-watch to thunder up to join the on-watch hands, Lewrie gazed off the larboard bows to wee HMS *Osprey,* already more than a league away and making a pretty way on up the Dutch coast for the next warship in the close blockade, to relay her supposedly glad tidings.

It was cold, it was nippy, the sea was cross-patch, and dollops of cold water showered down to plop on his hat and shoulders with each roll or shudder of tops'ls and t'gallants, but, of a sudden, it was a joy. One he feared he'd lose, and never recover.

"Ship's comp'ny, off hats and face aft to hark to the captain," Lt. Farley directed.

At least they'll *be glad enough,* Lewrie told himself as he began to speak; they've *something t'go home* to!

CHAPTER THREE

*O*f course, the happy homecoming didn't happen right away. Admiralty, justifiably leery of French intentions, was loath to reduce the Fleet quickly, even though the wish to save funds and reduce annual expenditures on the Navy's maintenance pressed *some* returns and de-commissionings.

Ships of the line were the first to depart, the oldest and weariest 56s, 58s, and 64s of British Third Rate, or those warships bought in after capture from their foes. No, it was the 74-gun two-deckers of the line which were the standard, and, should war break out again, the older, smaller ships might never be put back in commission. Yet even after the weakest and oldest were gone from the North Sea Fleet, it was not a fortnight later that the 74s were called home, too, leaving the frigates, brigs of war, and older sloops of war to carry the burden of showing the flag, with two-masted lighter "despatch" sloops and single-masted cutters to bear orders and mail back and forth.

It could be worse, Lewrie could conjure with growing impatience; *we could be in the Indian Ocean, or the China Seas!* Even a fast packet or frigate might require six months to bear word to Royal Navy units on far-off stations. Those ordered out to distant oceans *before* the peace articles were ratified, those still cruising halfway round the world, just naturally would assume that the war was still on, and would attack any enemy National ship they encountered, make prize of any enemy merchantman . . . and what the courts-martial might make of those engagements, and what the Prize Courts could demand as damages from unwitting captains was best not thought about!

At least Lewrie and HMS *Thermopylae* had learned of the peace in a matter of days; even ships on the North American Station at Halifax, the West Indies Station on Jamaica, or the Leeward Islands Station at English Harbour, Antigua, or the squadrons at Gibraltar might not know for another four or six weeks after October 12.

So, *Thermopylae* still cruised through the rest of October and well into November, her stores slowly diminishing, and the North Sea, ever a beast, growing colder and windier, and the winter winds howling over the many wide and shallow banks to stir up truly immense seas in bilious grey-green rollers, white-flecked and shattering alongside in icy sheets of spray.

They've forgotten we're here, Lewrie glumly thought one afternoon as his crewmen struggled to strike top-masts and reef in, gasket and lower upper yards almost to "bare poles"; *or, that bastard Nepean does know, and means t'punish me past Epiphany!*

"Drogue is ready, sir," Lt. Farley reported, looking half like a drowned rat in his sodden tarpaulins.

"See to its deploying, Mister Farley," Lewrie ordered, even more of a drowned rat in a camphor-and-rotting-hide reek of his own, for it was so chilly he'd had to dig out some of his furs from the solo dash into the Baltic weeks before the Battle of Copenhagen.

The frigate had thrashed out fifteen miles to seaward from the shoals of the Dutch coast before the gale had turned into a shrieking Nor'westerly storm, against which *Thermopylae* could make no progress. Their only choice was to lie-to under try-sails and a thrice-reefed main tops'l, letting out a canvas sea-anchor to check her inexorable drift sternward towards those sand and mud shoals 'til the storm blew itself out . . . and pray that it did before they were run aground and wrecked. Pray *most* earnestly!

"The bare yards will act like sails," Lt. Farley hopefully said, peering upward. "'Gainst a wind like this, well . . ."

"Quite so, Mister Farley," Lewrie replied, though still wondering if Sir Evan Nepean, the long-time First Secretary to Admiralty (no fan of his) who had served the former First Lord, the Earl Spencer, and now served Admiral Lord St. Vincent, "Old Jarvy," might not *wish* that he come a cropper; Nepean had despised him more than cold, boiled mutton for years, and Lewrie's acquittal at King's Bench for the crime of stealing a dozen Black Jamaican field slaves to man his old ship must have set Nepean's teeth grinding in frustration. *Could Nepean be that petty?* Lewrie asked himself; *for damned sure, I certainly could be!*

"Full 'trick' for the Quartermasters on the helm, sir," Lewrie snapped as the buoyed sea-anchor was paid out over the bows. "Trouble always seems t'come with inattention . . . when fresh hands take over."

"Very good, sir."

The sea-anchor was a modern one, a large canvas cone held open with an iron barrel hoop worthy of the largest water butt, weighted to keep it under the surface with a light iron boat anchor, at the end of an hundred-fathom cable of four-inch manila. As the cable was let out it felt ineffective for the longest time, 'til the painted buoy bobbed up about one hundred yards ahead of the bows, and the cable went taut, hauling *Thermopylae*'s bows closer to windward.

"Brace yards close-hauled to weather on the larboard tack, Mister Farley," Lewrie ordered, his left hand shoved into the pocket of his fur parka . . . with his fingers secretly crossed. He had never in his naval career been reduced to using bare yards as substitutes for proper sails, so it was an experiment to him—a life-or-death experiment! *Pray God my sham doesn't catch up with me . . . with us!* Lewrie silently wished, for he had never been one of those gladsome sailors who revelled in heavy weather, had never become so thoroughly salted as a tarry-handed "tarpaulin man" a fearful crew should look to as their sure and certain hope of salvation. In 1793, when the war with France had begun, after four idle years ashore playing an equal sham of being a farmer, his first daunting sight of HMS *Cockerel*'s intricate rigging had made Lewrie quail and had left him gawping and grasping for even the proper terms to *call* them, and many hours off-watch in his little dog's-box cabin poring in secret over his tattered copy of Falconer's *Marine Dictionary* and other beginners' guides, to keep from being revealed as an *utter* fraud, and a cack-handed, cunny-thumbed dangerous *lubber*!

"That seems to ease her, sir," Lt. Farley said at last, sounding as if he'd been holding his breath to see if the sea-anchor and braced bare yards would really work.

"How's her helm?" Lewrie asked Beasley, the Quartermaster of the Watch, and his Mate, Elgie, who stood braced wide-stanced either side of the double-wheel drum and spokes.

"Stiff, with th' relievin' tackle rigged, sir," Beasley replied, shifting his quid of tobacco to leeward, "but she's steadyin', aye."

"Very well, thankee," Lewrie said. "Mister Furlow?" he called for the Midshipman. "Pass word to my steward, Pettus, and Desmond, my Cox'n, and I'll have my deck-chair brought up."

"Aye aye, sir," Midshipman Furlow answered, then stepped to the break of the empty hammock nettings—the ship's people needed their dry bedding for their scant hours belowdecks between calls for All Hands—and bawled the summons to men in the waist.

Lewrie *knew* he could trust his First Officer, Lt. Dick Farley, his Second Lieutenant, James Fox, as well, to do their best for their ship, but . . . should things go completely to shambles, he felt he had to be present. Even if he had to engage in one more of his eccentricities. A *proper* Royal Navy captain should be so stoic a paragon as to stand and pace the windward side of the quarterdeck to set a stout example and inspire confidence . . . even did he not have the first clue. Lewrie, though, had always been an *idle* sort. So, after the canvas and wood collapsible deck-chair had been fetched up, spread out, and lashed securely in place, Lewrie sat himself down in it, spread a scrap of oiled canvas like a blanket to keep the sleeting, showering spray off him, and sprawled his booted legs out, as seemingly at ease as a passenger aboard an East Indiaman on a fine morning, and a calmer ocean.

Or, as much at ease as a man could appear as the frigate heaved her bows skyward with showers of salt spray cascading over her, then plunging like a seal with her jib-boom and bowsprit and beakhead rails under, and even larger bursts of white-out clouds of spray bursting to life, and the very fabric of the ship thundering, juddering, and groaning like a tormented ghost at each plunge or rise.

Lewrie tucked his chin down, slanted his hat firmly down atop his eyebrows, and even tried closing his eyes. *No, sir!* he decided after a minute of that; *eyes on the horizon . . . wherever that is, or I'll go sick as a dog!* Which thought made him smile in spite of the circumstances, the well-contained fear, and the danger of wrecking; it would not inspire confidence in the crew if he had to "cast his accounts to Neptune"!

"Some hot broth, sir?" Pettus asked, looking as if the very idea of victuals would empty his stomach, too, but he had to offer.

"I'm fine for now, Pettus, but thankee for asking," Lewrie let on with a forced smile. *And damn his eyes for the very mention*, Lewrie thought, feeling a brief spate of biliousness that made him belch. "Ah, hmm! Bloody brisk, ain't it, Mister Farley?"

"Amen to that, sir!" Farley shouted back, sounding pleased; as if he was truly one of those odd'uns who *relished* foul weather. "Off-watch hands below, now, sir?"

"Aye, make it so, Mister Farley. Let 'em dry out and thaw out for a spell," Lewrie decided. "Hot broth for *them,* if Sauder thinks he can trust a fire in the galley."

"I will see to it directly, sir," Farley agreed.

Lewrie doubted the roughness of the storm would allow fires to be lit below, but perhaps the offer might mollify *Thermopylae*'s people. With no recall in the offing, they were sullen enough already. For better or worse, this storm, and the risk of drowning in the surf of a Dutch beach, would take their minds off thoughts of de-commissioning and freedom.

Damn Nepean, Lewrie fumed inside, again, as the ship shuddered and tossed, and the storm showed no signs of easing; *it'd please him did we all drown!*

CHAPTER FOUR

*T*he Dog Watches came and went with no relenting of the storm; full dark, as black as a boot, and the Evening Watch was a roaring and soaking horror. So much spume, spray, and solid waves broke over the weather decks that the tar and oakum in the seams between the planking could not keep out a constant drizzle on sleeping off-watch men and their violently swaying hammocks. From the sick-berth and livestock manger under the forecastle right aft to the great-cabins, the decks bore puddles that were swept to either beam and fore and aft, so that the black-and-white enamel-painted chequered canvas deck covering in Lewrie's cabins became as slick as the marble tile design that it emulated, and the good Turkey or Axminster carpets had long been rolled up and stowed atop the transom settee.

It was only at Two Bells of the Middle Watch that the winds and seas seemed to ease, and the vast explosions of spray over the bows with each thundering, timber-cracking plunge diminished, allowing Lewrie to go below at last for a cold glass of tea, some cheese and a couple of soaked pieces of ship's biscuit . . . eaten in the gloom of a single candle, and the weevils in the biscuit considered "out of sight and out of mind." His bedding in the wide-enough-for-two hanging bed-cot was cold and damp despite an oiled canvas covering, so Lewrie, in all his clothes, tried to nap on the starboard-side collapsible settee for an hour or two.

It was hopeless, of course, for the settee was only long enough for two, only deep enough for sitting, and that in the proper mode of the age, which was to say erect, and mostly on the forward edge. He ended in a sprawl with one leg up, the other braced on the deck cover, and *thought* he'd wished his man Pettus a rest of his own, and to wake him should anyone need him before dropping off in a slouched, snoring bundle.

By Four Bells, though . . .

"Sir? Captain, sir? 'Tis Mister Privette, sir," Pettus said.

"Mmph? Bugger 'im."

"Mister Fox's duty, sir," Privette piped up as Lewrie pried an eye open, blinking away grit. "He wishes to make a tad more sail, sir."

"Sail," Lewrie said with an uncomprehending grunt, sitting up and rubbing his eyes with both hands.

"Aye, sir," Privette added. "Mister Fox believes we could bare stays'ls, spanker, and inner jibs, and begin to make a way, full and by."

Lewrie was woozy with exhaustion and lack of sleep, despite his brief nap, so it took him a long moment to listen to his senses. The ship was no longer rising and plunging like a manic child on a hobbyhorse, and the sickening roll was less. The hiss and roar of the sea down the hull, and the thunder of her bows meeting hard, steep waves, no longer made it hard to hear, or speak.

"Aye," Lewrie allowed at last, staggering to his feet. "Tell Mister Fox I'll come up. May *take* a moment, but . . . ," he added, wincing as muscles and joints too-long tensioned against the motions of the frigate complained loudly, making him wonder if he had caught the long-time sailor's plaints of arthritis and rheumatism, both.

"Very well, sir," Privette replied.

It was still cold, and icy spray still sheeted cross the deck as Lewrie attained the quarterdeck. The sea and sky were ink-black, and the only lights came from the two taffrail lanthorns, another by the foc's'le belfry, and the binnacle cabinet to illuminate the compass. Only now and then did the taffrail lanthorns glint off fleeting white-caps and sea-horses, mostly abeam the mizen mast or astern.

"Eased, has it, Mister Fox?" he asked.

"Aye, sir, or so I do believe," the Second Officer told him as he raised a bent finger to the brim of his hat in casual salute. "Her motion has most certainly eased, as has the velocity of the winds. I wish to replace storm trys'ls with stays'ls, hoist the spanker at two reefs, and hoist the inner jib."

Lewrie looked into the binnacle to discover their present course: Nor'East. "Wind still out of the Nor'West, Mister Fox?"

"Aye, sir. Though it does show sign of backing."

"Aye, hoist away," Lewrie decided, rubbing his chin and feeling two days' worth of stubble rasping. "With any luck, full and by, we'll be able to steer Nor'east by North. And take in the sea-anchor, too," he added, turning to look astern for the Dutch coast, as if the drift might have put them close to the shoals already. "Rate of drift?"

"Nigh a mile each hour, sir," Lt. Fox told him with a grimace.

"Then carry on, sir! Carry on, smartly!" Lewrie urged. They had set out the sea-anchor about Three in the previous afternoon, and if they'd drifted sternward a mile per hour since—it took Lewrie another long moment to do the simple math in his woozy head—that meant eleven hours of drifting, and they'd only been fifteen miles off Holland when they'd begun!

Mercifully for the weary and groggy hands, hoisting jibs and stays'ls, and baring the spanker at two reefs, could be done by the sailors of the current watch, not an "All Hands" manoeuvre requiring men to go aloft at their peril. The off-watch people could sleep in as best they could under the circumstances, and be a *tad* fresher when the watch changed at 4 A.M. Hoisting was fairly easy; it was sheeting home to cup that still-boisterous wind that would cause the hernias.

Lewrie stood out of the way by the after-most shrouds of the mainmast, crossing his fingers as the Afterguard hoisted and reefed the spanker. With but a bit more sail exposed, *Thermopylae* was forced to heel a few more degrees to leeward, but after putting her shoulder to the sea, she felt stiffer and no longer rolled to larboard like a metronome; no, the ship came fully upright with each windward roll, and seemed steadier. He looked overside to the amber-tinted glimmers of lanthorn-light on the heaving wave crests. The wind drove them by as they chopped and broke upon themselves, making it *seem* as if the frigate was making way, but was she? Lewrie staggered aft towards the cross-deck hammock nettings at the forrud edge of the quarterdeck, peering out-board, hoping . . .

"Two and a quarter knots, sir!" Midshipman Plumb called out in a thin, piping voice from the taffrails.

"Bow lookouts!" Lewrie bellowed through a brass speaking-trumpet. "Is the sea-anchor cable taut?"

"Slack, sir!" one shouted aft. "Runnin' up on th' buoy, sir!" cried another.

"Just thankee Jesus!" Lewrie said under his breath, then turned to Lt. Fox. "Take in the sea-anchor, sir, 'fore we run her under the forefoot."

He uncrossed his fingers with a whoosh of pented breath, grinning for the first time since mid-day. Even at a bare two knots' good to windward, they could be eight miles clear of the Dutch shoals by the change of watch!

"Watch your luff, Mister Hook, Mister Slater!" Lt. Fox warned.

"Can't hold her head Nor'east, sir!" the Quartermaster shouted. "Wind's veerin' on us." He and his Mate, Slater, heaved on the spokes of the wheel, easing a full quarter turn of helm leeward. "Steady on Nor'east by East, sir . . . best she'll manage."

Sailin' parallel t'Holland, not makin' sea-room, then, Lewrie thought with a groan; *we'll have t'tack, stiff as the winds are, and hope for the best!* The winds were too stiff, and the spray too thick, to spread a chart on the traverse board in the dark. The best Lewrie could do was picture the chart in his mind, and groan again as he realised that, should they continue on this course, they'd encounter those islands East of the Texel, Vlieland and Terschelling, Nor'east of Den Helder and Harlingen, that jutted Northwards, smack on their bows!

"We'll have to tack, Mister Fox," Lewrie said, about the same time that Lt. Fox opened his mouth to suggest the same thing, grimacing again. "Loose another reef in the spanker, pipe 'All Hands,' and shake a reef from the main tops'l, as well, so we can build up enough speed t'get her round without gettin' caught 'in irons.' "

"Aye aye, sir! Bosun! Pipe 'All Hands'!" Fox yelled.

Five Bells chimed before all was ready, before *Thermopylae* had accelerated to five knots, and "Stations for Stays" had been piped. Despite the heavy weather, and the continual shipping of seas over the bow, the larboard hawse buckler for the best bower had been removed, and the heavy-weather lashings on that anchor freed, with a cable of thigh-thick rope affixed to the anchor stock, and bound about the capstan. Men in hawse breeches swung lead lines from either channel of the foremast, just in case the *Thermopylae* could not cross the eye of the wind, and the sea-bottom might be close enough for them to anchor—to save the ship from drifting helplessly shoreward if unable to tack, or to try to box-haul her over to starboard tack so they could sail away, even if it meant cutting the bower cable and losing it altogether.

"Ready, sir," Lt. Fox reported. It was still his watch, though all watch-standing officers and Midshipmen were on deck, along with the Sailing Master, Mr. Robert Lyle, and his Mates.

"Pick your moment, Mister Fox," Lewrie allowed. "I have every confidence in you."

"Thankee, sir."

And I don't trust myself t'choose it, Lewrie wryly told himself.

"Pay her off half a point loo'rd, Mister Hook," Lt. Fox said.

"Half a point loo'rd, aye, sir!"

"Chip-log, Mister Plumb!" Fox shouted aft. "Smartly, now!"

"Five and uh . . . five and a *half* knots, sir!" the young Midshipman shouted back after a long minute or two to toss out the log, turn the sand-glass, check the line, measure the knot-marks, and report.

"Good as it'll get, right, Mister Fox?" Lewrie asked.

"Aye, sir! *Ready* a-*bout!*" Lt. Fox bellowed through a speaking-trumpet. "Ready, ready! Ease down the helm!"

God only knows her trim, Lewrie queasily thought, watching the helm spin round, noting the faint trembling of the spokes, as regular as the works of a good pocket-watch, that bespoke a decent balance to the ship, despite the shifting and consumption of stores, and all the water she'd shipped aboard over the long day and night.

"Helm's alee!" Lt. Fox shouted forward.

"Over, in the name of the Lord," the Sailing Master said in the old usage of the fisheries.

"Rise, tacks and sheets!" Lt. Fox yelled. The Afterguard hauled taut the lee spanker topping lift, the main tops'l's clew garnets were hauled up, and the jibs and stays'ls windward sheets were hauled taut, the lee sheets' binds round the belays undone yet held firmly, waiting for the proper moment when the bows were right up to the eyes of the wind, and they luffed and shivered.

"Come up, ye darlin' lass, come up, I say!" Quartermaster Hook crooned, as he and Slater let go the spokes and watched them almost blur as the wheel spun, even with relieving tackles rigged belowdecks, a sure sign that *Thermopylae* would go up to the wind ardently.

She's goin' t'make it! Lewrie exulted.

"Haul taut! Mains'l haul!" Fox all but screeched. "Haul of all!"

It was so dark, it was impossible to see the bows sweep round, see the proper trim of the sails, or the yard-cloths to mark the angle of the yards, but . . . one could *feel* her lift on the fierce-scending sea, stark upright for a long moment, then begin to heel to *larboard*; *feel* the *wind* as it shifted from right-ahead to one's right cheek; hear the rustling crackle of icy-stiff canvas as it whooshed over the deck, the groan of starboard sheets as they took the new strain, then a second *whump* and *whoosh* as they and the reefed main tops'l filled with wind and bellied out as stiff as sheet metal!

"Ease her, ease her, there! Helm down half a point loo'rd!"

Thermopylae shook herself like a wet dog, heeled hard onto her larboard side for a moment, then came back more upright, steadying with the deck canted about twenty degrees from plumb according to the inclinometer on the binnacle cabinet—on starboard tack!

"Steerin' West by North, half North, sir!" Quartermaster Hook cried with relief as he and Slater steadied her up.

"Another cast of the log, Mister Plumb!" Lewrie ordered.

About two minutes later, Midshipman Plumb could report the good news that *Thermopylae* was now making *three* knots!

"I think she'll bear the main topmast stays'l and the middle stays'l, Mister Fox," Lewrie opined aloud. "And I'd admire did ye add the fore tops'l and mizen tops'l at three reefs."

"Aye, sir."

"A perfect tack, Mister Fox," Lewrie congratulated him. "Timed to a tee."

"Uhm, thankee for saying so, sir," Lt. Fox said, tucking in his chin and ducking his head in modesty . . . false or otherwise.

"Permission to mount the quarterdeck, sirs?" Lt. Eades, their Marine officer, enquired. "Now all the excitement's done?"

"You did not wish to get in the way during the manoeuvre, sir?" Lewrie asked him, now in much better, relieved takings.

"I leave all that to proper seamen, Captain sir," Lt. Eades said with a grin as he came to amidships forward of the helm. "Besides, we had some scraps of yesterday's breaded and toasted cheese, and I admit all the tossing about made me feel peckish."

"Hungry? In *this* weather, sir?" Lewrie said with a gawp.

"Well . . . aye, sir," Eades admitted. "With the galley shut down . . . didn't everyone?"

"The ship's rats and Mister Eades own constitutions are of much the same nature, sir," Lt. Farley japed. "They can eat anything, at any time, with no ill effects."

"No sense in drowning hungry," Lt. Eades said with a shrug. "I do, though, gather that drowning is no longer an immediate threat?"

"Aye, and if the weather continues to moderate, we'll all have hot breakfasts by mid-morning," Lt. Farley told him.

"Good, ho!" was Eades's joy at that news.

Nigh as dense as a mile-post, Lewrie thought, shaking his head in wonder; *but he'll do.*

HMS *Thermopylae* continued on her course of West by North, half North 'til dawn and beyond as the winds eased and the seas moderated, slowly adding sail 'til she was making a good six knots. By Two Bells of the Forenoon Watch (9 A.M.) it was judged safe to light the galley fires and serve up a late breakfast for one and all. The low clouds lifted a bit and lightened in colour, and the rain ceased; not that it made much difference belowdecks, for the seams still dribbled water here and there, after all the flexing and strain put on the hull and the planking by the storm. And if Lewrie sat halfway down his dining table, he could find a dry spot to drink several very welcome cups of hot coffee and spoon up hot porridge.

The ship's motion was even steady enough to allow him a shave!

Then, back on deck in clean, dry linen, slop-trousers, and uniform, and feeling human for the first time in days, he could dispense with both furs *and* tarpaulins, for the temperature was just about warm enough to be stood with his coat doubled over and buttoned.

"Sail ho!" a lookout shouted down to the deck. "Two points off th' larboard bows!" Midshipman Furlow was sent aloft with a glass to report, and moments later he shouted down that she was a cutter, one of theirs to boot, the much-belaboured *Osprey.*

"She signals 'Have Despatches,' sir!" Furlow cried.

"Very well, Mister Furlow!" Lewrie shouted back, then turned to the taffrails. "Mister Pannabaker, send her 'Come Under My Lee.' I'd imagine she'd welcome our shelter if she's been through the same weather we've suffered."

Osprey quickly replied "Acknowledged" by flag hoist, and steered for *Thermopylae.* One hour later, she had come almost abeam to larboard, came about to starboard tack, and eased into *Thermopylae*'s lee off her larboard quarter, to lower a boat and send her across.

It was sick-making to watch poor HMS *Osprey* pitch and toss even so, or to watch her rowing boat rise, swoop, and fall amid showers of spray from wave crests and white-caps, 'til the boat was close-aboard, and the very same Midshipman from mid-October came scrambling up the battens and man-ropes to the larboard entry-port, and handed over his canvas bag of mail and orders. With a brief doff of his hat, he was back in his boat in a twinkling, making way back to his wee cutter.

"Mister Furlow, pass word for my clerk, Mister Georges," Lewrie instructed as he took the bag. "We'll sort everything out, then pipe the crew to receive theirs."

"Aye, sir."

He didn't feel all that hopeful, though. The canvas bag was not weighted, first of all, as it would be to prevent secret instructions or orders for future operations from being taken by an enemy. Second, there wasn't much mail to sort out. Lewrie and his clerk piled what contents there were into three quick heaps: officers and warrants in one pile; seamen in the second; and his own in the third, with the official letters the first to be opened and read before anyone else got a peek at theirs.

The one that took Lewrie's attention first off was from Admiralty, this time properly addressed to him and HMS *Thermopylae*. With a pen-knife, he sliced off the wax wafer seal and unfolded it.

"Hallelujah, at last!" he muttered, a broad smile breaking out on his phyz. "See to the rest, Georges. I'll go on deck."

Once there, he ordered Acting-Lieutenant Sealey to have 'All Hands' piped, then paced along the forrud edge of the quarterdeck by the iron stanchions of the hammock nettings, which were now filled, 'til everyone, both on- and off-watch, was gathered in the waist, on the sail-tending gangways, and the forecastle.

"I trust you lads've dried out, thawed out, and eat a fillin' breakfast, at last, hey?" he began in a loud, quarterdeck voice. "We have orders from Admiralty, lads! We are 'required and directed to make the best of our way' . . . we all know that means—pull yer bloody finger out and get a move on . . . ," he japed, which raised a laugh, "to Sheerness and the Nore . . . a few days West of here . . . there to lay His Majesty's Ship *Thermopylae* in-ordinary! To land ashore all of her artillery and small arms, to consign to His Majesty's Dockyards all stores not yet consumed, with a strict accounting to be—"

He was drowned out by the tremendous cheer that erupted, but he didn't have to say more or cite more from the officialese of those orders; it was not like he was "reading himself in" as Post-Captain or standing beside another who would relieve him.

"Mister Sealey, . . . Mister Lyle, sirs," Lewrie bellowed at last as the din died down a bit. "Shape the most direct course for the Nore, sirs, and lay us upon it. We are going home, lads! We're going home!"

BOOK I

O quid solutis est beatius curis,
cum mens onus reponit, ac peregrino
labore fessi, venimus larem ad nostrum
desideratque acquiescimus lecto?

O what is more blessed than to put cares away when the
mind lays by its burden, and tired with labour of far
travel we come to our own homes and rest on the
couch we longed for?

GAIUS VALERIUS CATULLUS,
POEM XXXI, 7-10

Or,
Whatever your gall, you're cock-of-the-walk
only on your own dung-heap.

LUCIUS ANNAEUS SENECA,
THE APOCOLOCYNTOSIS OF THE DIVINE CLAUDIUS

CHAPTER FIVE

*D*e-commissioning a warship demanded stacks of paperwork worthy of the weight of an 18-pounder gun; reams of it from the Victualling Board as they took possession of all consumable stores, butts, kegs, and tuns of salt-beef or salt-pork, of hard ship's biscuit, weevily or otherwise, spoiled or fresh. Salt-meat marked "Condemned" as too rancid to be eaten would, Lewrie was mortal-certain, be dumped into new kegs, to be foisted on some unwitting captain in the future. Their motto at the Victualling Board was "Waste not, want not."

Spare upper masts and yards were sent ashore to the warehouses first, then sails and cordage, and all bosuns' stores and lumber. The frigate was stripped down to her fighting tops and main, lower trunks of her masts, "to a gant-line." The magazine was carefully emptied of kegs of gunpowder, pre-made flannel cartridge bags already filled, and bales of empty bags, all meticulously indented for and counted.

Next went the artillery, the 18-pounder main guns, the lighter 12-pounder bow chasers, the 32-pounder carronades, and the quarterdeck 9-pounders, along with their truck-carriages, gun-tools, flintlock strikers, and all breeching ropes and handling tackle blocks. Heavy barges from Gun Wharf spent two days rowing back and forth to bear all the guns away, leaving *Thermopylae* high in the water, and her weather decks, the foc's'le, the quarterdeck, and Lewrie's great-cabins yawningly bare and empty.

By the end of the first week of December, there was no more need of crew, for there was nothing left to remove with muscle power, and no reason to keep her manned. Clerks and paymasters from the Port Admiral came out to muster the hands to issue them their pay chits. That required another chestful of paperwork, for every sailor owed the Navy something, right from the moment he'd been pressed or had taken the Joining Bounty. Deductions had been carefully kept by the Purser, Mr. Herbert Pridemore, and his Jack-in-the-Breadroom clerk of every quid of tobacco issued, each wool jacket, blanket, each pair of shoes and stockings, each broken plate or mug, each worn-out shirt or pair of trousers. The Surgeon, Mr. Harward, offered his own list of treaments beyond the usual; a dubious Mercury Cure for venereal disease was fifteen shillings, to be deducted when the rare chance for pay to be issued occurred. Surgeon Mr. Harward and the Purser had their own accounts to square, for though they might hold Admiralty Warrant, they could be considered as independent contractors, to be reimbursed for goods, medicines, or services expended; were they *not* allowed a profit, it would be almost impossible to lure anyone to the posts!

As *Thermopylae*'s captain, Lewrie was held to the most acute accounting, with reams of forms to be filled out and Admiralty satisfied that each item marked as Lost or Broken, each cable of rope rigging used up, each sail blown out or torn in heavy weather, each back-stay shifted since the moment he'd read himself in—all tallied with what he'd received and what remained to be landed ashore at the instant of his frigate's decommissioning, at the instant of his surrender of command, with penalties deducted from his own pay owing if he had been remiss.

The weather was cold, there was a faint swirl of snow falling, so the mustering-out was held below on the gun-deck. Each man came forward as his name was called; there was much hemming and ahumming 'twixt the Purser, the Surgeon, and the shore clerks, before a chit was filled out and a final sum announced, carefully noting whether a sailor had dependents to whom he'd authorised a deduction already for their support whilst he was away at sea.

"They'll be cheated, of course, poor devils," a senior clerk from the Port Admiral's offices muttered to Lewrie as they watched the proceedings from the door to the officers' gun-room.

"The Chatham Chest, deductions for Widows' Men . . . the jobbers," Lewrie sombrely agreed.

"Most of them will never *see* the Councillor of the Cheque, but will sell off their chits for half their value to the first jobber they meet," the senior clerk said with a sniff of disdain for the practice.

Selling them off was cheaper and more convenient than travelling to London for the whole sum owing; a wad of paper fiat money and a hefty handful of real, now-rare solid coin was simply too tempting to a tar who hadn't seen money—real money!—since his ship had set sail years before, even if was but a pittance of what a man earned.

"Aye, and they'll drink up half o' *that* the first ev'nin'," Lewrie added. "Find a whore and a tavern . . . and end up 'crimped' on a merchantman. Only trade most of 'em know, really . . . the sea."

"Aye, poor fellows," the senior clerk said with a grave, sad nod and another sniff. "Though," he added with a wry grin, "if the war begins again, they'll be much easier to find, and press back into the Fleet, hmm?"

"Uhm, Captain Lewrie, sir," a fubsy official from the dockside warehouses interrupted. "Your pardon, gentlemen, do I intrude upon a conversation, but . . . I do not see these iron stoves listed as naval property, and I must have a proper accounting of everything aboard."

"They aren't Navy issue, sir," Lewrie informed him. "Captain Speaks, whom I relieved when he fell ill, had purchased them for the crew's comfort for service in the North Sea winters."

"Most charitable and considerate of him, I vow, sir, but . . . I cannot accept them into Admiralty possession, these two . . ."

"There are four, actually," Lewrie further informed him. "One in the gun-room here, and one in my cabins as well. Mostly to keep his pet parrot from freezin' t'death, I imagine."

"Four, sir? Four? My word, he was profligate!" the fubsy old fellow vowed, scratching his scalp under his wig with a pencil stub. "And the coal, well! Why, there must be at least two hundredweight bagged up, to boot. What am I to *do* with it all, sir?"

"Leave 'em for the Standing Officers," Lewrie hopefully suggested, "t'see 'em through the winter?"

Once *Thermopylae* was officially de-commissioned, Mr. Pridemore the Purser; Mr. Dimmock, the Bosun; Lumsden, the Ship's Carpenter; the Master Gunner, Mr. Tunstall; and the Ship's Cook, Sauder, would watch over her in the Sheerness Ordinary, along with a small crew of other ship-keepers to manage her maintenance, paid by the dockyard at their full pay-rate for as long as their frigate sat at anchor, for as long as Admiralty deemed her valuable enough to keep in reserve. Wives and children would accompany them, of course. Unless those worthies asked for transfer to a new construction, wangled an exchange with another ship-keeper in a Navy port more desirable to them, or outright retired from service, they had full employment 'til *Thermopylae* rotted away or was stricken and sent to the breakers. Indeed, they'd been assigned to *Thermopylae* even as she had been constructed on the stocks, and were "hers" for the ship's entire life.

"Quite impossible, Captain Lewrie," the dockyard offical pooh-poohed, "for, without a regular issue of coal with which to stoke them . . . absent the kindling and firewood issued for the galley . . . they're useless, and His Majesty's Dockyards are not responsible for the cost."

"Stow 'em on the orlop, then, and let the next captain sort it out," Lewrie replied, sensing that there was bad news coming.

"Franklin-pattern iron stoves are *not* carried on our books as naval property, sir, and must be removed ashore," the official pressed. "If, as you say, the former captain purchased them at his own expense, then they remain *his* property, and should quite properly be sent on to him, wherever he may be."

Oh, good God! Lewrie thought, wondering how much that'd cost, for he had no idea whether Captain Speaks had survived his pneumonia, or where he resided if he had. *Lands' End, John O' Groats?* Lewrie speculated, worrying what the carting fee would be for four *heavy* metal stoves all that way. His own carting charges would be steep enough, to bear away all his furniture, wine and spirits remaining, his tableware, chests, and boxes . . . and, there were all the luxury goods, the dainties that those Russian counts, Rybakov and Levotchkin, had left aboard when he'd landed them close to St. Petersburg. They'd bought as if preparing for a six-month voyage to China on an Indiaman, not a two-week dash up the Baltic, and Devil take the cost, to boot. There were two-gallon stone crocks, five-gallon wooden barricoes, and costly cased *bottles* of vintage wines and champagnes, crocks of *caviar*, bags of coffee beans, cocoa beans, and assorted caddied tea leaves by the ten-pound lot, . . . along with lashings of vodka and gin, of course; so much that he might clear a nice profit in selling most of it off once he got to London. Why, the brandies, the rarely seen, expensive liqueurs could fetch a—

"Shall we say, for now, sir, that the stoves are of a piece with your personal stores, and will be removed when yours are landed, sir?" the rotund older fellow decided for them with an oily little smile.

"Just damn my eyes," Lewrie muttered, but had to nod an assent. Were the stoves still aboard a week from now, after his own departure, there'd be Hell to pay, and a full two years' worth of angry letters flying back and forth 'til *someone* claimed them.

"*Most* satisfactory, sir!" The dockyard official beamed.

"I'll be in my cabins," Lewrie announced. "I leave it to you, sirs, to continue the mustering-out. Pray inform me when you're done, and I'll say a few last words. The boats will be alongside by . . . ?"

"By Two Bells of the Day Watch, sir," the Port Admiral's senior clerk assured him.

"A final 'Clear Decks and Up-Spirits,'" Lewrie decided. "Later than usual, but . . . later, gentlemen," Lewrie decided, meaning a last issue of rum, full measure for all with no "sippers or gulpers," given to his crew to "splice the main-brace" just one last time.

CHAPTER SIX

As if things weren't gloomy enough! No sooner had Lewrie gotten to his cabins, now almost stripped of all his goods, and filled with piles of chests, crates, and boxes, than he had to deal with Pettus, his steward, and Whitsell, his twelve-year-old cabin boy.

"Hot coffee and a dollop of brandy with, sir," Pettus offered, his own canvas bag, his tight-rolled bedding and hammock, and his sea-chest before the door of the wee pantry.

"Thankee, Pettus," Lewrie replied, taking a welcome sip.

"Uhm, sir . . . might you be needing my services ashore once the paying-off is done?" Pettus asked rather tentatively.

"I do need a man, aye, Pettus, are you of a mind," Lewrie told him. "Couldn't ask for a better, really."

"Well, sir, I'd rather not, if you could find another," Pettus replied, looking cutty-eyed. "For I was of a mind to go to Portsmouth . . . to look up Nan, if she's still employed there. I've a fair amount of pay due me, enough to keep me for a time before taking service with some household, and . . ."

"And take up with the girl where you left off, aye, I see. If you need a letter of recommendation . . . ," Lewrie said.

"That'd be most welcome, sir, thank you," Pettus said, perking up with relief. "Sorry to let you down, sir, but . . .'twas only drink and the

Press Gang that made a sailor of me, an accident, that, not in my usual nature. If it's peace, I don't intend to go to sea again."

"I'll write it for you right now," Lewrie said, going to what little was left of his desk in his day-cabin. There to find Whitsell, idly playing with Toulon and Chalky, and looking hang-dog miserable.

"C . . . could ye pen one fer me, too, sir?" Whitsell plaintively enquired. "I'll need a place, meself, without the Navy."

Wee Whitsell was an orphan, a street waif who'd been begging on the streets of Yarmouth when Captain Speaks's recruiting "rondy" in a pier-side tavern had scooped him up almost two years before. Whitsell had eat his best meals, his only regular *meat*, aboard ship, and had no prospects in civilian life except for poverty, starvation, and exploitation. "Aye, one for you as well, Whitsell," Lewrie promised.

"Back to Yarmouth, Will?" Pettus asked the lad.

"Well, I dunno . . . ," Whitsell waffled, looking down at his scuffling shoes.

"Might come to Portsmouth with me," Pettus suggested, grinning. "A gentleman's servant, and a page or link-boy, together. Or Mister Nettles."

"Nettles?" Lewrie asked, intent on his writing.

"He's a standing offer as head cook for a posting house in his old town, sir," Pettus told him. "In Ipswich. Nettles might have need of an assistant . . . an apprentice, Will. Learn to be what the French call a *chef*? It ain't a bad life, head of a grand kitchen, with grub on either hand, whenever you like, hey?"

"Aye, I'd like *that*!" Whitsell exclaimed, beaming with joy and avarice for hot vittles. "Ya kin stay *warm* in kitchens!"

"He'll be missed, by God," Lewrie told them. "I've never eat so well aboard any ship at sea in my life."

There came a rap on the deck outside his cabin door. Lt. Eades and his Marine detachment had departed days before, so one of the Ship's Corporals, either Duncan or Luck, now stood guard over his privacy.

"Th' Cox'n an' Landsman Furfy t'see th' cap'm, sir!"

"Enter!" Lewrie bade in a loud voice.

In came Liam Desmond, a dark-haired, blue-eyed "Black" Irishman, and his long-time mate, the overgrown great pudding Patrick Furfy. Both were turned out as fresh as Sunday Divisions in taped short sailors' jackets, flat tarred hats in their hands, clean chequered shirts, snowy white slop-trousers, and their shore-going best blacked buckled shoes and clean stockings.

"Beggin' th' Captain's pardons, sor," Liam Desmond, easily the sharper of the two, began with a bright-eyed grin on his phyz, "but me an' Furfy, here, we're a'wond'rin' if ye'd have any need o' us ashore, sir, oncet th' auld girl's paid off, d'ye see? I'm minded that ye've a farm, where a brace o' stout, hard workers'd be welcome. If ye've beasties, Furfy here's yer man, sor. He could charm a chargin' bull to a kitten, for so I've seen him done, sure, sor . . ."

"You wouldn't enter a merchantman, Desmond?" Lewrie asked as he sat back in his chair and took a sip of his laced coffee. He felt an urge to smile, for Desmond was laying on "the auld brogue" thick, as he usually did when "working a fiddle," or talking himself, or Furfy, out of trouble. "Or take the opportunity to go back to Ireland for a spell? See your home folk?" he asked with a solemn face, instead.

"Faith, sor, dear as we'd desire t'see Erin, agin, well sor . . . ," Desmond said with a brief appalled expression and a disarming shrug, "they may be, ah . . . some back home who'd take exception t'th' sight o' us . . . do ye git me meanin', sor, so *that* might not be a good idee."

The law, a jilted girl, Lewrie wryly surmised; *one with a bastard or two . . . or the Army, lookin' for escaped rebels from the '98 uprisin'?*

"As fer *merchant* masters, arrah, they're a skin-flint lot, sor, nothin' *a'tall* like yer foin self, sor, an' Furfy an' me've got used t'gettin' paid an' fed regular. So, sor, do ye have need of us, we'd be that glad t'keep on in yer service, Cap'm sor," Desmond concluded.

"As a matter of fact, Desmond, Pettus here just told he that he plans to 'swallow the anchor' and take civilian domestic service back in Portsmouth, so I *do* have need of a man," Lewrie told him. "As for Furfy, though . . ."

Desmond swelled with happy anticipation, though he got a frown on his face when Lewrie mentioned his mate.

"You're good with horses, Furfy? With all manner of beasts?"

"Wi' me Mam's pigs an' chickens, sor," Furfy piped up, almost pleading to convince him, sharing a worried look with Desmond that he might be separated from him. "An' me first job o' work when I was but a lad was stableman, Cap'm sor. Nursed many a horse, colt, calf, or lamb through th' bad patches, sor, an', ah . . ." Furfy swallowed loudly, as if he'd lose Desmond, the one mate who looked after him.

"Th' critters follow 'im round loik a Noah, sor, so they do," Desmond stuck in quickly, "don't they, Pat? An' even fightin' dogs go puppy-sweet on 'im."

"Better a stableman I already know than one I'd hire blind back in Anglesgreen," Lewrie decided, relenting with a smile. "So be it, me lads. After all, *somebody* has t'keep an eye out for Furfy, and keep him in mid-channel. You've done the work before, when we coached to Yarmouth t'join. Well, we're off to London again for a few days at the Madeira Club, then down to Surrey. I trust that Anglesgreen won't be *too* rustic for you? It's a small and quiet place. Only the two taverns, the last I know of it, and I'm not welcome in one of 'em."

"They've a good local ale, sor?" Furfy asked.

"A hellish-good ale, Furfy," Lewrie assured him.

"Fine with us, sor," Desmond exclaimed, sealing the bargain.

Barely had Desmond and Furfy turned to go when there came another rap outside his door. "Mister Harper, from the Port Admiral's office, t'see the Cap'm, sir!"

"Enter!"

The senior official ducked under the overhead deck beams as he clumped aft to Lewrie's desk. "The mustering-out is done, sir."

"Very well, Mister Harper," Lewrie said, taking a peek at the face of his pocket-watch just as One Bell of the Day Watch was struck up forrud at the belfry. "Coffee with a splash of brandy?"

"That'd be most welcome, sir, welcome indeed," Harper said with joy, rubbing chilled hands together in anticipation. No matter those modern Franklin-pattern stoves, a few feet away from them and the cold below-decks could be a damp misery.

"Pettus, a laced coffee for Mister Harper, then pass word to the First Lieutenant," Lewrie instructed. "He is to have 'All Hands' piped, then 'Clear Decks and Up-Spirits.' The Purser's parsimony bedamned," he added with a grin.

"Aye, sir."

"This damnable peace with the Frogs won't last," Harper griped after a deep sip and an appreciative sigh.

"Not above a year," Lewrie sourly agreed. "The only reason Bonaparte asked for peace was to re-gather his forces, build up his Navy again, after the way we've savaged it since Ninety-Three."

"Perhaps two years, Captain Lewrie," Harper countered. "After all, he's a lot of building, and re-building, to do, and a proper navy is like Rome . . . not built in a single day."

"Aye, two years, then," Lewrie gloomed. "Refit what he already has and get them to sea in early Spring . . . drill and train their officers and sailors at *sea*, for a change, 'stead of harbour drill. Send squadrons round the world to re-claim all the colonies we've conquered so far. I haven't seen a newspaper, yet, regarding what we are to surrender to them. Have you?"

"Nothing official yet, no," Mr. Harper admitted. "Though I am sure we must restore all French West Indies islands, Cape Town and all that to the Dutch . . . the Guyanas in South America, too. Lord, when the war erupts, we'll have to do it all *over* again. Senseless! Plain senseless!"

"Makes one dearly miss Pitt as Prime Minister," Lewrie scoffed. "Even Henry Dundas as Secretary of State for War . . . the arrogant coxcomb!"

They both took deep sips of their drinks, in silence for a bit, each wondering *why* the new administration had felt it necessary to end the war when England held the upper hand.

"I've only de-commissioned one ship, long ago, Mister Harper, so I may be a tad rusty when it comes to the details," Lewrie confessed. "Now the mustering-out of the crew is done . . . what?"

"The boats come to fetch the hands off will ferry aboard an officer in charge," Harper told him, shifting clubman fashion in his seat and crossing a leg. "Most-like, a deserving old tarpaulin man with no future prospects. He will bear orders and will read himself in as the ship's new captain, relieving you. A full-pay retirement for *some* old fellow."

"Midshipman Furlow, sir!" his sentry shouted, rapping the deck with a musket butt.

"Mister Farley's duty, sir," Furlow reported crisply, hat under his arm, "and he reports that a string of oared barges are making their way to us. Mister Farley also reports that the Purser is prepared to serve out the rum ration, and that the Bosun is standing by to pipe the 'All Hands' and the 'Clear Decks and Up-Spirits,' sir."

"Very well, Mister Furlow," Lewrie said, finishing his coffee, and rising. "My compliments to Mister Farley, and I shall be on deck directly."

"Aye aye, sir."

The red-painted rum keg had just emerged on deck, its colour, and the gilt-paint royal seal of the Crown, with the gilt letters spelling out KING GEORGE III and GOD BLESS HIM the only vivid sight on a bleak and grey winter's day. Honoured much like the Ark of the Covenant was by the Israelites, it made its stately way forrud to the break of the forecastle before the belfry, past Able and Ordinary Seamen and Landsmen, ship's servants and powder monkeys, petty officers and rated men, all of whom were now in a festive mood, eager to depart the ship and gruelling naval service . . . but just as eager to drink their last issue of rum to warm their short voyage to the docks.

"Any debts left?" Lewrie cried out. "If there are, they are to be forgiven! Before we go our separate ways, *Thermopylaes* will splice the mainbrace one last time!"

That raised a great cheer.

"I don't know if we can trust the Corsican tyrant, Bonaparte, to *keep* the peace for long, lads," he went on, "but if England *does* face a future conflict, I can't imagine a surer way t'keep that snail-eatin' bastard awake nights than for him to know that the men of *Thermopylae* are at sea, and *that* eager t'rip the guts out of the best *his* navy can send against us!

"Wherever you light, you can be proud of what you accomplished here aboard *Thermopylae*," Lewrie told them after another great cheer had subsided. "*I'm* proud of you, and proud that even for a short time I was permitted to be your captain. Don't let the job—"

"Three cheers fer Cap'm Lewrie, hip hip!" interrupted him.

"A cup for you, sir?" Lt. Farley asked, for this once, the rum issue had made its way to the quarterdeck.

"Aye," Lewrie eagerly agreed.

And once the ship's crew had settled, Lewrie concluded, "Thank you kindly, men. I was *about* t'say, don't let the jobbers cheat you. . . . Don't spend it all the first night. . . . Make sure the doxy doesn't have three hands and pick your pockets blind . . . and go see your kin before you let yourselves get crimped!

"To *Thermopylae* . . . to you . . . and to us!" he shouted, lifting the wee brass rum cup to his lips and tossing its contents back whole.

Don't . . . cough! he chid himself, for the neat rum, with but a ha'porth of water to "grog" it this time, almost made his eyes water.

"Dismiss the hands, Mister Farley," Lewrie ordered, once he had control of his vocal chords again.

"Aye aye, sir! Ship's company . . . dismiss! Good luck and Godspeed to one and all!"

Taking leave of his officers, warrants, and midshipmen was much more genteel; handshakes and doffings of hats, a brief jape or two to the "younkers," and wishes for good fortune, promotion, another active sea commission soon, and hopes to serve together again someday.

"My Jack-in-the Breadroom's made arrangements for your cartage, sir," Mr. Pridemore told Lewrie, "and there will be a good-sized barge alongside within the hour for all your dunnage."

"Might have to make it *two* barges, Mister Pridemore," he had to confess. "The dockyard won't accept the stoves, and thinks I must send them on to Captain Speaks at mine own expense."

"Oh, really, sir?" Pridemore said, brightening. "If that is so, sir, might I suggest that you leave all that to me, for I have Captain Speaks's address, already, and made arrangements for most of his goods to be sent on to his home in Yorkshire months ago."

Just knew *it'd be a long, long way off!* Lewrie told himself.

"In point of fact, sir," Pridemore went on, "two of them would be more than welcome whilst we're laid up in-ordinary this winter. If I . . . *lease* them from Captain Speaks for my comfort, and the comfort of my fellow ship-keepers, it goes without saying," the Purser quickly added, "and, so long as *we* purchase our *own* coal, the dockyard people can have no objection, d'ye see, sir?"

"That leaves me two t'haul off," Lewrie glumly replied.

"Well, not *really*, sir," Mr. Pridemore schemed on, "not if Captain Speaks authorises me to *sell* them for him. So many warships laid up in-ordinary . . . so many shivering ship-keepers right here in Sheerness, or a quick sail up to the Chatham Ordinary? I'm certain their usefulness, and their rarity, shall allow me to turn a good profit, to the benefit of Captain Speaks, and myself, of course. All that is needful is for you to sign a chit consigning Captain Speaks's property to me, and all's aboveboard, so to speak."

"Really? That'd do it?" Lewrie marvelled, though there was the dread that Pridemore *was* a Purser, a skillful man of Business and Trade after all, and undertook nothing without a scheme to "get cheap, then sell dear." Pursers were not called "Nip Cheeses" for nothing!

"Do it admirably, sir," Pridemore assured him. "And, whilst we are at it, I believe the Russian gentlemen gifted you with nigh half a bargeload of dainties and luxury goods? Should you wish to dispose of some of them, and save yourself the carting fee to the London market, where you are certain to be 'scalped,' I assure you, Captain, for I am a veteran, and a victim, of sharp practices in the city."

"Not a big market for Roosky *vodka*, Mister Pridemore," Lewrie said, now sure that he might be being "scalped" on his own quarterdeck, "nor for *caviar* and *pâté* in Sheerness, I'd think, though. And, there is some of it I'd like to haul along home."

"But of course, sir!" Pridemore said with a little laugh, "for so would I. The bulk of it, though, I could purchase from you."

"With the bill of sale, though . . . ," Lewrie said, reminded by the word *bulk*, as in "breaking bulk cargo"; unlawful for a warship to do aboard a ship made prize, and the penalty for landing captured goods. "There are the King's Custom Duties to be paid. Do *you* undertake to pay them, once the goods are transferred to your possession, and note such in your bill of sale . . ."

Did I just pinch his testicles? Lewrie had to wonder, to see a brief wince twitch Pridemore's face.

"But, of course, sir, it shall be as you say," Pridemore agreed.

"Let's go below and sort it all out, then," Lewrie suggested, "and have my clerk, Georges, draw up the paperwork, with copies to all before I depart."

Whew! Lewrie thought; *once bitten, twice shy. Maybe with age wisdom* does *come. The last thing I need is another brush with the law over smuggled goods!*

CHAPTER SEVEN

*A*dmiralty in London was very crowded with so many ships being de-commissioned at once, so much so that it had been necessary to make an appointment for a set date and time to begin the process of turning in all his ledgers, forms, logs, punishment books, and pay vouchers. Thankfully, a fortnight shy of Christmas, Lewrie met with the *Second* Secretary to Admiralty, William Marsden, not his nemesis, Sir Evan Nepean, and the whole thing was a fairly business-like and pleasant affair, not the ordeal Lewrie had expected.

Well, there was a half-hour stint in the infamous Waiting Room on the ground level, but the tea cart was set up in the courtyard and doing a grand business, with its tea lads whipping round with hot pots, mugs, and sticky buns, right-active. Lewrie had even found a pew bench seat right off after but a single glare at a Midshipman, who'd gotten the hint and sprung from his place to accommodate a senior officer.

Is he the same snot-drizzler I saw, the last *time I was here?* Lewrie asked himself, for the Midshipman bore a strong resemblance to the mouth-breather with whom he'd shared a bench in February. *Damned if he ain't!* Lewrie marvelled with a faint grimace of distaste to see him snort back a two-inch worm of mucus, then gulp. *Has he been here every day* since? Lewrie wondered, shaking his head at the no-hope's persistence at seeking a sea-berth, even as two-thirds of the Navy was being laid up. *Don't he know there's a war . . . off?* Lewrie japed.

To make more room for Lewrie a Lieutenant shifted over a bit, a very tall and painfully thin young fellow with dark hair and eyes, and dressed in a shabby and worn uniform coat, with a very cheap brass-hilt small-sword on his hip. *Must bash his brains out on ev'ry overhead beam,* Lewrie thought; *maybe one too many already?* he further decided as the gawky "spindle-shanks" stared off into space, lips ajar, and damned near mumbled to himself with a gloomy, vacant expression on his phyz.

"Good morning," Lewrie said, to be polite—and to see if the fellow was truly addled. *Will this'un drool?* he thought.

"Er ah, hem . . . good morning to you, sir," the Lieutenant said with a grave formality, then returned to his dark study.

"Captain Lewrie? Is Captain Lewrie present?" a minor clerk enquired from the foot of the grand staircase.

"Here," Lewrie answered, springing from the pew bench, giving the officer not another thought as he followed the young clerk abovestairs with his bound-together stack of books and papers.

A pleasant ten-minute chat with Mr. Marsden, then Lewrie was passed on to a succession of underlings, from one cramped office to another, even right down to the damp basements where clerks would work on stools and makeshift plank passageways when the Thames flooded in Spring; to file his navigational observations, to hand over ledgers and charts, the final muster book to make official those crewmembers Discharged, Dead, or so injured that they were merely Discharged, and for what reason. Finally, long past his usual dinner hour, Lewrie saw the Councillor of the Cheque, where his final accounting was toted up, the last full-rate pay of a Post-Captain of a Fifth Rate was signed and handed over in full (an assortment of ten-, five-, and one-pound notes on the Bank of England, with only a few shillings and pence in real coin) and his whereabouts, should Admiralty have need of him, noted, thence placing him on half-pay for the near future—minus all the deductions for the aforesaid Chatham Chest and crippled pensioners, robbing him of the eight shillings per day of an active commission, reducing him to six shillings per day of half-pay, but really amounting only to a low three shillings!

By then, with the money in his pockets, and his stack of books and such much reduced, and sure that he had seen almost all thirty of the employees who ran the entire Fleet, Lewrie made his adieus and trotted down the stairs to get his hat and cloak from the hall porter, looking over the Waiting Room in hopes he might espy at least *one* old shipmate before departing, someone who'd shared privations, dangers, and high cockalorums, if only to stave off the dread that there would be *exceedingly* dull times ahead, on his own, without such companionable "sheet anchors" linked to the bulk of his adult life.

One'd think so, Lewrie thought as he took his time buckling on his sword belt, settling the heavy and enveloping boat-cloak upon his shoulders; *an hundred ships o' the line, an hundred frigates, sloops o' war, and brigsloops . . . less'n a thousand active Post-Captains, Commanders, not ten thousand Lieutenants . . . ye'd think I'd know one of 'em in here!*

Well, there were some he'd rather *not* encounter, *this* side of the gates of Hell; Francis Forrester, who'd made Post *years* before he had, the idle, well-connected bastard; that idle "grand tourist" Commander William Fillebrowne; that Captain Blaylock of the rosaceaed phyz back in the West Indies. . . . Come to think on't, there were rather more than a few fellow Commission Sea Officers listed in Steel's *Original and Correct List of the Royal Navy* who'd be more than happy to play-act the "Merry Andrew," glad-hand him, then spit in his tea on the sly, or worse!

There was the drooling, drizzling Midshipman; there was that gloomy, tall, and skeletal dark-haired Lieutenant, now taken to wringing his hands, and there were an hundred strangers. Fie on it!

Lewrie clapped his cocked hat on his head and left, going out to the courtyard, feeling as he imagined an aging foxhound would when left in the run and pen whilst the younger, spryer dogs set out for a hunt . . . to be idly, lubberly, civilian-useless!

"An' there's a proper sea-dog for ye, young ginn'l'men. Merry Christmas t'ye, Cap'um," the old tiler bade him, doffing his own hat and making a clutch of Midshipmen round the tea cart turn to gawk and grin in polite confusion. "Merry Christmas, an' a Happy New Year!"

Christ, will he never *retire?* Lewrie wondered; *or just drop the Hell dead? He's been doorman here since I paid off the* Shrike *brig in '83.*

"And a Merry Christmas t'you," Lewrie answered back, with a doff of his own hat to the old fart, then in responding salute to the Mids as he trudged past for the curtain wall and the street beyond, looking for a hired carriage to bear him to the Strand, his last-minute holiday shopping, and an excellent, but late, dinner at a chop-house in Savoy Street, one introduced to him by his barrister during his legal troubles. Bad memories or not, their victuals were marvellous!

Well, after his dinner, *before* shopping, he would have to drop by Coutts' Bank to deposit his accumulated earnings, then call on his solicitor, Mr. Matthew Mountjoy, to settle his shore debts with notes-of-hand. Then, the day after. . . ?

There would be no more reason to put off going home . . . home to Anglesgreen and the dubious welcome of his wife and dour, disapproving in-laws, all of whom held him in as much regard as a sack of dead barn rats! Lewrie would have thought "a sack of sheep-shit," but . . . sheep-shit was *worth* something, as fertiliser!

CHAPTER EIGHT

*I*t was a long, slow, and muddy road from London through Guildford and on "sutherly" towards Portsmouth, before taking the turning to the Petersfield road. It was cold enough for the ruts to freeze in the nights, then turn to brittle slush by mid-day; to lean out of a coach window was a good way to have one's face slimed by the shower of wet slop thrown up by the coach's front wheels.

The sky was completely overcast, the clouds low, and the winds held a hint of snow in the offing. Indeed, it had snowed sometime in the past two days, for the trees—the poor, bare trees—along the way cupped it in the fork of their branches, and the piles of leaves on the ground were half-smothered in white, as were the fallow pastures and fields last plowed into furrows in Spring. All the crops were harvested, now, the last good from them raked and reaped and gleaned, with only a hayrick here and there, topped with scrap tarpaulin to keep off the wet.

Most of the feed livestock, Lewrie knew, would have been slaughtered by now, too—the beef, mutton, and pork salted, smoked, sugar-cured, or submerged in the large stone crocks filled with preserving lard. It was only the young and breeding beasts that remained in the pastures by the road, in the styes or pens within sight from the rumbling, jouncing coach, and the dray waggon that followed.

"Fair lotta sheep, hereabout, ain't they, sor?" Liam Desmond enquired with a quirky uplift of one corner of his mouth.

"Thousands 'pon thousands of 'em," Lewrie told him. "The comin' thing in the North Downs, since before the American Revolution. We've about two hundred, last time I got an accounting."

"Nothin' like good roast lamb, sor, sure there ain't," Desmond said with a chuckle. Liam Desmond no longer was garbed in a sailor's "short clothing" but wore dark brown "ditto," his coat and trousers of the same coloured broadcloth. He sported a buff-coloured waist-coat, a white linen shirt, even a white neck-stock, and, with triple-caped overcoat and a grey farmer's hat, could almost be mistaken for a man of the squirearchy . . . one who rented his acres, not owned them, at least.

"You'll *founder* on lamb and mutton by Easter," Lewrie said with a wry laugh, for by previous experience, in the country, he'd seen that particular dish on his table rather *more* than thrice a week. In spite of the risk to his complexion, Lewrie let down the window glass and took a quick peek "astern" to see how Patrick Furfy was doing with the dray waggon. Furfy and the waggoner, swathed to their eyebrows with upturned overcoat collars, wool scarves, and tugged-down hats, seemed to be having a grand natter, and he caught the tail-end of a joke that Furfy was telling, and his deep, hearty roar of laughter at its successful completion. Patrick Furfy loved a good joke or yarn but had a hard time relating them onwards, leaving out details that he had to jab in in the middle, and overall had but a limited stash of jokes he could reliably tell.

". . . loight th' candle, help me foind me bliddy equipage, an' we'll *coach* outta this bitch's quim, har har!"

"That'd be Number Twenty-One, sor," Desmond said with a grin, "and I thought he'd nivver git it right." He tugged uncomfortably at his neck-stock and the enveloping folds of his overcoat, not used to such perhaps in his whole life in Ireland, then the Navy.

"Where the Hell did that come from?" Lewrie gravelled as their coach came even with a field that Lewrie recalled as a thinned-out wood lot, bounded by a low hand-laid stone wall. Now, the wood lot was taken over by several new buildings, a brick-works, and a wide gate open in the wall. About an eighth of a mile later, past a stretch of woods, and there was a *tannery*, thankfully down-stream from Anglesgreen. "My eyes, the town's gone . . . industrious! All that's the local squire's land, or it was . . . Sir Romney Embleton's. *He'd* not abide that. Did he pass over, and his son Harry set them up?"

"They good people, sor, the Embletons?" Desmond asked, peering out the windows himself.

"Sir Romney is," Lewrie commented, not sure whether he liked the changes round Anglesgreen; it was a bucolic, boresome place, full of predictable and sometimes tiresome folk, but he'd *hoped* to find it as reassuring as an old shoe . . . just long enough to get tired of it before Napoleon Bonaparte, and Admiralty, snatched him back to active sea service. "Harry delights in killin' horses at fox-huntin', and at steeplechasin', they're no matter t'*him*. Last I was home, he was the Leftenant-Colonel of the local Yeoman Cavalry. Ye can't miss him. . . . He's the chin of an otter, talks louder'n an angry Bosun, and laughs like a daft donkey."

"Faith, sor, but one'd think ye had a down on him!" his Cox'n wryly commented.

"Of long standing, hah!" Lewrie told him with a barking laugh. He took the risk to his hat and hair and stuck his head out the coach window once more, looking back at the brick-works and tannery, grimacing with displeasure to see the steam and stinks rising from them like a pall of spent gunpowder from a two-decker's broadside, hazing off to a flat-topped cloud that slowly drifted eastward.

God help us, does the wind change, he thought, just as a glob of muddy slush plopped against his cheek from the front wheel, eliciting a snarl that had more to do with the new-come industries. He swabbed the muck off with his wool scarf and sat back as he noted several new brick cottages on the left of the road that hadn't been there before, where once there had been a common-shared pasture before the Enclosure Acts that had taken away poor cottagers' grazing and vegetable plot rights, and turned so many from hand-to-mouth self-sufficient to common day labourers on *others'* farms, or driven them to the cities, where the new manufacturies might employ them. At least the dozen or so cottages were on decent plots of land, picket-fenced, with wee truck gardens and decorative flower beds. They were substantial-looking, well-painted, with flower boxes at each window sill, and in the Spring might appear quite pleasant, he decided.

To the right, at last, and there was mossy old St. George's parish church, as stout and impressive as a feudal manor or Norman conqueror's keep, with its low stone walls marking the bounds, now topped by new iron fencing. The expansive graveyard was further bound with iron fencing, too, though the oldest headstones were still lime-green with moss, and tilted any-which-way, as if braced "a-cock-bill" in eternal mourning.

St. George's had marked the eastern boundary of the village the last time Lewrie had been home—*Christ, my last time here was back in '97?* Lewrie realised with a start—but it seemed that that had changed, too, for, hard by the church's fenced boundary there was a lane running north, then a row of two- and three-storey brick and slate-roofed, bow-windowed shops that hadn't been there before, either.

"Milliner's . . . a tailor's . . . a tea shop?" Lewrie muttered half under his breath. "And what's this?" There had been four row-houses just east of the Olde Ploughman public house, but someone had re-done the fronts, closing off half the entrances, and turned two of them to double doors, all to allow entry to a dry goods! "A dry goods?"

Before, anyone wishing to do serious shopping would have had to coach, ride, or hike to Petersfield, the closest substantial town, or go all-in and stay over at Southampton, Portsmouth, or Guildford, but now. . . ! Why, in the dry goods store's windows Lewrie could espy *ready-made* clothing, china sets, and—

"This th' public house ye told us of, sor?" Desmond asked as the coach drew level with the Olde Ploughman. It had been touched up with white-wash recently, sported a new, swaying signboard over the entrance, and new shutters.

"Aye, Desmond," Lewrie told him. "The side yard's a grand place in warm weather, tables outside and . . . coachee! Draw up here, I say!" Lewrie cried, thumping his walking-stick on the coach roof. "As long as we're here, we'll try their ale, the coachee and waggoner, too."

At that welcome news, Liam Desmond sprang from the front bench seat and opened the door, jumping down to lower the folding metal steps for Lewrie, who was out not two seconds behind him, and walking round the head of the coach's team of four to take it all in, bare-headed.

"Ale, Pat!" Desmond cried. "The coachee and yer friend, too!"

"Ale, arrah!" Furfy chortled.

The Olde Ploughman fronted on the large village green that ran along the stream that bisected Anglesgreen, spanned just a bit west of the public house by a stout stone-arch bridge. Across the stream sat a second street, fairly new from the 1780s, once mostly earthen, mud and now and then gravelled. Now the street was cobbled, several row-houses had been turned into even more shops, and there were even more streets south of them, lined with even more of those handsome cottages, situated on spacious acre lots, with room enough for coach-houses and stables, chicken coops and runs, truck gardens, and walled-off lawns. Lewrie gawped in awe, slowly turning to look upstream towards the Red Swan Inn (where the squirearchy and landed gentry did their swilling, and Lewrie was most unwelcome) and found that the village had grown in that direction, too, though the smaller green of the Red Swan was yet untouched, and the groves of giant oaks still stood.

"Neat li'l place, an't it, Pat?" Desmond asked his mate.

"Fair-clean'un, too, Liam," Furfy replied, spreading his arms and expanding his chest to inhale deeply. "Nothin' like th' reeks o' London. Smells . . . farm-y . . ."

"A bit like our auld Maynooth, hey?" Desmond said with a grin.

"Smells *ale*-y," Furfy decided.

"Ale, aye," Lewrie announced. "Ale for all, 'fore we go on to the house."

Spiteful as Caroline's most-like t'be, I might as well go home foxed, Lewrie decided; *it mayn't matter, one way'r t'other.*

The Ole Ploughman was *ancient*, a public house since the days of the Norman Conquest, some speculated. Its interior walls were whitewashed over rough plaster, the few windows Tudorish diamond paned, and the ceiling was low, the overhead beams black with kitchen, fireplace, candle, oil-lanthorn, or pipe smoke.

Or so it had been. During his long absence, old Mr. Beakman and his spinster daughter had added fair approximations of Jacobean Fold wood wainscot panelling. The walls were now painted a cheery red, and the beams, and the barman's counter, looked to be sanded down to fresh, raw wood, then linseeded and *polished* to a warm honey-brown. Beakman had gone with the times and had set aside a dining area round the fireplace on the right-hand half of the vast room, with new tables covered by pale tan cloths, whilst the left-hand half had been re-arranged to accommodate drinkers and smokers round the other fireplace, with double doors leading out to the trellised and pergolaed side garden, which was no longer a scraggly attempt at lawn, but brick-paved and railed in by low picket fences.

There were brass spitoons for those who chewed their quids, and even more brass candleholders along the walls, and brass lanthorns hung from the overhead beams, making the public house much brighter, warmer, and more welcoming a place than ever it had been before.

"My stars," Lewrie breathed as he shrugged out of his cloak and hat, noting the framed pictures hung on the walls, too; old pastorals and race horses, prize bulls and boars, and hunting scenes featuring packs of dogs gathered round mounted riders. "Who did all this?"

"Will ye look at 'im! Cap'm Lewrie t'th' life!" a woman cried from behind the long bar counter, past the customers bellied up to it. "Will, come see who's come home!"

"Maggie Cony?" Lewrie exclaimed, recognising the round-faced local lass who'd married his old Bosun, Will Cony. She'd thickened and gone "apple dumpling cheeked" but she was still the good-hearted and hard-working woman he remembered when both she and Cony had been in his employ 'tween the wars. "You work here now?"

"Tosh, Cap'm Lewrie, we *own* the place now!" Maggie said, wiping her red-raw hands on a bar towel and coming round to greet him.

"Old Beakman sold up?" Lewrie asked, puzzled, as he made her a showy "leg" and bow. Maggie dropped him a curtsy.

"La, 'e wuz gettin' on in years, an' not but 'is daughter t'inherit, an' 'er still a spinster, so, once Will paid off from 'is last ship, with all 'is pay an' prize-money, we made an offer an'—"

"Cap'm Lewrie, sir! Welcome 'ome, by yer leave, sir, why I've not clapped glims on ya in ages an' amen!" Will Cony said with glee as he emerged from the back kitchens. The tow-headed, thatch-haired lad he'd been had thickened considerably, too, and his forehead had grown higher, his top-hair thinned considerably, though still drawn back in a sailor's queue.

"Will Cony! My man! Damme, but ye look hellish-prosperous in a blue apron!" Lewrie told him, stepping forward to shake his hand. "When did ye—"

"Last year, sir," Cony told him, pumping away at his "paw" like a well-handle. "After I'd healed up an' got my Discharge." He stomped his right foot on the clean new floorboards, making a loud sound. "Th' Dons went an' shot me foot clean off, sir, but after a spell in Greenwich Hospital, they fitted me with a knee-boot an' an oak foot, and I 'peg' round as good as ever. Ya come for th' good old winter ale, I'd wager, Cap'm? Yer first taste o' 'ome, not a minute back, and ya come t'th' Olde Ploughman, an' bless ya for it."

"Ale for all my party, Will, and right-welcome it'll be, aye," Lewrie agreed, introducing Cony to Desmond and Furfy, explaining how they'd been with him all through HMS *Proteus*'s commission, then *Savage*, and lastly *Thermopylae*.

"Beakman's daughter, ehm . . . ?" Lewrie had to ask, for before Will had wed Maggie, he'd spooned round the mort (not all *that* bad-looking a wench, really) and though no promises were made, no gifts exchanged to plight a throth—"I give my love a paper of pins, and in this way our love begins"—wasn't this new arrangement prickly?

Happily, Spinster Beakman had found herself a husband at last, a widower with two children, a fellow of middle years hired on by the squire, Sir Romney Embleton, as both a surgeon for the inevitable accidental injuries on his estate, and as a dispensing apothecary in his off-hours. Both the brick-works and the tannery used this new-come Mr. Archer's services, sending their sick and hurt to him with coloured paper chits which required him to treat or dose them for free, though both establishments paid him an annual retainer, as did Sir Romney.

"They've one o' them new cottages, east near the brick-works," Will Cony told them, "an' ol' Beakman's set up proper by their fire in his old age, thank th' Lord . . . though he does tramp in 'ere when th' weather's good, fer th' newspapers, th' ale, an' th' ploughman's dinner." That would have been an apple, a slab of cheese, a pint of beer, and perhaps a hunk of bread; a fixture on every rural tavern's chalked menu board the whole nation over. "Fall off yer 'orse, Cap'm Lewrie, an' Mister Archer'll fix ye right up, no matter 'ow many bones that ye break!"

After the better part of an hour spent in pleasant nattering, it was time to get on. The day was drawing to a close, the sun was lowering, the temperature was dropping, and damned if it didn't smell like there might be more snow in the offing. The hired coach-and-four could put themselves up at the livery stables for the night (at Lewrie's expense), but it would take longer to unload the dray waggon of all of his goods, and most-like the waggoner and his beasts would have to put up in Lewrie's barns for the night . . . and he'd have to feed the man, to boot.

The little convoy clattered on westwards, past the much finer Red Swan Inn, then took the turning for the Chiddingfold road. A half mile onwards, in the vale 'tween two rolling ridges, and there was the drive that led to both Chiswick and Lewrie properties; over a wooden bridge that spanned a narrow, shallow creek rippling over rocks, half covered with skims of ice and now filled with fallen limbs and twigs. Just past the bridge there was a fork; the muddy, unkempt track to the left was Uncle Phineas Chiswick's—a man so miserly that gravel and proper up-keep was too dear. Lewrie's drive lay to the right. There was a muddy patch at its beginning, but beyond that, as the drive ascended the low ridge, it was properly gravelled, almost two coaches in width (quite unlike Phineas

Chiswick's, which was barely wide enough for one!) and lined by trees; trees that had grown in height and thickness since Lewrie had last seen them. At present they were bare, but in Spring, they'd be delightful, and provide both shade and a sense that the drive would lead to a welcoming establishment, with nesting birds twittering and flitting about their hatchlings.

And there was Lewrie's house, at last. It was of grey brick and stone, with a Palladian entrance façade, set back from a circular gravel drive and large, round formal flower bed, now bedraggled and not much to look at, unless one appreciated bare brown stalks and weeds. Lanthorns either side of the entrance and stoop and a single lanthorn by the edge of the flower bed gleamed off the shiny royal blue paint of the door and the large brass Venetian lion door-knocker that Lewrie had fetched back from the Adriatic in '96. Despite the cold, drapes were pulled back in the first-storey windows to display candles, and Christmas wreaths of red-berried holly, ivy, and pine. All three of the fireplaces, and the kitchen chimney at the rear of the house, were fuming as chearly as convivial pipe smokers in a very friendly tavern or coffee-house. Everything said "come in, be welcome," yet . . .

Agamemnon thought Clytemnestra'd be glad t'see him, *too,* Lewrie sourly told himself as he alit on his own land for the first time in years; *wonder if I should tell Cassandra t'wait in the carriage, like* he *did.* And it came to him, a most apt snatch of classical Greek play that he'd stumbled over in his school-days, from *Agamemnon,* in point of fact:

> *It is evil and a thing of terror when a wife*
> *sits in the house forlorn with no man by, and hears*
> *rumours that like a fever die to break again.*

CHAPTER NINE

*H*e thought it good policy to knock, not just barge in. It took a long two minutes, though, before anyone responded to the rapping of his door-knocker. A sour-looking older woman in a sack gown and mob cap opened the door, looked him up and down as she might inspect a drunken, reeling house-breaker, and in a pinched-nostriled and pursed-lipped *impatient* way, haughtily enquired, "Yes? And what is it that you want of *this* house, sir?"

"I live here. . . . It's *mine*," Lewrie snarled back. "Step lively and tell Mistress Lewrie that *Captain* Lewrie's home," he said, walking past the mort, swirling off his boat-cloak, and sailing his gilt-laced cocked hat at the hall tree. "Now?" Lewrie prompted the woman who was balking in prim outrage. "Devil take it . . . hulloa, the house!" Lewrie bellowed in his best quarterdeck voice. "Anyone to home?" He barely had time to take in the black-and-white chequered marble of his foyer, the family portraits on the walls, the twin Venetian bombé chests at either side of the staircase, before chaos befell him.

First, bugling in alarm, came a setter belonging to his elder son, Sewallis, closely escorted by a fluffy, yapping ball of fur he *thought* was a Pomeranian, with his younger son, Hugh, galloping down the stairs and squealing in eleven-year-old glee, whooping like a Red Indian!

"You're home, oh, you're home!" Hugh cried, all but tackling his papa. "Home for Christmas, huzzah!"

With Sewallis, ever a much more staid lad, now fourteen, came a second setter, sniffing arseholes with the first and circling about the reunion in a quandary whether to defend the house or go into paroxysms of delight. The fluff-ball, the Pomeranian, had no doubts about the matter; he would continue to yap, growl, and go for the boots of the intruder . . . once he'd worked up the nerve.

"Sewallis, give us a kiss, lad," Lewrie bade, arms outstretched to give his eldest a warm hug. "Best Christmas ever, ain't it? All of us home, for once? *Damme*, but ye've grown! You, too, Hugh. Two fine young gentlemen, ye've turned out t'be."

"What did you bring us for Christmas, father?" Hugh asked with an impish look.

"Me . . . peace . . . and a waggon-load o' presents," Lewrie assured him. "Where's Charlotte? Where's my little Charlotte, hey? And, can someone shut this wee hair-ball up?" he added as the Pomeranian at last worked up enough nerve to nip at his left boot, and get shoved by a swift leg thrust.

Just in time for his daughter to appear on the landing and let out an outraged squeal of alarm to see her beloved lap-yapper be assailed. She came dashing downstairs to scoop the little dog up in her arms, quickly step back a few paces, and glare accusingly.

"Charlotte, *there* ye are, darlin'," Lewrie said. "Won't ya come and give your papa a welcomin' kiss?"

"You hurt my dog!" she cried, cradling it like a baby; a madly barking, squirming, bloodthirsty little baby yearning for his throat.

"I never, dearest, he was . . . ," Lewrie objected, then quieted as his wife descended the stairs, seemingly in no great hurry to welcome her husband back from the wars, and the sea. "Caroline," he said in a much soberer taking. "I'm home for Christmas."

"For so we see, my dear," Caroline coolly responded, both arms folded across her chest. "Your only letter did not inform us of just *when* you'd appear. When your *affairs* in London would be done."

That citron-sour housekeeper came down the stairs to stand near her mistress, still scowling as fierce as a Master-At-Arms might at a defaulter due at Captain's Mast for his *fifth* Drunk on Watch.

Ouch! Lewrie thought, striving manful not to wince at the chill.

"Your timing is impeccable, though," Caroline continued, with a *tad* of relenting welcome. "Supper will be ready in an hour."

Desmond and Furfy came bustling in at that awkward moment, hands full of sea-bags and carpet satchels; the waggoner followed with a sea-chest, and the dogs went silly once more.

"Uhm . . . this is my man, Liam Desmond, Caroline . . . children," Lewrie told them, "My Cox'n since we fought the *L'Uranie* frigate in the South Atlantic. His mate, Patrick Furfy, who'll be tending to the horses and such. . . . He's a way with animals. . . ."

Sure enough, Furfy did, for right after he'd dropped his burden he whistled and clapped his hands, and the two setters trotted to him, tails a'wag, tongues lolling, and their hind-quarters squirming in joy as he cosseted them with soft words, pets, and crooning Irish phrases.

"We've a stableman already, husband, so . . . ," Caroline began.

"Then we've another, dear," Lewrie baldly told her.

"Oh, very well," Caroline resignedly replied, stiffening a bit. "Mistress Calder, pray show Captain Lewrie's men to his chambers."

"Yes, Missuz," the older mort said, her mouth rat-trapping.

"We've the dray to unload, as well," Lewrie said.

"Then pray do so through the kitchen doors, and do not let any more heat out through the front," Caroline instructed.

"I'll pay the coachee and have the waggon shifted," Lewrie said, hiding a sigh. "Quite a lot of dainties . . . liqueurs, caviar t'stow in the pantry?" he tempted her, hoping for *some* enthusiasm.

"Mistress Calder will show them where to put things," Caroline said, turning to head "aft" for the kitchens herself.

"The waggoner'll stay over for the night," Lewrie told her.

"I'll tell cook to lay three more places in the scullery," she announced, then turned and departed with nary a hug, a kiss, or even a a promise of one.

Petronius had it right, Lewrie sadly thought, recalling another snatch of Latin poetry: *"Reproach and Love, all in a moment, For Hercules himself would be a Torment!"*

An hour later and it was time for supper. Lewrie had hung his uniforms and civilian suitings in the armoire, stowed his shirts and such in a chest-of-drawers, and had made a fair start on emptying his heavy sea-chest . . . in a *guest* bed-chamber at the end of the upstairs hall right above his library and office. He'd borne his swords down to that office-library, just in time to witness Mrs. Calder remove the last of the linen covers from wing chairs and settee, and stoke up the fireplace . . . as if in his absence, the only thing used there was the desk and the leather-padded chair behind it, for farm accounting. Desmond followed him in with his weapons; his breech-loading Ferguson rifle-musket, the long-barrelled fusil musket, the rare Girandoni air-powered rifle, twin to the one that had almost killed him at Barataria Bay in Spanish Louisiana, and his boxed pistols.

From the stairs onwards, his children had followed him as close at his heels as Sewallis's setters, the boys goggling at the firearms and swords. Lewrie hung his French grenadier-pattern hanger above the mantel and stood his hundred-guinea presentation small-sword in a wooden rack, along with five more small-swords of varying worth and quality that he'd captured from the French.

"Ehm . . . are not surrendered swords handed back to the owners?" Sewallis hesitantly asked, tentatively fingering each one.

"They usually are, Sewallis," Lewrie told him with a grin, "but that's hard t'do if they're no longer among the living. That fancy'un there, that was *L'Uranie*'s captain's sword, but he was dead by the time we boarded and took her. A couple of them belonged to Frog Lieutenants, who perished, too. None of the French prisoners would be in a position t'take 'em home to their next of kin . . . on parole here in England, or refused, and ended in the hulks, so I kept them. Got the dead men's names jotted down, and stuck the notes in the scabbards, so I s'pose I *could* forward 'em t'Paris someday soon. No time for that, not as long as the war was still on. Don't play with 'em, Hugh. They aren't *toy* swords. Neither are any of these fire-locks."

"Sir Hugo lets us, when he's down from London," Hugh objected. "He lets us shoot, for real! *And* he's taught us some fencing, too. Said we should take classes from a fencing master."

"Then we'll give that Girandoni air-rifle a try, once the holidays are over," Lewrie promised, taking a welcome seat in a wing chair before the blazing fire, and motioning the boys to sit on the settee. "Mind, *it's* not a toy, either, but . . . if my father allows you use of muskets and pistols already, I think we could have some fun with it. It's *very* good for silent huntin'."

Charlotte had trailed him round the house, too, though silent as a dormouse, lugging her lap dog, by name of Dolly, as if restraining the little beast from attacking him. Now she was seated in the wing chair opposite

Lewrie's, legs sticking out and the dog in her lap, so it could glare and bare its teeth in comfort. Three setters—*Dear God, how many* are *there?* Lewrie asked himself—were sprawled before the hearth, and his cats were in the room as well. Toulon and Chalky were quite used to "ruling the roost," furry masters of both great-cabins and quarterdeck, but the big, slobbery setters' antics and curiosity had driven them to the mantel top—even Toulon, who was not all *that* agile—where they now lay slit-eyed, tail-tips now and then quivering, and folded into great, hairy plum puddings.

"Uhm . . . how long've ye had the pup, Charlotte?" Lewrie asked.

"Last Christmas," his nine-year-old daughter answered. "Uncle Governour and Aunt Millicent brought her from London."

"Takes a lot o' *brushin'*, I'd imagine," Lewrie observed askance.

"Oh yes, she likes it so!" Charlotte replied. "Every day!"

"Know why she calls her Dolly, Papa?" Hugh said with a snigger. "'Cause she's ripped all *t'other* dolls t'shreds, ha ha!"

"Jealousy, is it?" Lewrie japed her.

"Just the *one*, Hugh! Don't be beastly!" Charlotte cried, hugging the dog closer. "She doesn't much care for *cats*, Papa. Nor do I," she announced.

"Ehm . . . were you really at Copenhagen, Papa?" Sewallis asked. "And did you see Admiral Nelson?"

"Saw him, spoke with him the night before the battle, and then after it was over, too," Lewrie answered. "Did I not write you about it? And how they sent us into the Baltic t'scout the enemy fleets and the ice . . . all by our lonesome? Hah! Wait 'til ye see the *furs* that I had t' wear! Swaddled up like a Greenland Eskimo!"

"Ahem!" Mrs. Calder said from the door to the library, looking as if she disapproved of parents speaking with children. "Mistress Caroline says to tell you that supper is served. Come, children. Yours is laid out in the little dining room."

"Aw! We want t'eat with papa," Hugh griped.

"Yes, why can't we all eat together?" Sewallis complained. "He just got home!"

"It's not—" Mrs. Calder began to instruct.

"Aye, it's high time for a *family* supper!" Lewrie announced as he sprang from his chair. "Shift their place settings, and there's an end to it. We've catching up t'do, right?"

"Huzzah!" Hugh exclaimed, and even Sewallis, who'd always put

Lewrie in mind of a solemn "old soul" due to take Holy Orders, beamed with glee and chimed in his own wishes.

Beats dinin' alone with Caroline all hollow, Lewrie thought as they trooped out; *oh, it has t'happen soon, but for now . . . use 'em as so many rope fenders! She can't scream an' throw things at me if the* kiddies *are present . . . right?*

CHAPTER TEN

And thank God it's Christmas! was Lewrie's recurring thought as the Yuletide festivities spun on. His brother-in-law, Burgess Chiswick, now Major of a foot regiment, was down from London with *his* future in-laws and fiancée, the raptourously lovely Theodora Trencher, and Mister and Mistress Trencher, her parents, both of whom were solidly well-off and *immensely* "Respectable" in the new sense; hard-working (prosperous as a result of it), mannerly, high-minded, well-educated, stoutly Christian, involved in "improving" causes, rigidly moral, and more than willing to impose their prim morals on the *rest* of Great Britain!

Lewrie *could* have been treated like a *pariah* by his country in-laws, but for the fact that Uncle Phineas Chiswick, seeing how rich the Trenchers were and being delighted with such a fruitful match, had to grind his false teeth and simper at the black sheep of the family, welcoming Lewrie like a long-lost son! And Governour, his other brother-in-law, now as rotund and red-faced as the lampoonish cartoons of the typical country-bumpkin Squire John Bull, had to plaster a false face and play the "Merry Andrew," though without guests for the holidays he would have happily *shot* Lewrie!

It was immensely, secretly amusing to Lewrie to see his uncle by marriage and Governour bite their tongues whenever the Trenchers said anything favourable about Lewrie, for the whole family were enthusiastic supporters of William Wilberforce and belonged to his Society for the

Abolition of Slavery in the British Empire; Lewrie was their champion for his "liberation" of a dozen Black slaves on Jamaica years before, making them freemen and British tars, "True Blue Hearts of Oak," and for his acquittal at trial for the deed.

To rankle those two even further, Burgess was for Abolition, as well, and had always thought Lewrie one Hell of a fellow, an heroic figure and a wry wag to boot.

And what was even saucier to relish from Uncle Phineas's and Governour's mute fuming was the fact that Uncle Phineas was still invested in the infamous "Triangle Trade," and Governour had been raised in the Cape Fear country of North Carolina before the Revolution and felt that chattel slavery was right and proper!

Oh, it was a merry band of revellers they made, for Chiswicks, Trenchers, and Lewries went *everywhere* together. Did they not dine at Uncle Phineas's, they were at Governour's, or Lewrie's, along with some of the other worthy families of Anglesgreen. Did they not sup at home, there were parish and community suppers, even an invitation to Embleton Hall with Sir Romney (still among the living despite what Lewrie'd feared!) and Harry. And what *Harry* made of having his rival for Caroline's hand come for supper, music, and cards, Lewrie could only imagine . . . and *savour*. Indeed, having Caroline herself over might have galled the fool equally well, for she'd once lashed him with her horse's reins and made his nose "spout claret"!

There were carolling parties beginning at sundown, coaching from farmhouse to farmhouse; through Anglesgreen's snowy streets from the Red Swan to St. George's, and bought suppers in both the Red Swan and the Olde Ploughman, with a round dozen or more to treat at-table. And the hunt club ball, again at Embleton Hall, and the cross-country ride that preceded it!

Mr. Trencher was not quite the skilled rider that his wife and daughter were, but he was dogged at it, and wildly enthusiastic for a steeplechase's jumps. All in all, the Trenchers fit right in as well as a country rector or vicar, for, despite the initial impression of being *very* "Respectable," all delighted at dancing and (Theodora aside) could put away the wines, brandies, and punch like the most affable churchman!

And then, two days before Christmas Day, Lewrie's father, Sir Hugo St. George Willoughby, coached down from London to open his home, Dun Roman (his own horrid pun!), a large, rambling one-storey *bungalow* in the Hindoo style, to pour the rum over the plum pudding, as it were . . . and to light it!

On top of all that, Lewrie and his children went riding almost every morning before the day's planned activities; went shooting with the lighter fusil-musket or the Girandoni air-rifle. They could not *hunt*, not even over their own lands, for Lewrie was Uncle Phineas's *tenant*, not a freeholder, but . . . they could try their eyes at empty bottles and marks whitewashed on a tree. That was great fun for everyone except Charlotte. She insisted on going with her brothers, with her father too one might imagine, but was interested only in the riding part, on her horse-pony, and whenever Lewrie tried to include her, or jest, or merely converse, Charlotte seemed as uninterested as his wife! It was only when Sir Hugo joined their morning rides, with promises of a cauldron of hot cocoa at his place after, that Charlotte opened up and actually essayed a *laugh* or two! Sir Hugo had done much the same with Sophie de Maubeuge, Lewrie's orphaned French ward, years before; it was uncanny.

"You should've had daughters, too, besides me," Lewrie told him in a private moment as they rested their mounts after a spirited gait.

"*Had* one . . . Belinda. Recall? Yer bloody step-sister?" Sir Hugo said with a snicker. "Well, *step*-daughter, at any rate, and look how *that* turned out."

Belinda was still listed in the *Guide to Covent Garden Women*, a highly recommended, and costly, courtesan.

"You bring Charlotte out of her turtle-shell," Lewrie said. "I can't make heads or tails of her moods. The boys, aye, but . . ."

"She's Caroline's, body and soul, lad," Sir Hugo said, "onliest child still at home, and lappin' up her anger 'bout ye like it was my chocolate. How's yer happy *rencontre* with her goin', anyway?"

"Much like a winter's day," Lewrie had to scoff, "short, dark, and dirty. I'm in a guest chamber. We *talk* . . . of nothing, mostly. Thank God for house-guests and the children, else ye'd be measurin' me for a coffin. She *acts* jolly, but that's only 'cause of the Trenchers and Burgess's comin' marriage. Zachariah Twigg did coach down to explain things whilst I was in the Baltic, but there's no sign she took any of it to heart. Too much to forgive, really. And too American-raised. An *English* wife of our class'd be more realistic."

"Don't lay wagers on *that*," Sir Hugo said with a sour cackle. "Women are women, no matter where, or how, they're raised. She's sense, though. There's her place in Society and the children t'consider. Oh, speakin' of . . . what'd ye get the children for Christmas?"

"What?" Lewrie gawped at the shift of topic. "More slide sets for their magic lantern . . . a new doll for Charlotte . . . assumin' her bloody dog don't shred it like the others . . . some French chocolates, now we're tradin' again. Bow and arrow sets, toy muskets and pistols, some more lead soldiers and a model frigate . . . and a half-dozen oranges each. Why, what'd *you* do?" he asked, fearing the worst.

"Well, an open-backed doll house for Charlotte," Sir Hugo said, looking a touch cutty-eyed, "a castle, really, and for the boys . . . swords."

"Swords?"

"Small-swords," Sir Hugo said on. "It's time for them to learn the gentlemanly art of the *salle d'armes*, and there's a skilled man I know from my first regiment, the King's Own, near their school who can instruct them. Do ye not mind payin' half his fee, they should be taught . . . Hugh especially, since we both know he'll most-like end choosin' either the Navy or the Army for his living."

"Well, I s'pose . . . ," Lewrie muttered, seeing the sense of it.

"Started *you* early, I did, and swordsmanship came in damned useful to you," Sir Hugo stated. "Hugh shows promise with the sword, and he's both a decent shot and has a hellish-good seat. He's spunk, and intelligence—"

"Didn't get it from me," Lewrie said with a snort as they both turned to watch all three children in a rare moment of glee, tossing snowballs at each other and running in circles.

"Grant ye that," Sir Hugo wryly jested. "As I said long ago, I still have connexions at Horse Guards, and could have him an Ensign or Leftenant in an *host* of good regiments. Or, with your renown, you could get him aboard a warship captained by one of your friends. What Interest and Patronage is all *about*, after all."

Fellow captains who like me? Lewrie asked himself; *I can count them on the fingers of one hand!*

"Another year and he's twelve," Sir Hugo further speculated. "More school'd just ruin him—"

"Ruined me!" Lewrie barked sarcastically.

"And one can't make General or Admiral if ye start late," Sir Hugo pointed out. "Something t'think about. Hope ye don't mind."

"No, not really. I just worry what Caroline'll make of it when they open their presents," Lewrie said. "Perhaps the Army's best for Hugh. She's rather a 'down' on the Navy, 'cause o' me, and won't much care t'see him followin' in *my* footsteps. And it don't look like our Army's ever going to do all that much overseas, after the shambles we made of it in Holland a while back. Re-take French and Dutch colonies all over again in the Indies, aye, but . . ."

The British Army, in concert with the Russians during a *brief* alliance, had landed in Holland, but had been muddled about like farts in a trance, had been confronted with regular French troops for the first time, and had been humiliatingly beaten like a rug and run out of the country with their tails 'twixt their legs.

As for re-taking West Indies colonies . . . it was never the risk of battle that could worry Lewrie as a father; it was the sicknesses that had slain fifty thousand British soldiers and officers since 1793. The Indies—East or West—were not called the Fever Isles for nought.

"Gad, ye'll be chilled t'th' bone, th' three of ye!" Sir Hugo shouted to the boys, who had given up on snowballs and had gone for tackling each other and heaping armloads of snow over heads and shoulders, breaking off just long enough to chase Charlotte and make her screech. "Hot cocoa at *Dun Roman*! Leave off and saddle up!"

And off they went to Sir Hugo's estate, and his eccentric home with its wide and deep porches all round. It had been a Celtic *dun*, a hill fort, once in the early-earlys, then a Roman legionary watch-tower, then a tumbledown ruin, which Sir Hugo had incorporated into one corner of his home-site, and partially re-furbished; his folly some called it, like the architectured grottoes some very rich landowners had erected in their gardens, lacking only a hired hermit to make them authentic. Moated, once, outer fosse wall restored, though most stone work blocks had gone to make the foundation of Sir Hugo's house. The boys found it the very finest play-fort that any lad could wish.

When it was Phineas Chiswick's land, I courted Caroline there, Lewrie painfully recalled as they topped a rolling rise and the broken-toothed tower came into view; *spread a blanket outside the fosse . . . chilled our wine bottles in the stream . . . kissed her the first time. Where'd all that go? Oh, right. I'm a bastard . . . in more ways than one!*

"Last one t'th' door's a Turk in a turban!" Sir Hugo shouted, spurring his mount, and they were off, snow, slush, and turf spraying from their horses' hooves, and all, Charlotte included, hallooing and whooping with happiness—'til she came in last, of course, was dubbed that Turk in a turban, and got all sulky again.

CHAPTER ELEVEN

*R*espectability had altered the celebration of Christmas, even in Alan Lewrie's times. Gangs of drunken revellers invading a house, led by the Lord of Mis-Rule and bought off with food and drink, were not much seen any longer, even in tumultuous, unruly London. The old custom of church "ales" in which every communicant in the parish, wealthy or poor, honest or otherwise, drank and supped together were things of the past in all but the most rural places, mostly reduced to a supper hosted by landowners for their own cottagers and labourers, more of a post-harvest celebration than a religious one.

So the Lewries, the Trenchers, the Chiswicks, and several other families, direct kin or long-time neighbours, spent Christmas Eve at Uncle Phineas's, with gay dancing right out and carols and hymns round the harpsichord replacing merriment. Mostly due to the fact that Phineas Chiswick would not *pay* for musicians, and held that too much gaiety anent the Birth of the Saviour was irreligious and unseemly. There was not enough wine to enliven things, anyway, or wash down their mediocre supper.

They coached home round ten in the evening, gathered about their own harpsichord, and sang and played livelier airs on their own, with Lewrie on his penny-whistle, Charlotte scraping away on her small violin, Sewallis strumming a guitar, and Hugh making *odd* notes on his recorder.

There was hot chocolate, with scones and jam to make up for the supper, and . . . from the kitchens the competing sounds of Liam Desmond and his *uilleann* lap-pipes, the thudding of Patrick Furfy on a shallow bodhran drum, and someone on the fife.

"Sounds like they're havin' a good time," Lewrie said as their last passable effort at a carol came to a merciful end. "Let's have my lads in for tune or two, and a glass of something."

Mrs. Calder, who had been rocking and knitting in silent disapproval in the corner, gave a faint snort and looked to her mistress to scotch such nonsense.

"They're servants, my dear," Caroline pointed out, making her "my dear" sound strained and forced, said only for the children's sake.

"Who'll attend church with us tomorrow morning," Lewrie countered, "whom we'll gift the day after on Boxing Day, and . . . Desmond and Furfy are sailors, dearest . . . my sailors. Mistress Calder, I would admire did ye fetch a bottle of brandy and sufficient glasses, as you summon them to the parlour."

"Very well, sir," Mrs. Calder replied with a stiff nod, putting away her knitting as if she'd been commanded to set out drink for the Devil himself.

His wife and her chief housekeeper might not have approved, but Lewrie and the children enjoyed the improvement. Sewallis and Hugh learned a "pulley-hauley" chanty or two, and got instruction on how to do a hornpipe dance, then a bit of clogging Irish step-dance, at which the burly Furfy was surprisingly light-footed. The cook and her husband, the scullery girl, Charlotte and Caroline's maids, and the maids-of-all-work (who'd been nipping at a bottle of their own on the sly) got into the spirit of things too and wanted to dance, which required Lewrie and Caroline to play some lively airs to accommodate them. It was nigh eleven before Lewrie uncorked the brandy bottle and began to pour all round.

"Tomorrow, we'll be prim, proper, and serious," Lewrie told them, "and surely inspired by the vicar's homily, but tonight . . . on the eve of our Saviour's birth, let us count our blessings. All charged? May I and my wife wish you all a very Merry Christmas. Now . . . 'heel-taps' and then to our rest!" They all lifted their glasses and drank them down to the very last drops, glasses inverted at the last to show that "heel-taps" had been attained. "Good night, all, and thankee for the merriment."

The children were hugged, hands were shaken, Charlotte kissed and wished sweet dreams, then all were herded upstairs by the sour Mrs.

Calder—sure to hiss and take all joy from the previous hours before they were all tucked in for the night.

"Not sure I *like* that woman," Lewrie grumbled as he poured himself another glass of brandy. "Stiff as that'un we had years ago . . . Missuz McGowan, wasn't it?"

"You disapprove of my choice of housekeeper, or governness, do you?" Caroline snapped. "It is my house, after all . . . my housewifery, year in and year out, but for the few brief spells you allow us from the Navy. I am quite satisfied with Mistress Calder's management of both house and children . . . else the boys would be as wild as so many Red Indians . . . as wild as *you*, sir!"

Merry bloody Christmas t'you, too! Lewrie thought with a groan, his nose in his glass; *this ain't workin'. Never will, most-like. I might as well lodge in London at the Madeira Club 'til Hell freezes up.*

"The boys are only home 'tween school terms, these days," Lewrie pointed out. "And Charlotte ain't the wild *sort*, Caroline. She's more in need of tutorin' at dancin' and music than grim discipline."

The glare he got could have shattered boulders.

"But I will defer t'your wishes, your ways," he quickly added.

"For as long as you stay," Caroline grimly said. "Which is?"

" 'Til the French start the war again, I am *home*," Lewrie told her. "It's my home, too. And 'til the boys leave for Hilary term, I hope we can share it . . . in a *sham* of harmony, at any rate. After that, well . . . you're the 'Post-Captain' o' this barge, and I'll try to accommodate my ways to yours. Stay out from under foot . . . all that," he allowed in a soft voice that would not carry abovestairs, chin tucked in defensively. "I don't s'pose Zachariah Twigg's visit made any impression at all?"

"What a *horrid* man!" Caroline exclaimed, her own arms folded over her chest. "Like an oily . . . spider!"

"And a hellish-dangerous one, t'boot," Lewrie agreed. "And God help any foe or spy that crosses his hawse. Every time he hauls me in on one of his schemes, it's neck-or-nothing, and cut-throats and murderers on ev'ry hand. Fair gives me the 'colly-wobbles,' he does."

Zachariah Twigg, until his partial retirement from His Majesty's Government, had served the Crown in the Secret Branch of the Foreign Office for years, and had been Lewrie's bug-a-bear since 1784, off and on. Oh, he'd sworn he'd coach down to Anglesgreen to explain who had written the poisonously anonymous letters to Caroline—Theoni Kavares Connor—and the why, which had been spite that she could not have

Lewrie for her own; and how so many of the sexual dalliances she had accused Lewrie of—in such lurid detail—had been complete fictions, . . . or so richly embellished.

Twigg's promised expiation could not erase *all* of Lewrie's overseas doings, of course: his mistress in the Mediterranean when commanding the *Jester* Sloop of War, or the fact that Lewrie had indeed seeded Theoni Kavares Connor with a bastard son, but . . . the rest of it was a fantasy *meant* to harm.

"*Have* t'talk about us . . . sooner or later," Lewrie told her, shrugging as he took another sip of brandy. "After Epiphany or—"

"Yes, we do, Alan," Caroline softly agreed, looking down at the pattern of the parlour carpet. She looked up then, almost beseechingly, with the vertical furrow 'tween her brows prominent. "Do you *love* me, Alan? Even after all your . . . do you still love me?"

Caroline was not the sprightly young miss he'd first met during the evacuation of Wilmington, North Carolina, back in his days as a Midshipman in the American Revolution. Nor was she the lissome bride he'd taken vows with at St. George's. Yet . . .

"Aye, I do, Caroline," he told her, and felt his chest turn hot, his eyes mist a bit with the truth of it, no matter everything else he had done. "I still do. Not for the children, not—"

"Then we shall see, Alan," she promised, arms still crossed in protection. "Once Yuletide is done, we shall see. Good night."

She paused at the double doors to the foyer and looked back for a mere trice. "Merry Christmas," she said, then headed for the stairs, a very brief smile that might have been wistful, or rueful, turning up the corners of her mouth, wrinkling the riant folds below her eyes for the slightest moment.

"Well I'll be double-damned," he breathed, muttering softly in wonder. "Might be a beginnin' after all!" He tossed off his brandy to the last drop, set the glass aside, and went abovestairs to his own bed—down the hall in the guest chamber, still—where Toulon and Chalky at least gave him *some* affection after he'd rolled into a cold bed. "Merry Christmas to you, lads. Merry Christmas to us all."

Though they did not snuggle the way he longed for.

BOOK II

It was the best of times,
it was the worst of times...
CHARLES DICKENS,
A TALE OF TWO CITIES

CHAPTER TWELVE

*C*hristmas Day, and the opening of presents, had passed, as had Boxing Day on the twenty-sixth; most gifts had gone over well, but for the *toy* muskets and swords. Sir Hugo's real blades had made the biggest impression, and cause for chaotic tumult as Hugh and Sewallis practised their initial lessons on each other . . . swash-buckling through the entire house 'til Lewrie and his father took them in hand in the barren back garden and gave them both some sword exercises learned from hard and bloody experience. At least Charlotte was ecstatic over her new doll(s), books, and miniature fairy castle.

After Epiphany, though, the boys coached away to begin their new school term, with "grandfather" Sir Hugo as their avuncular escort, and it was back to the routine drudgery of village and farm life in a cold midwinter, and only Lewrie, his wife, and daughter in the house.

And, much like the descriptions he'd read of North American porcupines mating, Lewrie found the process of reconciliation, and the enforced "togetherness," a *prickly* endeavour. With few occasions for visiting about, or receiving callers in return, and with Charlotte busy at her studies with her hired tutor, there were simply *too* many hours in a day. Not that it was boresome . . . exactly.

Wake, rise, and dress in the guest bed-chamber promptly at six; a quick shave and scrub-up, and breakfast was taken in the smaller dining room, *en famille*, round seven. Farm accounts, worked on together in his office, occupied another hour or so, with Lewrie the student and she the master, striving manful to remember what little he'd known of managing a farm from years before; striving manful to stay awake and pay heed to Caroline's "surely, you recall how . . ." or "surely, you remember what I once told you of . . ." lectures on crop rotation, animal husbandry, and sheep. A full pot of strong, hot coffee was *very* necessary!

Round ten or so, Caroline was busy with Mrs. Calder, the cook, or the tutor, and Lewrie had time in which to read a book or take a stroll through the barn and stables. Half-past twelve, though, and it was time for dinner. It was only by mid-afternoon that he was free to saddle up his old gelding, Anson, and canter into Anglesgreen to the Ploughman to have a pint or two and read the daily papers coached from London.

And, damn his hide did he linger too long or come home in his cups, either. No, once the papers were read, and a natter or two with Will and Maggie Cony and the idle regulars, life with his wife went *so* much better did he ride back out to his farm and skirt the bounds over the fallow fields, streams, and wood lots 'til his phyz was chilled to rosy red, and the last, lingering fumes of ale were dissipated. After that, he could return, about an hour before supper, for a *stiff* session in the parlour with wife and daughter, now free of household chores or lessons. A doting fuss must be made over Charlotte's lap dog, Dolly, though the wee beast still bared her teeth and flattened her ears whenever he got *too* close. Toulon and Chalky would huddle with him on the settee for safety, for lap, and for affection, flattening *their* ears, bottling tails and hissing fit to bust whenever Dolly approached too near at her play. His cats got along much better with Sewallis's wee pack of setters, all three of whom would never make true hunting dogs, and were goofily lumbering playmates.

A little music, some teasing banter with Charlotte (and a stiff glass of brandy) and it was time to sup together, again. After that, it was usually back to the parlour for more music together, or teaching Charlotte the simpler card games, before Mrs. Calder herded her up the stairs, leaving Lewrie and Caroline alone together.

"Chess," Lewrie said, apropos of nothing, to fill a void. "Or backgammon. D'ye think Charlotte'd enjoy learning those?"

"She hates to lose, though, Alan," Caroline answered, looking up from her current embroidery project.

"Can't learn to win 'less ye lose a few first. And she ought to learn that Life don't always *let* ye win. Even if she is a girl, she mustn't be so cossetted, or spoiled, she ends up a sore loser. The boys know it . . . *have* t'know it before they enter adult lives and careers."

"You say I cosset her?" Caroline asked with one brow up.

"Not at *all*, Caroline!" Lewrie quickly countered, wondering how deep in trouble he was stepping. "It's just that . . . damn."

Caroline gave a rare, mischievous smile. "It's refreshing that you show concern for her improvements, dear. 'Damned if you do, damned if you don't'?"

"Something like that," Lewrie admitted, squirming.

"She's always been head-strong," Caroline explained, returning to her embroidery of a new handkerchief. "Though usually a sweet and bid-dable girl, well . . . with two older brothers to vie with before we sent them away to school, and now the only child in the house, she's developed a competitive streak . . . one which I've tried to scotch, as unseemly for a young lady. You may not have noticed, being at sea so long." And for once, that did not sound like a sour accusation.

"But you think introducin' her to new games'd not go amiss?"

"Even does she pout when she loses, I think she'd adore them," Caroline told him with another grin. "She's playing with her *father*, whom she hasn't seen in years, and with both of us cautioning her to be a better sport, well . . . !"

"Tomorrow, let's *all* go for a ride together," Lewrie suddenly suggested. "Hang the kitchen and still-room for a day, there's your capable Mistress Calder to oversee things. That new tea shop in the village . . . tea and sticky buns or muffins . . . the dry goods store to prowl? Ride the bounds together, maybe put up a fox and have a go at 'View, Halloo'? Away from her tutor and lessons for a bit, that'd be a treat, surely."

"That is a marvellous idea, Alan!" Caroline eagerly said. "We will tell her at breakfast. And I must own that some time away from household drudgery will suit me right down to my toes, as well."

"Good, then, we'll do it!" Lewrie exclaimed.

"Well," Caroline determined, gathering up her embroidery, "it is time for me to retire. Do not sit up too late. Goodnight, dear."

And, wonder of wonders, she actually crossed the short space 'twixt settee and her chair to lean over and give him a brief peck on his forehead before stepping away.

"Goodnight, Caroline," he replied, half-stunned, unsure whether he should respond in kind; she was walking to the doors and out of his reach before he could decide.

"You see, Alan . . . domesticity can be very pleasant," she said as she paused in the doorway once more, with yet another of those enigmatic smiles. "After so many years of grim war and separation, your family *can* be a source of joy and contentment."

Aye, it can, Lewrie thought once she was gone; *though nine parts outta ten just bovine boresome!*

CHAPTER THIRTEEN

"*H*uzzah, we've letters!" Lewrie cried as he entered the house after an hour or so at the Olde Ploughman. "Letters and newspapers."

"Who are they from?" Caroline asked, bustling into the foyer from the kitchens, pantry, and still-room, where Spring cleaning had kept her occupied.

"Uhm . . . one from Sophie and Anthony Langlie," Lewrie told her, shuffling through the pack, "one from his parents, too. Burgess has written us . . . one from my father . . ."

"Oh, give me Burgess's!" Caroline enthused, drying her hands on her apron as they went to the many-windowed office at one end of the house, for Charlotte was practicing with her music tutor in the formal parlour. The windows were open, the drapes taken down to be beaten on lines outside and air fresh, as were the carpets. After months with the house shut against winter's chill, the accumulated mustiness from candles, lamps, and fireplaces was being dispelled, replaced with the soft breezes of Spring that wafted in the scents of the first blossoms in the gardens, fresh-springing grass and leaves, the twitter of birds, and the soft cries from the nearest pens where sheep were lambing.

Along with the first wasps of Spring, which Lewrie spent time to swat or shoo before opening the letter from Sophie, their former ward, and his old First Lieutenant aboard HMS *Proteus* and HMS *Savage*.

"Yes!" Caroline shouted in triumph. "Alan, my brother is to be *wed*. . . . The first banns were published last Sunday! Oh, how *grand*!"

"And good for him, at last," Lewrie heartily agreed. "When do we expect the wedding, and where?"

"What a splendid match!" Caroline further enthused before giving him the details. "Uhm . . . at the Trencher family's home parish, in High Wycombe,"

"Not *so* very far," Lewrie replied, more intent on the Langlies' letter. "Didn't know the Trenchers were landed. Still . . . rich as he is, I'm sure her father's found some 'skint' lord with a large parcel that *ain't* entailed, and willing t'sell up t'settle his debts."

England was crawling with "new-made men" of Trade and Industry, men risen from the middling classes who aspired to emulate the titled and long-standing landowners, with country estates and acres of their own without *renting*. The law of entail, though, awarded the inheritance of the *income* that land generated, not the land itself, to eldest sons, who could not dispose of it; nor could *their* sons. It was only the grandsons of the heirs who could sell off land, but a new deed of settlement could stave off that shocking event to *that* heir's grandson for another *three* generations, and it was a rare thing to see land be sold outright.

"Uhm . . . perhaps some former commons land, taken 'tween deeds of settlement, under an Enclosure Act," Caroline, ever practical-minded, idly commented as she squirmed excitedly in her chair. "Oh! The first Saturday after Easter! The boys can be home and attend with us! A suitable wedding present, though . . . over Christmas, Theodora told me her paraphernalia is quite extensive already, hmm . . ."

Beds, linens, plate, and *a thousand pounds per annum, to boot,* Lewrie idly thought, imagining that the lovely and charming Theodora Trencher might fetch along her own coach-and-four, thoroughbred saddle horses, a likely entry in the Ascot and the Derby, *and* a townhouse of her own in London. *Lucky bugger, that Burgess,* he told himself.

"Good God!" Lewrie exclaimed after scanning the first page of Sophie's letter. "Sophie . . . she and Langlie have just come back from *France*! From Paris, and her old lands in Normandy. Them and Langlie's parents, both!"

"From *Paris*?" Caroline gawped. "And they didn't lop off their heads? What risks they took!"

Lewrie had rescued Sophie, her mother, and her brother from Toulon before the besieged forces of the First Coalition had evacuated; the poor girl had been, for a brief time, the *Vicomtesse* Sophie, pitiful "meat" for the guillotine and the murderous wrath of the Jacobin revolutionaries who were red-eyed-mad for eliminating every "aristo" family, root and branch, and anything that smacked of nobility. Such revolutionary sentiment and old grudges, Lewrie imagined, still held sway.

"Surely not t'get her lands back," Lewrie said, reading on. "I doubt . . . aha. Damme if she don't say they had a *grand* time, a proper honeymoon month. Evidently, they took her for an English girl who—"

"Would that not be risk enough?" Caroline quipped.

". . . who could speak fluent French. As Missuz *Langlie*, with an English husband, they hardly had a *spot* o' bother. Saw all the sights in Paris . . . ate *well*, attended balls and levees, all sorts of things. Hmm . . . ," Lewrie said, reading off salient points. "*And* it now seems there's t'be a *Langlie* heir in the near future, Caroline. Sophie says to inform you she is . . . *enceinte*. Or *grosse*, d'ye prefer the colloquial French. Expectin', ha! Here, I'll let you read it for yourself."

"Later," Caroline demurred. She and Sophie: once one of those lying letters had arrived declaring that Lewrie had been topping her, *too*, Caroline had turned from fond to outright spiteful towards Sophie, spurring the girl to flee to London into the dubious aegis of Sir Hugo St. George Willoughby, her adored, adopted *grand-père*. Even now, after Sophie and Anthony Langlie had wed and those slanders had been found to be utterly false, Caroline still seemed glad to be shot of her. Lewrie doubted if she *would* read that letter.

"What is the rest of the post?" his wife asked after putting the glad tidings from Burgess Chiswick aside.

"Oh, there's two from the boys," Lewrie told her, still engrossed.

"Oh, you!" she cried, only a *tad* vexed, springing from her seat to the desk to paw through the stack. "One would think you'd set them aside as if you were still captain of a ship! Official things first, and personal last. You'd deprive me of word from my dear lads?" she said, but it was a *teasing*, almost *fond* admonishment for his lapse.

"Apologies, m'dear," Lewrie told her.

"Hmm . . . dear old Wilmington?" Caroline puzzled, looking over a travel-stained letter. "Oh, your old friend, is he not engaged in business there? The one who sent a deposition for your trial?"

"Christopher Cashman, aye," Lewrie agreed. "He bought into an import-export and chandlery . . . Livesey, Seabright, and Cashman. Has offices and warehouses on Water Street, he wrote me. The sawmill on Eagle's Island cross the river . . ."

"Why, we *knew* the Liveseys . . . before the Revolution. Rebels, though decent people in the main," Caroline fondly reminisced of her girlhood home in the Cape Fear Low Country. "The only Seabright that I recall was a new-come from England . . . an officer of the Royal Artillery who'd emigrated for land. *Married* a Livesey, I think he did. *He* was a rebel, too. Helped manage the guns at Widow Moore's Creek bridge . . . when our friends and neighbours from the Scot settlements at Cross Creek and Campbelltown were slaughtered. Ah, well. And . . . who is Desmond McGillivery, from Charleston?"

"Say who again?" Lewrie started; he'd missed that'un when he'd hurriedly sorted through them, and, good as things seemed to be going with his wife, they could turn to sheep-shit the instant she learned that Desmond McGillivery was yet *another* of his bastards, a result of his brief, very unofficial "wedding" to a captured Cherokee slave of the Muskogee Indians when he'd been up the Apalachicola to entice them into war against the Yankee Doodle frontier. "Oh! I remember! He was a Midshipman in the American Navy I met back in Ninety-Eight. His uncle was captain of one of their cobbled-together warships going after the Frogs when America and France got huffy with each other. I felt sad for the lad. . . . His mother was *Indian*, don't ye know. We've corresponded . . . on and off. Wonder what he's up to now?"

Caroline paid that letter no more attention, enrapt by those from Sewallis and Hugh, and thought no more about it.

Whew! Lewrie secretly gloated; *cheated death again!* He *would* reply to Desmond's letter . . . very *much* on the sly. And pay stricter attention to the senders' names the *next* time he collected the mails.

CHAPTER FOURTEEN

*W*onder of wonders, domestic relations took an even sweeter turn as Spring progressed, as Sewallis and Hugh returned from their school for the summer and filled the house with japes, pranks, and laughter. There were more family rides together, more companionable breakfasts, walking tours of the farm through sheep, cattle, and foals, nattering with day labourers and their few permanent employees, and yarns from Liam Desmond and Patrick Furfy about battles and grand adventures.

The Lewries even went visiting, as a travelling troupe; first to High Wycombe to attend Burgess and Theodora's nuptials, then up to London for some major shopping, and, lastly, down to the Langlies' at Horsham, in Kent, to visit with Sophie and her husband and in-laws. Even Lewrie's father, Sir Hugo, had coached down for that'un, for he'd always been doting-fond of Sophie, as she had been of him, her replacement *grand-père*.

Lodgings, well . . . they *could* reach London in a day, but once there, their favourite old haunt in Willis's Rooms, convenient to all the best shops and sights, could only accommodate so many guests, in so many beds. Charlotte and the boys could be bedded down on cots or in one nearby room. Lewrie and his wife were forced to share a bed-stead of their own . . . together.

The same arrangements were forced upon them halfway to the wedding at High Wycombe, and in a posting house in the town, as well, and the jaunt to Horsham not only forced Alan and Caroline to sleep in the same bed on the way, but, once there, Mr. and Mrs. Langlie insisted upon putting them up at their house, assuming that Capt. and Mrs. Lewrie were just another typical married couple who *naturally* shared a bed-chamber!

Perhaps it was the joy of Burgess's wedding, perhaps the relit notion of Romance (and a slew of wines and brandies taken aboard during the day!) but . . . Alan and Caroline found themselves in such close proximity, in such companionable darkness, and in such *thin* summer sleeping clothes, that Nature at last had its way. And in the mornings *after* such enforced intimacies, Caroline expressed such fondness and affection that Lewrie could imagine that their years' long bitterness had been no more than a quickly forgotten little spat over her paying too much for a new bonnet!

And even more miraculous was the fact that, once back home in Anglesgreen, there was no more of that damnable guest chamber for *him*. Lewrie was back in his wife's good graces . . . though he hadn't a *clue* how it had come about! Indeed, so content with things did she seem that Caroline could even abide a mid-Summer visit from Sir Hugo, down from London for a spell of country life. He'd *never* been one of her favourite relations, yet . . .

"More cool tea?" Caroline asked Sir Hugo as they all sat in the shade of an oak near the back-garden of the house. "Or might you be more partial to the lemonade?"

"The tea, m'dear, thankee kindly," Sir Hugo replied, sprawled in a slat chair near the table, and idly fanning himself, for it was a warmish afternoon. "That rob o' lemon drink makes me *gaseous*. Just a *dollop* o' lemon in the tea's sufficient."

A wasp now and then hummed about the sweetness of the lemonade or the napkin-covered plates of scones or sandwiches. Horses snorted, neighed, and clopped as Patrick Furfy walked them in circles in the paddock. Cattle lowed as calves butted for their milk; and it was almost so quiet as to be able to hear sheep munching grass. Except for the children, of course.

Charlotte sat at-table primly enough, to all appearances in her style of hair and gown a miniature adult, though she *did* tend to prate cooing nonsense to her newest doll and that damned lap dog of hers. Sewallis and Hugh were on their knees, sailing their model frigates at each other over a close-mowed green "sea" and ordering their sailors about, just ready to open fire.

Lewrie sat sprawled in an equal un-tidyness in a chair on the other side of the table, a wide-brimmed straw farmer's hat set low on his eyebrows, one eye open for the shrill argument to come over "first broadsides" and what "damage" the boys' guns had done to the other one's hull or rigging.

"Have you ever been to Paris, or to France, Sir Hugo?" Caroline casually enquired.

Halloa, what's that? Lewrie thought.

"France?" Sir Hugo scoffed. "Can't say that I have, d'ye not count Calais. Was in Holland, for a time, d'ye see, and . . . found it more convenient t'return t'England through Calais," he breezed off.

Haw! Lewrie silently sneered.

Long ago, when a Captain in the 4th Regiment of Foot, the King's Own, he scampered off from his "wife," Elizabeth Lewrie, once he discovered that some of his fellow officers had bamboozled him with a "false justice," a sham wedding, and an elopement to Holland, there to wait for the riches that should have come with his mother's dowry and goods. Once Sir Hugo'd discovered that there would *be* no quick fortune, that a very pregnant girl was boresome, nagging, and a burden on his shrinking purse, and that he was, technically, as free as larks, he had fled her, taking her jewelry along, and *danced* his way back to London!

"Didn't know that," Lewrie commented. "I thought you'd sailed direct from Amsterdam." He tilted up the brim of his hat to peer at Sir Hugo's answer to that, tacitly jeering.

"Got distracted," Sir Hugo rejoined with a toothy fuck-ye-for-asking smile. "Why d'ye ask, m'dear?"

"Well . . . now we're at peace with France," Caroline tentatively said as she poured a glass of tea for herself, "and it seems that they mean for it to last . . . I was thinking on what Sophie and her husband told us of their jaunt over there. It may not be like a Grand Tour of the Continent, as wealthier folk than *we* undertake, yet . . . I must own to a certain . . . curiosity."

Very rich members of the aristocracy considered a Grand Tour of France, Holland, some of the Germanies, Spain, and Portugal, and, of course, the ruins of ancient Rome and the "artistic" cities of Italy, with a stopover in Vienna and Venice, a necessity for the "finishing" of their well-educated and polished children. And to seek bargains in paintings, sculptures, and gold and silver work to enhance the furnishings of their mansions and estates.

"*Seen* Toulon, at least," Lewrie harrumphed. "Spots ashore in the

Gironde, to boot. That's enough o' France t'hold *me* for a lifetime. A *squalid* damned place, Toulon. Dirtier than Cheapside or Wapping. No, I don't mean you, cat. *You* know t'bathe, if the Frogs don't," he had to tell his black-and-white tom, who, at the mention of his name, leaped into Lewrie's lap. Not to be left out of it, Chalky came trotting to join Toulon, abandoning his butterfly hunt.

"It would be educational for the boys," Caroline went on in an off-handed way. "Improve their French, which every civilised man *must* speak."

"*Je suis un crayon, mort de ma vie,*" Lewrie quipped.

"Oh, tosh!" Caroline objected. "So you're a pencil, are you . . . death of your life?"

"Papa's a *pencil*?" Charlotte gawped, then burst into titters.

In point of fact, Lewrie's French was abysmal; *execrably* bad.

"I s'pose a tour o' France might teach 'em something, m'dear," Sir Hugo told her. "How vile are the French . . . so they hate 'em as bad as the Devil hates Holy Water, th' rest o' their lives, haw haw!"

"Perhaps as a . . . *proper* honeymoon," Caroline said, lowering her eyes and going a tad enigmatic. "As Sophie and Anthony did not have when they wed, with his ship ready to put back to sea as soon as the wind shifted. As short as ours was . . . recall, Alan?"

There had been one short night at a posting house in Petersfield and two weeks at the George Inn in Portsmouth, with him gone half the time fitting out little HMS *Alacrity* for her voyage to the Bahamas.

"Hemm," uttered both Lewrie and his father, for both knew what she was driving at, and the reason for it.

"You're *sunk*!" Hugh yelled. "I shot you clean *through*!"

"Did *not*!" Sewallis loudly objected. "I *dis-masted* you, so you can't *move*!"

"Can *too*!" from Hugh, face-down on the grass to shove his ship.

"Ships don't *sink*!" Sewallis insisted, shuffling on his knees to move his model frigate. Hugh's followed, at a rate of knots.

"Do *too*! They burn . . . they blow *up*! You're on fire!"

"Lads!" Lewrie barked, springing from his chair and scattering cats. "Leave off!" Another instant and they'd be rolling and pummelling each other. "Here, let me show you how things go."

Lewrie knelt on the grass, green stains on the knees of his old and comfortable white slop-trousers bedamned. "Now, which of ye is the enemy?"

Both pointed at the other accusingly, faces screwed up.

"Let's say the wind's from there, from the stables and the paddock," he instructed, "so you both should be sailin' *this* way, on the same course. Sewallis has the wind gage, aye, but his larboard guns can't elevate high enough to dis-mast ye, Hugh. You, on the other hand, in his lee, *can* shoot high enough . . ."

And, as he explained to his sons, a couple of curious setters, and both cats, that it was very rare for a ship to be sunk in action, that extreme pains were taken to prevent fires, and that it might take an hour or better to batter a foe into submission, Caroline looked on with a fond smile on her face, the very picture of contentment as she absently jammed a fresh scone for Charlotte.

"Ye look . . . pleased with life, m'dear," Sir Hugo pointed out.

"In the main I am, sir, thank you," she told him with a grin.

"France, though . . . Paris?" Sir Hugo queried with a scowl.

"Perhaps a second honeymoon, . . . as I said. A proper one this time," she answered, Though she was smiling, the determined vertical furrow 'twixt her brows was prominent. "After all I've had to put up with . . . I believe we owe it to each other. A fresh beginning."

"That he owes *you*, more t'th' point?" Sir Hugo leered.

"Indeed," Caroline rejoined with a slow, firm nod.

CHAPTER FIFTEEN

*T*his'll most-like put me in debtors' prison, 'fore we're done! Lewrie rue-fully told himself as he delved into his wash-leather coin purse to tip the porters, once their luggage had been stowed aboard the hired coach—some in the boot and the most valuable inside the box. It was prime sport for vagrants and street thugs to slit the straps and leather covers of the boot and make off with the luggage, with the travellers all unsuspecting 'til they reached their last stop.

The porters were a surly lot, unhappy to accept British coinage and to deal with an *Anglais*, a "Bloody," a *Biftec* in pidgin French.

"All square?" Lewrie asked the porters. "Uh, *c'est tout? Bon?*"

"Uhn," growled one; "Grr," the other porter sourly replied.

"*Au revoir*, then," Lewrie concluded, boarding the coach. "And may ye all catch the pox . . . if ye ain't poxed already," he muttered under his breath after closing the coach door. "Such a warm and *welcomin'* people, the Frogs," he told his wife, Caroline, seated by herself on the forward-facing padded bench seat. "Feelin' a touch better, my dear?" Lewrie so-licitously enquired.

"The ginger pastilles seem to have availed, yes," she replied.

The crossing on the small packet from Dover to Calais had been a rough one. They'd had bright skies and brisk winds, but the narrows of the Channel when a strong tide was running could produce a prodigious

chop, and the packet had staggered and swooped over steep ten-foot seas
with only thirty or fourty feet between the swells. The last time that
Caroline had been at sea, returning from the Bahamas aboard the little
HMS *Alacrity*, a ketch-rigged bomb converted to a shallow-draught gun-
boat that would bucket about in any sort of weather past placid, she'd suffered roiled innards for days before regaining the sea legs she had found
on the stormy passage *out* in 1786.

The packet voyage had been so short that Caroline had had no time to
acclimate, and she had spent most of the trip past the harbour mole by a
bucket or the lee rails. Even last night, spent in a squalid Calais travellers'
inn, she could tolerate nothing more strenuous than cups of herbal tea and
thin chicken broth.

The ginger pastilles were made in London by Smith & Co., recommended by another couple crossing to France with them, Sir Pulteney
"Something Fruitish" and his wife, Lady "Starts with an I," both of 'em
of the most extreme languid and lofty airs, the sort that set *English* teeth
on edge. Worried about Caroline, Lewrie hadn't paid all that much attention to the social niceties and, once on solid ground at Calais, had been
more than happy to decline an invitation to dine with the "Whosits," on
account of Caroline's tetchy *boudins*. . . . A further vague suggestion to
meet again in Paris, he'd shrugged off, as well.

"Well, we're off," Lewrie said to fill a void as their coachee whipped up
and set their equipage in motion.

"Once out in open country, and fresh, clean air, I expect that we shall
enjoy this much better," Caroline opined, holding a scented handkerchief
to her nose as she looked out the windows. "It will be a fine adventure, I'm
bound."

"Sweeter smellin' than Calais, at any rate," Lewrie agreed with her.
"Seaports always reek." Though he suspected that every French city or
town would prove as noxious as Dung Wharf or the old Fleet Ditch in
London, long ago paved over. *And how the Devil did I end up chivvied into
this?* he asked himself for the hundredth time; *guilt most-like*. No one back
in Anglesgreen had thought much of their jaunt to France. Well, Millicent
Chiswick, Caroline's brother's wife, had deemed it a very romantic idyll,
but she was about the only one.

Weeks of, well . . . not *exactly* harping and nagging had preceded the
actuality. There'd been French maps and atlases turning up mysteriously,
then a weedy university lad to tutor the *children* in French, though he and
Caroline had somehow become pupils as well. Not that those lessons had

done Lewrie's linguistic skills all *that* much good. He had a smattering of Hindi from service in the Far East between the wars in '84, a dab or two of French from duty in the Mediterranean in the '90s (and several good public schools from which he had been booted!), and a few words and phrases of Russian from dealings with the delectable Eudoxia Durschenko and her equally appalling papa, and his most-recent service in the Baltic.

Curse words, mostly, foul oaths and the sketchiest, rudimentary necessities such as "I will order the . . . , fetch me . . . , too hot, too cold, hello, good-bye, d'ye have any ale," and the ever-useful "fetch out yer whores." Schoolboy Greek was still a mystery, too, though he had done rather well in Latin . . . mostly due to all the battles described, and the lurid and scandalous poems.

Caroline heaved a petulant sigh and knit her brows, creating that vertical furrow that was usually a sign of her anger. Lewrie'd gotten very familiar with that'un over the years, and involuntarily crossed his legs to protect his "wedding tackle."

"Somethin' troublin', Caroline?"

"Oh, the children," she replied, fretful. "I *know* I thought our getting away would help, but . . ."

"They're havin' a *grand* time, dear," Lewrie told her. "Don't fret about them."

His father, Sir Hugo St. George Willoughby, had agreed to spend most of the summer in the country, and would look out for the boys at his Dun Roman, with the help of his exotic "man," Trilochan Singh, a swarthy, one-eyed Sikh as randy and as dangerous-looking as the worst sort of Calcutta *baʐaari-badmash* who'd cut your throat just to keep in practise. To corrupt Sewallis and Hugh even further, Liam Desmond and Pat Furfy would be near to hand with their seafaring tales, yarns, and Irish myths. And though his uncle Phineas Chiswick and his brother-in-law Governour Chiswick deplored it, Charlotte would be included during the days, though Governour had insisted that she reside with him and his wife . . . accurately thinking that exposing a girl to too much of Sir Hugo's past repute would quite ruin her. To irk Governour even further, Sir Hugo would take all three of them into town to play with Will Cony's children, a rambunctious and rowdy set as wild as Red Indians. Now, was Caroline having second thoughts?

"Oh, is that not the grandest *chateau*, Alan?" Caroline suddenly enthused, shifting over to the other side of the coach to goggle at a substantial manse surrounded by pasture land, vineyards, and manicured green lawns. "And . . . do I detect that our coach is travelling upon a very well-laid road? Perhaps one of Bonaparte's decrees."

"Pray God he's more interest in roads and canals than armies," Lewrie replied, though his professional sense was that armies marched faster and farther on good roads than bad.

"And the peasants!" Caroline further enthused as their coach passed a waggon heavily loaded with hay, drawn by a brace of plodding oxen, and goaded and accompanied by several French farmers, their wives, and children. "Are they not picturesque? Native costume, do you think?"

To Lewrie's eyes, what they wore looked more like a mixture of embroidered vests, straw hats, voluminous skirts, wooden clogs, and . . . rags. Rootless Irish mendicants could be deemed better dressed!

"Catch-as-catch-can, I'd s'pose" was his verdict.

"Why, one would imagine you had no curiosity in your soul!" his wife teasingly accused. "Or . . . is it that you have fought the French for so long, you can't fake interest?"

"So long as they ain't tryin' t'kill me, I'll allow that they are . . . colourful folk," he said with a smirk. "Given a choice though, Hindoos win 'colourful,' hands down."

And so it went, all the way to Amiens, where they laid over for the night in a much cleaner travellers' hotel, where Caroline's appetite was much restored, and though the chalked menu, and the waiter's unhelpful explanations, might as well have been Sanskrit, they managed to order both excellent, hearty meals and a couple of bottles of very good wine. As for dessert, French apple pie was as succulent as English apple pie, and the Lewries went to bed in fine fettle just a bit past eight, ready for an early rising and the next leg of their trip to fabled Paris.

CHAPTER SIXTEEN

*T*he Lewries found good lodgings, a spacious *appartement* on the Rue Honoré, just a short stroll north of the Jardin des Tuileries and the Palais National and Palais de la Révolution. They found themselves a brace of English-speaking servants, a pleasant young fellow named Jules for him, and a dumpling of a girl named Marianne for Caroline. At Jules's suggestion, they engaged an English-speaking guide, too. Jean-Joseph, a very smooth customer and a veteran of the early Italian campaigns under the fabled Napoleon Bonaparte, led them to the best bank, where Lewrie exchanged a note-of-hand drawn on Coutts' in London, and his pound notes, for French currency, with a temporary account set up to cover their expected expenses. Then, with a programme of "sights" lined up by Jean-Joseph, they set off to experience Paris and its environs.

The Place de la Bastille, now an open space since the infamous old prison had been razed; the Faubourg du Temple, the Hôtel de Ville, and Notre Dame, of course, along with the Îles de la Cité, and the site of the Revolutionary Court and Palais de Justice. The Vieux Louvre of course, too, filled with artworks looted during many of Napoleon's famed campaigns. They did the Right Bank, all the grand churches and former palaces, the Champs-Élysées and Champs de Mars.

They did the Left Bank, cross the Pont Neuf; along the broad and impressive Quai d'Orsai and Quai de Voltaire, visited the Pantheon and the

Cordeliers Convent, the Abbaye de St.-Germain-des-Prés, the Luxembourg palace, and the massive Maison Nationale des Invalides. And every day-jaunt was interrupted with a fine meal at a *restaurant*, *bistro*, or *café* that Jean-Joseph just happened to know all about, and recommended highly.

There were carriage trips to Versailles, Argenteuil, and the bucolic splendour of St. Denis and Asnières-sur-Seine, which Caroline thought the equal of the willowed, reeded banks of the upper Thames, replete with swans and cruising geese.

It was all so impressive, so romantic, did wonders for Caroline and the complete restoration of her wifely affection, for which Lewrie was more than thankful, that he could almost be glad they'd gone.

But for the stench, of course.

Firstly, there were the open sewers flowing with ordure, and the unidentifiable slop down the centre of some streets. Evidently, Parisians thought nothing of emptying their chamberpots out the nearest window, with but the sketchiest warning of *"Garde à l'eau!"* Even the Seine, a very pretty river, even in the bucolic stretches, was filled with foul . . . somethings, yet, to Lewrie's amazement, people actually fished it, and seemed happy with their catches!

Secondly, there were the Frogs themselves. Oh, perhaps some of the better sort might bathe weekly, and might even be so dainty as to launder their underclothes and wear fresh . . . on Sunday, at least, then not change 'til the next Saturday.

Admittedly, there were quite a few English who were "high"; the common folk, and his sailors, held that a fellow needed only three complete baths, with soap included, in their lives: at their birthing, the morning of their wedding, and bathed by others before their bodies were put in winding sheets and the grave! Yet . . . the French! Whew! Soap might be rare, but colognes, Hungary waters, and perfumes covered the lack . . . among the better sorts. Common Frenchmen, and Frenchwomen, could reek so badly that Lawrie was put in mind of a corpse's armpit.

"It is said, *m'sieur*," Jean-Joseph gaily imparted with a snicker "that when Bonaparte sailed from Egypt, he sent his wife, Josephine, letters by several ships, saying . . . 'I arrive. Do not bathe,' hawn hawn!"

"You know a good perfumery?" Lewrie asked him.

"*La parfumerie, m'sieur, mais oui!*" Jean-Joseph exclaimed. "You wish the finest scents and sachets in all the world, *Madame* Lewrie, I know the very place. But, per'aps *m'sieur* would find such shopping a tedium, *non?*"

"And a milliner's, a dressmaker's, a shoemaker's," Caroline happily ticked off on her lace-gloved fingers, "and perhaps a dry goods, a . . . uhm, *les étoffes*, Jean? For fabrics before the dressmaker's?"

"But, of *course*, *madame*!" Jean-Joseph heartily agreed, "the very *best* of fashion artistes, the most *impressive* fabrics, from people whom I know are *most* skilled, and . . . ," he intimated with a wink, "the final works can be had *bon marché* . . . that is to say, inexpensively?"

Now, why do I get the feelin' we've fallen into the clutches of a French *version of Clotworthy Chute?* Lewrie had to ask himself; *we've not seen "inexpensive" since we left Amiens!*

"And it would not go amiss did you have a suit of clothes run up for yourself, Alan," Caroline suggested. "France sets the style for the entire world, after all. And, what you brought along *is* a bit long in tooth by now," she said, giving him a chary looking-over.

"Uhm, perhaps," Lewrie allowed. In his teens, before his father had press-ganged him into the Navy (there'd been an inheritance from his mother's side, and Sir Hugo'd needed the money *perishin'* bad!), Lewrie's clothing tastes had run to the extreme "Macaroni" styles. But after better than half his life spent in uniform, what fashion sense he'd had had dulled to more sobre convention.

"Perhaps your maid, Marianne, and I can escort you to the shops, *madame*," Jean-Joseph spritely babbled on, "and for *m'sieur*, perhaps he can be guided by Jules, to whom I will impart the location of the most stylish tailor in all Paris, *n'est-ce pas*?"

"Uhm, that'd suit," Lewrie said with a shrug. "Suit? Ha?"

"*M'sieur* is so droll," Jean-Joseph all but simpered.

"Isn't he?" Caroline agreed with a roll of her eyes. "And on your separate jaunt, Alan, you might see about your swords."

"Aye. Call on our embassy, too," Lewrie said, with rising enthusiasm. To be frank about it, Lewrie by then had had his fill of museums, grand cathedrals, and art galleries, monuments to the Revolution and its brutalities, and, in point of fact, their unctuous guide, Jean-Joseph, as well. And he'd always despised being dragged along on feminine shopping trips. A full day on his own would be very welcome.

"*M'sieur* wishes a sword-smith?" Jean-Joseph enquired, a golden glint in his eyes at the thought of more spending with his recommended artisans.

"The British Embassy," Lewrie told him. "We do *have* one here, do we not? Now we're at peace?"

"There is, *m'sieur*," Jean-Joseph replied, looking a bit mystified. "I can instruct Jules to direct you there, as well."

"Very good, then," Lewrie decided. "Today or tomorrow, dear?"

"Tomorrow," Caroline said, "so I may spend the *whole* day at it."

"Per'aps, then . . . *madame* and *m'sieur* desire dinner? Quite by co-incidence, there is an excellent restaurant nearby, and their food . . . *magnifique!*" Jean-Joseph enthused, kissing his fingers in the air.

"Lead on, then," Lewrie told him. "Lead on."

CHAPTER SEVENTEEN

One hopes that readers will be patient with a slight digression from Lewrie's foreign adventure, but a few people also in Paris must be introduced before the tale may continue.

As Lewrie discovered in London the winter before, when between seagoing commissions, even the greatest, most populated city in the civilised world can seem *too small* when, out of the blue (or overcast grey, in London's case) all the embarrassing people who should *never* be in the same place at the same time, or ever actually *meet, do* show up and share greetings. In London, it was an innocent trip into the Strand to purchase ink, stationery, and sealing wax, and a chance meeting on the sidewalks with his old school chums (they'd all three been expelled from Harrow for arson and riotous behaviour at the same time) Lord Peter Rushton, Viscount Draywick, and that clever scoundrel Clotworthy Chute. Which *rencontre* had been interrupted, in distressing happenstance, by the arrival of the lovely, delectable (and hot after Lewrie) Eudoxia Durschenko, better known as the "Scythian Princess" (but really a Cossack) who performed bareback (and damn near nude!) with Daniel Wigmore's Peripatetic Extravaganza as a crack shot with the recurved horn bow, seconding as the *ingénue* in Wigmore's theatrical troupe . . . along with her papa, Arslan Artimovich Durschenko, the one-eyed knife-thrower and lion tamer, a man who was determined to see his daughter *buried* a virgin, and who hated Capt. Alan Lewrie much like Satan hated Holy Water.

Despite that, they'd ended together in the same tea shop, at the same table, with sticky buns and jam; Lord Peter drooling over Eudoxia, Eudoxia batting lashes at Lewrie, Clotworthy finagling how much money he might screw from the Russians, and Eudoxia's father whispering low curses near Lewrie's ear, whilst Lewrie strove for "innocent."

As if it could've gotten *any* worse (oh yes, it *could*!) in had swept the former actress Emma Batson, now the Mother Abbess of the finest brothel in the city, with two of her girls . . . one named Tess, whom Lewrie, deprived of his wife's affections for several years, was regularly rogering. Oh, it had been so jolly!

But we *do* digress.

As for Paris, now . . . Lewrie would think it very slim odds that he would know anyone among its hundreds of thousands of residents, except for the new First Consul, Napoleon Bonaparte, and it was even slimmer odds that he and Bonaparte would ever come face-to-face.

Bonaparte's guns had sunk Lewrie's commandeered mortar ship off the eastern side of Toulon during the brief capture of the port during the First Coalition (blown it, and him, sky-high in point of fact) and temporarily made Lewrie a soggy prisoner on the beach before Spanish cavalry had galloped to the rescue.

Dame Fortune, however, has always found a way to "put the boot in" where Alan Lewrie is concerned, when he is at his smuggest and most content.

In the heart of the city, down both sides of the Seine, lay the government buildings and former royal palaces. Napoleon Bonaparte was living in the Tuileries Palace, now the Palais National, in the eight-room *appartement* formerly occupied by Louis XVI. The Lewries, quite by chance (or was it?), were lodging in a *maison* on the Rue Honoré, the main thoroughfare that leads past the Tuileries and the Constituent Assembly, and dining and shopping and gawking in the same environs where the better sort of French reside and conduct their business, where the most exclusive shops are found . . . where people seeking favour and government employment gather.

Is it any wonder, then, that at the very moment that Caroline, Alan, and their guide depart a *restaurant*, pleasingly stuffed with one of the First Consul's favourite dishes, a blend of eggs, crayfish, tomatoes, and chicken called *Poulet Marengo* in honour of one of Bonaparte's grandest battlefield victories, also pleasantly "foxed" with wine . . . and out nearly one thousand francs—that someone from Lewrie's past should just happen to be limping away from the Ministry of Marine to his miserly and squalid lodgings in the maze-like ancient quarter round the Hôtel de Ville?

"*Salaud!*" the limping man hissed in shock, his remaining hand jerking to the sudden twinge of pain in his ravaged and partly masked face, a stabbing memory brought on by the sight of his nemesis. "*C'est lui! Putain, c'est lui, espèce de petite vermine.* Lewrie. It *is* Lewrie!"

Other people who shared the sidewalk with him—strollers or the ones in more haste about their business—gave the hideous old cripple a wider berth than they usually would, one or two tapping their heads and telling their companions that the ogre was *débile* . . . insane, and best avoided.

Perhaps Guillaume Choundas, formerly a *Capitaine de Vaisseau* of the French Navy, *was* partly insane by then. And that *Anglais* bastard Lewrie was the cause of it, and his crippled state.

'Tween the wars in the Far East, in the 1780s, a handsome and whole Guillaume Choundas had armed and organised native Philippine and Borneo pirates, won them over as French allies should another war come against the British, as it had in '93, and ravaged British trade in the Malay and China Seas, both "country ships" and those of the East India Company. To counter their losses, the British had sent out a disguised warship to counter Choundas's own, and suppress piracy. Despite all of his Jesuit-trained cleverness, his Breton-pirate native guile, and his lust to succeed and advance in the old aristocratic French Navy despite his commoner birth as a fisherman's son, he'd been bested, his allies slaughtered, and their *proas* sunk or burned. Lastly, he and his Lanun Rover pirates had been surprised on Balabac Island in the Philippines, and, on a beach, Choundas had made his last stand against the *Anglais*, and that *ignorant* bastard Lewrie had fought him face-to-face.

Outclassed, on his back in the surf and one cut or thrust from death, Lewrie had somehow risen, his hanger slashing upwards, silvery and trailing glittering seawater—for Choundas's blind eye could still *see* it—and laying Choundas's face open to the bone, cutting clean across one eyeball, laying *him* in the acid-burning salt surf to scream, writhe, and shriek!

An angry, petulant kick to Lewrie's shins had drawn another cut in response, and Guillaume was not only mutilated but ham-strung, and left a limping cripple for life!

They'd met again in the Mediterranean in 1795. Choundas, amply rewarded by the Ministry of Marine and the Directory in Paris for his zeal at rooting out Royalists, reactionaries, spies, and traitors to the Revolution during the Terror, was placed in charge of all coasting convoys, and their protection, from Marseilles and Toulon into the Ligurian Sea and the Gulf of Genoa, to support and supply Napoleon's First Italian Campaign.

And, dammit, but Lewrie and his Sloop of War *Jester* had been a leader in ravaging his coasters, his lesser gunboats, had sailed right into protected harbours to take, sink, or burn, making Choundas appear incompetent! His greatest feat—taking a British packet full of silver meant to prop up their allies, the Austrians, and pay their own sailors—should have won him laurels. Choundas had snuck it into Genoa to pay volunteers to join the *French* Army, but . . . to escape and return home in glory, he'd had to sail a civilian lateen-rigged tub back west, and there *Jester* had been. Choundas had been rowed ashore to a friendly port village, but Lewrie had taken the *lateener*, sailed it right onto the rocky shore, and pursued him with a small party.

On horseback, miles inland, 'til Choundas had reached the safety of Napoleon's army, a cavalry squadron sure to gallop down and sweep his foe away. Yet . . . even as he'd sneered, Lewrie had dis-mounted an impossible two hundred yards or better away, had taken aim with his rifled musket. Surely the ancient Celtic gods had been with him and against Choundas that day, for the ominous raven had flown *on* Choundas's *right*—a dire portent—and Lewrie had *shot* him, spilled him from the saddle in fresh agony and rage, and the army surgeons had had to take his arm off! Better he had died then!

Lastly, in the West Indies in '98 and '99, at the height of the slave rebellion on French St. Domingue, *Capitaine* Guillaume Choundas commanded a fine frigate and coordinated the privateers and smuggling ships from Guadeloupe: raiding British commerce, arming the factions on St. Domingue, then dealing with the ungrateful Americans, who'd all but declared war on their saviour during the American Revolution owing to the French policy of stopping and inspecting Yankee cargo ships that traded with France's enemies, and making prize of the offenders. The Quasi-War, it had been termed.

Perhaps it had been the tropic heat, the touchy, dyspeptic state of his digestion, and his infirmities, but Choundas, once he'd learned Lewrie was there in HMS *Proteus*, could think of nothing else but his revenge;

especially after Lewrie had sailed *Proteus* right into Basse-Terre harbour and had caught Choundas and his frigate at anchor, had bow-raked her mercilessly and crippled her timbers as surely as he'd crippled Choundas! Without European replacement oak knees, futtocks, beams, stem-post, and timbers, she might as well have been burned to salvage her metal fittings!

Then Lewrie had been there, in concert with the Americans, at the moment Choundas's last escorted convoy to St. Domingue had been brought to battle. It had been a monstrous American frigate which had taken him, but Lewrie had come aboard to taunt and demand custody of him and thank God for those chivalrous fools, the Yankees, who would not give him up, but took him on his parole to Baltimore.

When Choundas came home to France after that final humiliation, griped in his guts, lamer, and older, his old compatriots from the early days of the Revolution were no longer there, driven from office and the public view . . . replaced by ambitious younger men who'd serve a *king* if it meant employment, promotion, and wealth, the *bourgeois* time-servers! The Directory of Five were dead or displaced, the later Consulate taken over by this upstart Corsican *salaud*, Bonaparte, and Guillaume Choundas was now a pensioner living hand-to-mouth, unloved and unhonoured for his grand contributions to the Revolution. He was *poor*, one step away from *begging*, reduced to the cheapest stale loaves, rancid cheese, and sour *vin ordinare*, which victuals he found hard to chew with inflamed gums and loose teeth. When he was whole and unmarked, any whore would accept his coins, any very young and virginal native girl could be forced into his bed. When he was powerful, albeit mutilated, prisoners' wives, girlfriends, and daughters (Oh, the daughters!) were his. On Guadeloupe he had had the power, and the money, to savage any whore and hush it up, but now . . . He might as well have become a monk.

And it was all Lewrie's fault!

Without allies, without friends and accomplices, though, what could he do about it, to take his revenge at last? To kill Lewrie . . . no! Seize him first; butcher him *near* death, then ravage that woman on his arm, whom Choundas suspected was his wife, right before Lewrie's eyes . . . before cutting her throat, blinding Lewrie, ham-stringing him as he had Choundas, and leaving him a worse cripple for the rest of *his* life! Oh, yes! But . . . how?

Former *Capitaine* Guillaume Choundas cast a glance over his shoulder towards the Ministry of Marine on the Left Bank of the Seine, wondering if anyone official might be concerned that such a successful and dangerous foe as Lewrie was here in Paris, this moment. Spying, perhaps? Would that make someone sit up and take notice? He looked back, just in time to see Lewrie, the woman, and a third young fellow entering a grand *maison* converted to *appartements*. If nothing else, Choundas knew where Lewrie resided . . . where he could be *found* when the time came for vengeance!

CHAPTER EIGHTEEN

*T*he next morning, it was Caroline's turn for an encounter with more people from her husband's past, one of whom was very well known to her, by name at least, as a result of a series of poison-pen letters over several years, and one of whom she would not recognise from Eve.

With her husband off with his manservant, Jules, to shop on his own and call upon their recently re-established embassy, Caroline, along with her maid-servant, Marianne, and the garrulous and charming Jean, began a shopping trip of her own . . . the sort of shopping which unfaithful husbands *owe* their wives, and long-suffering women *deserve*.

There was a *parfumerie* that Jean-Joseph had mentioned, the very best, most exclusive shop in all of Paris, which was to say, the best in all of France, which, also left unsaid the very best in the world.

It was called La Contessa's, just off the Place Victor, and its scents could be discerned even before the front of the store was reached. A bright red door—set between matching bow-windows filled with arrays of vials, jars, and droppers of scents, with sachets for armoires and dresser drawers, with scented soaps, face powders, and cosmetics—opened to the accompaniment of the gay tinkling of a shop bell hung over the transom.

"Oh, it smells grand, Jean!" Caroline enthused, pausing to inhale and gaze about.

"Madame?" a young clerk enquired, drawn by the bell. It fell to Jean-

Joseph to explain that Mrs. Lewrie's French was not all that good, and that he would be translating. The young girl lifted her nose and almost sniffed in derision, even while she maintained her smile. Dealing with *Anglais* travellers was odious enough, and those who could not even *attempt* to speak French, garbling as bad as hairy-armed Gascons, were even worse.

As Jean-Joseph glibly continued, requesting that La Contessa herself attend his charge, knowing that La Contessa was somewhat fluent in English, a couple entered the shop behind them.

The young fellow was a Major in the dark green, scarlet-collared and -trimmed uniform coat of the Chasseurs, very gay and charming. The young lady with him was stunningly beautiful, with blue-grey eyes and chestnut-coloured hair, done up in ringlets framing her face, *Chinois* bangs on her forehead, and a *chignon* behind.

". . . Madame Lewrie wishes to sample your scents, your colognes, and bath powders, *mademoiselle*," Jean-Joseph went on, tipping the girl a wink to let her know that Madame had money and would not know if she was being gulled. "Your very best, *n'est-ce pas?*"

At the mention of Caroline's name, the girl with the chestnut hair blanched and seized her companion's arm for support.

Lewrie! C'est lui? Impossible! she thought, her mind areel; *it cannot be!*

"Charité, you are unwell, *ma chérie?*" the young Major enquired.

"The uhm . . . the richness of the aromas overcome me," she told him, recovering her aplomb and plastering gay coquetry on her face; moving deeper into the store so she could look back, from beneath lowered lashes, at the woman who went by the name of Lewrie.

She is very attractive, Charité Angelette de Guilleri thought; *for a woman in her . . . fourties?* she sneeringly over-estimated. *Is she his widow or another* sanglante . . . a *"Bloody"?*

For here we meet someone else who'd "crossed hawses" with Capt. Alan Lewrie; Charité Angelette de Guilleri had once been the younger daughter of a rich Creole planter family in Louisiana, the *belle* of any gathering in her beloved New Orleans . . . even if that original French colony had been traded off long before to the grubby Spanish, an odious fact that she, and many other French Creoles, had resented.

Everyone wished to restore Louisiana and New Orleans to France. They debated it, talked about it, emoted over it, yet . . . so few tried to *do* anything about it, so long as the rice and sugar crops were good, the prices high, the ships came from round the world for their produce, and the moribund, lazy Spanish officials left them alone. As light and as weak as the Spanish yoke was, it was still an onerous occupation, so much so that, at last, Charité and her brothers—oh, her clever and active, handsome brothers, long dead now! . . . Hippolyte and Helio, with their impoverished cousin Jean-Marie Rancour, whose family had fled the slave rebellion and bloody massacres of whites and landowners on St. Domingue with less than a tithe of their former wealth—had sworn to take action, to set a patriotic example for everyone else of like, but timid, mind. The spirit of revolution stalked the Earth, after all . . . first among those barbarous Yankees in the American Colonies, then in the beloved *belle France*. To rise up, to strike, was their patriotic *duty*! The civilised world would be re-made!

Two old privateers from the French and Indian War, Boudreaux Balfa and Jérôme Lanxade, had access to schooners and their old crewmen downriver in the bayous and bays, and to raise the funds to start a revolution, to purchase the arms required for the time when the people would rise up, they had engaged in piracy.

Thrilling piracy, against all ships but French, which, admittedly were rare in the Gulf of Mexico in 1798 and 1799, Spanish ships the most preferred, but any nation's would suit, so long as they had rich cargoes to sell off, and money aboard.

Thrilling, too, was the life of a pirate, a secret sea-rover, an unsuspected rebel, like the bare-breasted heroine of the French Revolution, the emblematic Marianne with the flagstaff of the Tricolour in one hand and a bayonetted musket in the other, in the forefront of the battle line and urging the others on against tyrants and oppressors!

Exciting, too, had been living two lives: she was Charité the demure coquette in the city, but aboard their schooner *Le Revenant* she donned buccaneer clothes, riding boots and skin-tight breeches, loose flowing shirts and snug vests, with pistols in her sash and a sword on her hip, and she'd been a good shot, too, as much a terror to the crews of the ships they took as the fabled women pirates of an earlier age, Anne Bonny and Mary Read . . . even if they *had* been *Anglais*!

But that *sanglant,* that *Anglais salaud* Alan Lewrie had come upriver to New Orleans, play-acting a penniless but skilled English adventurer and merchantman mate, in civilian clothes, to spy out a source of their piracy. Unsuspecting 'til it was much too late, Charité had found him amusing, attractive, and *eminently* satifying at lovemaking.

She blushed as she recalled how she'd almost recruited the bastard into their covert band, considered him as something more permanent than a wicked fling, and, for a brief, naïve time, felt *love* for him!

To be betrayed at Barataria Bay when Alan Lewrie and his frigate and a schooner had turned up, landing sailors and Marines on the ocean side of Grand Isle, sailing in himself and killing poor old Jérôme Lanxade with a sword, taking his schooner, and ordering his men to kill both her brothers and her cousin in the *foulest* way!

She and that Laffite boy, and Boudreaux Balfa and his son, had fled in a *pirogue*. Lewrie had pursued them in a rowing boat, and with tears of rage in her eyes, she'd levelled a Girandoni air-rifle, taken aim square in the middle of Lewrie's chest, and, despite her tears, was *sure* she'd killed him! The range had been nearly fourty yards, he had been standing amidships of his boat, and had fallen backwards as if he had been pole-axed, not to arise as long as his boat was in sight.

The scandal had been hushed up, kept from the Spanish authorities, and Charité had been sent packing, declared *débile* by the murder of her brothers and cousin, allegedly by runaway slaves round Barataria. She was doomed to live a mundane life with distant relatives, the LeMerciers, in the "quaint" town of Rambouillet, outside Paris. She'd quickly fled *that*, had found a way to inveigle her way into the company of the elite of the late Directory period and the tripartite consulate; into the best *salons*, where, with her beauty, her outspokenness, her coquetry, and feminine charms, she had gotten close to the Director of National Police, the clever if ugly and bald Fouché, the elegant but lame Foreign Minister, Talleyrand, and, after his seizure of power, the First Consul, Napoleon Bonaparte himself!

Her "slaying" of the *Anglais* Navy Captain, her attempt at revolution in New Orleans and Louisiana, had made her a minor celebrity in her own right, and the loss of her brothers and cousin a tragic figure who pleaded for a restoration of the Louisiana Territory to France.

Now . . . would it all come undone? Did Alan Lewrie *live*? She *had* to know. She idly strolled closer to the English woman, sniffing at articles on display, listening closely, though to another person in the shop just another gay *coquette*, chuckling and teasing her handsome companion, the dashing young Major of Chasseurs.

La Contessa emerged from the rear of the shop, a petite brunette with large brown eyes, a fine, trim figure, and the face of a teenaged angelminx. Oddly, La Contessa bore a slim and wiry young white-and-tan cat in her arms, a cat with a diamond-studded collar round its neck.

"Ah, Jean-Joseph, *mon cher*, so 'appy to see you again," said La Contessa with a grand and languid air usually seen among the "aristos" of the pre-Revolutionary era. She presented her hand to be kissed. "You bring a distinguish' English lady to my 'umble shop? *C'est merveilleux!*"

"Allow me to present *Madame* Caroline Lewrie, a visitor from England to you, *madame*," Jean-Joseph smarmily announced. "*Madame* Lewrie, I present to you *Mademoiselle* Phoebe Aretino, famed throughout Paris as La Contessa de la Bastia . . . on Corsica, the 'queen' of *parfumeurs*."

"Phoebe . . . Aretino," Caroline exclaimed in a stiff tone, each word *huffed,* with her eyes suddenly a'squint and her brow furrowed.

"Madame Lew . . . ?" Sophie Aretino stammered, her mouth agawp in utter shock. "Ahem! You are, ah, ze uhm . . . related to, ah . . . ?"

"Toulon, seventeen ninety-four," Caroline flatly intoned, "you and my former ward, Vicomtesse Sophie de Maubeuge, escaped aboard *my* husband's ship? You're *that* . . . Phoebe Aretino?"

"For w'eech I am ze eternally grateful, Madame Lew . . ." Phoebe stammered some more, turning radish-coloured.

"I just *bet* you were!" Caroline snapped, turning to leave. "We will shop elsewhere, Jean. *Never* in *her* place!"

"But, *madame*, I do not—" Jean-Joseph spluttered.

"I will give my *husband* your *regards*," Caroline archly concluded with a snide smile. "Do *not* expect them to be returned. *Au revoir!*"

Give him your . . . ? Zut! Merde alors, he lives! Charité thought in sudden alarm, like to faint at that news.

"Really, *ma chérie*, you look as if you will swoon," her Major of Chasseurs worriedly said, more than glad to put an arm about her to support her, for, like most men who met Charité de Guilleri, the dashing young cavalryman, Major Denis Clary, was enamoured. "Perhaps a restorative brandy, or . . . ?"

"Ah!" Charité denied, taking in a deep breath. "No, *mon cher*, I am fine, truly. Excuse me for one moment? Ah, *Mademoiselle* Aretino. Who *was* that horrid creature? *Anglaise*, was she? They are such a *rude* people. Pardon me for asking, but . . . why would a stranger insult you so?" she solicitously enquired.

"It is no . . ." the "Contessa of Bastia" began to snap, setting her slim cat down on a glass-topped counter and delicately putting her fingertips to her temples. "*Oui*, she *was* rude. Such a shock, to hear her name, and . . ."

To Charité's amazement, Mlle. Phoebe Aretino's distress turned to a wistful smile of reverie as she absently began to stroke her cat.

"From so long ago, *n'est-ce pas?*" Phoebe Aretino said further. "Perhaps not *all* the *Anglais* are horrid. *Some* of their men . . . well." *That,* with even more wistfulness, almost a sheepish smile.

He had you, too! Charité wryly realised, and, for but a *brief* second, almost felt a pang of . . . dare she call it jealousy?

"I may help you select a scent, *mademoiselle?*" Phoebe Aretino asked, back to business. "Something new to delight your charming young man? More of a scent you purchased before?"

On the streets outside, Caroline Lewrie set a hectic, furious pace along the Rue Neuve des Petits Champs, to turn south cross traffic down the east side of the Palais Égalité to return to the Rue Honoré. Her apple-cheeked maid, Marianne, puffed along in her wake, as did her guide, Jean-Joseph, who took the kerb side to protect her gown from the muck thrown up from carriage wheels.

"*Madame* Lewrie, I do not understand," he said. "La Contessa's is *the* most exclusive . . . nowhere else in Paris is there such a variety. . . . Did she somehow give offence? If so, my pardons to you for taking you there, but . . ." Jean-Joseph had not walked all that fast since his last forced marches into Savoia in '97.

"I know *of* her," Caroline snapped. "Until you named her, I did not make the connexion." Under her breath, she added, "The baggage!"

Oh ho! Jean-Joseph intuited, carefully hiding a smirk as he fell behind her a step to mask his amusement. *Capitaine Lewrie is* un chaud lapin, *the hot rabbit? Mon Dieu, he 'dipped his biscuit' in La Contessa? Oh, I see! The lucky shit! Before or* after *he marries, hmm?* Then, with a Gallic shrug and an urge to whistle gaily, he wryly thought, *During, hawn hawn!*

"Fabrics, Jean, the best!" Caroline huffed. "Then dressmakers, milliners, *everything!*"

Oh, this will cost M'sieur Lewrie dear, Jean-Joseph gleefully thought, all but rubbing his hands with joy over how much she would be spending with his friends, and how large his kick-back would be.

CHAPTER NINETEEN

*B*efore it was re-established, the British Embassy had been in French hands for several years, from 1793 'til 1802, and had not been treated well. It had an odour of dirty feet and old socks, of barrack farts and sweat, as if troops of the Garde Nationale had been garrisoned there. Effort had been expended to clean it up and make it grand once more, but it was a continuing process. After announcing himself and the reason for his call, Lewrie had cooled his heels in the baroque lower lobby for an hour or better, before some "catch-fart" flunky saw him abovestairs to the offices of Sir Anthony Paisley-Templeton, who held the odd title of *Chargé d'Affaires*, which could have meant anything. Lewrie had met a few people who parted their last names, and had come away with a less than favourable impression . . . one reenforced by his first sight of the fellow. Sir Anthony was a wispy young fellow, at least ten or twelve years Lewrie's junior, with pale skin and a stylish thick head of pale blond hair, poetically curled on top, sides, and nape, but brushed forward over his forehead, his long sideburns brushed forward towards his cheeks, as well. He sported stylish suitings, too, it went without saying, in the latest French cut, with up-standing shirt collars.

"Captain Alan Lewrie, so honoured t'meet you, sir," Sir Anthony enthused as he offered a hand to be shaken, one so limp once taken in hand that Lewrie might as well have been shaking a dead fish. "Followed your trial last year, don't ye know . . . capital doings, capital, hah!"

With about as much true enthusiasm as a clench-jawed Oxonian of "the Quality" ever allowed out in Publick, Lewrie took note.

"Now, what is it you wish to do, Captain Lewrie? Meet Bonaparte? Sorry, but . . . that would be impossible, it just isn't *done*, old chap," Sir Anthony pooh-poohed.

"A *rencontre* with Bonaparte isn't necessary," Lewrie told him. "Didn't exactly enjoy the first, anyway. The point is . . . I've several swords, surrendered by French naval captains, and I'd like t'return 'em to their owners, or their heirs. In *exchange*, Bonaparte does have one of my old swords . . . my very first. Nothin' grand about it, but . . . it is dear t'*me*. Gifted me just before I gained my lieutenancy, d'ye see."

"You, erm . . . *kept* surrendered swords, sir?" Sir Anthony Paisley-Templeton asked, seeming tremulously appalled. "I thought the customary usage was to refuse, and allow the surrendee to maintain possession of his . . . honour, sir."

"It us'lly is . . . are they alive t'take 'em back," Lewrie said, crossing his legs at sublime ease in a chair cross the desk from the slim diplomat. "Most . . . weren't," he added with a shrug and a grin.

"I see," Sir Anthony said with a barely imperceptible gulp.

"Something could be arranged 'twixt me and their Admiralty . . . their Ministry of Marine, or whatever they call it?" Lewrie asked. "I didn't think just bargin' in on my own would be a good idea. In the spirit of our newfound peace, though . . ."

"Ah, yayss, hmm," Paisley-Templeton drawled, head cocked to one side in sudden thought, then brightened considerably. "Peace! That's the thing, is it not, Captain Lewrie? Hmm. You will take coffee, or tea, sir? And, will, pray, excuse me for a few moments whilst I consult with my superiors?"

That few moments turned into two cups of very good coffee, one trip down the hall to the "necessary" to pump his bilges, and a third cup before Paisley-Templeton returned.

"Consider this, Captain Lewrie," Sir Anthony said with genuine enthusiasm, hands rising to frame a stage like a proscenium arch. "A levee in the Tuileries Palace . . . music, champagne, French chittering and flirting . . . the First Consul, General Napoleon Bonaparte, is there with his cabinet, his coterie. You are presented to him and perhaps to his wife, Josephine, by my superior . . . *or* one of his representatives, hmm?"

Like yerself, d'ye mean, Lewrie sarcastically thought, even as he kept his phyz sobre and nodded sagaciously; *goin' up in the world like a Montgolfier balloon, do ye hope?*

"Bonaparte . . . forewarned through his Foreign Minister, *M'sieur* Talleyrand," Sir Anthony speculated on, "will be prepared to accept the delivery of your captured swords. With enough forewarning, perhaps he will be able to find *your* sword.

"*Then,* sir! Then, with hundreds of people looking on, you and he will make a formal exchange," Sir Anthony fantasised. "Your . . . how many? Five, good ho, five. Your five swords presented to *him*, then . . . after some kind and sincere words shared, some smiles 'twixt warriors . . . *he* will return to you your *old* sword . . . *or* one suitable enough to the occasion in value and style to satisfy you," Sir Anthony tossed off as if it was no matter. "Gad, what a place of honour *that'll* have in your house, Captain Lewrie! Yours, or a proper replacement, from the hand of Bonaparte, why . . . one could dine out on that for *years,* ha ha!"

"Hold on a bit, sir," Lewrie said with a gawp. "I'm t'meet the Corsican tyrant? Glad-hand the bastard?"

Sir Anthony Paisley-Templeton visibly shuddered and pouted.

"Now, Captain Lewrie . . . in the interests of continental peace and goodwill, surely you could find more . . . *charitable* expressions," he chid Lewrie. "Now he's First Consul, perhaps for *life* it is lately rumoured, and so involved with a sweeping reform of France's legal system, its roads, canals, harbours, and civic improvements, standardising its currency and all, could you not, perhaps, give Bonaparte the benefit of the doubt? Think of him as a great, new-come man?"

"Don't know . . . seems a bit theatrical t'me," Lewrie dubiously replied, shifting uncomfortably in his chair. "But . . . long as I get my old sword back, I s'pose I could play along."

"*That's* the spirit, Captain Lewrie!" Sir Anthony cheered. "Now, you must give me all the particulars about your old sword."

"Should've brought my dress uniform, d'ye think, sir?" Lewrie asked.

"Good heavens, *no,* sir!" Paisley-Templeton gasped, about ready to shudder again. "General Bonaparte *usually* dons red velvet suitings for formal levees . . . *most* un-military. The sight of an officer from a branch of his *recent* opponents in uniform might be . . . insulting, my superior believes. Something new, stylish . . . uhm, might I give you the name of my tailor here in Paris, sir?" Sir Anthony enquired, with an equally dubious expression as he looked Lewrie's suit up and down.

"Make my wife happy," Lewrie mused aloud. "A reason to purchase *court* clothing, hey?"

"You *and* your wife together, sir? That would be even *more* pacific," Paisley-Templeton gushed. "Dare she take wine with Josephine? Well, perhaps that might be a bit of a stretch, but . . . as to what the old sword looks like, then, Captain Lewrie?"

"It was a hanger, patterned on a French infantry *sabre-briquet*. Royal blue scabbard and sharkskin grip, the grip bound in silver wire, with silver throat, drag, and . . ."

An hour later, and Lewrie was at a tailor's, not the one recommended by Paisley-Templeton, but the one that Jean-Joseph had named. It didn't begin well, for the elderly tailor had very little English, Lewrie was nigh-incomprehensible in French, and his manservant, Jules, was not as bilingual as he'd been touted to be.

Before negotiations broke completely down, another customer and one of the tailor's journeyman assistants emerged from a change-room at the back of the shop, and rescue was at hand . . . of a sort.

"Stap me! I declare if it is not Captain Lewrie, to the life, haw haw!" the fellow brayed in an Oxonian accent, and an inane titter.

"Sir . . . Poult . . . Pulteney?" Lewrie responded, groping for the fellow's last name and only coming up with "Thing-Gummy." "Yer servant, sir, and I thankee for your kindly assistance 'board the packet."

"Pulteney Plumb, and your servant, Captain Lewrie," the foppish man said back, making a flourished, showy "leg." "I trust your lovely wife recovered from the *mal de mere*, sir? Ha?"

"Completely, Sir Pulteney, thankee for asking," Lewrie replied. "Those sweet ginger pastilles did the trick. Should I ever command a crew of pressed hands again, a case or two of 'em in the Surgeon's apothecaries might prove useful, hey?"

"Might Admiralty *reimburse* you for them, though, haw haw?" Sir Pulteney gaily countered. "A parsimonious lot, officialdom."

"Indeed," Lewrie agreed, with a wry roll of his eyes.

"You seek new suitings, Captain Lewrie?" Sir Pulteney asked as he came closer to look Lewrie's current suit up and down. "Then you have come to one of the finest establishments in Paris, one which it was my utter delight to patronise in the years before the Revolution. You see?" Sir Pulteney spun himself slowly round most theatrically, modelling the new suit he was having fitted, and indeed it was a marvel to behold, of subtle grey and black striped watered silk over a burgundy satin waist-coat.

Light on his feet . . . ain't he, Lewrie thought as Sir Pulteney preened. Sir Pulteney Plumb was perhaps an inch taller than Lewrie's five feet nine, still of a trim, active build for a man in his late fourties (or so Lewrie judged him), broad in the chest and shoulders without appearing too "common" or "beef to the heel."

"Cut to the Tee, haw haw!" Sir Pulteney crowed. "Old Jacques, *mon vieux,* you have done it again! *Félicitations!*" he congratulated the master tailor, kissing his fingers in his direction, then, in fluent French, urging the fellow to emigrate to London, where he could make an even greater, new fortune . . . at least that was the gist Lewrie got from it. Old Jacques ate it up like plum duff.

"Something for our newfound friend, here, Jacques? I dare say you'd look particularly dashing in something maroon, or burgundy . . .'less you'd *prefer* something more . . . everyday, what? Perhaps you and your lady wife envision some formal occasion whilst in Paris, in which case 'dashing' would be required?"

"*M'sieur* Sir Pulteney ees ze *très élégante, hein?*" the master tailor simpered to Lewrie.

Christ, ain't he just! Lewrie silently agreed.

"An occasion, aye, Sir Pulteney," Lewrie informed him, telling him of those swords he wished to exchange. "In short, one thing led to another, and we're down for some theatrical flummery at a levee at the Tuileries Palace with Bonaparte," he said with a wry shrug.

"Presented to the First Consul of France? Begad, sir, what an honour! Odd's Blood, haw haw!" Sir Pulteney brayed, tossing his head back and to one side to emit another of his donkey-bray laughs. "Now we simply *must* array you in the *very* finest!"

There was a palaver 'twixt Sir Pulteney and the master tailor to explain how fine a suit would be necessary.

"Jacques cautions that you must not out-shine the First Consul in splendour, Captain Lewrie," Sir Pulteney Plumb said with a cautionary wag of a long aristocratic finger, "and that Bonaparte is fond of his general's uniform, or red velvet, with white silk stockings and a pair of red Moroccan slippers . . . fellow caught the Turkish and Mameluke 'fashion pox' somethin' horrid during his Egyptian campaign. . . . Even fetched back a Muslim manservant, haw haw! *Or* sometimes he will don the plainest uniform of a Colonel of Chasseurs. Yayss," Sir Pulteney softly speculated as he paced a quick orbit round Lewrie, "you would be *splendid*, but not *too* splendid, in something dark red. *Vite, vite,* Jacques. Maroons and burgundies!"

Is he a Clotworthy Chute, a Jean-Joseph, a Captain Sharp? he had to ask himself as assistants came with tapes to take his measure, and his dimensions were carefully noted in a ledger, should Lewrie be a return customer. "*Hang* the cost, Begad!" from Sir Pulteney, "Lud, a once in a lifetime occasion, haw haw!"

Fabrics were fetched, stroked, draped over his shoulders to display how a fine broadcloth wool would mould to him; how watered silks or embroidered and figured satins might complement the basic colour motif. Not knowing just how he'd been cossetted into it, Lewrie ended with all the makings for three suits. Hang the cost, indeed!

There would be a dark-red doubled-breasted tail-coat with a wide collar and lapels, snug matching trousers, and an electric blue waist-coat in moiré silk beneath. There would be a grey single-breast coat with a stand-and-fall collar trimmed in electric blue satin that could be paired to the first waist-coat, or a second one in maroon satin. There would be a third, a black single-breasted coat matched with a cream-coloured embroidered waist-coat, which could be mated with those grey trousers or any old pair of black or buff breeches.

Not to mention the hats, new silk hosiery, elaborately laced silk shirts Sir Pulteney thought essential. The gloves or lace jabots, the new-fangled Croatian cravats and various coloured neck-stocks without which a *proper* gentleman would be deemed half-dressed, or only half finished.

I'll need a new leather portmanteau t'pack away all this bumf, Lewrie told himself, wondering how much that'd cost him, on top of all this? Appointments were made for further fittings before the delivery of the finished togs.

Sir Pulteney Plumb slightly made up for the pained look on Alan Lewrie's face as he goggled over the reckoning, offering to treat him to a late mid-day meal and extending an invitation for Lewrie and his wife to sup with them that evening, his treat, then take in a performance at the Comédie Française, where, Sir Pulteney grandly imformed him, his lady-wife, Imogene—*Knew it was somethin' starts with I!* Lewrie told himself—had once "trod the boards" as a noted actress of some renown.

"French, o' course, Begad!" Sir Pulteney brayed, tittering over the fact. "Dash it, imagine an *English* gel on a Parisian stage, haw haw haw!"

A comedy, Lewrie thought, *that'll give the fop genuine call for that God-awful laugh o' his!*

CHAPTER TWENTY

*C*aroline Lewrie was waiting, rather impatiently, in their rented suite of rooms for her husband to arrive; pacing, frowning, *rehearsing* the wrath she would launch as soon as the faithless hound stepped into the parlour. Her purchases, those that could be carried away the same day, she had left scattered on settees, chairs, and table tops—pelts of her "kills," the expensive items that did not even come *near* to mollifying the rebirth of her anger after meeting Phoebe Aretino, his old mistress, and seeing her in the flesh! And to be so pretty and petite and *young-looking*, to boot, well!

"I'm home, dear!" Lewrie gaily called out, whipping his old hat at a row of pegs by the *armoire*, infuriatingly scoring a direct hit and hanging it up on the first try. "Have fun shopping, Caroline? Well, there may be need for a lot *more* of it, d'ye see—"

"I met an *old friend* of yours, today . . . husband!" she fumed.

"Did ye now? I say, that looks expensive, all that . . . stuff," Lewrie blathered on. "We've some formal 'to-do's' in our future. How would ye like t'meet Napoleon Bonaparte himself? The famous Josephine, too, most-like. *And,* we're invited to supper and the Comédie Française tonight. Recall Sir Pulteney Plumb and his lady, Imogene, from the packet? With the ginger pastilles? Ran into him at a tailor's . . . ," Lewrie said, grinning as he went to her, prepared to dance her round the room with his news.

"I *said* I . . . what?" said Caroline, flummoxed. "Napoleon Bonaparte? When?"

"Don't know yet, but our Embassy'll be sendin' round an invitation to a levee at the Tuileries Palace in a few days," Lewrie cheerfully explained. "Those swords o' mine . . .'stead of an informal hand-over at their Ministry of Marine, it's got turned into a raree-show. Ye should see the bill from the tailor's t'get me suited proper for it. What's the current rate of exchange, francs to pounds, I wonder?"

"You just . . . just *barge* in here, full of yourself, and spring this upon me, like a Jack-in-the-Box?" Caroline blurted, her fury now re-directed on a fresh cause. "You expect me to be presentable at the *theatre* at the drop of your . . . hat?"

"Should I have sent you a note first?" Lewrie asked, confused.

"The theatre, *tonight*?" Caroline continued to rant, pacing the salon. "In one of my *old rags*? Why . . . ! Sir Pulteney Plumb and Lady Imogene, I vaguely recall . . . Oh! That *lofty* couple? They were, as I recall, extremely well-dressed . . . in the height of fashion. Lord, I might be mistaken for their maid-servant in comparison! Are they anyone?"

"Well, over dinner, Sir Pulteney *alluded* t'bein' on intimate grounds with the Prince of Wales," Lewrie told her. "And, he *seemed* t'be swimmin' in gold guineas, 'tween his purchases at the tailor's and him sportin' all for dinner. Supper and the theatre's his treat tonight, too. If they're a pair o' 'sharps,' then they're both out a pretty penny, and if they think t'trick us out of 'chink,' then they're barkin' up the wrong tree. He *seems* genuine . . . annoyin'ly *odd*, but genuine.

"Should I write him a note and ask for a couple nights' delay?" Lewrie offered, sure that something else had set her off, and he ran better-than-good odds that he was "in the quag, right to his eyeballs" over *something*.

"You will not!" Caroline snapped, after a long moment to mull it over. "If the Plumbs *are* as well connected and as wealthy and aristocratic as you say they appear, to turn them down would be unseemly. People on close terms with the Prince of Wales, perhaps even with the King himself . . ."

So are pretty whores, and Eudoxia Durschenko by now, Lewrie had to imagine, though he dared not say *that* aloud. The winter before, in London, the Prince of Wales—"Prinny" to his friends and "Florizel" to himself, God alone knew why!—had taken a keen interest in Eudoxia, and despite her evil-looking father's Argus-eyed watchfulness over her virginity, the mort *did* sport a few more baubles than before!

"I'm in the same boat, Caroline," Lewrie told her. "*Boat*, see?"

That was met with another roll of her eyes.

"I'd be wearin' me own best, and my new'uns won't be finished for days, so . . . ," he went on. "Well, there's new stocks and such, hats and gloves, but . . ."

"I *suppose* I could throw a suitable *ensemble* together at short notice," Caroline allowed at last, with an exasperated, wifely sigh. "The Comédie Française? Gawd, it will all be in French!" she wailed, turning to sort through her new purchases to see if there was anything that would avail, instanter, to liven the best of her supper gowns.

Met an old friend o' mine . . . *in Paris?* Lewrie tried to puzzle out as he began to change clothes. He couldn't imagine who *that* would be, but . . . he had the uncomfortable feeling that he'd just dodged a broadside and that his wife, despite this new distraction, was still swabbing out, reloading, and just waiting 'til the range was shorter to fire off another!

Meanwhile, in the former offices of the Committee for General Security, just outside the eastern wall of the Tuileries, along the Quai Galerie du Louvre, *Mlle.* Charité de Guilleri was paying a call upon the head of the National Police, Joseph Fouché. It was not one that could be called a social visit, nor was it one done casually, for Fouché was a very clever, cold-blooded man; he had to be, to have survived from the earliest days of the Revolution, one of the last of the "old stagers" so steeped in the blood of discovered or denounced *aristos*, Royalists, and reactionaries. He'd created bloodbaths at Nevers and Lyon, had threaded a wary way through the denunciations and deaths of Marat, Danton, Robespierre, Saint-Just, and the other Jacobins, and had prospered.

"*Mademoiselle* de Guilleri, *ma chérie*," Fouché gravelled as she was at last let into his offices. He stayed seated, though, intent on the papers on his desk, scanning *fresh* denunciations of suspected plotters who still hoped to supplant the First Consul, undo the Revolution, and return royal rule to France. Joseph Fouché was an ill-featured man, rather short and stocky, some might say rotund due to his barrel chest. He cared little for fashion or the proper fit of his clothes, and still wore his shirt collars open, with a loose stock tied more like a sailor's kerchief. He was also completely bald, and shaved what little stubble or fluff remained.

"What can I do for you, *citoyenne?*" Fouché asked, reverting to the form of address created more than a decade before at the start of the Revolution; unlike some newly risen *arrivistes*, Fouché was a dedicated common man of the Republic.

"The British captain I thought I shot, do you recall, *citoyen*?" Charité baldly began, knowing that coquetry and idle niceties before business were wasted on Fouché, and would irritate him further than she dared. She took a deep breath, waiting.

"*Ouais*?" Fouché said with a leery grunt, intent again upon his paperwork. He'd always been unimpressed and dubious of the little self-made heroine's tale, thinking Charité a foolish dabbler, too full of herself, and too ready to push herself and her "cause" forward.

"I was mistaken," Charité meekly declared. "The air-rifle . . . my shot was, perhaps, too weak to *kill* him, as I dearly wished. I met . . . I met his wife today, *citoyen*, here in Paris, and she spoke as if he is still alive, this very moment! He spied on us once, in New Orleans. Who is to say he is not here to spy on us again, you see?"

"You suspect he is here in Paris, to *spy* on us, *citoyenne*?" the policeman responded, setting aside a document and folding meaty hands atop his desk. He seemed amused, and a touch irritated, by Charité's assertion. "Would it not make more sense for this fellow . . . what is his name?"

"Alain Lewrie, *Citoyen* Fouché," Charité said, un-nerved by the man's chary tone and expression. "An *Anglais* naval captain."

Fouché made a pencilled note on a fresh sheet of paper, then looked up again with a scowl on his face. "Would it not make more sense he . . . this Alain Lew . . . however you say it . . . spies in our seaports, our navy yards, than Paris, *citoyenne*? Perhaps you mis-heard what the *Anglaise* said. You've seen him yourself?"

"*Non, citoyen* . . . I have not seen him myself," Charité rejoined, bristling a little to be patronised or dismissed. "But I speak very good *Anglais*, from dealings with the barbarous *Américains* in New Orleans, and I know perfectly what *Madame* Lewrie said. In anger, you see? Surprised by confrontation with another woman whom she suspects was once her husband's mistress, *n'est-ce pas*?"

Charité de Guilleri explained the circumstances in "La Contessa" Phoebe Aretino's *parfumerie*, how icy and angry *Madame* Lewrie had become upon her introduction . . . and how flustered Mlle. Aretino had become in turn at the mention of Alan Lewrie's name!

"I quote, *citoyen* . . . 'I will extend your regards to my husband, but do not expect them to be returned,'" Charité told him. "Lewrie is alive, *Citoyen* Fouché, and most likely travelling with his wife, here in Paris. I thought the presence of an *Anglais* officer who put aside his uniform to spy on us in Louisiana should be brought to your attention, lest he do so again against us."

"These other people rescued by this Leew . . . whatever," Fouché asked, scowling more deeply. "Do you remember their names?"

"*Madame* Lewrie alluded to many *royalistes* escaping Toulon on 'her husband's ship,' she said, *citoyen,* though the only one she gave name to was a *Vicomtesse* Maubeuge . . . her former . . . ward, I believe *Madame* Lewrie said," Charité easily recalled.

"*Citoyenne* Phoebe Aretino . . . hmm," Eouché said with a grunt of displeasure. "Corsican, *oui.* Of noble birth? *Non.* A common *putain* in Toulon, as I recall. There is a *dossier,*" Fouché said with an idle wave of one hand. "An avid supporter of the Revolution in Toulon had no *reason* to flee. Service the invaders' officers, for they were the only ones with money at the time, *but* . . . did *Citoyenne* Aretino *deny* any of the accusations?"

"No, *citoyen,*" Charité told him, shifting uncomfortably on her hard chair. She'd come to warn the authorities and to get vengeance on the bastard who'd slaughtered her kin and ruined her plans for revolt, but . . . Charité hadn't planned on sending anyone *else* to prison—or the guillotine! "She seemed very upset by the confrontation, but . . . after, she . . . I asked her, not in so many words, *n'est-ce pas? Mada—* . . . *Citoyenne* Aretino seemed . . . *wistful. La tristesse?* A woman can *see* the look of a former lover who is still fond . . ."

"Womanly intuition," Fouché sarcastically said with a sneer.

"In this instance, *oui, citoyen,* I am sure she was once Lewrie's mistress, or lover," Charité could firmly state. "But so many years ago, surely . . ."

"You have given me some things to look into, *citoyenne,*" Fouché told her, making more pencilled notes.

"I failed the Revolution, *Citoyen* Fouché," Charité declared with a clever bit of frankness, and a becoming sniff into a handkerchief drawn from her left dress sleeve. "I truly did believe that I killed him with my shot. I am ashamed to confess my failure, one that puts you to extra work."

Fouché tilted his shiny head to one side and peered at her for a long moment, unsure whether to laugh out loud at her pretensions as a patriot, and her theatricality. "I will look into this . . . Lewrie person's presence in Paris, *citoyenne,*" he said at last. "I thank you for your honesty and your alacrity in bringing this matter before me. Perhaps it is nothing, yet . . . for the safety of the Republic, and the First Consul, enquiries must be made. Is that all, *Citoyenne* de Guilleri?"

"It is, *citoyen* Fouché, *merci et au revoir*," Charité said with a sense of relief as she rose from her chair and escaped from the foul spider's immediate grasp . . . though not his web, for it spanned all of France. In the heady early days, the French newspapers that reached New Orleans had limned Fouché in her pantheon of heroes with men such as Marat, Danton, Robespierre, Saint-Just, and the other brilliant lions of the Jacobins, people she wished to emulate. It was only once she got to Paris and *met* some of those rare, surviving revolutionaries that Charité had had the scales torn from her eyes. Joseph Fouché was an ice-hearted executioner, plain and simple, and no coquetry, no beauty or grace, no flattery could make an impression upon him.

She would *love* it if Fouché found cause to arrest Lewrie as a spy, to hunt him down, fetch him into court in chains, and put his head on the block, ready to be shorn and tumbled into the basket at last.

Yet Charité already rued her coming to Fouché if Mlle. Phoebe Aretino was swept up as a reactionary, a secret *royaliste* traitor to the Revolution, perhaps even now in league with her former lover, the *Anglais* spy! Charité intellectually knew of the excesses of the Reign of Terror, of the slaughter in the surf with shot, bayonet, and sword as those refugees who had not found a ship tried to flee Toulon. Three thousand men, women, and children in the space of two hours, the rumour related! And twice that number perished under Gen. Dugommier's guillotines over the next month after the city was re-taken.

But she had not been in Paris during those times, hadn't seen, heard, or smelled the holocaust, which was now mostly a bad memory to the French, uneasily shrugged off as a temporary necessity. But for men like Fouché, it would never be over, so long as displaced *aristos* overseas, beyond his grasp, schemed and plotted to overthrow the Revolution and its new leaders. And there were those to aid them, in France!

"*Mon Dieu*, I have denounced an innocent!" Charité whispered to herself as she reached the clean air along the banks of the Seine, recalling how lovely and petite, how vivacious and charming Mlle. Aretino was, had been whenever she'd visited her shop. Would *her* glorious hair be shorn at the nape, would *she* die under the guillotine, for *nothing?*

Fouché rang a small bell on his desk to summon a clerk. There must be enquiries made about this Lewrie, even so. *Laisser-passers* were now required of all foreign visitors, and this Lewrie *must* have one, issued by the Foreign Ministry, registered at the city gates, and noted by the municipal authorities at the Hôtel de Ville. And every *concierge* at every hotel or lodging house, no matter how grand or how mean, might as well be in Fouché's employ, and this would make locating the man and his wife very easy.

Fouché would send for information from the Ministry of Marine, as well, which kept *dossiers* on enemy Captains and Admirals, to see if they considered this Lewrie dangerous, beyond the scope of naval combat. He paused in his written demands, wondering if *Citoyen* Pouzin at the Foreign Ministry, a spymaster and *aristo* hunter well known to him, might have some information; he had been in the Mediterranean in the 1790s, when the de Guilleri chit said that this Lewrie had been.

"All these enquiries I wish answered by this time tomorrow," Fouché demanded with an even fiercer scowl. "See to it, *vite, vite.*"

Oddly enough, at about that same time of late afternoon, *Citoyen* Philippe Pouzin (though no one was ever sure if that was the name he had been given at birth) was sharing a bottle of brandy with an old compatriot from his time in the Mediterranean, though with a certain well-hidden sense of distaste. Pouzin's mission to subvert the Genoese, Savoyards, and Piedmontese in order to aid Gen. Bonaparte's First Italian Campaign had been a smashing success, destroying their will to fight for the British, and buying their zeal to ally themselves with France. He and his underling spies, male and female, had even penetrated the elusive and ultra-secret Last Romans movement, which aspired to unite all Italy once more, and turn it into a world power which would re-take everything that had once been under the old Empire in the Balkans and Greece, in the Holy Land, Egypt, and North Africa. Not only penetrated the movement, but turned it to France's advantage!

For that, Pouzin had been rewarded, promoted, and allowed to be among the living as the various feuding factions of the Directory slit each others' throats and sent each other to the guillotine. He'd been overseas, like Napoleon, *safe* from the treacherous games. Now he held an elevated position in the spy organisation under the aegis of the Foreign Ministry, and had thickened on a rich, safe salary.

His unfortunate compatriot, however, had not been so succssful, and had, if appearances were reliable judges, fallen even further than anyone but the unfortunate Job could dread.

"The West Indies, Saint Domingue, and Guadeloupe were not my areas of concern, *Capitaine* Choundas," said Pouzin in apology for not being cognisant of Choundas's troubles. "The undermining of the Kingdom of Naples and the Two Sicilies, the retention of Malta, and the Adriatic took all my attention at the time of the Quasi-War with the *Américains*. You have my condolences for your, ah . . . lack of success."

At least in the Med, Guillaume Choundas had still seemed vital, an active and hearty fellow despite his crippled leg with its rigid iron brace, the stiff black mask which covered his maimed face and dead eye. He'd had *two* arms the last time Pouzin had seen him, as well! Now Choundas was a grey-haired, creased, and stooping ruin, easily mistaken in his shabby remnants of naval uniform for a street beggar; as pruned and wrinkled and *aged* as a poor fisherman's *grand-père*.

"You say this Lewrie, the author of all your misfortunes, is here in Paris, eh, Choundas?" Pouzin asked between sips of an excellent brandy.

"I saw him, Pouzin," Choundas insisted in a harsh rasp. "Sure as I know you, did I see you on the street. He lodges in the Rue Honoré, he and his wife. Recall, *citoyen*, it was a close-run thing that I got the pay chests intended for the Austrians to your agents in Genoa, a hair's breadth *ahead* of Lewrie's pursuit, and would have made my escape to report to you, but for him. And what he did to our cause in the West Indies . . . ! All our vessels lost, our cargoes captured by the cursed, ungrateful *Américains* . . . *led* to them by that *salaud*. And my defeat and capture. We *both* know this peace is only a brief pause. The First Consul grows impatient and angry that the faithless *Anglais* delay the return of our former colonies, stall their evacuation of the island of Malta . . . which *is* in your area of expertise, *n'est-ce pas?*

"Trust me, *Citoyen* Pouzin," Choundas gravelled, his remaining hand clawed about his glass and his one good eye glaring, "when war comes, that *salaud* Lewrie will be at our throats once more."

"I gathered, though, *Capitaine* Choundas," Pouzin replied, "that when we worked together in the Mediterranean, you were dismissive of his cleverness . . . that you put his interferences in your enterprises down to blind, dumb *luck*."

Frankly, Pouzin had always been leery of Choundas's excuses for his set-backs and losses, for they were based more on ancient Celtic Breton superstition than anything else. The man saw signs, *portents*, and omens in the flights of birds, like an ignorant peasant, despite his vaunted level of education, imparted by cynical and worldly Jesuit tutors, of all people! Pouzin also knew that once Choundas was aware that this Lewrie was in the vicinity, he'd allowed his wits to be focussed more on the man's destruction than upon the job at hand. Pouzin could plainly see *why* Choundas might wish revenge, having been so ravaged and made to match his old nickname of *Le Hideux*—The Hideous—by anyone, much less his *bête noire*, his imagined nemesis, Lewrie.

"You have spoken to people at the Ministry of Marine, *mon cher Capitaine*?" Pouzin asked him, feeling sympathetic enough to top up the poor ogre's glass.

"Bah, those indolent and smug *bourgeois* new-comes! They arrive at nine, do no work 'til ten, then depart for *déjeuner* at twelve, not to return 'til three, and go see their wives and mistresses at *five*, the bear-skin slippered. . .!" Choundas almost howled with rage, choking on his beverage, and his bile. "They have no time for the likes of me these days, Pouzin, *mon vieux*. I upset their *digestion*."

Choundas's hideousness was certainly upsetting Pouzin's senses, and the time he allowed the old fellow (*wasn't he younger than me*, he thought?) was cutting into *his* supper, and time with *his* mistress.

"So long as he is here on innocent sight-seeing, *mon chere*, he is of no concern to my Ministry," Pouzin had to tell him, if only to hasten his departure.

"Even though he and that foul *Anglais* spymaster, Zachariah Twigg, who fooled *you* when he play-acted the part of Silberberg, a *Juif* banker from London, have been joined at the hip for decades?" the old cripple accused. "Though I lacked proper support from well-placed spies in the West Indies, we did know that two of Twigg's underlings were active, and that both of them, at one time or other, took passage with Lewrie . . . one to Saint Domingue to deal with that rebel general, Toussaint L'Ouverture. Lewrie and the *Anglais* secret service, Pouzin. Their *lackey*! *Not* clever, *not* all that intelligent, *but* . . . he does their bidding *extremely* well."

"I will look into it, then, *mon cher Capitaine*," Pouzin allowed as an *ormolu* clock on the mantel over his large marble fireplace began to chime the hour. His mistress would be distressed by his lateness. "After all, what are old comrades for, if not to help each other safeguard the Republic, *heu*? I will look into it. If there is something to his presence in France, well . . . perhaps we can find some way to re-pay you for your bringing this to our attention, *n'est-ce pas?* An increase in your naval pension and a financial reward, hmm?"

Guillaume Choundas tossed back the last of his brandy, his ugly face split with a rough approximation of a pleased grin, which hideous attempt made Pouzin shudder.

CHAPTER TWENTY-ONE

*W*hat an odd but charming couple," Caroline determined as they read-ied for bed. She yawned a couple of times, for such late hours in the almost-midnights was foreign to her rural life of early rising and early retiring. They had supped *divinely* well, with lashings of wine beyond her usual partaking, at one of the most elegant *restaurants* in Paris, packed to the rafters with the most fashionable and lively of Paris's elite, and had been regaled by Sir Pulteney's and Lady Imogene's quick wit and repar-tee. Silly though half of it had been.

Afterwards, there had been the theatre, and a grand comedy—Molière, of course, an immortal of French theatre—which the Lady Imogene, who indeed had once been a star on that very stage a decade before, still knew by heart; she had translated the cleverest, funniest parts for them in gay whispers in their box closely overlooking the stage.

Lewrie was yawning, too, though he'd managed a few short naps at the *Comédie Française, despite* Lady Imogene's excited whispers and Sir Pulteney's cackles, guffaws, and donkey brays. Sir Pulteney also had the annoying habit of making idle comments on just about everything and everyone, disparaging a badly tied neck-stock on one gentleman in the box opposite theirs, or the colour of some fetching young woman's gown, the tackiness of too much jewelry—"Cheap paste, most-like, Begad, that! What was she *thinking?*"

Charming, aye; annoying, as well. Still, the Plumbs *had* paid for everything, so what was one to do?

"So fortunate that Sir Pulteney married her away from France, before the Revolution, and the Terror," Caroline said as she brushed out her hair. "And she is lovely . . . in a way. Or was, once."

Meow! Lewrie thought, grinning. Lady Imogene Plumb was petite and wiry, with large, elfin green eyes and a wealth of shining raven-black hair, though her face was that of a slightly "over-the-hill" pixie. "She uses paints . . . the actress in her, I'd s'pose," he said to show Caroline that he agreed with her, and had *not* found her pretty.

"Yes, she does!" Caroline agreed. "Even so, though . . . Lord, that gown of hers! Sir Pulteney must be hellish-rich, indeed, I'd not *wish* to ascribe Lady Imogene's motives for marrying such a . . . daft fellow like Sir Pulteney," Caroline cattily said, pausing her brushing, looking pensively into the mirror as if drawing a comparison, "but . . . a chance to flee France and all the bloodshed, *and* to a man with so much money . . . seeming money, rather . . ."

"Silly as a goose," Lewrie agreed again.

"He does laugh rather a *lot*, doesn't he," Caroline said, chuckling, beginning to under-brush. "I must admit, though . . . they seem to be besotted with each other, still. Did you not notice, Alan?"

Usin' my first name, hey? Lewrie exulted; *that sounds promisin!*

"Can't say that I did, my dear," he said, tossing his shirt at one of his old sea-chests, and donning a dressing robe. "But it takes all kinds, don't it?"

"I suspect a great, mutual passion," Caroline said, done with her hair, and swivelling about on her stool to face him. It sounded wistful.

I'm up for passion! Lewrie told himself, feeling frisky; *should I break out the dental powder or settle for a swill-out with brandy?*

"Did you think her fetching, Alan?" Caroline teased; it *seemed* like romantic teasing, at any rate, Lewrie hoped.

"Well, I was too busy tendin' to you on the packet, Caroline," he replied with a non-committal shrug. "Only really met her tonight. Aye, I s'pose she's handsome . . . in her own way."

"Lady Imogene and I will go shopping tomorrow," she said as she put her toiletry items aside in a roll-up "house-wife," then stood to go to the far side of the inviting bed, nearest the last candle. "You will have another day to yourself. If we are to be presented to that ogre Napoleon Bonaparte, I will need something *truly* grand to wear, and she has promised to advise me. We cannot let the French form a low opinion of how British people dress. Oh, she has such an *exquisite* sense of style and taste . . . as does Sir Pulteney."

"Well, I s'pose I could find something t'do with myself," he allowed, sweeping back the covers on his side of the bed.

"So long as you don't go in search of scents," Caroline said, much more coolly.

"Scents? Hey?"

"Most especially at a shop called La Contessa's in the Place Victor," Caroline said on, her expression and tone hardening, the furrow 'twixt her brows appearing. "A shop run by a Corsican baggage by name of Phoebe Aretino?"

"Uhm, er . . . ! Who? Honest t'God, Caroline, how was I to know she was in Paris?" Lewrie flummoxed. "Mean t'say, rather . . . !"

Shit, there it is! Lewrie quailed; *fourty-two-pound coast guns!*

"And it did not give you pause that Lady Imogene and your . . . *whore!* . . . resemble each other remarkably closely . . . my *dear?* Here!" she snapped, handing him the candle from the night-stand. "It trust you find the settee in the parlour a pleasant bed for the night!"

CHAPTER TWENTY-TWO

*B*y mid-morning two days later, whilst the unsuspecting Lewries were coaching along another bucolic stretch of the Seine, an increasingly concerned Joseph Fouché was receiving a summary report on what his agents had been able to glean about this troubling *Anglais* visitor.

"The Ministry of Marine notes that this *gars* was instrumental in destroying a secret alliance with native pirates in the Far East, back in the bad old days of the *Ancien Régime*," Matthieu Fourchette, one of Fouché's cleverest and most persistent agents, related to his chief. "A dumb idea, anyway, that wouldn't have lasted a year once war broke out again and the *Biftecs* put enough warships out there to escort a China convoy," Fourchette told him with a sneer. "Only a Lieutenant, but the *Anglais* force *was* directed by secret agents from their Foreign Office. Just a lackey at the time, I'd suspect."

Matthieu Fourchette was one of the few people in France who did not cringe at the mention of Fouché's name or shudder in fear when in his presence or carefully guard every utterance. Fourchette was too *insouciant*, too casual and carefree to fear the man he served so well, and it was against his wry and sarcastic, cynical nature. Fourchette did not sit upright, but slouched with his legs sprawled in the chair in front of Fouché's desk, making free with a Spanish *cigarro* and knocking ash to the marble floor.

"Now, there's this retired *Capitaine* Guillaume Choundas's notes, but he's *débile* on the subject of this Lewrie *mec*," Fourchette breezed on, "and thinks the *Anglais* is a demon from Hell, sent specifically by the Devil to torment him. I can see why he thinks so, since this Alain Luray . . . *Lew*-rie . . . was the one who sliced him up like a veal sausage and crippled him. Odd, though . . . how often Choundas was put in charge of something that smacked of spy-work combined with combat, and Lewrie just happened to turn up . . . like a bad penny, as the *Anglais* say, hmm?"

"Anything recent?" Fouché pressed.

"We're getting there, *citoyen*," Fourchette said with a grin. "In the Mediterranean, he put a hitch in Pouzin's plans, again with connexions to the same *Anglais* spymaster that ran things in the Far East. Poor old Choundas lost his arm to Lewrie that time. Poor old *salaud* . . . this fellow just keeps whittling Choundas down to a nub. It's good our Navy retired him, hawn hawn! Anyway . . .

"This Lewrie did rather well in the West Indies, taking prizes, keeping the *Négres* slaves on Saint Domingue, so their uprising did not spread to Jamaica," Fourchette went on. "I spoke to that *Citoyenne* Charité de Guilleri, as you ordered. . . . *Mon Dieu, citoyen,* what a *fine* young thing, and thank you for the assignment! I'd love to 'dip my biscuit' in *that*. The fellow *did* dress in civilian clothes and go up the Mississippi to New Orleans as a spy, though there was no *provable* direction by *Anglais* spy agencies, but it is hard to believe that he did it on his own, *n'est-ce pas?* Then, when we and the *Américains* had our little disagreement, Choundas was out there on Guadeloupe, and, again, Lewrie was instrumental in his *last* downfall. Crippled the fellow's frigate in his own *harbour,* and rolled up many of his privateers and smuggler vessels before the *Américains* captured him and his last convoy."

"Perhaps this Choundas is not so demented, after all," Fouché rumbled. "After that, then?"

"Strictly straightforward," Fourchette said with a shrug, brushing his loose shock of dark hair back from his broad forehead and his oddly pale green eyes that sometimes, in the right light, looked yellow. He was lean and fox-faced, not much above middle height, but despite his *insouciance*, there was an air about him that made others tread as wary about Fourchette as most did about Fouché. "A time in the South Atlantic, escorting China convoys, a fight with one of our frigates, which he won. . . . Uhm, there's a note from the Gironde that he was responsible for the reduction of two forts in the bay of the river, a bombardment of troops dug in on the

Côte Sauvage that resulted in heavy casualties, and one of our naval officers who was spying on the *Anglais* blockade ships, pretending to be a poor fisherman who'd trade with them, sent a letter to the Ministry of Marine to say that the man is a clever liar.

"Which does not agree with Pouzin's, or Choundas's, opinions, *citoyen*," Fourchette pointed out. "They think this Lewrie just lucky, or well-tutored. *Un type de* poorly educated *Anglais* officer, one who will do anything to avoid being called 'too clever by half,' *n'est-ce pas?*"

"Which public face can disguise a wealth of cleverness," Fouché snapped, ill at ease with what he'd heard so far.

"This Lewrie did run into legal troubles last year," Fourchette told him. "He stole a dozen *Nègres* slaves from an *Anglais* planter he'd duelled with . . . from the family, that is . . . to crew his ship, then was tried *in absentia* and sentenced to be hung, but . . . the Abolitionists in England got him off."

"Perhaps he *is* lucky, as well," Fouché commented.

"Two medals, participated in the battles off Ushant, at Cape Saint Vincent, and Camperdown, and lately at Copenhagen," Fourchette tossed away. "Got sent into the Baltic, alone, to scout the Danish, Swedish, and Russian fleets before the battle . . . the new *Anglais* head of their Ministry of Marine is said to have appointed him to the duty directly. It is also rumoured that he carried two Russian nobles home . . . men who are *further* rumoured, so the Foreign Ministry *dossiers* say, to here participated in the assassination of the late Tsar."

"What? Assassination, you say?" Fouché perked up, going into an instant rage. "How *sure* are those *dossiers*, Fourchette?"

"Oh, *citoyen* . . . ," Fourchette disparaged, flicking more ash on the floor, "speculative, at best. The Foreign Ministry people whom I talked to about it don't believe the *Anglais* could ever undertake anything *that* simple and direct. The Russky *aristos* most likely wangled a rapid way home, *promising* a diplomatic solution . . . so they could be in at the kill, and prosper on their own. That's how Talleyrand and the rest of the Ministry interpret it."

"Talleyrand and his *grands légumes* are a pack of simple *fools*, Fourchette!" Fouché barked, rising to pace with his hands in the small of his back, head down, and unconsciously imitating his idol, the new First Consul, Napoleon Bonaparte. "Limp-wristed, over-educated, closeted *aristos*, and *arrivistes*! They would not recognise a rampaging *bear* in their dining room. . . . They'd call it a hungry foreign *visitor* with no fine *manners* such as theirs! You have placed this *salaud* under observation, Fourchette?"

"Since the first moment I spoke with you, *citoyen*," Fourchette assured him. "A rotating crew of watchers, so he will not take alarm, even should he be here to spy on us, and has been instructed in tradecraft. The *concierge* at his lodgings reports he and his wife mostly spend their time here in touring cathedrals, palaces, and such, with shopping and dining. The Comédie Française a few nights ago, accompanied by another *Anglais* couple, uhm . . ."—Fourchette had to refer to his notes for a moment— "neither of them are fluent in French, and he is the biggest offender. Both need the aid of bilingual servants and guides for even the simplest exchanges. Hardly what one would expect of a man sent to spy on us," Fourchette said with a shrug and a sniff of derision.

"No, it is not, is it?" Fouché said, raising his head and ceasing his frenzied pacing, calming as quickly as he'd raged. "What are they doing today?"

"Coaching along the Seine, *citoyen*," Fourchette told him. "Taking the air. Under observation by at least six watchers."

"Well, then . . . perhaps . . . ," Fouché allowed, sitting back down behind his desk and running his heavy hands over his bald pate. "Our terrified *Capitaine* Choundas . . . our deluded *Citoyenne* de Guilleri . . . both have good cause to seek revenge on this *Anglais*, and imagine him an agent of the Devil. In so doing, they magnify this Lewrie's cleverness and guile. To get *me* to do their dirty work, *hein?*"

"*Pardon, citoyen*." One of Fouché's clerks, a fellow much warier of his employer than Fourchette would ever be, tremulously rapped on the half-open door. "You are busy, *citoyen*? A letter has come from Minister Talleyrand, at the Foreign Ministry?"

"*Oui*, bring it," Fouché snapped, waving the man in impatiently and snatching the folded and sealed letter, winking at Fourchette as he did so. "*More* foolishness from that oily, lame bishop, the lecher. *Mon Dieu!*" Fouché exploded a moment later. "*Zut alors! Putain! Mort de ma vie!* The fucking fools! Get out, get out, get out!" he barked at the little clerk, and threw the letter at Fourchette, startling the wiry younger man to his feet. "At the next levee, two days hence, the First Consul will greet the very man we discuss, Fourchette! They've come up with a piece of diplomatic *theatre*, in the name of peace, bah!

"The *Anglais*, this *espèce de merde*, this *fumier*, Lewrie, will present to Bonaparte some swords he'd taken from defeated French captains, asking for one of *his* taken by Napoleon from *him* years ago! So everyone can *applaud* and *fawn* and simper about what good friends we and the *sanglants* now are! Within the reach of a *dagger* to Bonaparte, within a point-blank shot of a hidden pistol!"

"Are they mad?" Fourchette exclaimed.

"*Non*, Fourchette . . . deluded by their own foolishness," Fouché accused, eyes darting about the room for something he could smash, and not regret later. "Suddenly, it all makes sense, that this man is a spy, an assassin sent to destroy our head of government, and start the overthrow of the Republic! If the *salaud did* have a hand in the assassination of the Tsar, last year. . . . ! The faithless, perfidious British have *sent* him to do this."

"Uhm, *citoyen* . . . how might he plan to escape, once the deed is done?" Fourchette pointed out after a brief, quiet moment. "And would a man, even a mad *Anglais*, endanger his wife, as well? If she is here in Paris, will she not be presented with him? I do not see how anyone could be ordered to face certain death for both himself and his woman. And for England to *envision* such an act, *hein?* Surely, they know it would mean immediate war."

"Which they might be planning on," Fouché hotly rasped. "Their army and navy might even now be mobilised, just waiting for news of the success of their murder!"

"Have we seen any *sign* of that, *citoyen?*" the more practical spy suggested. Fourchette suspected that Fouché saw plots where *he'd* put plots were he in their enemies' shoes, and had spent so many years at sniffing out opposition where there really was no opposition, that he had become as fixated as that *débile* old sailor, Choundas.

Despite what Fourchette publicly espoused about the Revolution and the Republic, he was too pragmatic a fellow to give heart and soul completely; such sentiments—for a fellow who held very few sentiments— were the social oil necessary to keep his delightful career, and gain him plum assignments which guaranteed his steady rise in the Police Nationale. The Committee of Public Safety, the Directory, the Triumvirate, and now the First Consul, Hell . . . they could bring back a king, an emperor, and he could really care less.

Fouché, though, Fourchette considered; he owed his life to the continued good health and firm grip on power of his master, Napoleon Bonaparte. Fouché was his man . . . for as long as it looked like Bonaparte held sway. After that, perhaps he would jump ship and espouse another leader, but . . . for now, Fouché would go to any lengths to protect the fellow. *Too* devotedly, *too* slavishly, Fourchette thought him. A cool head was needed here.

"This *gars* Lewrie wishes to present captured swords? Let us ask for them to be held by the Ministry of Marine 'til the levee," he breezily advised his chief. "Before the presentation, call the fellow aside and check him for weapons. What can he do after that, leap and try to *strangle* the First Consul, *hein?* In the meantime, I will keep him under the strictest surveillance, and look into anyone that Lewrie speaks to . . . for any connexion to reactionary elements, *n'est-ce pas?*"

"One to keep watch on will be his former lover, the owner of a *parfumerie* in the Place Victor, a woman . . ."

"Well, I should hope so," Fourchette japed, "though so many Englishmen prefer boys."

"This is no laughing matter, Fourchette," Fouché cautioned him. "A *Citoyenne* Phoebe Aretino. She fled Toulon aboard his ship as our army re-took the city, fled good Republicans with *aristos*. In fact, assign one of your men to look into her, no matter whether this *fumier* contacts her or not."

"I will do so, *Citoyen* Fouché," Fourchette vowed, and, departed, after stubbing his *cigarro* out on the fireplace surround. And wondering, if the woman *had* been Lewrie's lover, would she be entertaining enough and pretty enough to interview himself?

BOOK III

Their hearts battered by this din.
Were torn in two and much afraid.
Flight by land, said one...
The sea is better, said another.

GAIUS PETRONIUS,
THE ROAD TO CROTON, 380-33

CHAPTER TWENTY-THREE

$\mathcal{N}$apoleon Bonaparte, all-conquering general and the First Consul of France, always rose at dawn, when the brain was keenest. After one cup of tea in his bedroom, he spent an hour in the marble bath tub, in water kept so hot that Constant, his valet who read the morning papers to him, sometimes had to open a door and duck out into the hallway to escape the thick, foggy steam.

". . . at the levee this afternoon, the First Consul will receive an embassy from Great Britain, represented by *chargé d'affaires* Sir Anthony Paisley-Templeton, escorting *Capitaine de Vaisseau* Alan Lewrie of His Britannic Majesty's Navy, and his lady . . . ," Constant intoned.

"A prissy, primping *pédé*," Bonaparte grumbled. "A shit in silk stockings. They send me titled boy-fuckers, not a real ambassador . . . and how long has it been since the peace was ratified? Even though my man, Andréossy, has been named to them for months? This *salaud*'s old sword had been found?"

"It has, First Consul," Constant told him. "Rustam has it."

"Well, let me see the damned thing," Bonaparte snapped. Usually his steaming bath relaxed him immensely and eased his constant problem of needing to pee, yet being unable for long, impatient minutes. But today, it was one vexation after another.

Rustam, his Mameluke servant brought back from his Egyptian

Campaign, stepped closer, dressed in magnificent native garb, holding out a scabbarded sword. "Cleaned and polished, General," Rustam assured.

A hanger-sword, no grander than the *sabre-briquet* a Grenadier of the Guard might carry on his hip: royal blue scabbard with sterling silver fittings, its only decorative touches being a hand-guard shaped like a sea-shell, silver wire wound round its blue shark-skin grip, and a matching sea-shell catch on the throat to fit it into a baldric, or a sword belt. The pommel was the usual lion's head, also in silver.

"And where the Devil did I get it? Remind me, Constant," Napoleon demanded. Young General Bonaparte had always awed his troops with a steel-trap memory for names, ranks, faces, and past heroic deeds. . . . Unknown to them was his preparation, and prompting by officers on his staff to provide those names, ranks, and deeds.

"Toulon, towards the end of our siege, First Consul," Constant read from notes made in Napoleon's own hand in the inventory of his personal armory. "The British officer was in command of a commandeered French two-decker, lowered by one deck and converted to a mortar ship. She was shelling Fort Le Garde, quite successfully, until you gathered General La Poype's heavy artillery and shelled her in return, scoring a direct hit and blowing her up."

"Ah, *oui* . . . now I remember." Napoleon brightened up, enjoying the memory. "The survivors swam ashore, and we rode down to take them prisoner. The officer. . . . ?"

"Lewrie, General," Constant provided. "Your note says that despite your offer of parole, he preferred to surrender his sword and go with his men."

"He looked like a drowned rat . . . but he had hair on his ass." Bonaparte hooted with glee. "*Oui*, just after I took his sword, those 'yellow-jackets,' Spanish cavalry, approached from Fort Sainte-Marguerite, and we had to scramble for our lives, hawn hawn! It was quite a day, Constant . . . quite a day. Doesn't look all that valuable, though, to me. Not enough sterling silver to make a tea-pot, really. The blade is more valuable. Unsheathe it, Rustam, aha! Made by Gills's. Even better than Sheffield or Wilkinson, or a German's Kligenthal. Now I see why that *Anglais fumier* wants it back."

When Napoleon Bonaparte shaved himself (not using a servant to do it), he secretly preferred pearl-handled razor sets smuggled in from Birmingham, England, since French steel could not take so fine an edge.

"Put it where we remember it, Rustam," Bonaparte ordered. "Any more interesting items, Constant?"

"Indeed, First Consul. Shall I continue?"

"Red velvet suit today, General?" Rustam asked.

"*Non*," Bonaparte decided. "If that preening fop Talleyrand is desirous of a theatric with the *Anglais*, then I must dress for my part . . . and I do *not* wish to portray the smiling, peaceful dunce. No one pulls my strings like a puppet! The British lie, stall, and delay . . . with such *wonderful* smiles. They play the same game they did with the *Américains* after they lost the Revolution over there. They keep hold of French, Spanish, and Dutch colonies the same way they kept New York and New England, the settlements on the upper Missouri and Mississippi . . . on the *Américain* side of the Great Lakes. Do the British even say *when* they will evacuate Malta, for instance? Pah, they do not!

"Today, Rustam," Napoleon Bonaparte instructed, wiping his face free of sweat with a fresh, dry hand towel, "I will appear more martial . . . as a sign of my displeasure. Lay out my Colonel of Chasseurs uniform."

Though it was but a short distance from their lodgings in Rue Honoré to the main entrance to the Tuileries Palace, a coach-and-four was *de rigueur*, laid on by the embassy and Sir Anthony Paisley-Templeton.

"Oh, *lovely* suitings, Captain Lewrie," Sir Anthony gushed once they'd gotten aboard. "You used my tailor? But, of course you did . . . and Mistress Lewrie, *enchantée*! Your humble servant, Mar'm, and allow me to tender my regrets that we have not, 'til this instance, met. I beg your pardons, but I must also express how lovely you look today, as well. Congratulations. My, won't it be fine, though, as I said to Captain Lewrie, for you to be presented to the First Consul? A day to remember the rest of your lives, aha!"

Stop yer gob, 'fore I do it for ye, Lewrie thought, in no better takings than the first time he'd been exposed to the simpering young twit; *Christ, but he* will *prattle on!*

"I am led to understand that a factotum from the First Consul's staff came round to retrieve the swords you are to present to him. . . . All is in order, Captain Lewrie?" Paisley-Templeton enquired.

"Aye, all done," Lewrie told him. "Shifty-lookin' cove."

"You will be thrilled to learn that the First Consul's office sent me a letter, informing me that your old sword has been discovered in Bonaparte's trophy room," Sir Anthony further enthused (languidly), "and will be on-hand to return to you, once the pacific speeches about our new relations are done. Erm . . . you would not mind looking over a few thoughts that might go down well, were you to express them to the First Consul during the time he gives you, Captain Lewrie?"

"Some actor's lines t'be learned, sir?" Lewrie balked. "Why is this the first I've heard of 'em?"

"Just a phrase or two, some hopes for a long, continued peace," Paisley-Templeton assured him, producing a sheet of paper from his velvet and embroidered silk coat.

"Well, Hell," Lewrie said with a put-upon sigh, quickly looking them over. "Damn my eyes, sir! Do people . . . *real* people ever talk in such stilted fashion?"

"Well, erm . . . ," Sir Anthony daintily objected, blushing a bit.

"Captain Lewrie will phrase things his own way, Sir Anthony," Caroline told the prim diplomat. "With luck, he will be able to get the gist of what you wish said across. Won't you, my dear?"

She was too impressed by the grandness of the occasion to be angry with him today, and sounded almost supportive, as if she'd tease the young fop, too. Almost like a fond wife of long-standing content.

"And, here we are!" Paisley-Templeton said with overt relief as the coach rocked to a stop and a liveried palace lackey opened the kerb-side door. This sea-dog was being a bit *too* gruff this afternoon for Paisley-Templeton's liking.

"You *do* look lovely, Caroline," Lewrie whispered to her as they debarked from the coach, into a sea of onlookers and other attendees garbed in their own grandeur. "Especially so."

That put a broader grin on her face and a twinkle in her eyes as she lifted her head to gaze over the incoming crowd. Lady Imogene had done her proud, with a choice of gown in the latest Paris fashion, with the puffy half sleeves, low-cut bodice, and high-waisted style of the moment. Caroline's gown was a delicate light peach colour, trimmed with a waist sash and hemmings of braided gilt and amber twine, with an additional trim of white lace; all carefully attuned to her complexion, her sandy light-brown hair, and hazel eyes. A gilt lamé stole hung on her shoulders, draped over long white gloved arms, and nigh to the bottom hem of the gown. Some of the late Granny Lewrie's gold and diamond jewelry adorned her ears and wrists, while a gold and amber necklace encircled her neck. Her hair was done up in the convoluted Grecian style, with a braided gilt and amber circlet sporting egret plumes bound about her forehead. And, in the style of the times, her gown was racily shimmery semi-opaque, which, in the right light, revealed almost all of a woman's secrets. In Caroline's case, her gown hinted at a woman who, despite three children and a hearty cook, had kept her figure slim and *nearly* girlish.

She did frown for a second, though, to look down at her feet to see if her white silk knee stockings or gilt lamé slippers had gotten scuffed or stained. Satisfied that all was still well, she looked back up and rewarded both Sir Anthony and Lewrie with another pleased grin.

"Beard the lion in his den?" Lewrie japed in a whisper to her.

"The ogre in his cave," Caroline quipped right back.

"The troll under the bridge," Lewrie added.

"The dragon in his golden lair," she said with a chuckle, and leaned her head close to Lewrie's for a moment.

"Those feathers'll make me sneeze," Lewrie said.

"*Pardon, m'sieur. Permettez-moi, s'il vous plaît,*" a uniformed officer in the Police Nationale said to Lewrie, once they were in the large formal receiving hall. "*Un moment?*" the young officer beckoned to draw him into an alcove, away from the others.

"What for?" Lewrie asked. "Sir Anthony?" He looked for aid.

"I do not know, Captain Lewrie. *Un problème, m'sieur?* Damme! He says no one presented to the First Consul can do so without being searched for weapons, Captain Lewrie! This is outrageous!"

"But understandable," Lewrie said, after thinking about it for a moment. "Proceed, sir. *Produit, m'sieur,*" he told the officer as he held out his arms to cooperate. Muttering to himself in English, "And I hope ye're not one t'prefer the 'windward passage.'"

Lewrie got a rather thorough pat-down, though it was obvious that the snug tailoring of his suit precluded hidden weapons; even the inside of his lower sleeves, the tops of his half-boots held nought.

"*Lui, aussi, maintenant, m'sieur?*" Lewrie asked in his halting French, pointing to Paisley-Templeton. "Him too, now?"

"They will not dare!" Sir Anthony snapped. "This is an insult to his Britannic Majesty, King George, and all Great Britain! A stiff note of displeasure will be on Minister Talleyrand's desk before nightfall, dare they man-handle *me*, sir!"

"*C'est de rigueur, comprenez, messieurs?*" the officer said with an apologetic shrug, waving them both back towards the hall doors, and the two men rejoined Caroline at their place in line before those tall double doors, as tall as a longboat stood on end. They were surrounded by a rainbow of brightly coloured uniforms of the various branches of Napoleon's army, some clanking with spurs on their boots and swords at their hips, which raised Lewrie's eyebrows over his recent search. By those officers and ornately dressed civilian gentlemen stood an host of elegantly gowned women, some of them young, lovely, and flirtatious as they waited for *entrée*; lovers and mistresses, Lewrie determined. Wives seemed more dowdy, even though gaudied up something sinful in the same semi-translucent fabrics as the young and firm-bodied. And there were so many egret plumes in hats and hairdos that Lewrie could conjure that every bird in Europe was now bare-arsed.

A majordomo or master of ceremonies loudly announced each pair as they were allowed in, crying above the soft strains of a string orchestra over in one corner of the vast baroque hall. Their turn came at last; first Sir Anthony, then, "*Capitaine de Vaisseau à la Marine de Guerre Britannique*, Alain Lui . . . Lew-rie, *et Madame* Caroline Lewrie!"

That turned quite a number of heads, made officers grip their sword hilts or pause with their champagne glasses halfway to their lips, forced women to goggle or comment behind their fans, and flutter them in faint alarm, as if a fox had been allowed into their chicken coop.

"Are we *so* infamous?" Caroline had to ask in a soft mutter near his ear once more, her cool and regal smile still plastered on her face.

"We're English. . . . We *must* be," Lewrie chuckled back. "How do, all," he said to the crowd in a soft voice, nodding and smiling, almost waving in their general direction as they paced down the centre of the reception hall. "Now, Sir Anthony . . . where the Devil do they keep the bloody champagne?"

First Consul Napoleon Bonaparte had completed his toilet after leaving his bath; his usual routine followed to the letter. He washed his hands with almond paste, his face, neck, and ears with scented soap (from La Contessa's, in point of fact, in the Place Victor), picked his teeth with a boxwood stem, brushed twice, with paste then powdered coral. Stripped to the waist, dressing robe tossed aside and standing in a flannel vest and underdrawers, he had Constant trickle *eau de cologne* over his head (also from Phoebe Aretino's) whilst he brushed his skin with stiff bristles, and had Constant do his back.

Napoleon donned stockings, white cashmere breeches, and a silk shirt with a fine muslin cravat, with a white cashmere waist-coat over that. He spent his morning at work 'til eleven, when he dined lightly. Then, still in a foul mood, he at last made his decision about what he would wear to the levee. The scarlet-trimmed dark green Chasseur uniform was militant, but not nearly enough.

Bonaparte ordered his dress general's uniform, the long blue tail-coat with the lavish gilt lace trim and scrolls of acanthus leaves. Top-boots, and a red-white-blue Tricolour sash about his waist, over the double-breasted uniform coat.

"*Bon*," he decided, looking in the *cheval* mirror. Lastly, he stuck a scented handkerchief in a pocket and a small snuff box into another, nodded to Constant, and headed down to attend the levee . . . and put those damned *Anglais*, those lying *sanglants*, in their place.

Oh, it was an *elegant* crowd attending the levee! Lewrie expected a scruffy Jacobin mob of *sans culottes* in ill-fitting coats and red Liberty caps, perhaps leaving their scythes and pitchforks at the door, a bunch of old peasant women knitting and rocking where they could get a good view of the next beheading, but . . . there were frosty foreign ministers from half of Europe (minus the Prussians and Austrians, of course) with their wives or temporary local *courtesans*; there were all those aforementioned officers from the Guard, the Chasseurs, the Line infantry, Lancers, and Light Dragoons, the heavy cavalry Cuirassiers and allied officers from the Dutch Batavian Republic, and all of Napoleon's Italian allies . . . the conquered but cooperative.

Instead of ragged commoners with unshaven chins and loose, long hair, the civilian male attendees were dressed so well they could give Sir Pulteney Plumb a run for his money, and a fair number of them had the graceful and languid airs that Lewrie thought more commonly seen at a *royal* reception, a gathering of *aristocrats*, which all the world knew were so despised by staunch French Republicans.

"One'd think they were all titled . . . waitin' for King Louis the Sixteenth t'come dancin' in," Lewrie pointed out to Sir Anthony as the three of them made a slow counter-clockwise circuit of the hall. "What happened t'all that 'noble commoner' nonsense?"

"Most of the great voices of the Revolution are now conveniently dead, sir," Sir Anthony simpered back. "Napoleon has even gone so far as to allow the churches to re-open, and the Catholic Church to restore its presence . . . with power only over its priests and nuns, *not* over the state, and of course, without its former wealth. *That's* gone for muskets and cannon. The *joie de vivre* of your common Frenchman cannot be suppressed. The draconian edicts of the Jacobins against riches, their dour insistence on Equality and Fraternity, were too much a pie-eyed idyllic dream, d'ye see, Captain Lewrie. It's against all human nature to believe that one could invent a *classless* society, with all individual effort directed in support of the state!

"Besides, drinking, eating, and living well, having fine things, and making money is every man's fondest wish," Sir Anthony said with a wry chuckle as he touched his nose with a scented hendkerchief. "Next thing you know, this Bonaparte will make himself First Consul for Life, and surround himself with a *royal* court. *Titles* will come back, just you wait and see. It'll be *m'sieur vicomte* and *madame baroness* 'stead of *citoyen* and *citoyenne*, you mark my words."

"Pity our own politicians, like Fox or Priestley, who *admired* the French Revolution," Caroline said. "How disappointed they must be to see the French slip back to having aristocracy."

"We should begin to introduce you and your good lady about," their young diplomat announced. "The civilian sorts, I'd expect. The military types might be a tad too gruff with us."

"Sounds good," Lewrie began to say, then froze in his tracks.

Holy Christ, it's '96 all over again! he thought, goggling at two people he hadn't seen since a night ashore in Genoa in one case, and a night in bed at shore lodgings in Leghorn, in the other.

It was *Signore* Marcello di Silvano, that hefty and handsome Italian *millionaire*, once the most powerful senator in the Genoese Republic, the man the old spymaster Zachariah Twigg had identitied as the prime leader of the Last Romans. Lewrie could not be mistaken; the fellow was wearing the same glaring white figured-satin suit with the royal purple trim, the same heavy gold medallion and chain of office atop an aquamarine moiré-silk sash. It appeared that Silvano had picked up a few more baubles of honour to pin to his coat breast, too, most likely from Napoleon.

On his arm, though, was the woman who'd spied on Lewrie and influenced him, pretending to be a North Italian Lombard, but really French from near the Swiss border . . . ! Claudia Mastandrea, looking almost as young and fetching as ever—she of the large, round, and firm breasts that she'd pressed either side of Lewrie's face, of the wealth of sandy blond hair, of large brown eyes, nipples, and *areolae* the size of Maria Theresa silver dollars! The spy Twigg had *ordered* him to bed, to pass on disinformation, and a good round lie or two, blabbed in the drowsy afterglow of throbbing, thrashing, hair-tossing, "View, Halloo!" sex!

Signore Silvano (now Duke of Genoa under one of Napoleon's kin) bestowed upon Lewrie a curled-lipped smile and a grave inclination of his head. "Get to you later!" that smile seemed to promise.

From Claudia Mastandrea, Lewrie got one of those momentary gasps and a *most*-fetching upward heave of her impressive mammaries as she recognised him, as well. Then came a sly, seductive smile, a tilt of her head, a lowering of her chin and lashes.

"Ma'am," Lewrie managed to mutter as he nodded. Thank God but Silvano was of no mind to wait for an introduction, but strolled past, tucking his long-time *paramour* a little closer to his elbow.

Lewrie took a cautious look over his left shoulder after they had passed, and . . . Claudia Mastandrea *winked* at him!

"Someone *else* you know in Paris . . . my dear?" Caroline asked.

"Ah, hem . . . met that fellow in Genoa, when I had *Jester*," he replied, thinking himself quick on his feet for so saying. "A senator at the time . . .'til the French bought him off. Already owned half or more of the damned place. A *nasty* article, *Signore* Silvano."

"Oh, now this is a good show," Paisley-Templeton excitedly told them, jutting his chin towards the space before the orchestra, where a few younger couples had begun to dance. "Not for them your everyday *quadrille* or *contre-danse*, such as we have at home. They're doing the *gavotte*, a *most* intricate dance. Takes years of study and practise to perform properly. I fancy myself as a dab-hand at dancing, yet . . . it is *so* complicated, the *gavotte*! I despair of ever learning it."

You look *the sort*, Lewrie told himself uncharitably.

"Napoleon, did you know, refuses to dance unless they play the *monaco*," Sir Anthony tossed off, intent upon the dancers with glee in his expression, his champagne glass hand gently marking the time, and even essaying a sway and faint shuffle of his feet. "The *monaco* is simple . . . as is the new dance that comes from Vienna, the *waltz*. Means 'walking,' I suppose, or something near it. One actually *embraces* one's partner . . . with a discreet space between, of course," he said, lifting his left hand in the air, extending his right. "A couple holds hands . . . here, the lady places her hand on her partner's shoulder, and the gentleman places *his* hand on his partner's waist. One dances a box, One step forward for the man, one backwards for the lady . . . one step to the right for both, then back for the man, forward for the lady, and then left back to where one started, before performing a half-turn to the right, and beginning the box again. Swooping . . . elegant. Romantic . . . yet perhaps too racy for English society, more's the pity."

"It has been Christmas since we danced," Caroline said, quite taken with the dancers' movements. "Perhaps if they do play something familiar to us . . . once we're done with Napoleon . . ."

"After I've had more champagne," Lewrie said. He'd once been a dab-hand himself in the parlours, at the subscription balls, but it had been years, and stumbling about canted decks on his sea legs was not conducive to elegance or fine style. He was sure he would *clump*!

As if he'd said "open sesame" a liveried waiter appeared with a tray bearing fresh glasses of champagne. Lewrie gallantly clinked glasses with his wife and turned away to sip deep . . . and spluttered and coughed.

"*M'sieur,*" Charité Angelette de Guilleri said as she dipped in a graceful curtsy, on the arm of an officer of Chasseurs, who knocked off a faint bow, wondering who the Devil his girl was greeting.

"*Mademoiselle,*" Lewrie managed to say, bestowing a "leg" in reply, suddenly feeling the heat of the room in late summer, and its crowded body heat of hundreds of attendees. Breaking out in a funk-sweat would be more to the point!

"*Madame,*" Charité continued with a maddeningly serene smile on her face, curtsying to Caroline this time. "*Enchanté.*"

"*Mademoiselle* . . . ?" Caroline said, responding in kind, confused, feeling a flush of heat herself, and wondering if she was being twitted by an impudent mort who wished to insult a Briton.

It didn't help that Charité was in an Egyptian-pleated gown of such thin, shimmery pale blue stuff that Lewrie didn't have to use his imagination to recall every succulent inch of her. Her hair was up in the ringleted style *à la Joséphine*, a plumed, wide-brimmed hat on her head, a furled parasol in one lace-gloved hand, and a tiny reticule hung from an elbow.

"*Pardon, Madame,* but I was also in the *parfumerie* La Contessa the other day," Charité said with wide-eyed, lash-batting innocence, "and wish to express my regrets you did not find anything satisfactory, for it is the grandest establishment. A thousand pardons for my boldness, but . . .

you are English? How marvellous that we are at peace, and you may enjoy the splendours of Paris, the most magnificent city in all Europe, *n'est-ce pas?* I may make your acquaintance?"

She got a pistol in that reticule? was Lewrie's prime thought, quickly followed by; *Christ, just open a hole in the floor, and let me through it! Who-the-bloody-else is goin' t'turn up?*

He surreptitiously gave Charité a careful looking-over; in New Orleans, she'd had a habit, when carousing in men's suitings, of keeping a dagger up a sleeve; did she today have it strapped to one of her shapely-slim thighs?

". . . and Captain Alan Lewrie, of his Britannic Majesty's Navy, *Mademoiselle* de Guilleri," Sir Anthony was happily babbling away, glad to have *some* Frogs to present. "Captain Lewrie, may I name to you *Mademoiselle* Charité de Guilleri, and Major Denis Clary."

"Your servant, *Mademoiselle* de Guilleri . . . Major Clary, your servant, as well," Lewrie was forced to respond with another "leg" to both of them, gritting his teeth to appear polite.

"Captain Lewrie will be presented to the First Consul today," Paisley-Templeton grandly announced. "An exchange of captured swords. General Bonaparte once made Captain Lewrie a prisoner, temporarily, at Toulon, and still has Captain Lewrie's sword."

"You refused parole, *m'sieur?*" Major Clary asked, amazed that a man would not accept the relative comfort of a very loose sort of imprisonment in civilian lodgings, with his pay continuing 'til exchanged for an officer of his own rank.

"I would not abandon my sailors to the hulks, Major," Lewrie responded. "It would've cut a bit rough t'just walk away from them and be . . . comfortable."

While Major Denis Clary was trying to sort out the phrase *cut a bit rough,* Charité stuck her own in. She *seemed* to find his choice honourable—wide-eyed astonishment and all—but, "The *Capitaine* Lewrie is surely courageous. As ferocious as Denis, here, a hero of Hohenlinden and Marengo, *n'est-ce pas?*"

She batted her lashes nigh-fit to stir a small breeze, playing the innocent minx, eliciting congratulatory coos from Sir Anthony, and a *moue* and shrug of false modesty from her companion to be so praised.

"*Quel dommage,* such choice was not given to my brothers, Helio and Hippolyte," Charité continued, suddenly turning solemn and all but dabbing at one eye with a handkerchief. "Or, my *cousin* Jean-Marie . . . who perished for the glory of France." Charité glared directly at the author of their deaths, making Lewrie purse his lips and frown, sure that she'd claw his eyes out, given half a chance. "You will exchange swords with Napoleon, *n'est-ce pas?* I only hope that some of those swords are not *theirs*, Capitaine Lewrie. That would be so *tragique*."

She's gotten teeth, Lewrie thought, fighting a wince, recalling those names; *Good God A'mighty, can this get even worse?*

"I do not recall those names being associated with the swords I brought, *mademoiselle*," he told her, glancing at her soldier companion. "These were surrendered by *naval* officers, at sea . . . well, picked up more than surrendered, since their owners had fallen."

Major Clary curled a lip in faint disgust over the fate of fellow French officers, even if he held a low opinion of his nation's navy, and how little it had accomplished since the war's start in 1793.

"Yayss, well . . . ," Paisley-Templeton placated.

"Honour to make your acquaintance, *m'sieur*," Major Clary said, eager to end their chat. "*Madame, Capitaine?*"

"Your servant, sir . . . *mademoiselle*," Lewrie replied with one more bow to each, hoping that *that* was over and done with.

"That little . . . whore!" Caroline muttered as they departed.

Oh shit, she's plumbed to it! Lewrie gawped to himself; *now she knows about Charité, too! Oh yes, it* can *get worse!*

Lewrie tried to bluster his way out of it. "Why call her a—"

"Her!" Caroline snapped, flicking her fan open in the direction of the orchestra, and the dancers. For there, now the orchestra had ended the long *gavotte* and gone on to a simpler *minuet* or *quadrille* air, was Phoebe Aretino, swanning gracefully through the figures, partnered with a tall, mustachioed Colonel of the Guard Infantry . . . and sneaking brief but longing glances at Lewrie, before his wife caught her at it!

Christ, it'll be Emma Hamilton next! Lewrie miserably told himself; *Irish Tess, Lady Cantner . . . even Soft Rabbit's ghost! Lord, but I need another drink! Now!*

"And . . . here he comes now," Paisley-Templeton said with enthusiasm as the orchestra quickly ended their air, and the tall double-doors at the far end of the long hall opened. People scampered from the centre of the floor to form up on either side as the First Consul made his entrance, hands behind his back and looking as if his boots were pinching his toes. "Now, what does his choice of uniform mean? Oh! Perhaps he expected

you in uniform, and means to honour you, sir," Sir Anthony whispered
with a hopeful smile.

It took better than three-quarters of an hour for them to find out what
Napoleon's martial appearance meant, for there were other luminaries
for the First Consul to greet; and Sir Anthony was more than happy to
point them out and name them for the Lewries. There were generals, of
course, the odd French admiral, men high in Bonaparte's government,
along with composers, scientists, philosophers, and academics; civil engineers enrolled to expand the French road and canal systems, as well as
actors and actresses, famed singers, and playwrights from the Comédie
Française, even a scruffy, artistic poet or three. There was the crafty (some
might say duplicitous) Foreign Minister, Charles Maurice Talleyrand-
Périgord, a tall and spare former *aristo* and former powerful bishop with a
taste for silly, and impressionable, young women. There were members of
distinguished and titled old families of France, mostly those who had
somehow escaped the rabid purges during the Reign of Terror, whose
sons had atoned for their sins of privilege on the battlefield, and were now
held blameless.

Finally, an elegant young fellow from the French Foreign Ministry approached Sir Anthony Paisley-Templeton, whispered in his ear, and indicated that that worthy should herd his presentees to a prominent place in
the centre of the hall, before a set of chairs and settees quickly cleared of
people, one chair in particular that would serve as a *throne* 'til the real
thing was dusted off and dragged down from the garret.

"Not very big, is he?" Caroline whispered to Lewrie as they were led
to the makeshift seat of honour.

Napoleon Bonaparte stood about two and a half inches shy of her husband's five feet nine. To Lewrie's memory, Napoleon had put on a few
pounds since '94, but still appeared slim. His hair was now more carefully
dressed, no longer a *sans culottes* page-boy; frankly, Bonaparte's hair was
thinning, and was combed forward over his brow, shorn closer to the
ears, with longer sideburns.

Forgot he and I have much the same blue-grey eyes, Lewrie told himself as
they approached. From one side of the seating arrangement, a liveried servant came with a long bundle wrapped in dark blue, gilt-edged velvet. From
the other, there came another man, bearing a much slimmer package.

Paisley-Templeton, presented first by a simpering Frog diplomat underling, responded in his excellent French with over a minute or two of "gilt and be-shit" diplomatist-speak, with so many subordinate clauses that Lewrie's head began to reel trying to follow it. At last, he recognised that he and Caroline were being named to Bonaparte, and made a "leg" with his hand over his heart, as Caroline performed a very fine curtsy (she had not imbibed as much champagne as he!) with a fetching incline of her head.

"Your servant, sir," Lewrie spoke up, in English, in English fashion, and he heard Paisley-Templeton making excuses for their lack of fluency in French.

"The First Consul says you are welcome, Captain Lewrie. . . . He expresses enchantment with *Madame*, and finds her beauty, and her gown, delightful," Paisley-Templeton translated. "He remembers you, he says. Toulon . . . Fort Le Garde exploding . . . firing upon your ship, blowing her up, as well, uhm. . . . You would not accept parole, and he told you then that, ehm . . . 'you have hair on your arse.' Had, rather," their representative said, deeply blushing at the crudity, while the gathered audience tittered and chuckled.

"Tell him that I recall, vividly," Lewrie said, not even trying to tangle his tongue with his French, not after four glasses of wine. "Say that I am honoured that he would remember such a minor incident, such a minor encounter. Say also that, had I known who he was then, or to what heights he would rise, I would have tried to be more pleasant, even given the soggy circumstances."

"Of course, sir," Sir Anthony said, before launching into one more long simpering palaver. Lewrie noted, though, that Bonaparte had his lips curled in a faint expression of dislike for this pantomime. Unconsciously, one finger of Napoleon's left hand tapped on his thigh.

"He says that you appeared a half-drowned rat, sir," Paisley-Templeton translated, "with your stockings round your ankles, and your breeches draining water."

"Aye, I expect I did," Lewrie agreed with a grin. "Though, as I recall, General Bonaparte looked natty. Does he still have that white horse he rode? A splendid beast."

The pleasantries went on for another minute or so before Sir Anthony got to the meat of the matter, expressing a well-rehearsed preamble about Lewrie's wish, now there was a lasting peace between their respective countries, to return the swords he had taken, restoring them to France and to the families of the fallen.

At a nod from Napoleon, the liveried servant with the large bundle came to lay it across Lewrie's arms, just long enough for him to re-take possession before the draped bundle was formally laid at Napoleon's feet and spread open to reveal all five scabbarded blades, with paper tags bound to the hilts to indicate who were the former owners.

At another nod, the other servant came forward and gave it to Napoleon. He whipped the cloth covering off and tossed it aside, then held up Lewrie's old hanger for all to see before stepping forward—Sir Anthony gave Lewrie a slight nudge to make him take a step towards Napoleon to meet him halfway—and Napoleon held it out to him. But, before he actually let it go, he began another long speech, this time with his lips slit to nothing whenever a pause came, and he didn't look all that happy.

"Oh Lord, sir . . . he asks what sort of peace is it when England stalls and delays fulfilling its part of the terms. I won't bore you with *all* of it," Paisley-Templeton said with a very good imitation of a placid expression on his stricken phyz, nodding now and again as the First Consul had himself a little rant at Lewrie's expense. "He *hopes* you never have cause to use your sword against France again, but . . . does Great Britain continue in its perfidious course, the need to draw it will become more likely, and he . . . he expresses a desire that England sends him a proper ambassador, and accepts his own in London, else . . . before mistakes and confusion engendered by *junior* diplomatists do irreparable harm to the amity between our nations."

Napoleon clapped his mouth shut for a moment, his lips pressed closer together, and his expression stormy, whilst the gathered crowd sounded quite pleased with his rant, the generals that Lewrie could see sharing wolfish, eager glances between them.

"He presents you with your old blade, sir," Paisley-Templeton said at last, looking as if he wished to daub his face with a handkerchief. "From one warrior to another."

A quick imperative shake of the sword and Lewrie reached out to take it. He had enough wit to bow again and express his utmost thanks along with some of those phrases Sir Anthony had written for him: great honour to be presented; so pleased the exchange could be made; thanks for his excellency's indulgence; let us pray that peace prevails, and all that tom-foolery.

Lewrie stepped back at last, with a final bow in *congé*, as Caroline did a parting curtsy, and Sir Anthony led them away from the Presence. "It don't look like we'll have tea with Josephine after all," Lewrie whispered to his wife. "Sorry 'bout that, m'dear."

"To see her was quite enough," Caroline told him. "She's not as fetching as we've heard." An incline of her head led Lewrie's eyes to a woman in a pale pink and white *ensemble,* with her hair up in Grecian style, and roses in her hair, who was now joining Napoleon.

"Should we scamper, now it's done?" Lewrie asked their chaperone. "Or must we circulate and *try* t'be polite any longer? I don't think he cared much for it."

"A quarter-hour or so, a last glass of champagne, and we could depart," Sir Anthony told them, looking troubled and whey-faced. "And not appear to be fleeing with our tails tucked."

Once back in his *appartements* in the Tuileries Palace, Napoleon Bonaparte had his body-servant, Rustam, peel him out of his sash and uniform coat. He tore away his own cravat and tossed it on the floor, crossing to the fireplace (Napoleon loved a fire, even in temperate weather) and furiously jabbing at the coals and embers with the poker. He even kicked one of the mostly consumed logs in anger, an act that cost him many ruined shoes and boots.

"*Monsieur* Bourrienne! *Monsieur, monsieur!*" he called for his private secretary. "*Allez vite!* Bring me Talleyrand and Fouché. I wish to know who thought that . . . charade a good idea!"

And it did not do his simmering temper any good that it took a good quarter-hour for Fouché to appear . . . without Talleyrand.

"Where is the *salaud?* Still fumbling under that silly *Madame* Grand's skirt again, Fouché?" Napoleon snapped.

"I would suspect so, General," Fouché sarcastically replied. "Is this about the Englishman? I am relieved that the affair is over, and that he had no ulterior designs upon your life. All my careful precautions proved un-necessary," he added, almost preening, awaiting his master's thanks. "A day or two more of sight-seeing and they will be gone, now the exchange is done." Bourrienne had warned him that the First Consul was angry, and why.

"I will not be settled in my mind 'til the *fumier* is back across the sea," Napoleon spat, poking at the fire again. "Much better would it be that my troops had slaughtered that Lewrie and all his men right there in the surf as they came ashore! I *read* the reports you sent me from the Ministry of Marine . . . about his connexions with the *Anglais* secret service, Fouché. That fellow is more dangerous to France than he appears! Not the sort *I'd* leave alive or turn my back on without finding a way to neutralise him, did I run across him on the field of battle. What an insult to the honour of France, to lay dead and conquered men's swords before *me* . . . to *smile* and speak of *peace* when what was *really* meant was to flaunt their navy's superiority to my face and present me with the blades of abject *failures*! As a warning to France what will happen at sea should we contemplate a vigourous response to their continued perfidy."

Napoleon paced at a rapid gait from one end of his offices to the next, pausing to jab or kick at the fire at the middle of every circuit.

"The fellow is not a Nelson, General," Fouché pointed out. "He is only a minor frigate *capitaine* . . . a very fortunate one, we learn."

"Fortunate?" Napoleon scoffed, giving the fire another poke. "A soldier or sailor makes his *own* fortune, Fouché! *Non non,* what the Ministry of Marine reports of his doings shows me a man *born* for war. In time, he might *become* another Nelson . . . another pestilent, obnoxious, poorly educated and piss-proud . . . Englishman! As poorly as our navy has done so far . . . *non.* It might be better for us that this *salaud* does *not* . . . that he drops dead of something would . . . Ah, *ohé*," Bonaparte barked. "Here at last, are we, *Monsieur* Talleyrand? I wish for you to explain to me what gain there was in that ignoble theatric you recommended so highly . . . that you forced me to endure!"

"I will see to it at once, General," Fouché said, certain that he understood his master's command to a tee. He was anxious to depart, no matter how much pleasure could be derived from seeing the arrogant, languid Talleyrand being scolded, and a strip of flesh torn from his arse.

"Fine, fine, Fouché . . . good work, your precautions," Napoleon offhandedly said with an abrupt wave of his free hand, too intent on scolding Foreign Minister Talleyrand to consider how Fouché might interpret his idle, spiteful wish. "Now, *monsieur* . . . tell me what . . ."

Fouché left the offices and quickly made his way out of earshot, his keen mind already laying plans, contemplating the methods and means, and organising a list of likely personnel to fulfill the First Consul's order.

CHAPTER TWENTY-FOUR

*I*t had been a grand jaunt up along the Seine to Melun and Fontainebleau to tour the pristine forests and the grand hunting lodges of the displaced nobility; over thirty English miles each way, but more than worth it, for the side-trip had soothed Caroline into calmer takings. That, and several smaller vineyards' best wines, and heartier provincial dishes than the effete kick-shaws found in Paris.

Still, it felt grand to kick off shoes, coat, and waist-coat and sprawl on one of the settees in their rented parlour—Lewrie upon one, and Caroline on another, in stockinged feet, too. She was tucked up with a new book in her lap when there came a rapping on the hallway door. Jules went to answer it.

"Stap me, if the Lewries *didn't* get eaten by the Corsican ogre!" Sir Pulteney Plumb brayed as he swept in, bestowing an elaborate bow to each with a flourish of his hat. "Imogene and I are *dyin'* of curiosity as to how your levee at the Tuileries Palace went, so much so that we simply *had* to barge in and enquire, haw haw haw!"

"Main-well, if ye like 'icy' and 'threatenin',"" Lewrie said as he got to his feet. "You find us not quite ready to—"

"And, to extend an invitation to supper this evenin', where you may reveal *all* the juicy details to us," Sir Pulteney blathered on. "I have discovered a *pearl* of a wee *restaurant* in the Rue Saint-Nicaise. Odd's Fish, but their *vol-au-vent*, their *bouchée à la reine*, and their *sauté à la provençale* are simply *divine*, and you *must* try the place . . . before you leave Paris. Oh, *do* say you will join us. . . . Our treat?" Sir Pulteney tempted, then added, "Imogene and I have news to impart to you, as well, which news you will find *astounding*, sir and madam."

"Well," Caroline said, cocking her head to one side and looking at her husband. "If you do not find our travelling clothes too plain, Sir Pulteney."

"Begad, Mistress Lewrie, no fear o' that, for you are always elegant," Plumb pooh-poohed. "It is we Plumbs who may shame you, haw!"

Indeed, Sir Pulteney was garbed in darker, soberer fashion than was his usual wont.

"'Tis a splendid evenin' for a stroll before we dine . . . grand for both appetite and the digestion, to which the French pay particular care," Sir Pulteney further suggested. "A turn along the Seine in the twilight?"

"Yes, let's," Caroline agreed, deciding for them.

A quarter hour later, after they'd dressed, the three of them slowly ambled along the Galerie du Louvre, enjoying the coolness of a breeze off the Seine and the soft, lingering amber sunset. Sir Pulteney had babbled, brayed, and japed most amusingly, plying his walking-stick with the *panache* of a regimental drum-major, but then fell into an unaccountably gloomy silence. At last, he turned his head to look at the Lewries, and muttered through a fool's smile.

"Pray, do not react at all to what I have to impart to you, or make any sign of distress. Pretend I tell you another amusing tale—can you do that? There may be people watching us this very instant."

"Watchin'? What the Devil for?" Lewrie asked, frowning, fighting the urge to peer about. Caroline put her hand in his but kept a silent shudder well hidden.

"Years ago, as the Revolution turned violent, and right through the Reign of Terror in Ninety-Three," Sir Pulteney Plumb explained in a softer voice, "there was a grand English lord who was so appalled by the injustice and bloodshed that he organised a league of gentlemen dedicated to the rescue of innocents from the guillotine and the Mob . . . which league was *quite* successful, right up to the death of Robespierre and the outbreak of the war with France in February of Ninety-Three. Of course, this league sometimes depended upon the aid, and the intelligence passed on, from well-disguised Royalist sympathisers here in Paris, throughout

France. I confess to you only that I was once a member of that league then, and *now*, able to make cautious *rencontres* with former French supporters . . . even under the noses of the Police Nationale."

"What the bloody—" Lewrie began to flummox.

"Hist! Listen carefully, I pray you!" Sir Pulteney cautioned, then continued. "The rebel Georges Cadoudal's failed attempt to kill Bonaparte with a hidden bomb a while back—quite near here in point of fact, at the intersection of the Rue Saint-Nicaise and the Rue de la Loi—has tightened the surveillance of the Police upon any who might still harbour Royalist, anti-Bonaparte feelings.

"Yet!" Sir Pulteney went on with a louder bark, as if getting to the punch-line of a jape, "one of our old confidants sought me out whilst you were away, and told me that whatever it is you did or said to Napoleon has made him *exceedingly* wroth with you, . . . and he has given orders that you are to be . . . *eliminated* for your insult to him."

"My insult?" Lewrie gawped. "But what the Devil did—"

"Dear God!" Caroline softly exclaimed, blanching.

"Now laugh. Laugh as if I just told you the grandest amusing tale!" Sir Pulteney hissed, breaking out his characteristic donkey's bray. The Lewries' amusement sounded much lamer, as if they were merely being polite or the tale had not been all that amusing.

"Therefore, you both must flee Paris, instanter," Sir Pulteney said, leaning closer and urging them to begin strolling again. "Pack as if you haven't a care in the world, wind up your accounts, *without* showing any *signs* of haste. Above all, do *not* let on to your hired servants or the *concierge* of your lodgings back yonder that you are departing in a panic. *Most* importantly, do not discuss the matter if a servant is anywhere within earshot, for you may trust *no one* whom you do not know, even a fellow Englishman whom you suddenly encounter here in Paris. . . . He may be a skilled, bilingual Police agent. I will arrange for your bulkier possessions' shipment back to England, and I have already begun the scheme to spirit you back to England. If you will trust to my experience and abilities in this matter?"

"What? Well, erm . . . hey?" Lewrie stammered, thinking that only a feeble idiot would trust this braying ass with an *empty* pewter snuff box, for Sir Pulteney Plumb gave all evidence of losing it within the hour; too scatter-brained to keep up with a pocket handkerchief!

Part of a secret league, him? Lewrie thought, incredulous over the very idea; he *arranged hundreds of escapes? Best we abandon all our traps and run like Blazes, this instant! I made Napoleon angry? He wants me dead? Or, is it Charité de Guilleri's doin'? Yet she's no real power here . . . does she?*

"Alan, if what he says is true . . . ," Caroline almost whimpered, squeezing his hand like a vise. "What must we *do*? This is impossible!"

"Softly, Mistress Lewrie, softly!" Sir Pulteney cautioned her, "and do not lose heart. You must believe that what I say is true, and that what our old league accomplished in years past we shall be able to accomplish now. Plans are already afoot, soon as I was informed of Bonaparte's wrath by someone well placed in his *entourage*. I've sent word to some of our old compatriots in England to cross over to help, and once we reach the coast, we shall be met by a schooner, mastered by yet another of our old compatriots. Royalist sympathisers and old supporters, though Minister Fouché and Réal *imagine* they have eliminated our, and Cadoudal's, networks, I assure you that whichever route we take, there will be many along the way to aid us.

"Will you believe me, sir, madam . . . for your lives? Will you trust me to see you safely out of France, and home to England?" Plumb pressed them.

"Christ, I . . . s'pose we must," Lewrie gravelled, still unable to take it all in. "Trust *someone*, at any rate. Though it beggars all belief that Bonaparte'd go t'such lengths, *knowin'* such an act would re-start the war. 'Less . . . that's what he wishes . . . ," Lewrie trailed off, his mind reeling.

"*You* didn't insult him, Alan, I don't think," Caroline said in a distraught whisper, looking deep into her husband's eyes. "It was more our government's delays that irked him, but surely he can't hold that against *you* . . . against *us*! Oh, why did I ever insist that we come to France? This is all my fault!"

"Still, sir and madam . . . do you trust me to make good your escape?" Sir Pulteney pressed with uncharacteristic sternness.

"Don't see how you can, yet . . . they say drownin' man'll clutch even the feeblest straws," Lewrie decided, puffing out his cheeeks in frustration. "Aye, I s'pose we must. . . . We do. Though, how . . . ?"

"We have our ways, stap me if we don't!" Sir Pulteney assured them, then cackled out loud. "Begad, but we do have our ways!"

Charité de Guilleri, in the meantime, had been having a grand few days. Firstly, she had finally allowed the dashing Major Clary of the Chasseurs to have his way, discovering that Denis was a most pleasing lover. Secondly, her beloved New Orleans, her Louisiana, was now rumoured to almost be back in France's grasp. While she could not fantasise that her continued hints, suggestions, or pleas for France to reclaim Louisiana from the dullard, corrupt, and incompetent Spanish had been the *sole* cause, Charité had, in the best *salons*, found allies who felt the same as she. A couple of Napoleon's brothers, Talleyrand (though that had taken an affair with the crippled, arrogant, and dismissive older *fumier*—an affair which had become almost unendurable before Talleyrand had discovered Madame Grand!), and a few others—all had coaxed, cajoled, and spoken favourably for an expansion of empire on the American continent.

Two years before, soon after Napoleon had become First Consul, talks had been opened with Spain for an exchange. Charles IV of Spain desired a kingdom for his new son-in-law, and Bonaparte had offered Tuscany, now firmly occupied by French troops, in exchange for Louisiana. An agreement had tentatively been signed then, at San Ildefonso, yet it still lacked the formal signature and approval from the dilatory and suspicious Charles IV.

Now, though . . . wonder of wonders, Talleyrand had dropped her a hint at the levee where she had confronted that imp of Hell from her past, Alan Lewrie, that Charles's final approval would soon come!

She could go home in triumph, not as an escaped felon from Spanish justice for piracy, not as a failed revolutionary, but as a confidante of Napoleon Bonaparte himself, a member of the official delegation which would accept the turnover in the Place d'Armes, before the Cathedral of St. Louis, to the cheers of her fellow Creoles, her fellow Frenchmen and Frenchwomen! She would be a heroine at last!

So it was that Mlle. de Guilleri felt as if she could float on air as she breezed into the quay-side entrance to the offices of the Police Nationale, at Fouché's invitation. After all his sneers at her pretensions, let him eat crow that she had succeeded in reclaiming her dear home!

"*Citoyenne,*" Fouche began with his usual grouchiness and testy impatience. "You have met *Citoyen* Fourchette."

"Indeed, *Citoyen* Fouché," Charité sweetly replied, dipping one brief curtsy to the slouching, greasy-looking agent who had questioned her about that *salaud*, Lewrie. "A pleasure to greet you again, *Citoyen* Fourchette."

"*My* pleasure to see *you* again, *Citoyenne* de Guilleri," the man replied with an appreciative, up-and-down stare, openly leering at her. He did not fully rise from his chair, though he did sit up straighter and continued to draw on his *cigarro*.

"Fourchette has had this Lewrie *gars* under constant watch for the last few days, *citoyenne*," Fouche gruffly told her, waving her to a chair, a touch too uncomfortably close to the lusting Fourchette for Charité's comfort.

"Indeed, *Citoyen* Fouché?" Charite asked, with one brow up.

"His presence in Paris . . . his history of involvement with the British spy establishment . . . what the Ministry of Marine knows about him from their *dossiers*," Fouché grumbled. "My thanks to you, *citoyenne*, for alerting us to him. For a time, we suspected he was here to kill the First Consul. How close he got to him during the exchange of old swords?"

"I was there, *Citoyen* Fouché," Charité pointed out, letting him know once more that she travelled in the best circles.

"Thankfully, we escaped that, but . . . perhaps you also witnessed how angry the First Consul was, as well, *n'est-ce pas?*" Fouché went on with a mocking grin over her comment. "Later, he gave me orders that this *mec* should drop dead of something, *hein*? Since you already know—"

"He will be done away with at last?" Charité exclaimed in sudden joy. Could her prospects be even more blissful? *"Bien! Très bien!* You have just made me the happiest woman in all of France!"

"Despite *Citoyenne* de Guilleri's enchanting beauty and seeming innocence, Fourchette, she is a fire-eater, a veteran of armed revolution back in Louisiana, *hein*?" Fouché told his agent, almost winking on the sly even as he praised her. "She and her brothers went to sea to pirate Spanish ships . . . raised funds and took arms so the patriots of Louisiana could rise and throw off the Spanish yoke, *comprenez*? I assure you, *Citoyenne* de Guilleri is a *very* dangerous young woman."

"Then all France must owe you a great debt, *Citoyenne* Charité," Fourchette said with slow and sly surprise, and an incline of his head to her, in lieu of a bow. "A slim sword, hidden in a silk scabbard."

"How? When does he die?" Charité demanded impatiently, feeling irked by Fouché's sarcasm and Fourchette's suggestive ogling. "May I be there, when it's done? My brothers, my *cousin*, must be avenged at last," she insisted, shifting eagerly on her chair.

"Not here in Paris, *non*," Fouché told her. "That's too public. Fourchette's watchers say that he and his wife will soon take coach to Calais, now the exchange is done, and their touring is over. The last trip, Fourchette?"

"Two days in the forest of Fontainebleau. Very romantic, I suppose," Fourchette answered with a chuckle and roll of his eyes. "They pay the *concierge* the final reckoning and may depart by the end of the week. A highway robbery may be arranged . . . *tragique, hein?*"

"The *both* of them?" Charité had to ask. That bastard Lewrie was one thing, but his wife was quite another.

"Might be best," Fourchette suggested with a tentative shrug of his shoulders. "And the coachmen, too. Better they simply disappear and are never heard from again. Hmm?"

"Pity they do not coach towards Normandy or Brittany," Fouché grumped. "It could be blamed on Royalist bandits, like Cadoudal and his compatriots, reduced to robbery to fund their schemes against the Republic. Ah, well, I suppose the Calais highway must do. You are sure that is their destination, Fourchette?"

"It is what they speak of with the *concierge*, the port to which they have already sent off their heaviest luggage," Fourchette assured his chief. "They will travel lighter, departing. Else it would take a second coach, she's bought so much in Paris. Understandably."

"I have summoned both of you, who know the man and his wife by their faces," Fouché continued, "just in case something goes wrong *en route*. You see, *citoyenne*, you *will* be in at the kill, hawn hawn!"

"A thousand thanks, *Citoyen* Fouché," Charité said in heartfelt and genuine gratitude, though she had her doubts about travelling with the leering Fourchette. "For that matter, Major Denis Clary, of the Chasseurs, was with me when I spoke with Lewrie at the levee, and *he* knows his appearance, as well." She thought she would have to put up with a lot less cloying attention should Denis be at her side.

"Uhm . . . perhaps," Fouché allowed, leery of involving anyone too official, in uniform, though; of any slip-up that might lead back to the First Consul or the French government. "I sent for another *gars*, who also has intimate knowledge of Lewrie's appearance, though . . ."

"*Pardon, citoyen*," the meek clerk intruded, rapping hesitantly on the door before sticking his head in. "But that naval fellow you sent for is here. Should I show him in?"

"*Ah bon!*" Fouché perked up, clapping his meaty hands together and getting to his feet. "Come in, *Capitaine*, come in! A man from the earliest days of the Revolution, you see? A zealous hunter of *aristos* and traitors, is . . . but here you are, *Capitaine*.

"Allow me to introduce you to *Citoyenne* Charité de Guilleri and one of my best agents, *Citoyen* Matthieu Fourchette," Fouche continued. "But of course you and Fourchette *have* met before, *hein? Citoyenne*, I give you *Capitaine de Vaisseau* Guillaume Choundas."

Charité shot to her feet in sudden, shivering horror as she got sight of the monstrous caricature of a human being, her face blanching. Surely, this . . . this *hideux* could not be real!

Guillaume Choundas limped into the office, his stout cane tapping on the marble floor, his crippled leg in its stiff iron brace making a dragging *swish-clomp, swish-clomp* . . . with a leer on that half of his dissipated, twisted, and aged face that he still showed to the world. "*Citoyenne* de Guilleri, *enchanté*," the horror said to her with an evil smile, clumping close to her, flipping his cane to the elbow of his sole arm and reaching out to take her hand as if it had been offered to him, he bestowed a kiss upon it, a kiss that, to Charité, felt like the crawling, maggoty lips of a rotting corpse. It was all she could do to not jerk her hand away, to recoil in disgust from his monstrosity . . . to flee the office and go light candles at Notre Dame and make her confession to a *curé* in hope of deliverance from one of Satan's demons!

"*Capitaine* Choundas, like you, *citoyenne*, is also a victim who has suffered at the hands of that *salaud*, Alan Lewrie," Fouché informed her.

"In . . . indeed, *citoyen?*" Charité managed to say, stricken with terror and revulsion.

"This is about Lewrie?" Choundas snapped, dropping her hand and regaining the use of his cane so he could turn towards Fouché, a feral gleam in his remaining eye. "Something is to be done?"

"He insulted the First Consul, *Capitaine*," Fouché told him. "He is to be done away with. Somewhere lonely and quiet, out of sight on the road to Calais. The three of you know what he looks like, so . . ."

"*Sacre bleu!*" Choundas exclaimed. "And I will participate in his end? *Mort de ma vie*, all I have asked of life, for so *many* years, and it comes to pass? Perhaps there *is* a God!"

He spun about, more nimbly that Charité imagined that he could, to face her again. "All the ravages you see, *Citoyenne* Charité, have been at *his* hand . . . my face, my laming, my lost arm! The ruin of my life's *work*! *Oui*, I will *gladly* help you murder him!"

Another quick turning to face them all. *Swish-clomp!*

"But it must not be an easy death for him," Choundas demanded. "With forethought . . . he must be taken alive. Only for a time, *hein?*" he specified with an anticipatory cackle. "Give him to me for half a day . . . a full day, and I will take from him what he took from me so long ago . . . and make him beg for death's release, oh *mais oui!*"

"That, uhm . . . might be a bit beyond what is necessary," Fouché hesitantly countered as he fiddled uncomfortably with his loosely bound neck-stock. "We had thought to make it appear as a highway robbery by *aristo*-lovers and criminal elements."

"And so it may, *citoyen*," Choundas quickly countered, his mind a'scheme as he haltingly paced in anxiety, *swish-clomp, swish-clomp.* "Is the crime brutal enough, it can be *blamed* on Georges Cadoudal and his conspirators against the Republic, financed by the Comte d'Artois with *Anglais* gold, from his lair in England . . . to . . . to foment anger in Britain against France, because their government wants to begin the war again, *hein?*"

"Their Prime Minister, Addington, pays the Comte d'Artois for a murder of one of their naval officers and his wife?" Fouché scoffed at the notion. "Too complicated. They disappear, everyone in the coach, with no one ever the wiser. The First Consul does not wish a new war with Britain . . . at least not yet. I have his personal, spoken assurance on that matter."

"His wife, *too. Oui,* I *saw* her with him!" Choundas crooned with an evil hiss, shrugging off the quick dismissal of his initial scheme. "If they *must* disappear, the coachmen, horses, carriage, and all, then an out-of-the-way place *could* be found where all that could be disposed of . . . an hour or two with *her,* before his eyes, before I begin on *him,* and that swaggering lout, that *despicable fumier* would *beg*—"

"Ahum!" Fouché pointedly coughed into his fist. "You will be in at his demise, *Capitaine* Choundas. That must be enough."

"If you insist, *citoyen,* then . . . it must be so." Choundas seemed to surrender—too quickly for Matthieu Fourchette or Charité to believe. Choundas set the exposed half of his face in a wry smile of contentment, but . . . she and the police agent shared a quick, dubious look and an even briefer nod in mute agreement that, if they *had* to be saddled with this hideous monster, they would have to keep a sharp eye on him at all times . . . and keep his half-insane fury on a tight leash!

I must *have Denis with me,* Charité de Guilleri vowed to herself; *to keep this "hot rabbit" Fourchette from laying his hands on me, and . . . to keep this disgusting beast from killing anyone who denies him his revenge.*

A sour taste rose in her throat, a chilly feeling in the pit of her stomach, and a weak, shuddery feeling that forced her to sit down in her chair once more, with only half an ear for Fouché's plan being revealed.

As dearly as she desired Lewrie to die before her eyes, for her own revenge, still—completely innocent coachmen, *Madame* Lewrie, and any unfortunate peasant who happened by at the wrong moment must die as well? Callous as she had been over the fates of those taken in the merchant ships by her and her brothers, her *cousin*, and the old pirates Jérôme Lanxade and Boudreaux Balfa, this just didn't enflame her former passion or hatred of all things English.

It felt to her, of a clarifying second, as foul as the touch of Choundas's lips on the back of her hand!

CHAPTER TWENTY-FIVE

*T*he hired servants, Jules and Marianne, were paid off, the last funds in their temporary bank account had been withdrawn, and a coach had been arranged for their journey to Calais. With their travelling valises at their feet, Alan and Caroline waited in the foyer of their lodging house for their coach's arrival, whilst the *concierge* and her servants were busy abovestairs; so far as Lewrie knew, fumigating the *appartement* after being occupied by "Bloodies."

Yet the coach-and-four that drew up by the kerb outside was not theirs, for a French couple emerged from it with some hand-carried luggage, and began to palaver with the *concierge*, announcing, so far as Lewrie could follow the conversation, that they wished to take lodging for a fortnight, and would she show them a vacant *appartement*. Barely had they gone abovestairs before a second coach rolled up, and out of it popped Sir Pulteney Plumb and Lady Imogene, as well as two other couples whom Lewrie didn't know from Adam and Eve. They also bustled in with hand-carried luggage, as if they would seek lodgings, too.

"The *concierge* is busy, is she? Good!" Sir Pulteney said with a snicker. "See why we asked specifically what you would be wearing for your departure, haw haw? All ready? Names are not necessary for now, but these fine people are old companions, summoned back to work in our endeavour. All change now, quickly!"

The women, one with sandy blond hair and the other a brunette, had entered in light travelling cloaks over their gowns, their faces and hair obscured by long-brimmed, face-framing sun bonnets. Valises were opened, and the cloaks stowed away in them, revealing that both women wore plain light-grey gowns very similar in colour and cut to the one that Caroline wore. The brunette further produced a wig from her valise, changing herself to a sandy blonde, too.

The men had entered in broad-brimmed hats more suited to a day on horseback, and light riding dusters to protect their suitings. At the same moment, they revealed themselves in black coats, buff waist-coats, buff trousers, and black top-boots. A quick change of cravats to match the dark blue one that Lewrie sported, a change of hats to a taller model with short, curly-brimmed hats much like Lewrie's, too.

"You've both sets of *laisser-passers*? Good!" Sir Pulteney said to the first couple. "Off you go, then, Thomas, you and your lady and we shall see you in Dover."

At that, "Thomas," or whoever he was, picked up his valises and offered his "wife" an arm. They stepped outside into the Rue Honoré, and entered the waiting coach, which, Lewrie could note from a vantage point back in the foyer's shadows, quite blocked the view of any watchers. The coach clattered off, heading west.

Not half a minute later, a second coach, almost the twin of the first, with a four-horse team of the same colour, drew up, facing the other direction.

"Andrew, you and Susannah next. You're on!" Sir Pulteney urged, almost shoving them towards the doors. "Last one to the Queen's Arms Inn pays the reckoning for all, haw haw!"

He tapped his long walking-stick on the parquetry foyer floor impatiently as the second couple of "Andrew and Susannah" exited and got into the coach, which headed east, whip cracking.

"Now for you and your lady, Captain Lewrie," Sir Pulteney said hurriedly, cocking his head and ears as the rattle of a *third* carriage could be heard. "Calm as does it. Show serenity and unwitting blandness to the guards at the *porte*. They'll have orders to report your passing . . . all of them will. After they allow you to leave the environs of Paris, which I expect they will, for any attempt in the city would be too incriminating, let your coachees proceed at their normal pace. You'll be using the Argenteuil gate, so you must say that you will be taking ship at Le Havre. We will catch you up on the Pontoise road, before your coach crosses the river

Oise, where we shall put into play *other* measures to throw the authorities off your scent. Now be on your way, quickly! Go with God, and we shall see you shortly!"

Lewrie heaved a deep breath and picked up his valises whilst Sir Pulteney shrugged out of his elegant suit coat, tossed his hat to the sideboard table, and whipped out a white porter's apron, to play a servant's role to carry the rest of their luggage to the coach that was, that very instant, drawing rein right by the doors. Lady Imogene gave Caroline a fond, assuring hug, then shooed her out to join Alan, with a last instruction to smile and be gay. "You are going home to England, *n'est-ce pas?*"

Once inside the coach, though, and under way, Caroline pressed her hands together and shut her eyes as if in prayer, looking wan and pale, whilst Lewrie fussed and shifted on the leather seat beside her, to rearrange his coat and waist-coat, trying to get comfortable.

"Alan . . . ," Caroline muttered in a fretful, conspiratorial whisper, "will they *really* let us pass, not snatch us out? Or murder us in one of the poorer stews? We've seen them, passing through. Crime is surely rampant in them . . . unremarkable!"

"Still too public," Lewrie decided, patting her knee. "*Casus belli* . . . or *bellum?* Plumb's right about that, at least. It'd mean war, even if they put me on trial as a spy and slung me into prison. From what Bonaparte said to us t'other day, it sounds as if things're tetchy enough already. As Plumb says, their best chance'll be out in the countryside."

Seeing how fretful Caroline still seemed, he took her hand and gave her an encouraging squeeze. An instant later, and she turned to lay her head on his shoulder, silently demanding to be held, no matter if the sight of one of his former lovers had put her off intimacy the last few days. Nigh sixteen years of marriage—no one could call it "wedded *bliss*," exactly— counted for something, he supposed.

"We *never* should have come to France!" she fiercely muttered on his coat lapel, and he could feel her body shudder at the brink of hot tears of remorse. "I'm sorry I ever . . . !"

"Oh, tosh, m'girl," Lewrie calmly objected, though his own guts and heart were about to do a brisk canter. He kissed her forehead and muttered into her hair. "It was half my idea, d'ye recall? And . . . if ye dismiss *this* little problem, hadn't we a grand time? Well, *fairly* a good time, in the main?"

Her answer was a tearful snort and a closer snuggling.

"Mean t'say, it's been *me,* traipsin' halfway round the world, havin' all the adventures," he cajoled, "and gettin' paid main-well by King George for it, too. You haven't had a whiff o' danger since you whipped Harry Embleton with yer reins . . . or came nigh t'shootin' Calico Jack Finney's 'nutmegs' off when he burst in on ye and Sewallis when he was a baby. We get back t'England with our scalps, why . . . we could dine out on this for *years*!"

Caroline uttered another snort, this one tinged with amusement. Lewrie gently tilted her face up to his and kissed her for reassurance, though, to his surprise, that kiss quickly turned to a warm and musky one of passion.

"That's my darlin' lass," Lewrie told her, grinning. "Here now . . . ever do it in a carriage?" he added, to jolly her further.

She punched him in the ribs, almost hard enough to hurt, but . . . she smiled at last; she laughed, even in "gallows humour," and said, "And I suppose that you *have*? Don't answer! Your lewd suggestion is clue enough to your past, you . . . wretch."

"Well, later perhaps . . . ," Lewrie allowed with an easy chuckle.

"Uhm, Alan . . . ," Caroline said, snuggling up to him. "Do you imagine that Sir Pulteney is *that* capable? Mean t'say, he *seems* as if he's done this sort of thing before, he *seems* to have the connexions, but . . . might he be in league with the French, too? Are we to be his *victims*? His wife's French—Lady Imogene was a famous actress *during* the Terror, and she'd have known a lot of the brutal revolutionaries, and . . ."

"Don't think we've anything t'fear on that score, Caroline," Lewrie quickly dismissed. "At first, I took him for a 'Captain Sharp' who plays on unwary travellers, lookin' t'skin us broke, but . . . look at all they've spent on us. Suppers? Theatre? And if he meant to lay hands on our goods we sent off to Calais, then that'd be a damned bad trade. No, all these matchin' coaches and horse teams, the clothes the Plumbs came up with at the drop of a hat, and people who *somewhat* resemble us at short notice? Puttin' themselves to as much risk as us if they're exposed? No, I'm beginnin' t'think he's the genuine article . . . even if he *is* daft as bats half the time. We get home, we could look him up in Debrett's . . . see if he's authentic."

The coach began to slow, and Lewrie turned his attention to the environs as they drew up into a line of dray waggons, coaches, and farm carts at the Porte d'Argenteuil.

During the Reign of Terror, under the hideously mis-named Committee for Public Safety, then even later under the Directory of Five, France had become a suspicious police state, fearful of counter-revolutionaries and spies, of *saboteurs* and each other. Paris, and the great cities, had closed and barricaded their medieval gates completely at night, and only the market carts that fetched fresh produce from the countryside were let out. Travellers not known to locals were instantly suspect, and soldiers of the Garde Nationale or Police Nationale inspected every basket or valise for contraband, bombs, smuggled weapons, or coded messages.

Even now, in the autumn of 1802, the city gates were manned by policemen or soldiers, though passage was usually much easier, even for foreigners, and thorough questionings and searches were a thing of the past. At least Lewrie hoped!

"Buck up, now, Caroline," he told her. "It's time to play the snooty English tourists. Bland, serene, stupid . . ."

A Garde Nationale soldier with a musket slung on his shoulder, a *sabre-briquet* on his hip, and a cockaded shako tipped far back atop his head, rapped on the left-hand coach door, demanding papers.

Lewrie handed them over in a languid, limply bored hand through the lowered window, and the guard, a Sergeant by the tassel hung from one shoulder, moved his stubby pipe from one corner of his mouth to the other, tugged at a corner of his impressively long and thick *mustachios*, and gave out a grunt. He looked up, locking eyes with Lewrie for a second, then peered into the coach to assure himself that it contained only the two people declared by their *laisser-passers*.

"*Anglais, m'sieur?*" he gruffly asked.

"*Oui,*" Lewrie replied.

"*Et vous retournez en Angleterre?*"

"*Retourn* . . . yes, we're going home," Lewrie replied pretending even poorer command of French. "Back to Jolly Old England, what? Mean t'say . . . *oui.*"

"*Au revoir, m'sieur . . . madame,*" the guard said, handing back their *laisser-passers* and sketching out a salute before waving to the coachmen and his compatriots to signal that they were allowed to exit Paris.

"No worse than any other day-coach jaunt we made," Lewrie told Caroline. "We're on our way, one way or the other."

Matthieu Fourchette had placed three covert watchers in close vicinity to the lodging house in the Rue Honoré; feeding pigeons, taking a stroll, sullenly sweeping horse dung. As the first coach came to a stop by the doors, the senior man tipped an underling the wink, and he was off, quick as his legs could carry him, to alert the band waiting for his news in the Place du Carrousel.

The second coach, then a third, bollixed everything, throwing the remaining two watchers into feetful confusion. The *departure* of those three coaches, with *three pairs* of Lewries, less than a minute apart, threw those two agents into a panic. Try to pursue them? Try to catch up with Fourchette and his men, who had most likely started off for the Porte St. Denis, the logical exit for the Calais road, or raise a hue and cry? The senior man decided that his best choice, if he wished to continue his employment, was to run to the headquarters of the Police Nationale on the south side of the Tuileries Palace to pass the burden on to Director Fouché— well, not directly to his *face!*—and let him despatch riders to sort it out.

If Director Joseph Fouché had had a single hair on his head he would have been sorely tempted to yank it out in frustration as contradictory news came in in mystifying dribs and drabs.

Horsemen from *three* of the *portes* had come to report the departure of the *Anglais* couple the guards had been ordered to be on alert for? Another horseman had to be sent off to catch up with Fourchette and his party to warn them that a massive charade was being played on them. Of a sudden, Fouché needed two *more* parties of pursuers, with no time to brief them on the purpose of their urgent missions or to scrounge up the proper men who could manage the elimination of those perfidiously clever *Anglais!* All their plans had put that task into the hands of Fourchette, that *salope* de Guilleri, and that foul fiend, Choundas.

"Damn, damn, damn!" Fouché roared, flinging an ink-pot at the nearest wall. "Even if they catch them, they won't know them from Adam! Their papers give nothing away! *Merde alors! Merde, merde!*"

"*Citoyen?*" his meek clerk timorously asked, cringing a little. "You have orders?" he dared to pose.

"Another rider!" Fouché demanded, grabbing for pen and paper and realising he no longer had any ink with which to write new orders. "*Putain!*" he roared in even greater frustration. "Ink, fool! Bring me more ink, *ballot, vite, vite!*"

He took a deep breath to calm himself as the clerk scrambled to fetch a fresh ink-pot. Fourchette could sort it out; he'd *better*, or it would be his neck! Three coaches to pursue, so . . . he would split his party, of course, and make haste, Fouché assumed. The girl, with a few agents to help her; thank God she'd talked him into including her Chasseur, Clary, who could chase after the second with a few more men . . . though he'd been included to *identify* them, to *trail* them, and had not been in on the *conclusion* of the plan. Would he balk? Fourchette and that beast Choundas could chase after the first coach . . . *before* all three of them got too far away from Paris, *before* the roads diverged too far *apart*!

The clerk returned with the ink, and Fouché scribbled furiously to impart his new instructions, then . . . issued a second order. There was a chance that the *Anglais* couple *would* get so far along that there would be no catching them if the first lead was false. He needed more men, with orders to arrest them; he would leave the elimination to his man, Fourchette. For that, he would send an urgent request to the general in charge of the Garde Nationale garrison in Paris, no . . . no request, but an *order*, for at least three troops of cavalry!

"Send them off at once, at once!" Fouché snapped, thumping down into his chair with his head in his thick hands, staring at the middle distance, and wondering if things could go even more awry!

Fouché's first despatch rider caught up with Fourchette and his party no more than two kilometres past the Porte St. Denis.

"*Putain, quel emmerdement!*" Fourchette spat once he'd read it, balled it up, and shoved it into a side pocket of his coat. "Our quarry must have been warned, but I do not see how! Three couples at three *portes* presented papers declaring themselves as the Lewries."

"With the help of *Anglais* spies, I *knew* it!" Guillaume Choundas growled, thumping his rein hand on the low pommel of his saddle. He had never been a decent horsemen, even when in possession of both his arms and working legs, and even a little more than one hour astride a horse was beginning to be an agony. "He's in league with the Royalist conspirators. How *else*? In league with the Devil!"

"Make haste," Fourchette decided quickly, "The coach bound for Calais from the Porte Saint-Denis can't be that far ahead. We'll see whether we're after the *real* Lewrie, or another. *Allez vite!*"

Fourchette spurred his horse to a gallop, quickly joined by the girl, and her Chasseur Major. Both revelled in the sudden chase and the kilometre-eating pace and the wind in their faces. Still unaware of their true purpose, Major Denis Clary delighted in showing off his superb cavalryman's mastery of a horse, and Charité was just as eager to impress him with her seat. For a few moments, she could shake from her mind the image of what would occur at the end of their chase and take a little joy. She looked over her shoulder and laughed out loud to see that foetid monster, Choundas, jouncing almost out of control in only a bone-shaking trot as she left his hideous form and mind behind!

"There it is!" Fourchette bugled, espying a slow-trotting coach-and-four on the road ahead. "Hurry!"

Fourchette, Charité, Major Clary, and half a dozen agents garbed in civilian clothes thundered up to the coach, catching up easily and passing down either side of it as Fourchette bellowed demands for the coachee to draw reins and stop. He sprang from his saddle and was at the carriage door before one of his men could take his reins.

"*M'sieur et madame,* I order you to present your *laisser-passers* at once, and . . . oh, *merde alors.* Who the Devil are you?"

"Sir, I do not know who you are, but you will not use such foul language in my wife's presence, do you hear me?" the gentleman with the mid-brown hair inside the coach shot back with an imperious back and in perfect French, with but a touch of *Anglais* accent.

"Your papers, at once!" Fourchette shot back, fighting down his shock to find utter strangers. Once handed over, he read them over quickly and got a sinking feeling. The man and his wife *were* English . . . but not the ones he sought. "You are . . . ?"

"Sir Andrew Graves . . . sir," the Briton said, looking at Fourchette with that maddening supercilious air of a proper English lord looking down at a chimney sweep. "My lady wife, Susannah. And what is the meaning of this . . . sir?" Irking Fourchette so much that he *wished* this arrogant *Anglais* was his real prey, and he could just put the *salaud* into a hastily dug grave. Yet . . . the *laisser-passers* he had been presented were authentic, with entry dates and a departure from Paris showing that they had been in France two weeks, and with all the proper signatures and stamps depressingly authentic, to boot!

"A thousand pardons, *m'sieur, madame,* but we seek escaping criminals thought to be fleeing justice on this highway in a coach quite like this one. Adieu, you may proceed," Fourchette said, though that galled him to no end.

"And you apologise, *m'sieur,*" Sir Andrew pressed, a brow up.

"A thousand pardons for . . . my choice of words, as well, and my apologies to *madame,*" Fourchette was further forced to say.

"Well, I should bloody-well think so, dash it all!" Sir Andrew huffed. "Whip up, driver! *Avance, cocher, vite vite!*"

"One down, two t'go!" his wife, Susannah, who was really better known round Drury Lane as Betsy Peake, chortled to her companion, who was also better known on the Shakespearean stages of London and its nearer counties as Anthony Ford, as the party of horsemen clattered far enough away for them to revert to their natural accents and glee to have fooled the Frogs so thoroughly.

"Must say, m'dear, but these roles we play give life a zest!" Ford said with a satisfied sigh of contentment and a bit of relief that they were free and clear.

"Here, I'll shred these lyin' packets t'wee bits as we bowl along," Betsy offered. "And, yes! It is very . . . piquant!"

"Showin' off, again! Piquant, my eye! Hoy, Bets . . . ever do it in a carriage?" Ford leered.

"Wif th' likes o' *you?* Hmmph!"

CHAPTER TWENTY-SIX

*O*h," Caroline said with a start, after sitting silently tense for more than an hour as their coach rolled past the last outskirts of Paris and into the pleasant countryside 'tween the Seine and the Oise.

"Trouble?" Lewrie bolted erect, thinking she had seen some sign of pursuit. "What?" he demanded, wishing that he'd thought to pack a *single* pistol in his bags before leaving England. Even the hanger he had gotten back from Napoleon was in a round-topped trunk on its way to Calais.

"No, I don't believe," Caroline told him, delving into her reticule. "Forgive me for being remiss, but I quite forgot the note that Lady Imogene slipped me just as we were leaving." She produced a wee folded piece of paper, when opened no more than four inches square.

"Oh!" Caroline exclaimed again. "Sir Pulteney has additional instructions for us. Here, see for yourself."

> Once you pass through Pontoise, there is a quite nice coaching inn on the far bank of the Oise, called Le Gantelet Rouge. Stop there for refreshment. Linger! I arrive anon.

"Hummph!" Lewrie huffed. "What's that, down at the bottom?" Lewrie asked his wife, once he'd read it. "That blob, there."

"It looks like a flower of some kind," Caroline said, peering more closely at the note, which was written in black ink; the flower petals, though, were coloured yellow with chalk or pastel pencil.

"Should we *eat* the note, now we've read it?" Lewrie japed.

Caroline rolled her eyes at him for making jest in such circumstances, but at least she did it with a grin. She began to shred it, feeding wee pieces of the note out the window on her side of the coach, bit by bit. "That should be sufficient, enough so for the likes of your mysterious old friend, that hideous Zachariah Twigg!"

"Never a friend," Lewrie countered. "I wonder if they'll ask for our papers when we enter Pontoise . . . cross the bridge, or when we order dinner at the inn?"

The authorities in Pontoise evidently could have cared less of a damn anent the identities of travellers, for there were no soldiers posted on the southern outskirts, nor on the bridge which spanned the Oise. The carriage trundled through the heart of the town's business district, to the northern outskirts, then . . .

"There it is!" Caroline exclaimed as Le Gantelet Rouge came in sight on the right-hand side of the road, out where the homes were humbler and further apart, where stone-fenced or hedged pastures and farm crops began to predominate.

"Uhm . . . *cocher?*" Lewrie called, leaning out his window. "I say, *cocher. Arrête, s'il vous plaît . . . à le Gantelet Rouge.* For *déjeuner.*"

"*Mais oui, m'sieur,*" the lead coachman laconically replied as he slowed the horses and turned the coach into the large, shady yard in front of a two-storey stone inn with a slate roof, with a cool gallery to one side, and many outbuildings and barns.

"We will be awhile, erm . . . *quelque temps?*" Lewrie said to the coachmen once they had alit. "Ah . . . you're free to . . ."

"*Faites comme vous voudrez, messieurs,*" Caroline provided for him, explaining that while they took a long dinner and a rest from the ride on the hard benches, the coachmen could do as they will; have a bite themselves, some wine, and such. "Give them a few franc coins, Alan."

"Oh, right-ho," Lewrie agreed, handing up coins from his purse.

"The gallery looks inviting," Caroline commented as the entered the travellers' inn.

"Perhaps an inside table, Caroline. Out of sight from the road."

"Yes, of course," she agreed, then looked at him with amusement.

"Right-ho, Alan? The Plumbs must be wearing off on you. You will be saying 'Begad,' 'Zounds,' and 'Stap me' next."

"Well, uhm . . ."

They shared a bottle of wine, lingering over it and making but guarded small talk. Half an hour later, and they ordered a plate of *hors-d'oeuves*, then a second bottle of wine when that was consumed. They ordered soup and bread, then opted for breaded veal and asparagus, to while away another hour. Le Gantelet Rouge boasted an *ormolu* clock on the high mantel, and its ticking, the *slow* progression of its minute hand, was maddening, after a while, 'til . . .

A coach could be heard entering the inn yard, wheels hissing and crunching over the fine gravel, and chains tinkling . . . bound to the *rear* of the inn, nearest the stables and well. Was it Sir Pulteney, was it soldiers? Both Alan and Caroline began to tremble despite their efforts not to, ready to bolt!

"Zounds, but there you are!" Sir Pulteney Plumb exclaimed very loudly as he bustled in the rear entrance, now in more modest travelling clothes and a light *serge de Nîmes* duster and wide-brimmed farmer's hat, which he swept off elegantly as he made a "leg" to them. "*Told* you the 'Red Gauntlet' sets a fine table, haw haw! And, here is my good lady! Begad, m'dear, but look who has stopped at the very same inn as us! Allow us to join you, for we are famished and as dry as dust." The Lewries had to sit and sip wine, order coffee to thin the alcohol fumes from what they had already taken aboard as Sir Pulteney and Lady Imogene ordered hearty full meals and dined as if they had all the time in the world.

"Now, for your coach and coachmen," Sir Pulteney said at last as he rose and moved to the front door. Lewrie followed him to see Sir Pulteney paying off their hired coach and ordering their luggage brought to the inn. "I told them that you found the inn so delightful, and the arrival of old friends so pleasant, that we would all be staying on the night, and coach to Le Havre together in the morning." Sir Pulteney explained after he returned. "They will rack back south to Paris a touch richer than they expected, and, God willing, your whereabouts ends here, haw haw!"

"What happens tomorrow, then?" Lewrie asked him.

"Not tomorrow, Captain Lewrie . . . what happens *now* is more to the point," Sir Pulteney said with a sly expression as their luggage made its way *through* the inn, to the rear stableyard, and into the Plumbs' coach.

"Sated, my dear? Excellent! Now we will all pay our reckonings and resume our journey, what?"

There was no coachman for Sir Pulteney to pay off, for once he had handed Lady Imogene and Caroline into the coach, he sprang to the coachee's bench and the reins most lithely, and got the team moving with a few clucks, a whistle, and a shake of the reins.

Lady Imogene crossed herself as they got under way once more. "Pulteney *adores* playing coachee . . . though I fear he's not as talented as he imagines himself, and he rushes on much too fast sometimes."

"Good Christ," Lewrie said, shaking his head in dread.

Sir Pulteney got the coach on the road and began to set a rapid pace, whipping up like Jehu, the Biblical charioteer, putting the wind up Lewrie, who'd had his share of harum-scarum whip-hands like Zachariah Twigg and his damned three-horse chariot. Twigg was in his *sixties,* for God's sake, usually aloof, staid, and cold, but hand him the reins and he'd turn into a raving lunatick, screeching like a naked Celtic warrior painted in blue woad, revelling in how close he came to carriages, farm waggons, and pedestrians, as if re-enacting Queen Boadicea's final charge against the Roman legions.

Sir Pulteney took the eastern road from Pontoise, following the north bank 'til reaching a crossroads that led north towards the smaller towns of Méru and Beauvais, slowly climbing into a region of low and rolling hills that were thickly forested . . . and the roads were windier.

Did it matter a whit to that fool? Like Hell it did, for their coach sometimes swayed onto two wheels, and those inside were jounced, tumbled, and rattled like dice in a cup. Lewrie's testicles, it must be admitted, drew up in expectation of the grand smash to come.

At long last, and at a much slower pace, Sir Pulteney steered the coach off the road to a rougher and leaf-covered forest track, some few of those new-fangled Froggish *kilomètres* short of Méru, or so the last mile-post related, before they drew to a very welcome stop, deep in a forest glade.

"What now?" Lewrie had to ask, easing the kinks in his back from keeping himself as stiff as *rigor mortis* the last few hours, as he and Sir Pulteney went into the woods in one direction, the ladies another, to tend to the "necessities."

"Why, we become other people before we reach Méru, sir," their rescuer told him, beaming with pleasure as he took a pinch of snuff on the back of his hand. "Then, once there, we change our mode of travel. Ten years ago, during the height of the French Revolution's bloodiness, there were more than a few residents there, Royalist in their sympathies, who aided our endeavours at spiriting the blameless to safety. In such a rural place, I rather doubt the Committee for Public Safety, or the later Directory, even bothered to root out so-called reactionaries, or hold their witch-hunts. No no, I'm certain there are still many of our old allies ready to speed us on our way. Ah-ah-*achoo!*" Sir Pulteney paused for a prodigious sneeze into a handkerchief, with all evident delight. "You will partake, Captain Lewrie?" he said, offering a snuff box. "*Zounds,* but that's prime!" he said, sneezing again.

"Never developed a liking for it, thankee," Lewrie said. "You say we're t'become other people?"

"Your trail goes cold at the Gantelet Rouge in Pontoise. Now, it will go even colder at Méru," Sir Pulteney confidently told him as they went back to the coach. "My trail, and Lady Imogene's, as well. We will openly sup in Méru after obtaining a much humbler conveyance, then travel through the night to put as much distance between us and Paris, and any pursuit, before tomorrow's dawn. That will require new aliases, and some, ah . . . costume changes, to transform us into a *most* unremarkable party of travellers . . . French travellers, Begad!"

"I'm t'play a Frenchman?" Lewrie gawped in dis-belief. "*Me,* sir? That's asking rather a lot!"

"I took that into consideration, Captain Lewrie," Plumb replied, "just as I noted that your wife's French, though not fluent, is much better than yours, which suggested to me the very *personas* which must be assumed, haw haw! Imogene and I shall do most of the talking."

"Wouldn't we need new documents or something?" Lewrie wondered.

"For foreign visitors, of a certainty, but for innocent and up-standing Frenchmen? Hardly! Aha!" Sir Pulteney exclaimed, hurrying them to the boot of the coach, "my lady has already begun the alteration of your wife's appearance!"

The leather covering of the boot had been rolled up, revealing several large trunks, one of which was open, whilst a second served as a seat for Caroline as Lady Imogene fussed over her, now and then having a good dig down through the open trunk's contents. There were some gowns, many scarves and shawls, a heap of various-coloured wigs, and a smaller box of paints and makeup.

Caroline had changed into a sobre and modest, drab brownish wool gown, with a cream-coloured shawl over her shoulders and a dingy white apron. White silk stockings had been replaced by black cotton, and her feet now sported clunky old buckled shoes instead of light slippers.

"Good God!" Lewrie gawped again, noticing that Carolone's fair hair was now covered by a mousy brown wig, and atop that, there now sat a nigh-shapeless old straw farmwoman's hat. Lady Imogene had done something with her paints and powders, too, for Caroline looked at least ten years older, of a sudden.

"Lud, but that's subtle, m'dear!" Sir Pulteney congratulated.

"*Merci*, dearest," Lady Imogene sweetly replied, beaming. "What is necessary for theatregoers twenty rows back would be much too much for those we will deal with face-to-face. Artifice, as you say, must be subtle. Oh, I apologise for making you seem so careworn, Mistress Lewrie, but your natural beauty must *not* be remembered," Lady Imogene said, finishing up the additions, or slight enhancements, of furrows or crow's-feet, darkening the merry folds below Caroline's eyes as if she possessed weary, sleepless bags. *Et, voilà!* Done," she cried.

"Now, should any pursuers ask if anyone has seen a fair-haired Englishwoman, they can honestly say *non*, d'ye see, Captain Lewrie?" Sir Pulteney said with an inane titter. "Your turn, now, sir." He removed his own clothing and began to dig into another trunk. "I will now become Major, ah . . . Pierre Fleury, a retired officer of foot, now too lame to serve. I will be a very disappointed man, haw haw! Lady Imogene is to be, oh hang it, Imogene Fleury . . . a disappointed woman in her own right, because . . . because . . . aha, I have it!" he said as he paced in a small circle.

"You, Mistress Lewrie, are the *widow* of my eldest son, Bertrand, who found you in the Piedmont during Bonaparte's Italian Campaign, an *Italian*, of all things, and *not* the sort of match we had arranged for him. Being foreign, of course, your less-than-fluent French is plausible. M'dear?" he asked Lady Imogene.

"I simply adore it, *mon cher!*" Lady Imogene cried, clapping her hands in delight.

"I see . . . I think," Caroline said, sounding a bit dubious.

"You, Captain Lewrie," Sir Pulteney said, whirling to face him and already feigning the stiff fierceness of a retired officer and a disappointed father, with a strict martinet's snap to his voice. "*You* are my *youngest* son, our last hope of grandchildren and the continuation of our family's name, but you . . . Armand, yes, that'll do . . . *you*, Armand, *tried* to be a soldier. You can remember your name? *Très bien*. You enlisted as a private soldier in the cavalry, but proved so clumsy that you ended by getting kicked in the head by your horse, before you had a chance to go on campaign, and have recently been invalided out. We shall have papers to that effect. . . . Well, we will shortly. You will have to play a dummy."

It didn't help Lewrie's nerves, or his dignity, that Caroline let forth a cynical chuckle-snort, then a full-out hoot of laughter.

"You're addled as a scrambled egg, Armand," Sir Pulteney went on. "You must walk stiffly, as if afraid your whole head will tumble off. Slowly and stiffly. Be clumsy with anything you handle, forks and spoons and such. Be slow in speech, grasping for the proper names for things—"

"*Je suis un crayon,*" Lewrie interrupted, feeling sarcastic, too.

"With your poor command of French, I expect you'll grasp for a great *number* of nouns, yayss," Sir Pulteney snapped, still in character. "Do you rise from a chair, you might swoon a bit . . ."

"And wince, as if there's a sudden pain in your poor head, as well," Lady Imogene prompted. "We will cut your meat for you! Dribble a little wine so that I may wipe your chin."

"Should I *drool?*" Lewrie rejoined, growing tetchy.

"*That* might be a bit *too* much," Sir Pulteney said with a frown.

"Let me wrap this bandage round your head," Lady Imogene said, "then turn your complexion pale and wan."

By the time Lewrie had been "touched up" and his good suitings replaced with ill-fitting and older cast-offs, Sir Pulteney had altered himself into a stiff and stern-looking fellow in his late fifties or early sixties, with a shock of reddish hair and a large, gingery mustachio, a man who wore a sobre black ditto suit and limped on a stout cane.

"When I address you, Armand, it may be well for you to cringe into your collar," Sir Pulteney instructed. "Who, after all, would wed you now? What hopes of family martial glory for *la patrie* can come from one such as you? Will you give us grandchildren, or a life of caring for a lack-wit? Pah!" he stamped.

Lewrie ducked his head as if avoiding a proctor's rod, gulping a bit as he recalled that what he must play-act now was him to the life in his student days—when caught lacking at his studies, skylarking, or wakened from a nap in class. *Huzzah for an English public school education!* he told himself.

"Thank God for Napoleon Bonaparte," Lady Imogene said as she packed up her paints and closed the trunks, "the meddler! He imagines he will re-order so much of France . . . the civil law codes, the roads and canals, standardising the currency. . . . He has even given instructions to the *Co-médie Française* about costumes, makeup, and how roles must be played! All these cast-offs were available for a song!"

"Let's hoist these trunks back into the boot and be on our way, Capt . . . Armand," Sir Pulteney snapped.

Not all that many kilometres, or miles, away at that very moment, Matthieu Fourchette was gazing across the fields to the river Oise, at a small crossroads place called L'Isle Adam on the main road to Amiens, and cursing under his breath as they watered their tired horses and eased sore fundaments. He had been forced to split his already small pursuit party after the incident with that English lord and his wife; some went on up the road to see if a second coach containing their quarry had gotten that far along *beyond* the first they'd stopped. There was a slim chance of that, but Fourchette had to make sure that that trailing coach had not been a decoy to put them off the chase and turn their attention elsewhere.

He wished he could sit down and rest, wished he could reach back and massage his buttocks and inner thighs, but he would not admit that he was not as good a horseman as that damned Chasseur Major Clary or the girl. On most of his missions for Fouché, walking round Paris or coaching round France was sufficient, and when required to go by horse, the distances were usually much shorter, and at much slower paces.

Police agent Fourchette also wished he could get on with it, but he could not do that, either. Fouché had promised him a cavalry troop, and he had to wait for their arrival. He had to wait for his agents to return with a report from the other road. "Damn!" he spat.

"The coaches that left through the Argenteuil gate, and the gate at Saint-Germaine en Laye," Major Clary thought to contribute as he stood nearby, idly flicking his horse's reins on his boots while his mount sipped water from the poor tavern's trough. "The Englishman is most likely in one of those, *M'sieur* Fourchette."

"From the west gate? Pah!" Fourchette snapped. "Where would they run to, going west? Brest, Nantes, or Saint Malo? L'Orient or Saint-Nazaire? That would take them *days* to make their escape. That coach will prove to be a decoy. Fouché writes that he has requested a troop of cavalry to pursue that one, though it will prove fruitless. No . . . I think our quarry flees north for Dieppe, Boulogne-sur-Mer, or Calais. Those ports are much closer, and make their journey shorter."

"Then why do we tarry, *m'sieur?*" Charité asked him.

Fourchette began to round on her, but Major Clary spoke up as he pulled the horse back from the trough and began to lead him to the shade under the trees beside the tavern. "Beauvais, is it? Departing the Argenteuil gate, the direst route north leads to Pontoise, then to Beauvais. All the roads join there. We *could* go on, leaving word with the *tavernier* for your men, and the cavalry. *We* could cross the Oise and ride for Beauvais and be there by nightfall, *n'est-ce pas?* With your authority from *M'sieur* Fouché and my rank in the Chasseurs, we could order fresh mounts from the regiment garrisoned there. And request more men than a single troop."

"With *these* blown nags?" Fourchette gravelled, loath to take advice from a *soldier.* "We would be lucky to get to . . . what the Devil is the place?"—he snarled, unfolding a poor map—"to this little Méru. *Oui,* we'll go to Beauvais, when my men have checked the road all the way to Creil, when the cavalry arrive, and when our horses are rested . . . else we get stuck in the woods until someone comes and rescues *us!* We will have to wait a bit longer, Major."

Major Clary thought to tell Fourchette that cavalry sent from Paris in haste would arrive with blown horses, too, but was beginning to take a great dislike to the lank-haired, weaselly fellow. He would have said that, in his military experience, and with General Bonaparte and his many victories as a shining example, forces so widely separated *had* to act on their own initiative, and *quickly.* Bonaparte had trusted his generals and colonels to *think*, to play their disparate parts in the overall scheme before converging before the final objective, to the utter confusion of the enemy. In this case, Beauvais was the objective, the junction of almost every road their quarry might take to flee.

But Major Clary didn't think that Fourchette would be in a mood to listen to sound advice. Besides, he didn't much care for how this *insouciant*, leering *salaud* ogled Charité, either.

Major Clary came back from the hitching rails, letting his fond gaze assess his *amour* with a new lover's delight as she sat on a bench, impatiently jiggling a booted leg crossed over the other, idly pinning back up her wind-tossed coif. She rode astride, like a *man*, a pair of men's breeches underneath her gown. Charite rode as *good* as a man, he further marvelled. Yet . . . what was this chase all about, and what was so important to her about being a part of it—beyond the fact that she could recognise the Englishman and his wife—that that billiard-ball-headed Fouché had allowed her to come along? So this *Anglais* had insulted the First Consul, had he? Clary had heard their conversation, and Bonaparte had done most of the insulting to the smiling and bobbing "Bloodies." They were to arrest this *gars* for *that?* Horse-whip him, perhaps, or throw him into prison?

Asking Charité in the few fleeting quiet moments of this chase had resulted in vague answers, waved off with an impatient hand, and a change of topic. All Paris knew *Mlle*. de Guilleri's heroic history to raise a rebellion against the Spanish and reclaim Louisiana and New Orleans for France, the loss of her kin, and her banishment before the Dons garrotted her. Others said the Englishman was a spy, sent to kill Bonaparte, but that hadn't happened, so why the urgency?

Thinking back on what he'd seen at the levee, Major Denis Clary suddenly recalled being introduced to this Lewrie . . . and how Charité had spoken to him with such well-concealed anger. Had she known him before, in Spanish Louisiana? Impossible, Clary decided. Yet . . .

"Oh, *beurk*!" Charité exclaimed, standing quickly. She made a gagging sound. A light two-horse open carriage was trotting up the road to the tavern, with a saddled horse tied to its rear by the reins. "Can we not be *rid* of that obscenity? That disgusting . . . !"

Capitaine Guillaume Choundas had caught up with them, bleating in bile to run into them, demanding why Lewrie was not yet in their hands, and what did they think they were doing, standing about with their fingers up their idle arses!

CHAPTER TWENTY-SEVEN

*P*olice Agent Fourchette didn't think much of Méru, when they got there at last just before sunset; a wide spot in the road, most likely awash in pig-shit, inhabited by numbskulls in wooden clogs, he concluded, sharing the views of most Parisians with regard to their rural countrymen. They did call a halt for wine, bread, and cheese, water and feed bags for their horses, and a few questions.

The local policeman, the *only* policeman, was a corpulent, lazy jumped-up hay-scyther, stuffed into a uniform and a lax set of duties.

Yes, there were some travellers at the two foul inns, but none of them were *Anglais*, and no one even close to Lewrie's description had passed through. Of *course* he'd carefully looked at the registries (or he would once this intense Parisian and his entourage had departed!) and no foreigners of any kind had paused in sleepy little Méru.

A coach? A big, shiny black coach-and-four with a matched team of sorrels? *Mais oui*, a coach like that *had* passed through, but that had been three hours before.

That forced Fourchette, Major Clary, Charité, the police agents, and the befuddled troop of light cavalry into their saddles, some still chewing or pulling at spare canteens hurriedly filled with a raw local *vin ordinaire* a vague step away from vinegar.

"On to Beauvais, *allez vite!*" Fourchette demanded. "They're in a coach, three hours ahead, but we can still catch them!"

"If they did not change teams somewhere along the way, *m'sieur* Fourchette," Major Clary said as they began to clatter north, "we will be much faster, even on tired mounts."

"Fresh team? *Oui,* the livery," Fourchette snapped, spurring his horse for the stables. "If they obtained fresh horses here . . . !"

The old stableman was as much a slow-witted bumpkin as the policeman, interrupted from shovelling dung with a pitchfork from one of the barn stalls. "*M'sieur* wishes?" he asked slowly.

"A coach came through here a few hours ago," Fourchette began impatiently. "Did you provide them a change of horses? They are criminals, wanted in Paris."

"A coach came here, *oui m'sieur,*" the older fellow said, taking his own sweet time to puff on his pipe, take it from his lips, and look into the bowl to see if it was drawing properly, then spit to one side. "But, I did not change horses with them."

"So they will be slow, aha!" Fourchette started to cheer up.

"You wish to see the coach, *m'sieur?* The horses?" the old man asked. "They left it all with me and gave me three hundred francs to see it back to a livery in Paris. Is it stolen, perhaps? Will you be taking it? I was looking forward to going to Paris. *Quel dommage.*"

"Still here? Where?" Fourchette yelped.

"In the barn, *certainement, m'sieur,*" the old fellow said with his pipe stem for a pointer to the barn's interior. "The old fellow is a criminal, then? One would never have guessed."

"What old man?" Fourchette snapped as he dismounted and ordered some troopers to help him search the barn and the coach.

"The man who left the coach here, *m'sieur,*" the stableman said in his slow, laconic way. "A *m'sieur* Fleury."

"*How* old? With a fair-haired woman?"

"An old soldier, I took him to be," the stableman answered— maddeningly slowly. "Red hair and *mustachios?* In his fifties, I should think. Carried himself as an officer would. A colonel or general of brigade, I thought him. He travelled with his wife, but she had dark hair, mixed with grey, and quite stout. He had a limp and leaned on a cane."

"Lewrie could not disguise himself *that* much," Charité said in rising impatience, too. "Nor could his wife. Just the two of them?"

"No, *mademoiselle*" was the grunted reply, 'tween smoke puffs. "*M'sieur*

Fleury had his widowed daughter-in-law and his son with him. Poor fellow." Puff puff, look at the pipe once more, and spit.

"What about him?" Fourchette demanded, coming back from inspecting the coach and coming away without a clue.

"Why, he'd been kicked in the head by a horse, and let go from the army," the stableman related. "All his wits knocked from him."

"Fair, mid-brown hair, slightly curled . . . with a faint scar on his cheek?" Charité pressed, sketching a finger down her own face.

"No, mam'selle. Dark-haired. Didn't see a scar."

"Did they say where they were going?" Fourchette asked.

"Did they rent horses from you?" said Charité at the same time.

"Did they just walk on up the road?" came a croaking snarl from the open carriage from Guillaume Choundas.

"Hé, merde, what a sight!" The old stableman gawped at Choundas and made a gesture guaranteed in local lore to ward off evil. "One question at a time, pray you!" he pleaded with his hands before him.

"Did . . . they . . . say . . . where . . . they . . . were . . . going, you old fool?" Fourchette. "And how!"

"No reason to be insulting, m'sieur," the old fellow said in a sudden sulk. "M'sieur Fleury said they were going home to Rouen. He had taken his son to a physician in Paris, to see if they could do anything for him. As for how they went on, they rented an old two-horse farm waggon from me. They went up that way, the road to Beauvais."

"What is all this nonsense about these people, Fourchette?" Choundas demanded from his carriage, slamming his cane on the floor. "Lewrie did not come this way, he's on another road right now, laughing his head off at how feeble we are!"

"Who the Devil are we after and why, Major?" Capitaine Joseph Aulard, leader of the troop of cavalry, asked the only military man in the party. "Two Anglais or four French people? My colonel told me nothing but to catch up with this police fellow and follow his orders."

"Two Anglais . . . a capitaine in their navy and his wife. As to why, you might have to ask M'sieur Fourchette, for I see no sense in it, mon vieux," Major Clary replied in a mutter, with a shrug. "I am here simply because I met the Anglais and can recognise him."

"Incroyable!" the cavalry officer spat.

"There is a plot!" Fourchette growled as he fumbled to put his foot into the stirrup. "Three coaches, three couples, two to throw us off the scent! There's more to this than we thought. Organised by a cabal of Anglais secret operatives, paid for with British gold. This coach came from Paris, a match to the first one we came across. They are still ahead of us . . . Lewrie and his wife, and another pair that *aid* them! Going to Beauvais. We ride on!"

"All night?" *Capitaine* Aulard bemoaned. "*Merde*. We'll all be reeling in our saddles by the time we get to Beauvais . . . without a proper supper, too."

The farm waggon had no suspension straps to support its jolting solid axles. Its four wheels were badly greased, if greased at all, so the intermittent keening shriek could carry for miles at night. It had been used to haul hay, bricks, lumber, dung, everything. Now the bed was liberally covered with fresh-smelling straw, under which all those trunks and valises were hidden. Still, it remained a nasty conveyance, and a slow one, to boot, for the two large horses which pulled it were old, and Sir Pulteney, at the reins again, did not press them too hard.

The sun was down, the stars were out, and the moon hinted that it might rise above the trees and low hills several hours hence. The birds had gone to their nests and were silent. Innocent farm people were slurping their soups, dipping their breads, carving off slices of cheese and onions, and sipping their *vin ordinaire*, perhaps no more than an hour from retiring. The locals' own waggons and carts were in the barns, so the fugitives had the road pretty much to themselves. In the distance, only here and there, were there glims to be seen through opened shutters.

"Odd's Blood, *there* it is! Just as I recall it!" Sir Pulteney announced as he turned the waggon into a much narrower farm track off the Beauvais road, the entrance almost lost in overgrowth, and so bad a lane, evidently so little-used, that in the darkness anyone chasing them would have to know of its existence and peer hard to spot it.

Sir Pulteney shook the reins and clucked the team to a faster pace for a mile or so before slowing again. "It appears there's been a dry summer, so we *should* find one of the old fords and cross over the Thérain river. After that, there are a *thousand* farm tracks just like this, which will take us near Amiens, *round* it in point of fact, and, is our luck in, we'll be in Calais in a trice, haw haw!"

"How *long* a trice did ye have in mind?" Lewrie asked, clawing at a maddening itch beneath his dark wig and bandage, hoping that the last Frog actor who'd worn it hadn't had crabs, lice, or fleas. The paints that

Lady Imogene had daubed on him were greasy, too, and the cool night air made him conjure that his face was covered in bear fat like a Muskogee Indian's would be, to keep the mosquitoes at bay.

"Three days in this waggon," Sir Pulteney estimated as they shared the un-sprung bench seat of the un-sprung waggon behind their plodding team. "Slower than cold treacle tonight, of course. Farmer folk hereabouts would remark upon anything on the roads at night, especially one making good time. And we can't have that, Begad! Haw!"

If we can't make noise, then stop that brayin'! Lewrie griped.

"Horse, pray God, at some point?" Lewrie hoped aloud. "So we can make better speed?"

"Once we've altered our appearances and assumed new aliases, some-where up ahead," Sir Pulteney pooh-poohed. "You and your wife . . . pardons, Armand and Dorothea . . . should try to get some rest. Hello?" he said of a sudden, drawing the creaking waggon to a full stop. "Do you hear something back there?"

Oh, Christ, they've found us! Lewrie thought in dread.

He stood, facing to the rear. They had come more than an English mile, Lewrie reckoned, so he had no fear of being spotted right off; there was a lot of forest behind them. As he did at sea, Lewrie opened his mouth and breathed softly, cocking his head to either side. Even above the groan of timbers, masts, and yards, and the hiss of the hull through the sea, sound carried quite far, even something as faint as the dinging of a watch bell.

"Horses!" Lewrie said in a harsh whisper. "A lot of 'em. Jinglin'."

"Sword scabbards and musketoons . . . bit chains, and such, or so I recall from my days in the Yeoman Cavalry," Sir Pulteney opined. "Cavalry . . . at least a troop . . . and a coach, too? At a fast canter or trot, it sounds like. Lud, they fell for it! Old Simenon at the stables pointed them to Beauvais, possibly Rouen, as well, where Major Fleury *claimed* he lived! A party being pursued could take a boat at Rouen down the Seine to the sea and board a packet at Le Havre. Let us *pray* they take that as a better-than-fair proposition!"

"Once we get to Calais, though," Lewrie had to ask, losing his dread as the sound of their pursuers—if pursuers they truly were—seemed to continue on north, and coming no closer or louder along their miserably narrow and rough farm track. "How do we get aboard a packet ourselves if we have no false papers? If word gets out for the police and all to be on the lookout for us?"

"Recall, I mentioned that I'd arranged for a schooner to meet us?" Sir

Pulteney breezily boasted. "The former head of our league, the greatest of us all, has a schooner yacht of his very own, and had the eager cooperation of several other merchant masters. She will be off one of our old *rendezvous* coves near Cap Gris Nez, to loiter near the shore 'til we turn up, then take us off the beach, and away!"

"Uhm, Sir Pulteney . . . that was ten years ago, in the midst of the Terror, when the Frogs weren't anywhere *near* as organised, with so many police and guardsmen," Lewrie pointed out, a new nagging dread in his head. What also nagged him was that Sir Pulteney Plumb looked on their escape from France as a chance to re-live the antics of his youth, like *alumni* during Old Boys' Week, men of middling age who should *know* better, but would over-indulge in the old taverns and haunts, and dive into vigourous sports as if they were still not come to their majority.

One last chance t'be heroic, Lewrie sarcastically deemed this; *one last grand adventure . . . with us dead in a ditch if he fails!*

"They didn't have nigh a million men under arms back then, sir," Lewrie continued, "in their army, the Garde Nationale, and the police. There wasn't a *gendarme* on every street corner, and if there were, he was more like the Constable at Herne Bay, or a London parish Charlie. What do we do if even Frogs have t'have identity papers? Whip 'em up on the spot?"

Pull 'em out o' yer small-clothes? Lewrie thought.

What *really* gnawed at Lewrie, though—and even he would admit it—was that he was so completely out of his depth, and not a whit of his competence as a Commission Sea Officer, an experienced Post-Captain, would avail them. He was good with a sword, a dab-hand shot with pistol, musket, or rifled piece, but if it came to using those skills, the game was up; surrounded and out-numbered at the last resort, with his back to some wall!

And our lives are in the hands of this daft, play-actin' dolt? Lewrie almost angrily thought; *Good God, we're dead as mutton!*

"Listen!" Sir Pulteney Plumb interjected, raising his hand to shush him. "Begad, I believe they've gone on! *Fooled* 'em, haw haw!"

Not a single word had penetrated; the impossible *geste* was yet alive, in his mind; the game was still afoot!

Fourchette and his party, with *Capitaine* Aulard's light horse troop, reached the gates of Beauvais round midnight; even the skilled riders' thighs chafed, their legs shuddery-weak, and their fundaments saddle-sore. Their horses were certainly played out, by then capable of only a plodding, head-down walk, lathered with sweat and reeking of ammonia, Men swayed in their saddles, barely able to keep their eyes open, their balance astride, and some, once the pace slackened, had nodded off completely, trusting their horse to follow its fellows and keep its feet.

Beauvais was a fairly large town, a garrison town, and with so many roads passing through it, there were watchmen posted at its *portes* day and night. At one time before the Peace of Amiens, Napoleon Bonaparte had contemplated an invasion of southern England cross the Channel, so the town had been mindful of spies as the lead elements of the armies had started to assemble, before it was called off. Beauvais's authorities might have slackened their watchfulness after that, but that did not mean that they had let their guard down completely.

Yet with all that watchfulness at the city gates, there was no sign of a two-horse farm waggon with four occupants, no *M'sieur* Fleury and family declaring himself at the southern gate, and after checking with the town's constabulary, no one of that name or description noted in the registries at any of the town's overnight lodgings! No *concierge* could report any Fleurys taking an *appartement;* no landlord, hastily wakened, knew of anyone suddenly leasing a house at such a late hour!

"We would have caught up with them if they were ahead of us on the road," Major Clary sleepily muttered over a welcome cup of coffee as he slumped, exhausted, on his elbows at a rough plank table in the inn at which they had retired. "*Ergo*, they never were *on* the Beauvais road. *Another* goose-egg, *messieurs. Un zéro!*"

"That damned *villageois*, that *péquenot* stableman! Either he is in league with them, or he's an idiot!" Guillaume Choundas accused as he sat on a padded chair nearby, his hand clawed round a brandy glass. A few hours on horseback, even most of the day and night at ease in a comfortable carriage, had caused him even more pain than it had the others. His iron-braced leg throbbed, his abused bottom was between numbness and muscle spasms, and the cool, damp night air even made his ravaged face's nerves now and then spike with knife-like pain, forcing him to set down the glass and reach up to soothe it. "Someone should ride back there and have the fool arrested! Tortured 'til he talks!"

"He told us only what he was told," Charité de Guilleri numbly mumbled over her own cup of coffee. "His sort is too dense to lie, too much the ox to be curious . . . or risk his life for another." Her first bleak year spent with her distant relations in the village of Rambouillet had shown Charité the dimness of *rustique* French people!

This tavern had been about ready to shut its doors for the night when their party had clattered up, demanding hot food, spirits, and lodgings. The *tavernier* and his barman, cook, and waiters, now kept far past their bedtimes, clattered, clomped, and silently sulked and sneered, as only Frenchmen can, while the hot meal was prepared. Its arrival was delayed by the excuse that the cookfire had ebbed, and even though the interlopers accepted the quickly doubled prices and willingly paid in gold *franc* coins, their party was still unwelcome.

The door to the street opened, and Matthieu Fourchette and *Capitaine* Aulard clomped in, the cavalryman looking exhausted and Fourchette looking grim. Fourchette ordered brandy at the tin-covered bar counter, Aulard opting for a mug of beer, before they came to the table to join their compatriots and slouch in matching manner.

"The Colonel of the local regiment . . . the idle time-server!" Fourchette spat after a deep draught of brandy. "He *finally* allowed us audience, after more than half an hour!" Fourchette swiped impatiently at the hair that had fallen over his face. "It was only after we declared our mission was ordered by the First Consul that he got out of *bed*!"

"So we start out at once?" Major Clary asked.

"No, *mon cher* Major, we start at *dawn*!" Fourchette said with a snarl. "He's sending riders to Rouen, Amiens, Le Havre, and Dieppe as we speak, but will not send out his troops 'til the sun is up."

"We *do* get remounts, and he *did* offer my men use of the barracks for the night," Aulard sleepily told them. "That is something, I suppose." When he lifted his beer mug, his hand shook with tiredness.

"Such *bourgeois* . . . shop-keepers and clock-watchers would have lost their heads a few years ago," Guillaume Choundas told them with relish; in his heyday during the Terror, he'd sent more than his share from his own navy to such a fate, and looked as if he'd be delighted to see a few *more* heads tumble into the bloody basket. "Perhaps a report should be sent to Bonaparte, Fourchette . . . to encourage the others."

"Oh, for God's sake . . . ," Fourchette said with a weary groan. "I may lose *mine* if we fail, not you, you . . . !"

"Where will the good colonel *send* his patrols, *m'sieur*?" Major Clary said, his mind still sharp, even at that hour. "We did not catch up with them because, as I was telling the others, they were never *on* the Beauvais road. . . . They did not *come* to Beauvais. Perhaps did not ever have the intention of risking discovery at the gates. Yet there are dozens of farm lanes and un-mapped tracks. They turned off somewhere along the way. East or west? To skirt Beauvais and proceed to Rouen or Le Havre? It seems to me that, even if the entire regiment turns out and is split into files of only ten or fifteen men, it will be impossible to scour all of the lanes. And all the while, those we seek will make their way to the coast . . . in disguise, assuming we are not following *another* false lead."

"Denis is right," Charité sleepily mourned. "And if so many search parties are sent out, how will any of them be able to recognise the Lewries? There are only four of us who know what Lewrie and his wife look like! Are we to dash from one patrol to the next? Is half of France to be arrested 'til we can arrive and sort through them?"

"If that is what it takes, yes!" Guillaume Choundas demanded.

"Even given your coach, *m'sieur*, you could not *dash* after a *lame* snail," Fourchette angrily scoffed, "or a batch of *escargot* in *garlic* sauce!" He'd had more than enough of this bitter old cripple, his continual bloodthirsty eagerness, and more to the point, Choundas's snide and cutting comments, which galled sore.

Fourchette shut his eyes for a long moment, half nodding as he contemplated what Fouché would do when he reported back to Paris; the guillotine was no longer out in the public square, but it still was in operation.

"It very well *may* be your head, as you say, Fourchette," the old ogre shot back in a soft coo. "I will be delighted to see that. If I cannot have Lewrie, perhaps I will have *you*, for letting him escape!

"Yet . . . ," Choundas continued after a moment, "consider that he is a sailor, *hein*? We *know* he flees to the coast, but . . . perhaps not to a seaport. There is no point in galloping down every narrow country road, when we should be concentrating on the beaches, the inlets, and the lonely coves. Is France not on guard against threats coming *from* the sea?"

"We *let* them run," Major Clary understood quickly, "imagining that they elude us. Perhaps they become careless, or too confident, but . . . all the time, we double the patrols at the coast, and they will eventually have to take passage, hire a fishing smack or steal a boat from somewhere. The locals could arrest them, 'til we do arrive and . . . sort them out, as you say, *Mademoiselle* Charité."

"Does that mean I can go to bed?" *Capitaine* Aulard whispered.

"From Le Havre to Calais, the entire coast," Choundas insisted. "Like frightened gnats, they will fly . . . buzz-buzz-buzz . . . unsuspecting into our sticky web! Where the spider will bind them tightly and suck them dry!" Choundas happily conjured, looking like a beast having a blissful orgasm, so much did he like his fantasy.

Even the jaded Fourchette felt a shiver up his spine.

"*Oui*, I dare say we can all go to bed and get a decent rest at last," Major Clary told Aulard. "At dawn, we tell the good colonel to send out more riders to alert the coastal garrisons and police. It may still be necessary to scour the immediate area round Beauvais, but if they travel all night without pausing, they may be too far away for an exhaustive search hereabouts to matter very much. The only question is, where do we place ourselves along the coast to organise the search? Rouen? Amiens?"

"They landed at Calais," Charité suggested, perking up no matter how weary she was. "How much of France do they know how to travel?"

"The soup," a surly waiter growled as he set his tray down atop the rough table, bowls slopping onto the tray. He dealt them out with a glower on his face. "*Bon appétit*," he said off-handedly, making that sound more like a curse.

"*Hot* potato soup, aha!" Fourchette cheered, quickly spooning up a taste. "Rouen . . . Amiens . . . we can decide in the morning. *Hé, garçon!* Can we get some *good* wine?"

CHAPTER TWENTY-EIGHT

*T*hey got beyond Montdidier by farm roads as the unhappy Fleury family, then the Plumbs altered their disguises to those of a pair of old crones, Sir Pulteney doing a remarkable imitation of a woman for a whole day, whilst Alan and Caroline hid in the waggon bed under an even larger pile of pilfered straw. In that guise they crossed the river Somme, then let the Lewries emerge for another set of costumes and aliases. The way Sir Pulteney and Lady Imogene preened, giggled, and congratulated each other really began to cut raw with Lewrie.

Sir Pulteney became *M'sieur* André Guyot, a garrulous, somewhat simple and grey-haired "Merry Andrew" with but a muted version of his inane donkey-bray laugh, no longer in need of a cane.

Himself t'the bone, and he don't have t'act, Lewrie thought of that *persona.* Might we mention that Lewrie by this time was becoming a *touch* surly?

Lady Imogene became *Madame* Hortense Guyot, streaking her raven hair with touches of grey to play an elegant beauty, wed to an older, well-to-do man, and a silly goose herself, with fond toleration of her husband's foibles.

"Oh, such a clever ploy, m'dear!" Lady Imogene gushed as they studied themselves in a hand mirror. "And *so* distinguished-looking!"

Be pullin' rabbits out o' his hat next, Lewrie told himself.

Now they were in Artois and Picardy, so close to the border of the former Austrian Netherlands and the dead Holy Roman Empire (which after 1815 would become Belgium) Sir Pulteney thought it made sense for the Lewries to portray the Guyots' manservant and maid, Flemings or Walloons, half-German really, hired from cross the border years before. Lewrie became a flaxen blond in neat but worn brown woolen ditto; Caroline became a coppery redhead with her face subtley re-done to pinky-raw cheeks and chin. Again, their poor French could be explained by their supposed origins, and in Flanders, Ricardy, and in Artois, no one gave a tinker's dam or the slightest bit of notice to crude Flemish or Walloon folk—as bad as so many Germans to them!

Sir Pulteney allowed his goose-brained self to be cheated most sinfully at Albert, a small town on the road to Arras and Lille, on a solo trip, then returned to join them in a wood lot short of the town at the reins of a shabby canvas-topped *cabriolet* with a younger and fresher two-horse team, wishing to make a grand entrance in Lille, he told them as they re-loaded the remaining trunks and valises, which by then had been reduced to but one valise each, and one trunk that held the last disguises Sir Pulteney decided would be apt when they got to the coast.

Albert to Arras, the famed woolen industry town. But instead of going through it and proceeding on to Lille, as Sir Pulteney had told the *cabriolet*'s owner, they turned off the main road once more and resorted to backroads and farm lanes 'til striking a major highway near Béthune. There, they bought oats for the horses, bread and wine, cheese, a baked ham, and pair of broiled whole chickens, with all the necessities for a mid-day *pique-nique*, along with all the utensils and plates, the napkins, cork puller, and large basket necessary. By the looks on the faces of the various vendors by the time they were done, Sir Pulteney and Lady Imogene had made a distinct impression of a pair of cackling twits; so much so, Sir Pulteney whispered once back into the *cabriolet*, that no one would remember their silent servants! Then they rattled out of Béthune on the St. Omer road.

"We will find a place to lay up somewhere off the road," Sir Pulteney informed them. "It will mean sleeping rough tonight. Then I fear poor *M'sieur* Guyot will be cheated most horribly when he sells the *cabriolet* in Saint Omer, haw haw! One last change of disguises, then we're off for the coast! Begad, m'dear, ain't it grand to be in harness again? Livin' by our wits! What marvellous sport!"

⚓

They dawdled along the road for the better part of the day, 'til the sun began to decline and traffic began to thin. A mid-day meal was taken *en route*, without stopping; sliced ham and cheese sandwiches with a mild mustard and pickles, and but one bottle of wine shared by all. Sir Pulteney had forgotten to purchase glasses, and made quite a dither for their lack, japing over how they had to pass that bottle back and forth.

Finally, as it drew on toward sunset, Sir Pulteney began peering ahead and to larboard for a place to leave the road, muttering over and over, ". . . sure to be here, just about here, I remember it well, unless they've gone and cut the woods down. Now where is it?"

This part of France was looking less promising to Lewrie, when it came to a place to go to ground. It was mostly flat and not very interesting, with long gentle slopes that rose only slightly for what seemed miles, then fell away for what looked like even more miles, and the plowed fields they passed, the road bed, looked paler as they passed through a land of chalky soil. There were drainage ditches to either hand and enough windmills to put Lewrie in mind of the Dutch coast.

"Aha, there it is, Begad!" Sir Pulteney crowed at last. "*Knew* we'd stumble cross it sooner or later! See it, m'dear Imogene?"

"Hortense, *cher* André . . . *mon coeur*," Lady Imogene prompted.

There was a long, slow rise to the left, what passed for a hill hereabouts, thickly covered with forest, with the faintest trace of a path where waggons or carts had cut a sketch of a road in white, chalky earth. It looked so long un-used that new grass was growing in the ruts, not just the crest of the track, and a few seedlings from the forest had even taken root, some as high as the belly of the *cabriolet*. Sir Pulteney drew the coach to a stop, stood on the seat to peer up and down the main road, then, satisfied that there was no one visible for miles, sat down and clucked the team up into the woods.

By the time they had un-hitched the horse team and hobbled them it was sunset, a rather spectacular one of yellow, amber, and crimson, which made Lewrie feel a tad better; the day's dawn had been a clear one, no "red in the morning, sailor take warning." Given the febrile, goose-brained airs that the Plumbs displayed, he was about ready to hunt up a rabbit's foot or spit and dance about three times counter-clockwise for luck!

There was a spring at the foot of the rise on the western side, and they fetched canvas feed bags of water for the horses 'til they were sated, then gave them their oats.

From the summit of their low rise, looking down to the northwest and west, Lewrie could see quite a long way into the sunset, and the land round them seemed but thinly populated. There was a village, far off, and a manor house a mile or two away. But in the immediate vicinity, there was nothing but empty fields, with not even the yelp of a stray dog to disturb the bucolic quiet.

"We'll put up the bonnet and let the ladies sleep in the *cabriolet*," Sir Pulteney suggested. "Blanket rolls beneath for us . . . hard ground, dews, and wee crawling things. Odd's Blood, what I would give for a straw pallet tonight! Haven't slept rough in ages. It's a feather mattress for me, I tell you!"

They dug a pit and risked a small fire, hopefully deep enough in those old-growth woods that it would not be seen. In companionable fashion, they spread blankets to sit on and delved into their basket once more for a cold supper. The new bottle of wine that they passed back and forth even proved to be a fairly good *cabernet*.

"An early rising at dawn," Sir Pulteney mused after jointing a chicken for them all, and choosing a thigh for himself, eating with his fingers most commonly. "By the time the shops open, *pauvre M'sieur* Guyot, the old addle-pate, will be selling the coach and team. Money matters not at this stage . . . just enough to tide us over 'til we are at one of the coves. *Quel dommage*," he said with a grin and a little sigh. Followed by one of his irritating titters, of course.

"An utter fool," Lady Imogene said with a fond grin, snickering. "Still, a fool has his uses, and his good points. *Un bouffon*, a clown, will outwit all of Réal's, all of Fouché's, minions, no matter how clever they are, or think they are. That fellow, what is his name, m'dear, in charge of the pursuit?"

"Fourchette," Sir Pulteney said with a guffaw. "He is named Matthieu Fourchette. My old sources informed me he's been watching the Lewries long before the levee, and he's reputed to be—"

"Come again?" Lewrie blurted through a bite of chicken breast. "We're bein' chased by a man named 'Fork'? And there's been people watchin' us all *that* long? Think ye might've warned us *earlier*?"

"By now, Fourchette could be as hot on our trail as he is on yours, Captain Lewrie," Sir Pulteney rejoined. "Though not as famous as the instigator of our league, my sobriquet was not unknown to the French authorities in those horrid days. Who knows? Perhaps a paper record of the times ten years ago was kept, the connexion made from old *dossiers* and suspicions of my presence in France before the war closed off access for English visitors, and the disappearance of the intended victims of the

Revolution, say? Perhaps I *did* have a careless moment, leaving a note behind, as a cheeky taunt or by omission, dropping one in haste . . . one intercepted or taken from a collaborator . . ."

"Mean t'say you signed yer bloody *name*?" Lewrie gawped; this was getting even *more* lunatick. And he still hadn't gotten an answer to his question about the watchers!

"My insignia, rather," Sir Pulteney told them.

"That wee flower at the bottom of the note Lady Imogene gave me before we left Paris, do you mean, Sir Pulteney?" Caroline asked. "A part of a family seal, or . . . ?"

"Not so incriminating as a signet ring in wax, no, Mistress Lewrie," Sir Pulteney told her with a smile, and a bray. He sat up straighter, as if in pride. "Back then, we *all* had our secret names and signs. I . . . was known as . . . the Yellow Tansy."

If he was expecting awe, rushes of indrawn breath, or knowing nods, he didn't get them; the Lewries looked at him like an escapee from Bedlam, then at each other, shrugging at the same time.

"Well, it was a long time ago, *mon cher*," Lady Imogene said as she patted his thigh to comfort his deflated feelings. "And it was a secret from everyone, wasn't it? No mention of the league in the newspapers, no thrilling tales written after the fact. We laboured in the dark, and our successes were their own reward, *n'est-ce pas*?"

"Mean to say, you never heard . . . ?" Sir Pulteney said, crushed.

"Not an inkling," Lewrie rather enjoyed telling him.

Who the Hell runs about callin' himself the Yellow Tansy? he thought; *"the Shadow," or somethin' spy-ish, aye, but . . . mine arse on a band-box, who'd even admit t'such? They don't even call race horses at Ascot or the Derby such silly names!*

The search round Beauvais had proved fruitless, as Fourchette expected, and the quickly erected road blocks on all roads leading to Rouen had not turned up the fugitives, either. For a time he had hoped that this mysterious "Fleury" family might appear in Le Havre or some other seaport, and the coastal police or guardsmen might identify them, but a rider had come from Rouen's *hôtel de ville*; according to a census, there were several *real* Fleurys living there, but all were accounted for, and none matched the descriptions they had gathered from Méru. Again, as Fourchette dourly expected.

"How I wish that *all* France was linked by the First Consul's semaphore towers, the way it was when it was Gaul, and the Romans held us." Fourchette gloomed at how long messengers took to go back and forth.

"How Napoleon protects our coast with those new semaphore towers of his," Guillaume Choundas grumpily pointed out, stifling a belch of liquid fire that threatened to sear his throat. His digestion had been going bad during his last stint in the West Indies, and what the *Américains* served during his captivity had completed its ruin. On his own in his Paris hovel, and with his miserly excuse for a pension, he ate only the blandest, cheapest food. This hunt after Lewrie, though, and the lavish funds spent on it by Fourchette's employer, resulted in many hastily eaten meals in foul inns along the way, usually ordered by the policeman for all, with no individual choice, and guaranteed to be piquant and spicy, and insults to his stomach and bowels. Even with final revenge waiting at the end of their road, there were times that Choundas wished he'd stayed home with his tasteless broth. Some nights when the hunters could take lodgings, Choundas would spend half the hours that he should have slept in the outback *toilettes*, either squirting liquid and searing his hemorrhoids, or groaning in painful, bloated inability.

Charité wasn't enjoying the hunt much, either, for she had come away from Paris imagining that Lewrie would be taken no more than two hours outside the city, and that she would be home in her chic *appartement* by dusk. She had packed nothing more than a brace of pistols and their accoutrements. No valise, no tooth powder or brush, no spare clothes. Her one small carry bag held a comb, a brush, a mirror, and a scented face powder and puff! And no more than two thousand francs to purchase a meal in celebration! After three days, she was sure she was as "high" as the rankest cavalry *soldat*. Her one serviceable gown and her single pair of men's breeches were stained with ammonia horse sweat and the stench of wet saddle leather, and after the hard use to which their horses had been put, both originals *and* remounts, the reek of open and rotting saddle sores.

The cavalryman's cloak Major Clary had loaned her against the chill of night rides, and one afternoon of sullen rain blown inland from the Channel, had seen an entire year's hard field use on campaign, and it, too, gave off a *mélange* of odd odours, not a one of them that could be called pleasant, either.

All in all, Charité reckoned, she had managed to stay cleaner, sweeter-scented, better groomed, and a world more stylish aboard one of their pirate schooners in the Gulf of Mexico, and Denis could *have* this "glorious" soldier's life!

"What you said, *Mam'selle* Charité," Fourchette said suddenly, leaning intimately towards her at the breakfast table they shared at their lodgings in Beauvais, a seductive note to his voice and flirtatious glints in his oddly pale eyes. "How Lewrie only knows the roads from Calais to Paris?"

"*Oui, m'sieur?*" Charité answered, put off once more by his continual lusty looks, shifting a few *centimètres* further away, wishing she had a shawl with which to shield herself from his leering gaze.

"Calais, Boulogne, Dunkerque . . . perhaps even Abbeville and Dieppe," Fourchette went on as if amused by the reaction he elicited. "*Much* closer to England, *n'est-ce pas?* On a good day, one can see the cliffs of Dover from Cap Gris Nez, *n'est-ce pas?* I thank you for the suggestion. It is so astute of you, *mam'selle*. You are a treasure indeed."

He was so obvious that even Guillaume Choundas snorted in derision.

"*You, Capitaine* Choundas, remind me that Lewrie is a sailor," Fourchette said, turning to face that ogre. "He certainly cannot try to book passage aboard a packet, for we watch all departures by now, yet . . . is he a *good* sailor? One able to handle a small boat? And tell me, *Capitaine*, how small a boat might he need to sail it himself cross the Narrow Sea?"

"Every second day, the straits are so boisterous that anyone trying to cross in a small boat would be swamped and drowned, and if he managed to get far enough offshore, the swift tide race would take him either into the North Sea or halfway to Le Havre before turning," Choundas was quick to say, drawing on his nautical experience, which was long and expert. Choundas paused though, his evil sword-ravaged lips curled in sourness anent the first part of Fourchette's question.

Was Lewrie a good small-boat man? With a crew, even Choundas had to cede him tactical skill, and . . . daring, damn him! But he'd only seen Lewrie handle a jolly-boat, gig, launch, or cutter on his own once, so he did not know. His natural hatred of the man made him wish that he could say no, yet . . . the British Royal Navy was a demanding and hard school, and Lewrie had come up in it, successfully. Choundas could *not* let him make his escape *this* time by underestimating him or deprecating him.

"He has spent twenty years in their navy, most of that at sea, *Citoyen* Fourchette," Choundas slowly and carefully said, at last. "He most certainly can 'hand, reef, and steer' as they say, as good as any *matelot*. If he obtains a boat, then he *could* sail it to England.

"But . . . ," Choundas added, holding up his one hand and arm, "he would need a *decent-sized* boat, of at least ten metres' length, with a single mast . . . a typical fishing boat . . . to survive the crossing in any sort of rough weather. Such a boat would be hard for one man to handle without help. His wife could toss free the dock lines, while he could hoist the single lugsail. A woman *might* have the strength to hoist the much smaller jib for him while he mans the tiller. Your small rowing boat, your *small* ship's boat, would not avail him."

"Such are more likely to be found in the smaller harbours then?" Fourchette asked, looking pleased with Choundas's answers.

"In *all* harbours, *citoyen*. Unfortunately," Choundas told him.

"What if he travels with this mysterious second couple?" Charité fretted, though relieved that Fourchette had turned his mind to ideas other than bedding her behind Denis Clary's back. "How big a boat can *two* men handle?"

"If the seas are rough, as I just said, *Citoyenne* de Guilleri," Choundas told her with his mildest manners, "any boat much larger than ten *mètres* would be too much for two men to handle. For two men and two women . . . if we now believe that Lewrie and his wife travel with help . . . anything with more than *one* mast would also be hard for them to sail."

"We can send riders to alert the Guard Nationale and the local *gendarmes* to keep a closer watch on such boats, and pass word among our fishermen to guard their livelihoods from theft," Fourchette said.

"Hah!" Choundas scoffed with a mirthless laugh. "You might as well tell them to lock up all the smugglers 'til we've caught them, too, Fourchette! *Our* smugglers, who would drown their children for a purse full of coin, or the *Anglais* smugglers, who come and go as free as the wind and brazenly walk the streets of Dunkerque and Calais in full view, with the winking knowledge of police and customs men! How do plotters against the Republic enter France or escape back to England, like will-o'-the-wisps? On smugglers' boats, I tell you!"

"What of smugglers further down the Narrow Sea?" the policeman pressed, suddenly unsure of his clever idea.

"Our entire coast, their entire coast, is as infected with smugglers as this inn is full of bed-bugs," Choundas sourly replied. "In my own Brittany, in Saint Malo, the heroism and patriotism of my glorious Celts is corrupted by the lure of quick money. Brittany, where one may find the bravest, most skillful seafarers in all Europe since the days of Julius Caesar and—"

"Yes, yes, *Capitaine*, as you have told us," Fourchette said with a wave of his hands. Ever since this foul creature had joined their expedition, they all had been subjected to Choundas's tales of Breton derring-do and pagan myths and sagas. *More* than enough of it! "This Lewrie, though, stands a better chance from Calais and Dunkerque?"

"He does," Choundas sulkily said, nettled that no one would appreciate his people's glories.

"Then we shift to the Calais coast," Fourchette decided.

"God," Charité softly groaned, not looking forward to another long, hard ride on a reeking horse, in her reeking clothes.

"We will coach to Calais, *mademoiselle*," Fourchette informed her. "Once there, in more comfortable lodgings, we will *wait* for the quarry to come to us, instead of haring all over France as we have. And I think that Minister Fouché would not deny us clean clothing, barbers, or hair dressers, *n'est-ce pas*? It will be my treat to reward your cleverness, *ma chérie*."

Oh, gag me! Charité thought; *I'll owe him gratitude? A debt?*

The ladies went off deeper into the woods atop their rise just before bedtime, a last moment of modesty. Sir Pulteney Plumb produced a pint bottle from a side pocket of his coat, pulled the cork, and had a brief taste, then waved it to draw Lewrie down-slope northwest once more. "Will you partake, Captain Lewrie, as we give our good ladies a touch more privacy, what?

"Not a bad tipple, does one prefer apples to grapes. So near Normandy, their *calvados*, an apple brandy, is easy to find." He handed the bottle over to Lewrie, then tended to his trouser buttons for his own ease.

"Mmm, tasty," Lewrie had to agree after a taste.

"Whilst we're here, sir, in private . . . so we do not alarm the womenfolk, there is something that has been nagging at me this past day or so . . . ," Plumb hesitantly began.

Him? Worried 'bout somethin'? At this *late stage? How far up Shit's Creek are* we, *then, for* him *t'look worried?* Lewrie cringed.

"Since crossing the Thérain river, no one has given us even the slightest looking-over," Sir Pulteney said, sounding fretful and sombre. "What I took for success at eluding them may have been that they have guessed our final objective, the coast and the seaports, and have set watchers in place . . . so we stumble into their spider-webs."

Oh, just bloody grand! Lewrie sourly thought; *ye didn't think they wouldn't?* He took a goodly slug of the *calvados* before he gave in to the urge to curse, loudly.

"They'll guard the cross-Channel packets, the good-sized boats we could steal," Lewrie said. "But we ain't *plannin'* t'sail ourselves over, are we? Your schooner, waitin' off some beach t'take us off . . . like you told me, right? We *do* have a plan, hey?"

"Of course, Captain Lewrie," Sir Pulteney was quick to assure him; perhaps reassure himself on that head. "There's the very place I had in mind . . . a very lonely wee beach where we may hide in a maze of rocks above a small inlet 'til the schooner arrives. Used it in the past . . . though . . ."

"Though?" Lewrie felt like screeching.

"Ten years ago, it was totally abandoned," Sir Pulteney said in reverie. "There were some fishermen's shacks atop the cliffs, and the path down so steep and convoluted that hardly anyone even knew there was a shallow inlet, and a beach, at the foot of it. The shacks were falling in on themselves, un-used for years, as well, and, did a lone *gendarme* happen by and see activity, what could one man do, with help *miles* away at the next post? *Then*, at any rate. But, as you say, the French have thousands more police and army patrols now. And . . . now I can cannot say with any certainty whether it is unhabited, still."

Just bloody, fuckin' great! Lewrie gawped; *you clueless . . . !*

"I'd *thought* to take a look at the place, for old time's sake, but Imogene wished to get on to Paris, so I didn't," Plumb lamented. "Neither of us is quite as eager to forego our comforts as we did in our headier days, d'ye see. Yet who could have expected a visit to be necessary?" he added, to excuse himself.

"Well, you couldn't have known," Lewrie said, sighing heavily to the reality and taking another deep gulp of *calvados. You'll get us killed, for the lack of it, though, you hen-headed . . . !* he thought.

"Once we've donned our last disguises and gotten a new form of transport in Saint Omer, I must leave the three of you somewhere safe and make a reconnaissance on my own, before committing us to its use," Sir Pulteney decided aloud, waving a hand for the bottle, as if in need of "Dutch courage" himself. "In a *very* humble costume, haw haw!"

Hope it ain't clowns or mimes! Lewrie gloomed.

"So close to the sea, what better way to blend in than to play the part of common sailors?" Plumb said with a clever little hee-haw. "I trust our ladies will not be scandalised to become sailors' doxies!"

Sailors and doxies, is it? Lewrie thought; *no sailor is authentic without a good knife, no doxy without a wee pistol up her skirts! We get to Saint-Omer safe, the last o' my money's goin' for weapons!*

CHAPTER TWENTY-NINE

*P*lumb drove alone to St. Omer to dispose of the *cabriolet* and their last, now-empty trunk and leather valises, getting what he could for them. He came back, on foot this time, with a canvas sea-bag partially filled with *something*, and changed his clothes and appearance to match their own. Caroline and Lady Imogene had changed, in the meantime, to voluminous peasant skirts, with hems high enough to show a bit of ankles, clunky buckled shoes, and a froth of lace. They wore rough *ecru* blouses with be-ribboned and embroidered peasant vests over them, topped with tawdry shawls and hats. Caroline kept her coppery-red wig, whilst Lady Imogene went for frizzy, dishwater blond. Sir Pulteney and Lewrie wore tattered and dingy old-style slop-trousers, the legs so loose and baggy, and ending just below the knees, plain cotton stockings to hide gentlemanly legs that had not been bronzed by the sun, their feet crammed into buckle shoes, as well. Sailors of any nation were proud to be well-shod when ashore. Itchy fishing smocks atop striped pullover singletons completed their disguises, as did the tasseled red Jacobin Liberty caps proper to good French revolutionaries. The fact that they hadn't shaved in few days helped with versimilitude, though Lewrie thought Sir Pulteney's eye-patch *was* a bit much.

They walked into St. Omer on "shank's ponies" to do the last shopping and to purchase a rickety, two-wheel cart and a lone older nag to pull it.

The Plumbs took the front bench together, whilst the Lewries lolled in the rear, using sea-bags for bolsters, and, to make their disguises even more believable, all made an open show of wine or brandy bottles, tobacco in the form of *cigarros* or blunt pipes, and an air of merriment. On their slow way north out of St.-Omer, the Plumbs quickly taught them some semi-drunken songs to sing should the need arise when confronted by a patrol.

It was disconcerting, though to see how *many* cavalry patrols there were on the road that morning. Almost every hour, a file of ten or more troopers would come cantering south from the sea, or another file would go past towards Calais, but only now and then stopping the rare coach-and-four or the larger public conveyances.

The cavalrymen might look them over as their cart slowly plodded up the road, mostly to ogle Lady Imogene or Caroline and make lewd, suggestive japes to them, but Lewrie had to hand it to Lady Imogene, for she could hurl insults and gutter-French right back at them, insulting their manhoods in a way that made the troopers guffaw, not get angry, then canter on. Each time, Lewrie's stomach did back flips and a handstand, his mouth turned dry (which only another tipsy swallow of wine could assuage), and his "nutmegs" did their shrinking act, even as he swayed and scowled at the cavalrymen, striving for pie-eyed innocence.

The slightly soberer and more fluent Sir Pulteney always told them that he and his mate were bound for Calais to find a ship, since they'd spent the last of their previous voyage's pay, and, amazingly, every patrol, no matter how suspicious, had taken that as Gospel and ridden on!

And so it went, hour by slow hour, mile by plodding mile, each fetching them that much closer to the coast, the sea, and to the fisherman's hut, the inlet and beach, and freedom.

"Love what ye've done with yer face," Lewrie told Caroline as the afternoon wore on, and they finished off the last of the chicken, ham, and bread. Lady Imogene had "tarted" them both up with the sort of heavy makeup no respectable lady of worth would employ; red lips, kohl-outlined eyes, pale-powdered faces, and too much rouge. "And yer stockings!" Lewrie added. Caroline had her skirts up halfway to her knees, displaying blue-and-black horizontally banded hose. She flicked her skirt down quickly. "Arr, does yer warnt a l'il tumble roight 'ere in th' cart, missie?" he teased in imitation of a British tar. "Give a shillin', I will, fer a bit o' sport, har har!"

She tossed a chicken bone at him, grinning as she plucked some meat from a breast and chewed, looking impish, for a rare moment. She held out a strip for him to chew.

He took it, though chicken breasts were not as moist and tasty as dark meat. Playing a drunken sailor, and the many nips at a bottle to make that plausible, *had* made him hungry.

"More coming, from behind, Sir Pul . . . Henri," Caroline warned, recalling Plumb's new alias. "A *lot* of them!"

The Plumbs went into their drunken singing, swaying, and bottle-waving in time to their tune.

"Christ, shit on a biscuit!" Lewrie yelped as he looked astern at the party that was rapidly gaining on them. "Mine arse on a band-box! *Grope me, Caroline! Lay down and paw me . . . for our lives!*

"It's that de Guilleri bitch and that Chasseur Major we met at Bonaparte's levee. They'll know us, sure as Fate, if—"

Caroline fell on her back and pulled him half over her, arms round his neck to hide his face, one thigh lifted to stroke down his thigh. It was a lazy kiss, a sleepy one 'twixt two people too foxed to couple. Lewrie shut his eyes tight, with the inane thought that if he couldn't see Charité de Guilleri, she couldn't see him!

Rapid clops of hooves, coming closer! The chink of bit chains and metal scabbards, the squeak of saddle leather! A *lot* of horses, then the hiss and creak of a carriage's wheels and suspension, to boot! And they were slowing *down*, reining back to look them over!

"*Hé! Des Matelots ivres et leur putains,*" someone said dismissively, so close that Lewrie could imagine that he had leaned over close enough to smell the fellow's garlicky breath. *Drunk sailors and their whores . . . damned* right *we are, so sod the fuck off!* Lewrie thought in panic.

"*Hé, Capitaine* Choundas," another mocked. "Are *these* some of your heroic Celtic or Breton seafarers, *hein?*"

Choundas? Gawd! Lewrie thought, ready to squeak in stark terror; *him, too? Where'd they find* him, *floatin' face-down in the Seine?*

There was a slow palaver 'twixt Sir Pulteney—Henri—and the leader of the mounted party; intent questions from one and drunken mumbles from the other. Whatever was said, what little Lewrie could glean from their French, he hadn't a clue. He fully expected a rough hand on his shoulder, tearing him away to face them, then . . . !

Caroline turned her face to his, tucking under his shoulder to hide her own identity while he pretended to lamely nuzzle her neck, his own face hidden in her red wig, wondering if his own black one'd stay in place, and trying manful not to *sneeze*!

"*Merde*," said the leader "*Adieu. Allons vite, mes amis.*"

The clop of hooves picked up the pace from a slow walk to a canter, the carriage rattled past, and the Plumbs took up their mumbling song once more as their pursuers diminished on the road north.

"You, erm . . . know one of them, Captain Lewrie?" Sir Pulteney asked, once it was safe to speak in English again. "A de Guilleri?"

"The girl with 'em," Lewrie muttered, cautiously sitting up to look beneath the cart's driver's bench at the departing party. "Shot me once, in Louisiana. And if there was a crippled monster with a mask on his face and but one good arm, then, aye, I do. He's named Guillaume Choundas, and I'm the one who maimed him . . . several times. Known him since the Far East, in Eighty-Four . . . the Med, ten years later, and the West Indies in Ninety-Eight."

"One of the most disgusting creatures ever I laid eyes upon," Lady Imogene said with a delayed shudder.

"How many of them were there?" Lewrie asked, daring to sit up all the way.

"A whole troop of green Chasseurs," Sir Pulteney told him. "An open carriage for the ogre, a Major and a Captain of cavalry, and the young woman. *And* their leader, a fox-faced, lank-haired fellow, him I must imagine to be the very Matthieu Fourchette I mentioned to you last evening. Haw haw! *Zounds!* Odd's Blood, but we've just fooled the very people sent to catch you, Captain Lewrie! How glorious!"

There he goes again! Lewrie sourly thought.

"And just who is 'that de Guilleri bitch' to you, Alan? She *shot* you once?" Caroline asked, sounding *very* huffy and hard. "One may only *imagine* the *why*. You knew her *before* we encountered her at the levee?"

Oh, merciful shit! Lewrie quailed in alarm; *just when I think I'm back in her good books!*

The Plumbs shared a worldly-wise look, sure that it was none of their business, but . . .

Fourchette had been free with official funds at Beauvais. They improved their cleanliness and comfort, and hired coaches and teams to take them to Amiens, where he'd spent even more. *Capitaine* Aulard's cavalrymen had gone back to Paris, but they'd picked up a troop of Chasseurs at Amiens, and Denis Clary had been delighted to don a borrowed uniform and once more be a complete soldier. Charité had picked up a few new serviceable gowns, a fresh pair of breeches to allow her to straddle a horse, not perch daintily side-saddle, and fill a pair of saddlebags with not only fresh necessities but a few luxuries as well.

From Amiens on, though, they had set a furious pace, as rapid and demanding as the first dash from Paris to the Oise, to reach the coast, set a temporary headquarters in Calais, and coordinate with the *gendarmerie* and the local National Guard garrisons. So intent was the police agent, Fourchette, to get there that they performed only a cursory inspection of travellers on the road to Calais, trusting to the alerted cavalry patrols to nab any suspicious people matching the descriptions they had sent ahead by despatch riders.

Fourchette and his party *had* to depend on the vigilance of the local authorities; they could not be everywhere, on every road, or at every town gate, to spot their quarry.

It was only after they had taken brief lodgings at an inn at Calais, and Fourchette had bustled himself importantly to the *hôtel de ville*, the Chasseur troop had taken over a livery to see to the horses (and obtain lashings of wine, by fair methods or foul), and that beast Choundas had painfully, crookedly limped off to the out-house to ease his flaming bowels, that Major Clary finally had an idle hour to spend in private with Charité.

"Why you, *ma chérie*?" he posed over a welcome glass of wine on the inn's open-sided gallery as a soft, warm breeze redolent of fish and kelp and salt blew in from the sea. "You knew this man before, I suspect. Not from one brief introduction in Paris. What is he to you?"

She turned away, eyes closed in weariness and her face to the aromas of the breeze. She did not answer him.

"Why did Fouché insist that you come on this chase?" Denis went on. "Or was it *you* who insisted that you be included?"

"Denis, *mon cher* . . . ," she warned him, her lovely face stern.

"No, I must know, at last," Clary insisted. "We both know that the *Anglais* gave no real insult to the First Consul. He was not the assassin Fouché suspected, either. Yet we chase after him, and will drag him back to Paris in chains? And you seem to have such personal interest in being here, in the pursuit. As if you have cause to *hate* him. I must know, Charité!"

"He killed my brothers, my *cousin*, Denis!" Charité snapped in sudden venom, turning to face him. "He chased us down to Grand Isle in Barataria Bay, and his frigate destroyed everything and everyone. *He* ruined it all, *he* destroyed all hopes of taking Louisiana back from Spain. And for that I *despise* him! I had a chance to kill him once, and I *failed*! I *thought* I shot him full in the chest, with a miserable air-rifle, but, by all that's unholy, he lived, all right? Happy now?"

"And you took advantage of Fouché . . . so you could kill him at last, Charité?" Major Clary surprised her by speaking softly, with understanding, as if in sympathy. "Is that what you wish, *ma chérie?* To see him dead? The way that *hideux* Choundas wishes him dead?"

"*Yes*, I wish to see him dead!" Charité spilled out in rage. "He owes me *blood*! He came to New Orleans in disguise, to deceive, to *spy* and find all about our plans, our force! He . . . !"

Denis Clary leaned back a little, his face harder as he realised just *who* had been deceived in New Orleans, and surmised *how* this girl had been beguiled.

"So. We're to murder him," Denis Clary whispered. "And what of his wife? We must shoot her, too? The mysterious couple that they travel with? Leave no witnesses?"

"That is what Fourchette was told, Denis," Charité de Guilleri confessed with a bitter laugh. "You heard him *speak* of it before, so do not pretend that you are here unwittingly. He is a dangerous enemy of France, and you are a distinguished, patriotic soldier of France. It will be your duty."

"I will gladly obey orders to *fight*, Charité," Clary objected, his chin up. "I will happily shed a foe's blood in the heat of battle. But this . . . ! I already feel slimed . . . *mademoiselle*. Dear as I hold you in my heart . . . ," he trailed off, distancing himself with the formal address and suddenly feeling very sad, and badly betrayed.

"Perhaps . . . ," Charité relented, feeling a chill under her heart that she might lose him after such a wonderful, whirlwind beginning. "Perhaps you do not have to take an active hand, Denis *mon cher*, but . . . my revenge . . . and the First Consul's revenge, must be fulfilled."

"Ah, the cooing little lovebirds!" Fourchette exclaimed in glee as he breezed back into their inn, coming to the table to pour himself a glass of wine, not waiting for permission. "And where is that ugly old cow-hide Choundas? Dying in *les chiottes* again, *hein?* It's no matter . . . I've lit a fire hot enough under our local soldiers and police for the night, so we will split our party, each of us to go with five or six troopers to cover the city gates and the roads to Boulogne, Dunkerque, and Saint Omer. If we can reach the coast by now, then so can our quarry. I have a feeling about to-night. Eat a hearty meal, and then we'll be about it!"

Fourchette sat himself down a bit away from their table, taking another sip of wine and savouring the late-afternoon sea winds; hiding a grin as he shrewdly took note of the stiff and uncomfortable postures and the silence between the girl and her soldier. *Not as fond of each other as they'd been when I left? Bon! More hope for me,* Fourchette thought.

CHAPTER THIRTY

Sir Pulteney left them at a foetid inn a mile or so short of the sea, so old and begrimed that they were afraid even to speculate what simmered in the large iron pot over the fire in the hearth, settling instead for bread, cheese, and sour wine, over which they could linger 'til his return from his reconnaissance. The two bent-backed old prune-faced hags and the one white-whiskered old man who supposedly ran the place must have a "fiddle" on the side, Lewrie thought, for in the hour or longer that they sat there coughing in silence over their food in low-hanging haze of smoke from the fire, they were the only three customers. Lady Imogene whispered that they had used the inn as a way-station long ago, and . . . it appeared that the owners had not scrubbed the bare wood of the table top in all that time!

At last the door, leaning at an angle on loose leather hasps, creaked open, the bottom screeching on the wood floor as Sir Pulteney, in his one-eyed piratical sailor's disguise, slouched in to join them. He up-turned a somewhat clean glass to pour himself some wine, used a sailor's sheath knife to cut himself some bread and cheese, and dropped a silver coin on the table for his fee.

"That untrustworthy *Anglais* smuggler is not coming," Plumb, or as he preferred, "Henri," growled, well in character, talking through his food in raspy-throated French. "We might as well go on into Calais. . . . There are others who might be interested in our goods, *hein?*"

The old, whiskered man came to collect the coin and bend an ear to the conversation for a moment.

"We are full? *Bon.* We go."

They had left the two-wheeled cart and the weary horse in the side yard. Still grumbling about the perfidy of any *Anglais,* "Goddamn," or *sanglant* in business, or anything else, Sir Pulteney climbed up to take the reins, leaving Lady Imogene to clamber aboard on her own, still in character. The Lewries took their place at the tail-board as he clucked the horse to a slow plod once more, and the cart creaked off into the night.

For a late summer night, it was cool, with a soft wind wafting off the Channel, cool enough to make Lewrie shiver as his shoes dangled a foot or so above the road. Caroline was huddled into her shawl, her arms crossed—for warmth, Lewrie hoped. Since he had blabbed the name of Charité de Guilleri that afternoon, and had then had to explain how she and her kin had gone pirating in the West Indies, and how he'd ended them—how the girl had *shot* him!—leaving out the *bawdy* parts, of course, Caroline had acted very coolly towards him, rightly suspecting that there was a lot *more* to the tale.

He put an arm round her shoulders to warm her up and adjust her shawl, but she shrugged him off with a much-put-upon bitter sigh.

They came to a turning, another of those faint tracks, within sight of the lights of Calais, before the crossroads of the east-west Boulogne-Dunkerque road and their former St. Omer–Calais road. This jolting, grass- and gorse-strewn track led west, parallel to the main road, and Lewrie wondered how Sir Pulteney could even see it in the dark.

A mile or so more, and the track bent northwards, after a time spent in low, wind-sculpted trees and bushes. "We'll rejoin the road to Boulogne, soon," Sir Pulteney told them in a harsh whisper. "Missing any crossroads, where patrols might be, what? A mile and a bit more, and we'll be just above the cove, and stap me if it *still* ain't occupied!"

They had to get off the cart and almost drag it, and the horse, through a shallow ditch that ran alongside the Boulogne road, calming the skitterish old horse 'til it was back on solid ground, then boarded their cart for the last leg.

"Here!" Sir Pulteney cried at last, drawing reins. "Fetch out your things, and we're off, Begad!" They alit, and Plumb looped reins loose and slapped the old horse on the rump to send it plodding down the road on its own. "This way, smartly, now!"

They stumbled over uneven clumps of grass, small bushes, and a field of half-buried rocks, at first on the level, then gradually on a down-slope, northwards. Cape Gris Nez, "Old Grey Nose," stood high to their right, barely made out in starlight and the hint of a moonrise.

Yes! Ahead of them loomed a black, sway-backed mass, that hut that Sir Pulteney had mentioned; crumbling slowly into ruin, its roof half-collapsed, and its low front and back doors seemingly no higher than Lewrie's breast-bone, and the jambs leaning at crazed angles. A bit beyond, the coast was a darker mass, erose and bumpy-looking to either hand, but for a notch a little to their right, back-lit by some lighter something that seemed to stir and glitter in the starlight . . .

"The Channel!" Lewrie exclaimed as loud as he dared. "The sea!" And for the first time since their harum-scarum odyssey had started, he felt a surge of confidence; he was within reach of his proper *milieu*!

Matthieu Fourchette and five Chasseur troopers sat their horses at the crossroad, where the east-west highway met the St. Omer road, about a mile before the *porte* of Calais, with Fourchette showing a lot more impatience than the bemused, softly chatting cavalrymen. He could hear a horse approaching from the south, taking a damnably slow pace, one that almost made him spur out to meet it. At last, a rider emerged from the dark, a *gendarme*. "See anyone on the Saint Omer road?" Fourchette demanded.

"No one, *m'sieur*," the fellow said, making a sketchy salute to him. "It is very quiet, nothing moving this time of night. Even the Jolly Hound tavern had only a few patrons tonight. God help them if they ate there, though, hawn hawn!" he added with a laugh.

"What sort of patrons? Did you enquire?" Fourchette pressed.

"Only two sailors and their whores, the innkeeper reported to me," the local *gendarme* easily related, smiling. "Most likely, they were smugglers, looking for a ship, *m'sieur*. The Jolly Hound is one of the regular *rendezvous* points for smuggling dealings. . . . We keep a wary eye on it, I assure you, *m'sieur*. The innkeeper said that the older one, a *gars* with an eye-patch, told the others that some *Anglais* smuggler didn't come, as agreed, so they would go into Calais and try someone else. They had a two-wheeled horse cart. . . . They should have passed here, *m'sieur*, so surely you have—"

"Four people . . . two couples in a cart?" Fourchette said with a frown, shifting his sore bottom on his damp saddle. "Two sailors and two women? One with an eye-patch, you say?"

"*Oui, m'sieur*," the gendarme told him. "One woman with coppery-red hair, one fellow with black hair, much younger, with a scar down his cheek . . ."

"We passed them on the road south of here this afternoon," the frustrated police agent muttered, half to himself. "Drunk as *aristos* and . . . a *scar*?" *Mademoiselle* de Guilleri said that *Lewrie* had a scar, a faint one, but . . . "You're *sure* the innkeeper heard them say they would go to Calais?"

"*Certainement, m'sieur*," the *gendarme* said, mystified.

"Yet they didn't!" Fourchette spat, thinking hard.

Two couples, four *Anglais*, had dined together at Pontoise, then coached together, disappearing from the face of the earth, it seemed. Two couples had supped at Méru: Major Fleury, his wife and widowed daughter-in-law and . . . a *bandaged* son! The watchers on the Somme bridge had noted four well-dressed people, though oddly travelling in a hay waggon, going to Arras and . . . *morbleu*!

"Disguises!" Fourchette yelped, realising how gulled he'd been. "A whole set of disguises! The two sailors and their women, they are the ones we seek! If they didn't come through this crossroads, then they must be either east or west of us this very instant!"

"The criminals we seek are *disguised, m'sieur*?" the *gendarme* gawped. "If they change again, how can we ever—"

"Trooper!" Fourchette snapped at the nearest cavalryman. "Ride to Major Clary and his party and bring them here at once!" His burst of sudden energy made his horse fractious, beginning to circle. "You! Ride the other direction where we left *mademoiselle* and bring her here! And you . . . ," he ordered in a rush, "fetch that ugly thing Choundas and *his* party. We have need of *all* our men! They're looking for a smuggler to take them cross the Narrow Sea, but not in Calais itself. Someplace along the coast. . . . *Gendarme*, you know this coast well? What of side roads, farm lanes, that lead *round* Calais?"

"There are some, *m'sieur*," the local *gendarme* replied, his own horse beginning to rear and arch. "We . . . my unit and I . . . know *almost* all of

them. I should ride to fetch my officer and more men, to be your guides?"
he asked, eager to please this fellow from the splendours of Paris, and
surely a man of great importance.

"Go, go, go, *vite, vite*! I will wait for you here! Make haste, for the love
of God, though!" Fourchette demanded, in a lather. Poor as this lead was,
and as slim a hope, there was still a chance that the enigmatic foursome
would be in his hands before daylight!

They paused briefly at the tumbledown fisherman's hut to take a breath,
kneeling by its back side. It was a rough log structure, re-enforced with
scrap lumber and driftwood from the beaches. It looked, and smelled, as if
it had been a decade since anyone had even attempted to make use of it, or
maintain it. Sir Pulteney dug into his sea-bag and pulled out a battered old
brass hooded lanthorn and a flintlock tinder-box. "Remain here and rest,
ladies, whilst Captain Lewrie and I head down to the cliffs for a little look-
see," Sir Pulteney said in a harsh whisper, though cackling to himself in
his old manner.

They scampered bent over at the waist, as if dashing through a volley
of fire 'til they reached the edge of the cliffs, to the left of a deep, axed-out
notch that led down to the Channel, a deep, hidden inlet, and a rock-
guarded sand beach. Lewrie looked back and realised that the abandoned
fisherman's hut was below the long slope from their highway above, and
was invisible to any but the most intent searchers following the Boulogne
road.

Whoever fished from here, he most-like broke his damnfool neck! Lewrie
thought, espying a zig-zag path down from the notch, through a maze of
boulders, to the beach. Had the last tenant kept a cockleshell boat drawn
up above high tide, down there, he wondered? Or was he a simple caster
of nets?

"You've keen eyes, Captain Lewrie?" Sir Pulteney asked. "Fear mine
own are of an age, but . . . might there be a schooner out yonder? I *think*
there's a vessel of some kind, but it's hard for me to make out. If you'd be
so kind . . ."

Lewrie lifted his eyes to the vague horizon. The moon was rising at
last, that orb waxed half full, spreading faint blue light on the Channel
waters, illuminating the white chalk cliffs of Dover, far to the north,
twelve or so odd miles away! *Only!* So close, yet . . .

Lewrie cupped his hands round his eyes and strained to scan the sea, quartering near, then closer. "Wait!" he hissed. "Aye, there *is* something out yonder! I think . . ."

There was an eerie, spectral blotch of pale grey, about three or four miles offshore, a ship of some kind. Two trapezoids, like twin fore-and-aft gaff-hung sails? There was a smaller, thinner shape that *might* be a single jib, to the right of the trapezoid shapes, so she was making a long, slow board East'rd, up-Channel.

"Aye, there's something much *like* a schooner," he said at last. "But it could be a smuggler's boat, puttin' in to Calais, a Frenchie, or even one of their navy's *chasse-marées*, lookin' for smugglers. No," he said on second thought.

Chasse-marées had a short mizen, right aft, he recalled. Was it an innocent fishing boat making a long night trawl, to be first to the market come daybreak?

"We must have faith, Captain Lewrie," Sir Pulteney said with rising enthusiasm as he fluffed the lint in the tinder-box, cocked the firelock, and pulled the trigger. On his third try, sparks took light in the lint, which he carefully coaxed with his breath into a fire that caught in the oily rag, which began to glow with dark amber, which yet another breath turned to a flame! He opened the lanthorn and applied the rag to an oily wick . . . which, at last, flared up!

"Zounds!" Sir Pulteney crowed, standing erect, holding up his lanthorn and waving it to and fro for a bit, then he turned it round so the closed back side faced the sea. Rapidly rotating it back and forth, he sent some signal known only to him and one of his old conspirators, then lifted it high once more, the glass-paned side facing outwards.

"*Begad*, sir! Odd's Life, will you look at *that*!" Sir Pulteney yelped, almost leaping in joy as a tiny glim aboard that vessel leapt to life and began to flash a slow reply in a series of rotations much like Sir Pulteney's. "It's our *schooner*, Captain Lewrie. He has *seen* us, and, if God is just, we shall be away before the dawn! Let us go gather our ladies and make our way down to the beach, haw haw!"

Major Clary, Charité de Guilleri, and Guillaume Choundas had responded to Fourchette's urgent summons to join him at the crossroads, Choundas in such bilious haste that he'd demanded a Chasseur to carry him behind his saddle, no matter how painful it was. Now he was incredulous, and raging. "Costumes? Disguises? Pah!" he bleated. "Are we chasing phantoms, chimeras? The *Comédie Française?*" he snarled as Fourchette's suspicions were laid out.

"This Lewrie *salaud* was bandaged at Méru, most likely dismissed at the Somme bridge, and groping a red-headed whore in the back of the cart this afternoon, and we never thought to ask to see his face. But he showed his face at a smugglers' inn, and he had a faint scar. They *tried* to find a smuggler to take them over to England, but they *didn't* . . . they didn't enter Calais or pass this crossroad," Fourchette told them all. "You did not see two sailors and two whores in a cart on the Dunkerque road, Major Clary? Then we must admit that the older man of their party has an intimate knowledge of farm lanes and back roads from here to Paris . . . and that they are very near us, this moment, and desperate for passage. We almost—"

He was interrupted by a lone rider coming from the west, up the road from Boulogne, "*Qui va là?*" the rider called out nervously as he caught a glimpse of their large party.

"Police!" a *Capitaine* Vignon, commander of the local *gendarmes*, barked back. "Who are *you*, damn you?"

"Oh, there you are, *Capitaine*. It is I, *Gendarme* Bossuett," the rider said, spurring up to them and re-slinging his short musketoon. Evidently, the threat of dangerous, fleeing felons, *aristo* conspirators, or cut-throat smugglers had made him edgy.

"Report, immediately," *Capitaine* Vignon snapped.

"Pardon, *Capitaine*, but one cannot be too careful tonight, with so many . . . ," the *gendarme* began with a relieved chuckle.

"Have you seen anyone on the Boulogne road? Two sailors and two women, in a one-horse cart?" Fourchette pressed him.

"I've seen no one, *m'sieur* . . . *citoyen*," the *gendarme* said in confusion as to the proper form of address to use. "But there is a two-wheeled cart, abandoned, about a league back, just grazing along, with the reins . . . I thought it rather . . ."

"*Zut alors! Putain!* We have them!" Fourchette cursed, crowing with glee. "They *did* find a smuggler to carry them away . . . from some beach along the road! *Allez, allez vite*, at the gallop! Where they left the cart, they cannot be far from it on foot!"

Despite the faint moon and starlight, Fourchette spurred into a reckless gallop, leading the party of soldiers and police at a furious pace. Choundas whimpered and howled with pain, clinging desperately to his trooper's back; music to Fourchette's ears, as it was to Clary and Charité, as well!

Once they were over the edge of the cliff, the path down to the beach was not *quite* as steep as Lewrie feared, though it wound like a snake round large coach-sized boulders, in some places so snug between that he had to turn sideways and puff out his breath to squeeze through. At other points the flinty earth, gravel, and loose soil crunched and tumbled as soon as he set foot upon it. In the steepest stretches, someone had long ago used pick and shovel to carve out rough steps down to flatter ledges, before another uncertain descent.

Now below the line of the cliffs, and unable to be seen by any watchers along the road, Sir Pulteney kept the lanthorn lit and open to hasten their progress and to light the ladies' way.

"Thank God our last disguises called for stout old shoes, not slippers," Lady Imogene whispered, between deep breaths.

Halfway down, Lewrie told himself, helping Caroline down a set of steps, then looking out to sea again. That schooner *was* the one Sir Pulteney had arranged, by God! After that mysterious signal, it had hauled its wind and come about to approach the coast, and their notch-like inlet and cove. She was not more than two miles off now, and cautiously slanting shoreward, with a large rowing boat in tow, astern, and dare he imagine that it was already being led round to the schooner's larboard entry-port?

"Not much further, not much longer, all!" Sir Pulteney crowed as they reached the last of the boulders, and a faint solid path down through a dangerous scree slope where the going was all gravel, flat shards, and fist-sized rock where ankles could be turned, bones broken, and skulls smashed in an eyeblink if the way slid in an avalanche.

"There, there's the cart!" Major Denis Clary cried, pointing to the west, caught up in the chase despite his misgivings, as he caught sight of the weary horse trying to feed on the spotty, dry weeds and shrubs by the landward side of the road. The cart was crosswise upon the road, and the poor horse was fortunate that the cart had not gone into one of the ditches.

They drew rein short of the cart. "Is this about where it was first discovered?" Fourchette demanded, wheeling his mount to search for that sluggard dim-wit *gendarme* who'd found it. "Speak up, you!"

He wasn't much of a horseman, so it took the *gendarme* some time to thread his way through the others. "Uhm, near here, *m'sieur*. When I first came across it, it was on the right side of the road, back near a little cart track, uhm—"

"Show us!" Fourchette ordered impatiently. At the walk, they had to re-trace their way about two hundred metres east, 'til the *gendarme* at last pointed to two faint ruts in the poor vegetation. "It was here I saw it, *m'sieur*," the *gendarme* told him. "By this path to the old hut. The one down there, *m'sieur*."

"And you did not think to *explore* the hut?" Capt. Vignon snapped.

"By myself, *Capitaine*? Against four dangerous criminals? *Non*, I rode for re-enforcements. To raise the alarm."

"What about the hut?" Fourchette asked. Vignon quickly informed him that it had been abandoned for a decade or better, caving in upon itself. "And is there a beach down there, below the bluffs, *m'sieur*?"

"*Oui*, there is a beach, a small one," Vignon said. "And there is a path down to it. But *this* useless simpleton—"

"Dismount, everyone, and arm yourselves," Fourchette cried. "We must inspect the hut, find the path, and look for them. They are here, I know it, I feel it!"

Choundas insisted that his Chasseur stay mounted and take him to the edge of the cliffs at once. As armed troopers and policemen crept down the slope to surround the hut, as torches or lanthorns were lit to aid the search, Charité kneed her mount to follow Choundas, and Major Clary, fearing for her safety on the cliff edge, below the hut, where their quarry might shoot at her before the troopers cleared it, trotted his own horse after her, urging her to wait in a harsh whisper . . . to which she paid no heed. She'd drawn one of her long-barrelled pistols, intent on her revenge, as intent as that twisted monster!

Choundas reached the edge of the bluff first. His cavalryman drew rein with a gasp and fumbled for his scabbarded musketoon. One instant later, Charité came up alongside him.

"Here! Down here!" Choundas cried in a feral rasp. "There is a schooner! A boat! They are here! Come quickly!"

Charité used her rein-hand's wrist to draw her pistol to full cock, even though the range was far too great, and pulled the trigger.

CHAPTER THIRTY-ONE

*O*h, Christ on a crutch!" Lewrie groaned as he heard the shot, and the "View, Halloo" from the top of the cliffs. They had been discovered, and the rowing boat was still a half-mile offshore, and they weren't yet on the beach. "This'll be close as dammit."

"Sir, such language . . . ," Sir Pulteney objected, stiffening.

"Bugger me, that's that bastard Choundas up there," Lewrie went on, recognising his crow-caw voice, then Charité's, and paying the prim Sir Pulteney no mind. "And that Charité bitch, t'boot!"

They half-slid the last of the way, in a cloud of dirt, bounding reck-lessly through the last of the scree to hard, bare ground, then to deep, above-the-tideline sand! They would have rushed on to the surf, but for a second shot from above that ricocheted off one of the large boulders at the back of the cove, making them duck quickly into shelter of those boul-ders. "Lewrie! I have you at last!" Choundas howled.

Lewrie dug into his limp, mostly empty sea-bag to pull out the pair of old, used single-shot pistols he'd bought with his last French coin in St. Omer. They were big, blunt, ugly things, akin to the pistols dealt out from the arms chests aboard ship when a boarding action was likely; good for ramming into a foe's stomach or chest and fired, but unpredictable for anything much beyond ten or fifteen feet. "Pray God it'll take 'em about five minutes t'pick their way down that path. I don't s'pose you've a brace o' barkers handy, too, Sir Pulteney?" he said as he quickly loaded both with powder and shot, and primed their pans.

"No, there never was need of them back when I . . . ," Sir Pulteney confessed, huddled over Lady Imogene, who was cowering close against the boulder. "Lived by our wits, d'ye see?" he lamely added.

"Wit's played out," Lewrie snapped. "Got a signal for 'hurry up' to yer schooner? Best make it, if ye do!"

Fortunately, the crew of the rowing boat, the mate conning her in, had heard the shots, had seen the torches and lanthorns atop the cliffs, and were almost bending their ash oars to hasten their pace.

"*Tirez, tirez!*" Choundas was demanding as soon as he was set on solid ground. "Shoot!" he commanded. "Kill them before they get off the beach!" A few Chasseurs obeyed him, firing wildly.

"Hold your fire!" *Capitaine* Vignon ordered his *gendarmes*. "The range is too long, and we are to arrest them!"

"Hold fire!" Major Clary was ordering the Chasseurs in a firmer command voice than Choundas's. "Down the path, *mes amis*, and capture them!"

"No, Denis, no!" Charité shrilled, fumbling her re-loading with her furious haste. "Order your men to fire, for God's sake!"

"Down the path!" Clary ordered again, dismounting and drawing his musketoon from the saddle scabbard. "Right, Fourchette? *Capture* them?"

"Oh, Christ!" Fourchette cursed under his breath. It could've been *so* simple! One couple and two coachmen, buried in an un-marked forest grave! Now four people must die, along with the sailors from that schooner, yet the *ship* would still escape, and all Europe would hear of the First Consul's orders, hear and be outraged! But *taken* and privately executed *later* . . . "Marksmen! Keep them in hiding and away from that boat! *Oui*, capture them, Major Clary!"

"*What? Non*, dammit!" Choundas screeched. "You two . . . *carry* me down to the beach!" he ordered two Chasseurs. "I must be there to see them *dead*!" The Chasseurs looked to Major Clary, who nodded his assent with a sneer, and they hoisted him up, with a musketoon under his legs, and moved towards the head of the path down. Charité, at last re-loaded, dashed ahead of them with the first of the soldiers.

Fourchette shook his head in disbelief as he followed, shoving his way past cavalrymen to catch up with her and Major Clary.

⚓

"Might be able t'pick one or two off and block the path," Lewrie muttered, with one loaded pistol stuck in a pocket of his slop-trousers, and the second in his hand. He rose to a half-crouch to look up-slope. Torches and lanthorns showed him his pursuers' progress; it was damned slow, so far! Above the sounds of the surf, he could make out the noise the French were making, stumbling, tripping, and sliding, and setting off small showers of gravel. There was a surprised shout as someone up there turned his ankle!

Soldiers or *gendarmes* atop the cliff fired at him, and he ducked down again as lead balls spanged off the boulders. Once the volley was spent, he popped up again, taking quick note that the people coming down the path were armed with short musketoons, weapons about as in-accurate as his own pistols, at any decent range.

Yonder t'that boulder, Lewrie schemed; *up t'that big'un, then I will have a good slant at that sharp bend. Can't hope t'hit anyone, but they might waste a volley, duck, and have t're-load. That'd slow 'em down. Do it, damn yer eyes!*

"Hang on a bit . . . be right back," Lewrie told the others, ducking down as another blindly aimed volley came their way.

"Alan, no!" Caroline wailed as he broke cover and ran for the first boulder, her hand trying to snatch at his loose fisherman's smock. "Why must he be such a damned *fool*!" she cried.

Only one or two shots followed him to his first hide, and then Lewrie was up and scrambling to the second. A moment to get his wind back, to calm his twanging nerves, and he stood up, levelling one of his pistols over his left arm to steady it, cocking it, and taking aim.

Bang! and he dropped out of sight. *Spang-wail!* went the ball as it caromed off the rocks by the sharp bend, then the instinctive discharge of seven or eight return shots, and the rattle of balls round his sheltering boulder.

A quick pop-up for a look-see! Soldiers were hunkered down in the boulders, groping for cartridges and ramrods. More shots—from the top of the cliff this time. Once they were spent, Lewrie rose and took aim with his second pistol at a Chasseur with a torch at the head of the pursuit, squeezing himself through the first tight space. He fired and ducked. *Bang!* Then a meaty *Thunk!* and a frightened shout. He'd *hit* one of the bastards!

That summoned another ragged volley from the cliff top, and one from the pursuers on the path, and Lewrie dashed back to that first boulder, then back to rejoin the Plumbs and Caroline.

"*Pinked* one, I think!" he chortled, quickly re-loading pistols. "They're tryin' t'be quick about it, but they're clumsy," he told them. "Frog chivalry! There's two of 'em carryin' Choundas, and more takin' care that Charité don't fall and break her neck . . . please Jesus! One I hit was only at the first tight squeeze, and they'll have t'move him 'fore they get round it."

Another quick peek that drew more fire, and Lewrie put his back to their boulder to look out to sea. The schooner's rowing boat, with eight oarsmen stroking away like the Devil was at the transom, was only 150 yards off, and coming on strong. Another pop-up showed him that the leading French soldier was only halfway down the path, and behind him, there was a jam-up where the Chasseurs had to put Choundas down so he could squeeze through the first tight space on his own.

"Tide's out," Lewrie said. "It'll be round fourty or fifty yards to the boat when it grounds. Be a real dash t'get into her as soon as she grounds, which'll be . . .'bout a minute, or less. They'll not *have* us! When we run, go straight to the boat, no weavin' about, that's useless. Understand me? Caroline?"

Voices above were shouting; oddly, Lewrie could understand every word, for once. *French must be gettin' better,* he thought, sharing a joyful grin with his wife. There was another volley of about a dozen rounds from the cliff top, a ragged later shot from the soldiers on the path. He stood and fired over the boulder, not even bothering to aim this time, just to make them cower . . . to *fear,* and slow down!

He looked at the Plumbs; they were *not* taking this well. Lady Imogene was whey-faced, her teeth chattering. Sir Pulteney, holding her, looked glazed-eyed and ashen in the first hints of false dawn, staring off at nothing.

He claimed *t'be a soldier once!* Lewrie scoffed; *most-like the parade-ground sort, in a* fashionable *regiment, and* their *sort doesn't get sent to battle* that *often. Schooled in arms,* sometime *long before, but . . . playin' chameleon's more his style, not fightin' for his life!*

Lewrie waited out another volley, then rose and fired his other pistol, quickly tumbling down upon his back as a few cleverer French waited for his response and took pot-shots at him.

"Alan!" Caroline yelped, crawling to him.

"I'm *fine*! Get back against the boulder!" he told her, dusting himself off and taking his own advise to scramble back to cover, too, where he began to re-load with what little powder, shot, and wadding he had left; enough for four more shots, total, he reckoned.

The sea, the surf; it didn't look much higher than two-foot waves as the waters funnelled into the inlet and raled upon the sands. A bit choppy, but . . . their salvation was now within fifty yards offshore. Lewrie risked one more peek and saw that a Chasseur officer—damme but wasn't he the one he'd met at Bonaparte's levee?—another one with a torch, Charité, and a weaselly-looking man in a dark suit were at the bottom of the worst of the path, just about to hit the scree-slope. There was Choundas, too, in all his ugliness, past the last squeeze-point and being carried again by two soldiers. It would be a *very* close thing!

Time t'run! Lewrie decided for them all.

"We're breakin' cover, now!" he snapped. "Kiss for luck, m'dear?"

He put his arm round Caroline, she took his face in both hands and kissed him as fiercely as their first night wed; it was hard for Lewrie to break away, to gather his nerve, and let go of her!

"On our feet, ready?" He asked. "Ready, ready . . . *wait!*"

There was yet another volley from the cliff top. Lewrie stood and backed out into the open, bracing himself for any clever bugger up yonder. Presented with a good target at last, those last few clever Frenchmen fired, but, thankfully, they were *gendarmes*, not soldiers, and missed wide of him with their short-barrelled musketoons.

Now for the rest! Lewrie told himself, dancing further out onto the beach, capering and waving his arms. "*Va te faire foutre! Foutre* Napoleon! And God bless King George!" he yelled at the Chasseurs on the path, then lifted one of his pistols and fired upwards, striking a Chasseur carrying a lanthorn in one hand and his musketoon in the other. He yelped, dropped both, and clapped a hand to his thigh, losing his footing. The Chasseur in front of him, trying to aim and fire, was swept off his feet, too, as the first landed on his back, then began to slide down the scree slope, taking the lead man with him in a whirl of arms and legs!

"Shot their bolt!" Lewrie yelled as he rushed back to the rocks, followed by sharp cracks of musket fire and plumes of sand from misses. "Ready, ready, *go!*" With Caroline's hand in his left, and his last pistol in his right, they dashed for the surf line and the boat, which was now pitching in the shallows, not ten yards from grounding!

There were a couple of stray shots chasing them, but the party remained untouched. The deep sand above the tide line dragged at their feet like cold treacle, slowing them, and all the while, weapons were being re-loaded and desperate soldiers were all but throwing themselves down the path and the slope. Lady Imogene hitched up her skirts with both hands to run faster, and Lewrie let go Caroline's hand for her to do the same. Sir Pulteney dodged astern of his wife, to shelter her.

"Kill them, kill them, someone!" Guillaume Choundas was howling.

"On, men, on!" Major Denis Clary was urging with his sword out, his musketoon in his left hand. Yet another Chasseur slipped on loose rock and shale and went tumbling, arses and elbows, to join the first two who'd fallen and who lay at the base of the slope barely moving, still stunned. Clary came to a halt at the top of the scree, fearing that half his borrowed troopers would break their necks or legs if they went on.

Charité half-slid to a stop beside him, eyes wild and hair dishevelled, panting open-mouthed at the exertions. Fourchette thumped to a halt with them, too, then came another Chasseur with a torch.

"It's too steep to . . . ," Clary said, dry-mouthed.

"Shoot him!" Fourchette ordered. "You soldiers, *shoot* him!"

"Not loaded, *m'sieur*," the torch-bearer told him, fumbling for car-tridges.

"Shoot *which* one, *m'sieur*?" a second asked, also re-loading.

"The younger man, shoot *him*!" Fourchette snarled, nigh crazed. "Major Clary, you are loaded?"

"*Oui*, shoot him, Denis!" Charité shrilly demanded.

"I am loaded, *m'sieur*," Clary calmly told Fourchette. "But I will take no part in murder. Here . . . do it yourself," he added as he shoved his weapon at the police agent.

"They're almost in the boat!" Guillaume Choundas screamed with frustration as he stumped down to join them at last, leaning on one of the Chasseurs who had been carrying him. "Someone do *something* for God's sake!" he said, punching the soldier in the arm to urge him to raise his musketoon and use it.

As if in answer, the *gendarmes* atop the cliff let off a ragged volley, but at that range, their shots only struck sand-plumes round the fleeing *Anglais*, raised a waterspout or two somewhat close to the boat, which was now grounding, but fell wide of their marks. Choundas was almost whim-pering with rage, grinding what few teeth remained as the bow men sprang from the rowing boat into waist-deep water to steady it and help the escapees aboard!

Fourchette sneered at Major Clary's ill-placed ideas of honour and tugged the lock of the musketoon to full cock, then put it to his shoulder.

He reckoned himself a *decent* shot with a pistol or musket, and this *fumier* Lewrie would not be the first man he had had to shoot down, but most of his kills had been at much closer range. He put the rudimentary notch rear sight and front blade sight in line, on Lewrie's back, just at the top of his spine, trying to lead his target as he ran the last few yards to the waiting boat. A down-hill shot, fifty *mètres* or more off? Should he not hold even higher, to allow for the bullet-drop? he wondered, then lifted the sights to aim at the top of Lewrie's skull. Fourchette took a deep, steadying breath and let it out slowly, gently stroking the trigger . . . which did not move even a *millimètre* rearward. His own weapons were made by a talented Parisian gunsmith, and this musketoon was a crude, mass-produced military firearm. More pressure on the trigger, *then* the lock released with an audible *clunk*, then . . . *Bang!*

Sir Pulteney might not have been an impressive figure of a man, but he was wiry; when he and Lady Imogene reached the boat, he lifted her from behind, not breaking stride, and practically hurled her into the arms of the second-tier oarsmen, then scrambled over the larboard side, tumbling into the boat head-down. Lewrie reached it a second later, hoisting Caroline with both hands on her waist, his face in the small of her back for a second as a starboard oarsman took her by her upper arms to hoist her up and over the gunnel.

Sailors' shouts, the mate's orders by the tiller, the thud and rushing hiss of surf and . . . a *buzz-hum!* and then a meaty *thunk* of a bullet. Hot wetness sprayed his face, blinding him.

Christ, I'm killed! he thought, amazed that he'd neither heard the fatal shot nor felt the hammer-blow impact of his death.

"Sweet Jesus, *no!*" Lady Imogene was screaming.

"'Em murd'rin' Frog bashtits!" a sailor cursed while two men seized him by his arms and armpits and threw him into the boat, down onto the sole, with his legs atop a thwart.

"Alan?" a faint, weak, and fearful cry, almost lost in the rale of the next wave breaking on the beach, a phantom voice.

Go game! Lewrie told himself; *make a brave face for her!*

Lewrie lifted a hand from the sole, dripping with seawater from the splashing of the chop, and swabbed his face, wondering when pain would come. His hands came away almost black in the false dawn light.

What the Devil? If my head's blown open, how am I still able t'see? he goggled. Oarsmen were sitting back down to back-water, some were poling off the sand, and he was getting trampled, so he grasped the next-aft thwart and rose to his knees.

"We get her aboard quickly," someone aft was saying, "we might save her . . . even with no surgeon aboard."

"Alan?" came that phantom cry again, weaker and more fearful.

"What? Caroline? Good God!" he cried, scrambling aft to her. She lay on her back in an inch or two of seawater in the sole, head and shoulders in Lady Imogene's lap. "No! No, no!"

Her light-coloured blouse, so cheery that morning, was covered in large nigh-black stains that slowly spread, even as he crawled to her. Lady Imogene was pressing her shawl and bright kerchief to try and staunch the flood at its source, but there was so swift an out-welling that both cloths had turned almost completely dark, too!

"Caroline!" Lewrie cried as he got to her and took her hands in his. A thin trickle of blood sprang from the corner of her mouth, and she coughed, spasming and gasping. Her eyes opened and she looked up at him, eyes wide for a moment, and her hands squeezed back, then lost their strength. She let out a long sigh, then lay very still.

"Caroline?" Lewrie croaked, gathering her to his chest, knowing she was gone. "God damn them, God *damn* them!"

The boat was now off the sands, one bank of oarsmen stroking ahead, the other still backing water to turn her bows out to sea, and the mate at the tiller was judging the best moment to put the helm over between incoming waves, so she would not be upset, spinning her in her own length before both sides of oarsmen could row together.

"You bastards!" Lewrie howled, unaccustomed tears in his eyes. "You murderin' *bitch*, Charité! You foul *child*-fucker, Choundas!" he raged, searching for the pistol he'd lost, but he'd dropped it when he'd lifted Caroline into the boat. "Any guns aboard? *Any* sort of gun!"

"Aye, we've . . . ," the mate said, jutting his chin towards a pair of muskets near him, intent on his steering.

Lewrie snatched one up, jerked from the muzzle the cork used to keep out the damp, and tore off the greasy rag that sheltered the fire-lock and primed pan. He scrambled right aft to the transom, crowding the mate at the tiller, to kneel and drag the lock to half-cock, and check the powder in the pan and the tightness of the flint clasped in the dog's jaws.

The boat was rowing out now, swooping wildly as the incoming waves lifted her bows and the oarsmen dragged her through the troughs, making the stern soar upwards in turn. He braced one foot on the aft end of the sole boards and the vertical stub of the keel where it emerged. He had to try!

"Lewrie, no, what matters, it will make no difference!" Plumb was cautioning him.

He dashed a hand over his eyes once more, squinting away those tears; he had grim work to do. Then he'd weep. "Stop yer bloody gob!" he told Sir Pulteney.

There were several French Chasseurs on the beach now, some of them tending to their fellows who had slid or tumbled there, none with a weapon at the ready, as if they realised that firing would be pointless. With them was a man in a dark suit and narrow-brimmed hat, and *he* held a weapon at high port-arms. Lewrie could conjure that spent powder smoke still fumed from its barrel, but . . . up above the beach, at the top of the scree slope stood that Major of Chasseurs, Charité de Guilleri, and that bastard Choundas, who was crowing and waving his cane in triumph.

Seventy, eighty yards? Lewrie gaged it; *shootin' uphill, so if I take one of 'em . . . the man on the beach's closer. Which? Who do I kill? Who deserves it most? Please, Jesus, help me shoot true, help me kill just* one of 'em!

"We are damned," Major Clary whispered.

"Fouché will be furious, *oui*," Charité numbly agreed, "and the First Consul . . . ," she trailed off, numb and drained and horrified by how badly her vengeance had gone amiss.

"I speak of God and our *souls, mademoiselle*," Clary said with a rasp of anger. "*Mon Dieu*, does he intend to *shoot* at us? *Bon!*" Clary said, sheathing his sword and standing to attention, chest offered as a target.

"Is she *dead*, Lewrie?" Guillaume Choundas was cackling and huzzahing. "Do *you* suffer now, hawn hawn? *Weep*, lament! Suffer as I, *vous fumier!*"

Charité suddenly felt ill, sick at her stomach and exhausted beyond imagining. Even her long desire to kill Lewrie was gone, flown away, and all she felt was deep sadness, and revulsion to be a part of the deed, and those with whom she had shared it, and at everything—they had failed.

The boat was now over hundred *mètres* offshore, and there was nothing to stop it, short of a miracle. It was pitching and swooping wildly, yet Lewrie was still aiming at them? Charité took one step away from Denis

Clary and squared her own shoulders to make herself an open target, and crossed herself for the first time in a long, cynical time, in expiation.

There was a sudden tiny bloom of gunsmoke from the boat's stern-sheets, whipped quickly away by the wind.

"Stupid!" Choundas yelled seaward. "You always were a hopelessly stupid *salaud*, Lewrie! Mistaking muscle for brains! See your last hope dashed, and fear for my revenge! I will get you in the end. *Suffer*, and . . . *Eee!*"

Thunk! as lead slammed into flesh and bone! Choundas reeled on his good leg for a moment, looking down at the blood spurting from his chest before toppling forward, turning a clumsy pirouette as he slid down to the beach in a shower of loosed gravel and flinty stones, going over and over, head then feet, before thudding to a stop at the foot of the slope in the deep sand, his cloak spread out like a shroud and his corpse resembling a pile of cast-off laundry.

Major Clary let out a whoosh of relief, agog that *anyone* could kill with a smooth-bore musket at that range . . . and delighted that he had not been this Lewrie's mark!

"You see, *mademoiselle*, there *is* a judgmental God!" he said in wry delight, beginning to whoop with laughter for a moment. "We must thank Him for removing that *thing* from the earth. And pray that we've been allowed to live for a good reason."

"Denis?" Charité said, amazed herself, smiling and shuddering to be spared, as well. She reached out a hand to her *amour*. If Denis was now in good spirits, would he not wish to . . . ?

"*Non*," Major Clary told her with a sad shake of his head, that good humour vanishing as quickly as the gunsmoke. "I now bid you *adieu, mademoiselle. Au revoir.*" With that he turned and began to trudge back to the top of the cliff, summoning Chasseurs to help their injured comrades.

Below on the beach, Matthieu Fourchette lifted his re-loaded musketoon to his shoulder, but gave it up as hopeless after a second of thought. He un-cocked it and handed it to one of the dazed soldiers. There would be Hell to pay when he reported this fiasco to Minister Fouché. They'd killed a *woman* yet let the others escape to England, where news of the entire pursuit, Napoleon's involvement, and the murder would enflame British, perhaps world, outrage.

Fourchette heaved a deep sigh, contemplating the utter ruin of his promising career, shrugging and shaking his head sorrowfully, as he turned to face the cliffs, wondering if he should cross over the frontier and lose himself in the Germanies.

"What's that?" he asked a woozy Chasseur, who was aiding one of his mates with a twisted ankle, as he spotted the bundle of clothing.

"That's that *hideux* fellow, sir," the Chasseur told him, rather cheerfully. "Amazing, that shot. Be a trial . . . to get what's left of him back to the top of the cliffs."

"Don't bother," Fourchette told the soldier. "Leave him here, and let the crabs and gulls have him." And wondered if he could couch his report to place some of the blame for his failure on Choundas . . . well, a bit of it!

He went past the corpse, struggling to make his way up through the loose scree slope.

The Chasseurs, more practical and realistic, took a little time to loot Choundas's pockets, though they found little of value; seventy francs, a poor watch, some *cigarros*, a flint tinder-box, and a decent pistol with all accoutrements. The ogre's cane wasn't even scratched, and it, at least, was of good quality.

Then they walked away from him, too.

BOOK IV

Quid primum deserte querar?

Forlorn, what first shall I lament?

PUBLIUS VERGILIUS MARO,
AENID, BOOK IV, 677

CHAPTER THIRTY-TWO

*T*hough it was after Easter, in the year of Our Lord 1803, there was still need of a fire in the hearth in the office/library with its many large windows and French doors overlooking the side yards and the gardens. It was a bright day, if still a cool one, so no candles or oil lamp was necessary for Alan Lewrie to read the latest letters that had come, or take pen, ink-pot, and stationery and reply to them. The only sound in the comfortably well-furnished room was the ticking of a mantel clock, and the occasional *skritch* of his steel-nib pen.

The house itself was quiet, far too quiet and yawningly empty to suit him, with the formal parlour and larger dining room furniture under protective sheeting, Sewallis's and Hugh's bed chambers abovestairs un-used now they were back at their school, and Charlotte the only child still residing at home . . . though of late she had spent the bulk of her time with his brother-in-law Governour Chiswick and his wife, Millicent, and their children at their estate.

Lewrie felt no need to break his fast, dine, or sup in the big dining room, no call to set foot in that wing of the house; there were no visitors calling who could not be received in the smaller breakfast room, or this office. His world had shrunk to the foyer, the landing and stairs, his office, the kitchens and pantry, and his and . . . *their* large bed-chamber. In point of fact, Lewrie preferred to pass most of his days outside, or somewhere else; the stables and barns, on a long ride daily over his 160 acres, or to town and the Olde Ploughman.

Lighting himself up to bed each night with a three-candle lamp, with the last bustling sounds from the kitchen and scullery over, he found that the house in which he once took so much pride felt more like a tomb . . . an eldritch and eerie one. All winter and into the spring since he had brought Caroline home, the house at night let out odd wooden groans or ticks. Latched shutters rattled even in light winds, and there seemed an accusatory empty silence.

Reading in bed far into the night and partaking of perhaps a glass or two of brandy beyond his usual custom, he would look over to see *her* armoire and *her* vanity, empty of Caroline's clothing and things, and drawers in the vanity stripped to the last hair-curler or hat-pin, yet . . . they still stood in place, in what seemed to him to be mute condemnation.

The Plumbs' hired schooner had not sailed for Dover, but for Portsmouth, at Lewrie's request, to shorten Caroline's final journey to the Chiswick family plot in mossy old St. George's graveyard, in Anglesgreen, cutting a week off the time it would take to coach from Dover to Surrey.

In Portsmouth, one could also discover better carpenters who could fashion a finer coffin. There were more fabric shops for lining that coffin, and for a proper shroud, and professionals knowledgeable at the dismal death trade. And there would be perfume shops.

Lewrie had had no experience with shore funerals and the needs of the dead. When a sailor perished at sea, his corpse was washed by his messmates and the loblolly boys, sewn into a scrap-canvas shroud with rusty, pitted old round-shot at his feet to speed him to the ocean floor; a last stitch was taken through his nose to prove that he truly was gone. The sea-burial was done that very day, with the hands mustered, the way off the ship and her yards canted a'cock-bill; a service read from the Book of Common Prayer before the dead man was tipped off the mess table from beneath the flag, in brief honour.

In the heat of battle, sometimes the slain didn't even get that, and were passed out a lee gun-port so the sight of dead shipmates did not un-man or discourage the rest; then, only the names were read for their remembrance and honour.

There was no time for rot to set in.

Dear God, but that had been hard for Lewrie to bear! Despite a brief bustle of aid from the Plumbs, *too* damned many condolences and too much hand-wringing, "can you ever forgive us?" once too often, and watery, goose-berry-eyed speculations on what had gone wrong for the first time in *hundreds* of successful escapes, it was up to Lewrie to see her home, on his own. With the liberal use of a whole bottle of *eau de cologne* and nigh a bushel-basket of fresh-cut flowers in the coffin with her, he had set off with a dray waggon, riding beside the teamster, whilst the Plumbs had set off for London—thank God!—swearing that the news of Caroline's murder would set the nation afire, that they would speak to their friend, the Prince of Wales, etc. and etc., 'til he was heartily sick of the sight of them!

Travelling on the waggon seat, necessity though it was, made him cringe and burn with shame, though, for . . . how could he wish to bolt from a loved one, how could he do all the proper things if he wished that *he* had been the swift rider sent on ahead to alert the family and the vicar at St. George's and his sexton, who would dig the grave, instead of making the trip with a scented handkerchief pressed to his nose and fighting the continual urge to gag?

Once he was in Anglesgreen, others thankfully took charge, and Lewrie had been spared any more of the sorrowful details 'til the morning of the church service, and Caroline Chiswisk Lewrie's burial beside her parents, Sewallis Sr. and Charlotte. Even her old, hard-hearted and skin-flint uncle, Phineas Chiswick, had appeared to be moved to tears . . . or a convincing sham for family and village, for he'd never cared very much to be saddled with his distant North Carolina relatives who had fled at the end of the Revolution and had showed up on his doorstep destitute and with nowhere else to turn.

There was yet another cause to make Lewrie squirm, to this day; in church or at the graveside, he could not mourn her death so much as he grieved for how he had *failed* her, that he had not been man enough, or clever enough, to *save* her, and . . . that he had not been *husband* enough to make her life content and easy! He could easily conjure that what their vicar had said was ruefully true, in a sense; that Caroline was now at peace in Heaven . . . a welcome peace to be *shot* of him, at last!

As common as death was, *how* she, Caroline, had perished had outraged everyone, re-kindling the instinctive mistrust and hatred of the French to a white-hot blaze in Anglesgreen, for Caroline always had been quite popular with everyone . . . with the possible exceptions of Uncle

Phineas and Sir Romney Embleton's son, Harry, who had courted her after a fashion before Lewrie had come along and swept her away, and had
never forgiven either of them for refusing what he had desired.

Lewrie suspected that it had been Harry who had started a rumour that
her death had been Lewrie's fault for dragging her over to France and
enflaming Bonaparte's wrath by being his usual head-strong and reckless
self—a malicious slur that, unfortunately, had found a fertile field with
Uncle Phineas, his brother-in-law Governour Chiswick, who'd never
been in favour of the match, and, sadly, through Governour, his own
daughter, Charlotte.

Lewrie had thought it done after a week, and all that was left was to
order her headstone, but . . . people learning of her funeral too late to attend coached to Anglesgreen to console him. Anthony Langlie, his former First Lieutenant in HMS *Proteus,* and his wife, Lewrie's former
orphaned French ward, Sophie de Maubeuge, had come up from Kent to
see him. His other, much more likable brother-in-law, Burgess Chiswick,
and his new wife, Theadora, had come a week after, his letter to them
having arrived late at the barracks of Burgess's regiment.

And there were so many letters, some coming *months* later as word
crept its way from London papers to provincial papers in the far corners of
Great Britain, or overseas, each new missive clawing at the scabs, to the
point that he dreaded the arrival of a post rider or a mail coach.

Old shipmates like Commodore Nicely from his days in the West Indies, Commodore Ayscough and Captain Thomas Charlton; people from
his Midshipman days like Captain Keith Ashburn, former officers aboard
his various commands, like Ralph Knolles, D'arcy Gamble, Fox and Farley of HMS *Thermopylae,* former Sailing Masters and Mids, even one or
two Pursers had written, and, despite Lewrie's urge to crumple the letters
and toss them into the fireplace, he'd kept them, pressed flat together in a
shallow wood box . . . if only to save the home addresses after years with
no correspondence for the lack of them.

His solicitor, his former barrister from his trial, his banker at Coutts',
Zachariah Twigg and Matthew Mountjoy at the Foreign Office, even
Jemmy Peel, still up to something shady for King and Country in the
Germanies, had written. Eudoxia Durschenko had penned a sympathetic
letter (her command of English much improved) just before the start of
Daniel Wigmore's Peripatetic Extravaganza's first grand tour through
Europe in years; Eudoxia was sure that the circus and theatrical troupe
would score a smashing season. She *said* that her papa, Arslan Artimovitch,

sent his condolences, but Lewrie thought it a kindly lie; the one-eyed old lion tamer hated him worse than Satan hated Holy Water!

Alan Lewrie sanded the last of his correspondence, then folded it and sealed it with wax. One last dip of the pen in the ink-well and the address was done. He looked up from his desk to a sideboard, on which rested a silver tray and several cut-glass decanters; one for brandy, one for claret, and one filled with Kentucky bourbon whisky. He glanced at the mantel clock. It lacked half an hour to noon. He shook his head, thinking that he'd done too much of that, of late, to fill the hours of solitary quiet . . . to stave off the feeling that he now resided in a mausoleum. Ring for a cup of coffee? No.

He gathered up his letters and went out into the foyer, on his way towards the back entrance past the kitchens, but paused, once there, looking into the parlour and dining room at the cloth-shrouded furniture. The heavy drapes had been taken down and beaten clean, and the lighter summer drapes now graced the windows, drawn back to let light in, and the shutters open for the day. For a brief moment, he considered selling up and moving on . . . to flee this house.

'Tween the wars, when it was built, it had been to her desires of what a proper home should be, when he'd paid off HMS *Alacrity* and settled in Anglesgreen. Caroline had made allowances for his need for that office/study/library he'd just left, but the builder had deferred to her on almost everything else. *She'd* chosen the paint for all the rooms; *she'd* selected the new furniture and the fabrics for the new chairs and settees, the fabrics and colours to re-upholster their old pieces. They were *Caroline's* drapes, tablecloths, china pattern, and table ware, *her* collected knick-knacks and *objets d'art*, the paintings on the walls, of pastorals and Greco-Roman ruins, the portraits of the children and her kin; save for a couple of nautical prints and a portrait of Lewrie done way back when he was a Lieutenant on Antigua, there was little sign that he had ever lived there!

In point of fact, he ruefully thought, he had not lived there *much*. A few brief years from '89 to '93, and he was back at sea with active commissions, with barely six weeks at home between them. Last winter, before they'd gone to Paris, was the longest he'd spent under this roof in nigh twenty years!

Can't sell up, he realised; *the children need their homeplace. Some roots, and a* sense *of place. Even if I . . . don't.*

"Your pardon, sir, but you'll be havin' your dinner before you post your letters today?" the cook, Mrs. Gower, intruded on his musings as she bustled from the kitchen. "Steak and kidney pie!" she tempted.

"No, long as I'm to town, I'll get something at the Ploughman," he told her. "Does it keep, that might make a good supper, though."

"La, and I've a brace o' rabbits your man Furfy snared in the back-garden this mornin', sir," Mrs. Gower objected cheerfully. "And them skinned and all, and steepin' in an herb broth for your supper already."

"Well, don't let Phineas Chiswick know of 'em," Lewrie japed. Legally speaking, Lewrie rented his land as a tenant, not freeholding, and had no right to shoot, trap, or snare any game that strayed upon his property; those rabbits were Chiswick rabbits. Fish in the rills and creek, in the dammed-up stock pond, were Chiswick fish! "Rabbit does sound tasty, and we do have to . . . eat the evidence of Furfy's poaching. Let him and Desmond enjoy the pie."

One of the first things he'd done, once the first fortnight of mourning was over, was to dismiss that dour Mrs. Calder as housekeeper and semi-tyrant, with two month's wages. Caroline's maidservant had been let go, too, though with half a year's salary and her choice of Caroline's clothing, those that he had not donated to the church and the parish Winter charity, or let Governour's wife, Millicent, have.

Now his domestic staff was reduced to Mrs. Gower and her husband, who served as handyman, gardener, and doorman, should any caller ride up or knock. Little Charlotte still needed a maid-and-governess in one, and Mrs. Gower had need of a scullery maid and one maid-of-all-work to keep up with the cleaning, but, as for him, he felt no need for a manservant. He had Liam Desmond and Patrick Furfy, his former Cox'n and a sailor off his last three ships, to see to everything else about the stables, barns, the livestock, and the crops, with day labourers hired on as needed. It was not due to the expense of keeping a staff that he'd pared them down; it was rather that the presence of so many people bustling about the house, no matter how downcast or cheerful, *rankled* him!

Lewrie went on past the kitchens, still-room, and pantry, to the rear exit, and more of Caroline's handiwork. Her herb plots and her meticulously arranged flower garden, with the bricked terrace and the bricked walks through it, under the vine-covered pergola where wicker chairs and a settee sat ready for mid-morning contemplation or afternoon tea. A bit further out to the right there was another gathering of wood-slat furniture under the spreading oak boughs, which provided a splendid view of the fields and woods, the barn, stables, and stock-pens and paddocks.

"Aye, and there ye be, Cap'm," Liam Desmond called out as he led Anson, Lewrie's favourite horse, from the stable doors, saddled up and ready to go. "He's ready for ye, faith. Missed his mornin' ride, and that eager for a trot t'town, sure."

"Morning, Desmond . . . Furfy," he added to the good-natured side of beef who was Desmond's shadow. "Lashin's of steak and kidney pie for dinner, lads. And Furfy? We'll have your rabbits for supper, so the magistrate won't learn of it," he added with a wink as he took the reins. "Think we should bury the bones, once we're done with 'em?"

"Master Sewallis's dogs'd 'preciate 'em more, sor," Furfy said, looking furtive over his misdeed. "They must be a goodly warren about, though, for s'many rabbits raidin' th' gardens, arrah, sor. Mebbe we . . . I should keep snares set?"

"Damnedest thing, Furfy," Lewrie said as he swung aboard. "At this moment, I think I've gone deaf! Couldn't hear a thing ye said."

"I meant t'say, sor . . . ," Furfy began before Desmond poked him in the ribs. "Oh! Git yer meanin', sure, Cap'm Lewrie."

"Forget yer hat, sor?" Desmond pointed out.

"Oh. No threat o' rain, today, so . . . ," Lewrie said, shrugging and peering at the sky. "I can live without. Later, lads." A flick of the reins, a cluck, and a press of his heels on Anson's flanks, and he was off round the house to the circular driveway and the gravelled lane down to the junction and the bridge at an easy trot, posting in the stirrups. Though the day was cool, the breeze felt good on his scalp, and the sunshine scintillating through the fully leafed trees was delightful.

And it struck him then that the only time he felt like japing or smiling was when he was astride a horse . . . away from there.

CHAPTER THIRTY-THREE

*W*hy, Captain Lewrie!" Maggie Cony exclaimed as he entered the Olde Ploughman. "Just in time for the mail coach, and steak and kidney pie, t'boot! And look who's just arrived not a tick ago! My, but we must cut you a *goodly* portion and put some meat on your bones again."

"Hallo, son," Sir Hugo St. George Willoughby, seated by himself at a table near a side window, cordially said, hoisting a mug of ale in invitation.

"Father," Lewrie replied, crossing the busy dining room to join him at his table, and plunk himself down in a wood chair. "I wondered whose carriage that was, out yonder. What brings you down from town? Alone?" he added in a softer voice, with a raised eyebrow. Though Sir Hugo was now of an age, and played a Publick Sham of upright respectability, the lascivious old rogue's penchant for doing "the needful" with any courtesan, or mistress who would go "under his protection" still thrived quite nicely, and his fortune in Hindoo loot from his time in the East India Company Army assured him willing, even fetching, young things . . . some of whom fortunate enough to enjoy his offer of a fortnight of "hospitality" at his country estate, Dun Roman.

"Alone, aye, this time," Sir Hugo admitted with a shrug and a roll of his eyes, "though there's a delightful new one in London. As to my business here, why, I came to see *you*, lad. See how you're coping . . . speak of a few matters. Mistress Cony's right, ye know," his father added, reaching out to pluck Lewrie's coat and cocking his head in survey. "Ye *have* lost some weight. Several good feeds're what ye need. Seen the latest papers?"

"Ah, some," Lewrie replied as one of the waitresses brought him a brimming pint mug of the Ploughman's famed sale. "Thankee" for the waitress, who was a fetching brunette, and "What about the papers?" to his father. "Have I missed something or other?"

"Evidently," Sir Hugo drawled. "This business over Alexandria and Malta . . . the French ain't happy, and neither's our government."

"Bugger the French!" Lewrie snapped, which statement aroused a chorus of Amen and a few choicer curses from the public house's diners.

"Spoke with a few people at Horse Guards." Sir Hugo leaned over closer to impart his rumour in a guarded voice. "The general sense is that Pitt and his people—Windham, Grenville, and that crowd—and the King himself *want* the war t'start up again. The Prime Minister, Addington, is leanin' that way, and his cabinet, too. First week of March, the King said in his address that the militia should be called out, and ten thousand more men called to the Navy, hey?"

"Must've missed that'un," Lewrie said after a deep quaff of ale. And feeling a bit of hope. "But so many people were just *sick* of the war, the shortages and taxes . . ."

"England *ain't* one o' those damned *democracies*, as mob-driven as ancient Greeks!" Sir Hugo hooted mirthlessly. "And thank God for that! Recall what that scribbler Edmund Burke wrote . . . that intercourse with the French is more terrible than fightin' 'em? Give 'em leave and they'll spread their revolutionary ideas *everywhere*. Uhm, 'The spread of her doctrines . . . are the most dreadful of her arms'?" he quoted.

"Missed that'un, too," Lewrie replied, cocking his head at his sire. "Damme, when did *you* take up readin' so much?"

"I'm a retired gentleman o' means," Sir Hugo snickered back, "a fellow with the *time* for it . . .'mongst other, more pleasant things, o' course. At any rate, Bonaparte and the Frogs ain't happy, as I say. He evacuated Taranto, but we're still in Alexandria and Malta, a year after we were s'posed t'turn 'em over to the Turks, and the French. We gave France back her West Indies colonies, and we got Trinidad and Ceylon, but lately . . ."

"And the French are *more* than welcome to Saint Domingue," Lewrie stuck in. "Toussaint L'Ouverture and his generals're killin' Frogs by the ship-load, even if the French did capture the old bugger and rout his men.

They're *still* givin' General Leclerc fits in the jungles . . . ambushin' anything smaller than a brigade. That and Yellow Jack—"

"Of late, Addington's added Holland and Switzerland to our objections," Sir Hugo continued, "and Piedmont in Italy. Bonaparte'll get Malta *ten years* from now, if he pulls his armies out and lets the Dutch and the Swiss alone, and Bonaparte *can't* agree *t'that.* He's dead set on riggin' up all these damned republics, with his eyes on all of Europe, eventually. It's comin', Alan me son, it's comin', for sure.

"And, if it's as much joy t'you as it was t'me," Sir Hugo added with a grin, "there's word that General Leclerc, Bonaparte's brother-in-law, died of a tropic fever on Saint Domingue. People also told me that there's a General . . . or Marshal . . . Victor with a large army in Holland . . . Batavian *Republic!*" his father spat, "ready t'sail for the Indies. Perhaps Bonaparte will end up killin' as many French soldiers as Henry Dundas did of ours when he was Secretary of State at War, ha!"

"That'd be lovely," Lewrie wolfishly agreed. Before, his hatred of the French was personal, limited to only a few individuals he'd met and opposed face-to-face. Now, though . . . it was "damn 'em all, root and branch," with Napoleon Bonaparte at the top of his list.

"Horse Guards *rarely* talks with the Admiralty," Sir Hugo drolly said, "but there have been *some* discussions I've been made privy to . . . some folderol over increasing the size of the Royal Marines for duties at sea with the transfer of a battalion of foot to the Navy, doled out in platoons per each ship. Heard anything from the Navy yourself?"

"About another active commission? No," Lewrie had to tell him. "Dear as I *wish* it . . . give me something to *do* again."

"You very well may, soon," his father attempted to assure him. The old rascal had risen to Major-General and the senior military officer to the Lord-Lieutenant of Surrey for a brief time during the Nore and Spithead naval mutinies, when for a time it had looked as if French Jacobin revolution would come to England, too, and he'd done the Crown yeoman service in 1797. Retired he might be, but he was still on the Army List, and he still had good connexions, so . . . perhaps he was not being kind. Not that Lewrie could remember too many instances in their spotty past when Sir Hugo St. George Willoughby had *been* kind! *Only if it didn't cost him tuppence!* Lewrie not-so-fondly thought.

"Another matter . . . ," Sir Hugo said, after finishing his ale and waving for another. "Hugh's nigh thirteen, now. If the war begins again, I might be able to wangle him his 'set of colours' with a good regiment . . .

Ensign, first. Bit young for a Lieutenant . . . though, there are a fair number o' twelve-year-old Captains, if their parents have enough 'blunt' to purchase their commissions. Can't make Brigadier, or higher, if ye start late, ye know."

Lewrie delayed his answer by paying attention to his ale. They had spoken of this before, years ago, and after the funeral, before Hugh and Sewallis had had to return to their public school.

"I want to kill Frenchmen, father," Hugh had said in a shudder of barely controlled emotion, tears at the corner of his eyes. "If we ever fight them again, I wish to go to sea, like you, and kill as many of them as *ever* I may!"

And even Sewallis, his usually subdued and quiet first-born, had evinced stony-hearted anger, had whispered "Amen to that!" and stated *his* desire to avenge his mother. "Blood for blood," he'd whispered.

"A good shot, a decent swordsman, and possessed of a splendid seat," Sir Hugo reminded Lewrie. "Intelligent *and* daring is our Hugh. Active . . . a keen sportsman? Make a grand officer. Hmm?"

"He wants t'be me," Lewrie told the old rogue. "He'd prefer to be a Midshipman. When answering all those letters of condolence from my fellow captains and such, I requested they keep Hugh in mind, should they get a ship, in future. Thankee for the offer, but . . . his heart's set on the Navy. So he can kill a shit-pot o' Frogs, he said."

"Well then, I'll say no more about it," Sir Hugo said with a bit of a sigh. "Least Hugh's future's assured. And Sewallis'll inherit, so more schoolin's more suitable for him. University, perhaps?"

"'Ere ye go, sirs!" the fetching new brunette waitress declared as she delivered two heaping plates of steak and kidney pie, and a new round of ale. There was fresh white bread, lashings of butter with it, mashed potatoes with spring peas, and, the girl promised, figgy-dowdy for sweets, after. "Any o' ye gentlemen need anything, just call out!"

"Public schools're ruin enough for young lads," Lewrie objected with a growl. "University's a *good* deal worse."

After leaving the Olde Ploughman, Sir Hugo wished to go on out to his estate, and invited Lewrie to join him in his coach. Lewrie agreed to join him, but wished to exercise Anson, so he would ride by the coach instead, perhaps canter on ahead and meet him there.

His father had sent letters on to alert his house staff to have everything ready for his arrival from London. As his coach rolled to a stop in front of the wide and deep front gallery of the low, rambling one-storey *bungalow* built in imitation of an East India Company cantonment, there was his butler, cook, estate agent, stableman and groom, a brace of gamekeepers, four maids-of-all-work, some ten- or twelve-year-old lads who would assist at anything from the barns to the kitchens, and Sir Hugo's long-time Army orderly and manservant, the one-eyed old Sikh Trilochan Singh. Bows and curtsies, doffed hats, and wide smiles all round as the carriage box and boot were un-loaded, and the horses led off to the stables. Singh saluted and stamped boots, *sepoy* fashion.

"Better than I thought, what hey, Singh?" Sir Hugo exclaimed in joy over his latest improvements. "Damme, but the flowerin' bushes and such *do* make the place attractive." There were even hanging baskets of some sort of flowers strung from the gallery's overhead porch beams.

The summer wicker or bamboo furniture had been set out on the gallery, along with a couple of rope hammocks, too; both of them large enough to accommodate two people at a time.

Plan t'strum a girl in one of 'em? Lewrie had to think, grinning as he had a mental picture of a full-moon romp in the nude, neighbours and house staff bedamned. *Well, he* is *set in the middle of all these acres,* he told himself; *maybe he could pull it off with no one wiser.*

"Some o' your cool tea, here on the gallery?" Sir Hugo suggested. "Must admit, it's refreshin', that notion o' yours, so I took it up."

"Capital," Lewrie agreed, taking a seat as the tea was ordered.

"Ah, the country!" Sir Hugo said with a happy sigh, sprawling on a wicker settee and its canvas-covered padding, one booted leg atop a woven cane ottoman, with his neck-stock removed, his shirt collars open, and his coat off. "I'd love t'spend a whole fortnight, but I've business back in London. No more'n a week, this trip. Later on in the summer, well . . . might spend a whole two months! Clean air, refreshin' breezes . . . good horses, and long, open fields, what?"

"Absolutely," Lewrie had to agree, more by rote than anything else. He got the feeling that there might be one more "shoe to drop." His father was not one for small talk or idle invitations—unless he had a good reason for it.

"Yours, when I'm gone, lad," Sir Hugo reminded him as the cool tea arrived. Trilochan Singh must have been responsible for its brewing, for there were slices of lemon and a pot of light brown turbinado sugar from the first pressings, already ground fine. "All of it, lock, stock, and barrel. Ever, erm . . . ever given thought t'removing in here now? Mean t'say . . .

if Hugh's t'go for a sailor, and Sewallis is t'be away at school if you get a ship . . . well, it's *bags* roomier than your place. Charlotte's still lodgin' with Governour and Millicent?"

"Aye, but . . . that was only temporary, while Caroline and I . . . ," Lewrie replied, then paused, reminded again that there was no Caroline, and never would be. "If I *do* gain a new command," he slowly said, "it might be best did she board with 'em. I'd pay for her tutor and music teacher and all that, but . . . that's where she is now. Charlotte has gotten it into her head that . . ."

He sat up with his elbows on his knees, the cool glass of tea in both hands, squirming in shame to announce that evil rumour.

"There's *some* say it was *my* fault Caroline was killed," he told Sir Hugo, growing angry. "Damn 'em! Don't know what Millicent thinks, she's sweet and kind, most of the time, but Governour . . . he's always disapproved of my . . . well, ye know what he disapproved of. At their place so much, Charlotte thinks it was my fault, too! She was always Caroline's daughter, first and last, and with me gone so much, and . . . those letters comin' and makin' Caroline so bitter, the girl was dead-set against me and took Caroline as Gospel. Even after I came home last winter, Charlotte's been missish and stand-off-ish with me, and I don't know what t'do about it. The boys, I can understand, but her?"

"I leave her in Governour's clutches, I might as well give her up," Lewrie said with a bitter sigh. "Don't suppose you'd take her on in London, would you? Like you did with Sophie?"

"Not a chance in Hell," Sir Hugo baldly stated. "Young *ladies* I can deal with . . . not with head-strong little *girls*. Besides . . ."

"She might cramp your doin's?" Lewrie said with a mirthless chuckle.

"There is that," Sir Hugo cheerfully admitted. "Without a wife in yer house, without a step-mother t'rear her up . . . I don't suppose ye'd consider marryin' again."

"Not a chance in Hell," Lewrie assured his father. "Besides . . . how'd it look, with the first year of mournin' not *half* over? And who could I trust t'do right by her . . . and me?"

"Just a thought," Sir Hugo said, waving one hand idly to shoo his suggestion away. "Now, *do* ye let Governour and Millicent have her through an active commission, that's what . . . three years or more out at sea, halfway round the world, before ye have t'come home to re-fit?"

"About that, aye," Lewrie sombrely agreed. "A dockyard re-fit in England, but still held active, it might be five or six years."

"And all that time, yer house sittin' empty and idle? Left in the hands of an estate agent ye don't know whether t'trust?" Sir Hugo speculated. "Up-keep not done . . . rats and mice everywhere? Rent paid t'Phineas Chiswick, with little return? *That's* rum."

"What are you gettin' at?" Lewrie asked suddenly, thinking that that shoe was about to be dropped, and he wouldn't much care for it.

"Ye haven't spoken with Phineas Chiswick or with Burgess?" his father asked, brows up as if surprised that Lewrie was still in the dark.

"As little as possible to the first, and not since the funeral to the second," Lewrie answered. "Why?"

"Ye really haven't," Sir Hugo realised, sitting up straighter and seeming to squirm, his lined face turning pinker. "Damn! Would've thought ye'd heard."

"Heard bloody *what?*" Lewrie demanded.

"Phineas and Governour think that Burgess should have a country estate of his own, son," Sir Hugo began. "Near his kinfolk, d'ye see? Close t'London and Horse Guards, 'stead of way up at High Wycombe with his wife's parents. Handier for the Trenchers, t'boot, do they wish a week or two in the country, callin' on their daughter and son-in-law. And . . . ," Sir Hugo said with a sly, worldly look, "I do recall that the Trenchers are simply *un-Godly* rich, and ye know how Phineas Chiswick slavers like a jowly hound if he hears two guineas rub t'gether. What better sort of neighbours could he wish?"

"Phineas *can't* turf me out," Lewrie snapped, "not as long as I stay current in my rents, and there's no chance o' me fallin' behind! I've prize-money in the bank, interest from the Funds, and, thank God, we've had two years o' good corn crops, and the price o' wool's still high, despite the peace, so he can't. It's a *long-term* lease, dammit!"

"I vow I never thought t'hear ye speak o' crops and wool prices like ye knew what they were," his father said with a snicker. "Oh, he could *buy* you out, any time he felt like it, son. There's Burgess . . . come home from India a 'chicken nabob' with more'n fifty thousand pounds. . . . There's the Trenchers, who might've made a round *million* since the war began in Ninety-Three. Considerin' all the improvements ye've made over the years, Phineas Chiswick might have to pay ye twelve or fifteen hundred pounds. But he could turn round and offer it to Burgess as a lease, and make that back before he goes toes up.

"Phineas don't have anyone t'inherit, mind ye," Sir Hugo sagely pointed out. "His first two wives died without issue, so he's no sons t'leave it to, and he's the miserly sort who'd take all his property t'Hell with him, could he figure out how. Or keep it together after he's gone. It's good odds it'll all go to Governour, since he's the elder of his nephews . . . and Governour's been doin' the old bastard's will since he got here, *schemin'* t'be his sole heir. Eatin' his shit and runnin' his errands and smilin' all the while, haw haw!"

"Even so, I don't see Governour keepin' Burgess as a tenant," Lewrie said, frowning with concentration, "thinkin' t'prosper off his own brother in rents."

"Rent for now, then *will* the farm to Burgess when Phineas dies . . .'til then, Governour'd be responsible for up-keep and working the crops and herds . . . same as he does for his own lands, and Phineas's," Sir Hugo explained. "Then *both* brothers end up freeholders, and able t'vote in the borough. Hunt, fish, trap game . . . both end up country gentry. It ain't exactly the Christian thing t'do, turfin' ye out so soon after Caroline's passin', but . . . what can ye expect from such a purse-proud old miser?"

"And there's what ye leave the children t'consider," Sir Hugo added after a long, contemplative sip of tea, and a fond gaze over his own vista and acres. "Should the French manage t'kill ye before ye inherit Dun Roman, that is. Another twelve or fifteen hundred pounds in the bank, or the Three Percents, would help them along their ways."

"Why go to all that trouble, when Phineas could just sell it to the Trenchers, and Burgess could be landed right away?" Lewrie fumed, getting to his feet to stamp down the length of the gallery, shouting back over his shoulder before he turned to clomp angrily back to his father. "No matter how *land-proud* Phineas Chiswick is, he sold to *you*! First time in living memory, hereabouts, that. Like to've made local folk go into *fits*, it did! Thought he'd gone mad as a hatter!"

"He'd had a bad investment or two, crop prices were down, and he needed the money perishin' bad," Sir Hugo explained with a shrug. "Not his *best* land, you'll note. Too hilly to plow, too wooded, and thinner soil. Don't make tuppence from *workin'* this land, son, just barely break even. It's *ownin'* this much land, the house and my *view* is what matters t'me. Be the same for Burgess, long as he's in the Army. A pleasant country seat, that's all."

". . . that the Trenchers could buy, then give to Burgess as a weddin' present, and the deal's done, straightaway," Lewrie fumed, rocking on the balls of his feet and feeling like he wanted to hit something or kick furniture. Remembering how Phineas Chiswick had turfed out that sheeper tenant who'd had the place before he and Caroline had returned from the Bahamas in '89, and had needed a place to live . . . close to the bosom of her *family*, ha!

"*Bugger* Phineas Chiswick!" Lewrie growled. "Bugger Governour, and bugger Burgess, too, if he hasn't the 'nutmegs' t'speak with me about it! Just damn my eyes!"

"Bugger 'em all, aye," his father inexplicably hooted, laughing heartily. "No matter how they wish it, though, me son, they can't run ye outta the shire. Hark ye . . .

"Shift yer traps an' furnishin's up here to Dun Roman, and this will be yer new country seat," Sir Hugo schemed with a wry little grin. "They might *think* ye'll end up in London, at the Madeira Club, but yer children can consider this their new home whilst yer at sea, and ye'll be able t'come home and be up their noses 'til the Last Trump. When I go, you're heir t'twice as many acres as yer old place, *and*, do I *not* squander all the loot *I* brought back from India, you and yours'll sit in deep clover, haw haw! They'll *never* be rid o' ye!"

Lewrie thought that over hard, sitting back down in his chair and taking a long sip of the cool tea, considering how much "dear Uncle Phineas" might have to shell out to get him out. The house they'd run up had cost eight hundred pounds in 1789, and was surely worth more now. The old wattle-and-daub barn had been torn down before it collapsed or the rats ate it, and a new stone-and-wood barn had replaced it. The brick-and-stone stables and coach-house, the silage tower, had gotten added the next year. There were good horses for the team, and saddle horses; he'd keep those at his father's, but the rest of the livestock could go with the land. With no more rents owing at each Quarterly Assizes, *and* more money in the bank . . . !

Lewrie sat back in his chair and began to grin.

"Ye see?" Sir Hugo cajoled.

"Onliest problem, though, is that the children won't have *their* home any longer," Lewrie mused. "Where they were born and grew up. Oh, the *boys* . . . they love comin' up here t'your place, so I don't imagine it'd pain them too sore . . . perhaps Sewallis more than Hugh. It will be Charlotte who'll take it worse. Hard as she took losin' her mother, t'lose our old house, too, well . . . she'd never forgive me for that, on top of all that Governour's put in her head."

"Son . . . who's t'say Charlotte'd forgive ye, anyway?" Sir Hugo pointed out with a sad shake of his head and a reassuring tap upon Lewrie's knee.

"Well . . . there's truth t'that," Lewrie had to agree after a long moment to think that over. "There is that."

CHAPTER THIRTY-FOUR

*A*ll worries about being turfed out of his home became moot just two days later, when Lewrie went down to the Olde Ploughman after his daily morning ride for a rum-laced coffee, and found his old Coxswain, Will Cony, waving to him and wiping his hands on his blue publican's apron. "Mail coach brought ya somethin', Cap'm Lewrie!" Will declared, coming to meet him near the doors. "Letter from Admiralty, th' most important! Want a drop o' somethin' warmin' whilst ya read it, sir? 'Tis a raw sorta day."

"Aye, Will, I'd admire rummed coffee," Lewrie replied, quickly taking his letters and ripping the official wax seal to read it before even taking a seat at a table. Idlers in the public house's common room turned in their chairs at that announcement, worried that a resumption of the war might be coming, though none of the newspapers had yet declared it.

They offered him a *ship* . . . another frigate of the Fifth Rate, a 38-gunner with 18-pounder main-battery guns; HMS *Reliant*, now lying in-ordinary at Portsmouth!

He sat down with a smile on his face, an expression that local people had not seen since he'd come home from Paris, closed his eyes and slowly nodded, as if in a brief prayer of thanks, before hungrily reading his letter again, just to make sure that it was real, that the offer of active commission was true, and not a fantasy.

"Is it war, beggin' yer pardon, sir?" Cony asked in a whisper as he returned with his coffee.

"It doesn't say, Will, but . . . ," Lewrie informed him an a mutter of his own, "it may very well be, if they're re-commissioning me."

"There'll be a press, then. Soon," Will Cony speculated. "A hot press. Recruiters comin' t'town, from the Army, but what sorta lad'd go for a *soldier* when he kin be a *sea-dog*, by God! Lotta young lads hereabouts, Cap'm Lewrie . . . barely scrapin' by as day labourers, or down t'the tannery'r brick-works, since the Enclosure Acts took their folks' wee plots o' land, and the commons. I'd wager I could round up a couple dozen likely lads fer your new ship! What's her name, sir?"

"*Reliant*," Lewrie told him, "a Fifth Rate Thirty-Eight."

"A *big* frigate, aye!" Will Cony exclaimed for one and all in the common rooms. "HMS *Reliant*, the Cap'm's got, huzzah! Damme, did I have two feet t'day, *I'd* go back t'sea quicker'n ya kin say 'knife'!"

"Ye really think ye could?" Lewrie posed, knowing how hard it would be to recruit willing hands in a hard press, and thinking that a dozen or so volunteers from Anglesgreen, who'd known him and Caroline for years, might take the Joining Bounty as a way to get *their* revenge on the French for the murder of a local favourite.

"Even *wif* two feet, Will Cony, ye've too much *belly* t'shin up a mast these days!" a patron hooted.

"An' th' Navy won't let ye sling a keg o' yer best ale aboard!" cried another.

"Cony takes th' King's Shillin', who'd *make* our ale, I ask ye?" shouted a third. "We got t'keep 'im here. Tie him up 'fore he gits away!"

Lewrie opened a second letter, this one from his old superior in the Adriatic in '96, and a senior officer in the close blockade of the Gironde coast three years before: Captain Thomas Charlton. *He* was being given a commission, a two-decker Third Rate 74 (he wrote) and, did Lewrie still have need for a Midshipman's berth for his son Hugh, then Charlton would be honoured to accept him. HMS *Pegasus* was lying in-ordinary at Portsmouth (happy circumstance!) so make haste, etc.

"And my son Hugh has a ship, too," Lewrie told Cony.

"Runs in the fam'ly, th' sea, it do, sir!" Cony beamed proudly.

"I'll be all night, writin' all the people I have to," Lewrie said, hurrying through his coffee, "and get letters off on tomorrow's mail coach. That's a temptin' idea, Will, our local lads. If I could get 'em past the Impress Service into Portsmouth without half of 'em being stolen."

"An' robbed o' their Joinin' Bounty, aye," Will Cony agreed with a growl.

"I'm off, and thankee!" Lewrie said, springing to depart.

He rode at a fast lope to Dun Roman to inform his father, spending perhaps an hour arranging for Sir Hugo to serve as his representative, should Phineas Chiswick press the matter after he departed. The next stop was home, his news a delight to Liam Desmond and Pat Furfy, who, no matter how pleasant their lives were on the farm, found that a chance to serve at sea again suited them right down to their toes.

Then it was finger-cramp, ink smudges, and hot sealing wax on his fingers all through the day and early evening, with only a few very brief breaks for dinner, supper, and trips to the "necessary." First came his reply to Admiralty, the next to Capt. Charlton, then to his solicitor, Coutts' Bank, Sewallis and Hugh, urging them to come down to London and lodge at the Madeira Club 'til he arrived, and informing Hugh that his fondest wish would soon be realised. After all those, he had to write all the other naval officers from whom he'd asked a place for the boy, telling him that Charlton would take him.

"Note for ya, sir," Mr. Gower intruded into the library office.

"Hmm?" Lewrie perked up. "This late? From whom, d'ye know?"

"Governour Chiswick, I reckon, sir," Gower replied.

Lewrie tore it open and read what Governour's wife, Millicent, had penned; Charlotte wished to sup with *them* and sleep over with her girl cousin. They would fetch her home by mid-morning tomorrow.

"Awf'lly damned high-handed of 'em," Lewrie muttered, thinking that a *request* sent much earlier would have been more polite, not this "oh, by the by . . ." note, as if they were her parents, not him.

Christ, she's been over there all day? Lewrie realised; *I've eat dinner and supper and didn't even note she wasn't here? Well, maybe they are! Or will have t'be.*

Charlotte couldn't stay at Dun Roman, not if his father was not present; nor could she reside with him in London, as the old rogue had made very clear. *Somebody* had to take her on! And who better than "family," her only kin . . . disagreeable as most of them were?

Have t'ride over there and see if they'll board her, permanent, he told himself; *arrange for all her clothes, bed-chamber furniture and toys t'go with her. Have familiar things round her . . . poor tyke.*

Or, he reckoned for a long minute or two, he could do the right thing by his children, turn down *Reliant*, thus ending his active Royal Navy career. He could go on half-pay the rest of his life, live here in Angles-green, as farm agent at Dun Roman, perhaps, with an occasional jaunt up to London and the Madeira Club when country living got too boresome.

"No," he whispered, sadly shaking his head in the negative.

"Sir?" asked Gower, who was still hovering.

"Thinkin' out loud, no matter, Mister Gower," he told him.

"Right ho, then, Cap'm Lewrie," Gower said cheerfully, doing a sketchy bow before slouching off to the kitchens.

Lewrie heated the sealing wax and daubed it on the flap of his final letter, then snuffed the candle heater and leaned back, with an ache in the small of his back from sitting hunched forward too long. He rose and arched himself to work out the kink, fists in the small of his back, and decided that he'd done a fair piece of work and was now well deserving of a healthy measure of whisky. The sun was not only *far* below the yardarm by then, it was two hours past sunset! Desmond and a stable boy were going round closing the outside shutters for the night. As he poured himself half a glass of bourbon, they closed the shutters on the French doors to the back-garden, leaving his office lit only by the candelabra on his desk and the glow from the fireplace.

He paused after his first sip, looking round slowly at all his books and possessions, his furniture, his weapons, and the hanger he'd recovered from Napoleon, now hung over the mantel, where it had lodged years before.

After another sip, he stepped out into the foyer, looking over the side-board and mirror, the framed portraits, the Venetian bombé tables he'd brought back from the Adriatic, and . . . into the parlour and dining room in the other wing of the house, and all those ghostly pale sheet-covered furnishings. There was a bit of a moon that night, and before Desmond and his lad began to close the shutters over all those windows, he got the shivery feeling that he was looking at a coven of spooks.

"I will never see this house again," he whispered, with a new shiver trilling up his spine. Back in service and out to sea within a month, he'd not return for years, and when he did, it would surely be Burgess's and Theodora's house, in freehold. He would be invited over to dine or dance, at holidays, but by then it would look totally different, done to Theodora's taste; the nursery might even be occupied by *Chiswick* children, there'd be new servants, a lot more of them, too.

Ask my father t'close it down and move everything over to his place, in storage, Lewrie decided, making a mental inventory of furnishings he could use aboard his new ship.

That sense of finality was not dread; he felt those shivers for an ending, not like a premonition like the old adage of sensing that "rabbit running over one's grave." He knew what he was doing aboard a ship—even if he didn't know much ashore. Let the French *try* to do him in! He'd give them measure for measure, and more, to boot.

"Sorry, Caroline," he muttered, finishing his drink, and sure he would soon have another. "I'd've *liked* t'keep everything just as ye liked it, but . . . I can't. I can't live with all your ghosts, either."

Never see this place again? he asked himself; *bloody good!*

CHAPTER THIRTY-FIVE

It was a toss-up as to who peered out from the coach's windows more eagerly as it began the long descent from Portdown Hill to Portsmouth proper—Hugh, Sewallis, or their father. The lads squealed and oohed at the sight of the harbour so crammed with warships at anchor, so many water hoys and supply barges working to succour them, and the lug-sailed or oared boats dashing back and forth like so many roaches scuttling from a sudden flood of light.

And once they were on level ground before the George Inn, the one Lewrie preferred most, the streets leading into HM Dockyards were even busier with dray waggons and seamen, with parties from the Impress Service chivvying along their latest catches to the tenders to ferry them out to the hulked receiving ships, with files of Marines tramping along at the Quick-Step, with officers strolling together in twos and threes for whispered conversations, or sharing cock-a-whoop japes.

"Stay close or get trampled, now," Lewrie chid his boys, leaving it to his father, Sir Hugo—who had coached down with them for the nonce and who would see Sewallis back to London and the diligence coach to his school, once the necessities were done—to deal with the driver of the dray waggon, which bore all his personal goods and furnishings and Hugh's sea-chest, and to supervise Desmond and Furfy's unloading.

Lewrie closed his eyes and sniffed deeply, feeling a swell of satisfaction as he realised how different a seaport smelled, and how much he had missed it. Other than the horse dung, of course.

There was the fishy smell of tidal flats and the kelp and hard marine life that clung to wood and stone piers at low tide, the scent of salt, of cable-lengths of hemp or manila, fresh from weaving at the ropewalks; hot tar or pitch, turpentine and rosin, and the sweetness of new-sawn wood and sawdust. New-baked ship's biscuit, small beer by the keg, the heady aroma of a leaking rum cask from a passing waggon.

And there were the sounds; mewing, crying gulls, the clatters of sail, signal or flag halliards on masts, staffs, or poles. Far-off rustles of loosed canvas from one of the nearer ships as its rusty or newly impressed crew went through an exercise in Harbour Drill. Roars and shouts, barked orders, fiddle music and laughter, and the rumbles of a great many men of a myriad of skills all congregating to launch a great enterprise, and the bulk of them knowing what they were about.

I think I'm home, Lewrie told himself, opening his eyes to take it all in; *a damned* deprivin' *one, once we're out at sea, but . . . home just the same.*

"Yes well, let's see about our lodgings first, then we'll see my goods aboard *Reliant*," Lewrie said, abandoning his reverie. "I've written ahead, so the George *may* be able t'take us all."

"All of us, father? To go out to your new ship?" Sewallis asked him, looking more eager than was his usual wont.

"Aye, you can be there when I read myself in," he agreed.

And an hour later, with two hired boats to bear all his goods and the six of them, they went alongside HMS *Reliant*. She was still reduced "to a gant-line" with none of her upper masts set up, and her gun-deck empty of artillery, riding high in the waters not too far off Southsea Castle, in the deeper water 'twixt Spit Sand and Horse Sand.

"Boat ahoy!" one of her Midshipmen challenged; *pro forma*, that, for there was no doubt that the first boat carried a Post-Captain, and the second his possessions.

"*Aye aye!*" their boatman shouted back, showing four fingers to declare that a Post-Captain was indeed aboard.

"Might ye have need of a bosun's chair, father?" Lewrie teased.

"Bedamned if I will!" Sir Hugo snapped back.

"Last in, first out," Lewrie said, laying a restraining hand on Sewallis's shoulder as he stood to grope for the main channel platform, the dead-eyed main-mast stays, and the man-ropes of the boarding-battens. "Sir Hugo next, then Hugh, then you, Sewallis."

He tucked his sword behind his left leg, stood on the gunn'l of their boat, and stepped onto the main channel, then the battens, making a quick way up to the starboard entry-port. He was greeted with a side-party of Marines, a Bosun and his Mate piping a long call, and two officers and a clutch of Midshipmen.

Once safely in-board, Lewrie doffed his hat to the flag at the taffrails, the officers, and the crew hastily assembled along both sail-tending gangways above the bare gun-deck, and in the waist.

"Captain Alan Lewrie, come aboard to command," he told his two Commission Officers. "Mine arse on a band-box!" he gasped a second later, though, quite ruining the solemnity of the occasion. "Mister Spendlove? Last I saw of you 'twas Ninety-Seven, when we paid off *Jester*! Congratulations on your Lieutenancy, sir."

"Thank you, sir!" Lt. Clarence Spendlove proudly replied.

"Geoffrey Westcott, sir," the older officer said. "It appears I'm to be your First Officer . . . unless Mister Merriman turns up and proves senior to me. Your servant, Captain Lewrie, sir."

"Mister Westcott, how d'ye do, sir," Lewrie said with another doff of his hat to match Westcott's. "Well, shall we get on with it?" He turned to see that Sir Hugo had scaled the ship's side right handily, and both Hugh and Sewallis were behind him, too.

"One of ours, sir?" Lt. Westcott enquired as the both of them walked to the hammock nettings at the forward end of the quarterdeck, and amidships.

"No, my son Hugh's down for Captain Thomas Charlton and *Pegasus*, a two-decker," Lewrie told him. "His first ship. I've never very much cared for kin on the same ship." Lewrie was too busy extracting his precious commissioning document from the safety of his coat to see Westcott's approving nod. He had eyes more for his sons and Sir Hugo, who stood off to one side, as he unscrolled his paper.

"Ship's comp'ny . . . off hats and hark to the quarterdeck!" Lt. Westcott ordered in a voice that would carry in a full gale.

"By the Commissioners for executing the office of Lord High Admiral of Great Britain and Ireland, and all His Majesty's Plantations and *et cetera* . . . to Captain Alan Lewrie, hereby appointed to His Majesty's Ship, *Reliant* . . . by virtue of the Power and Authority to us given, we do hereby constitute and appoint you Captain of His Majesty's Ship, *Reliant* . . . willing and requiring you forthwith to go on board and take upon you the Charge and Command of Captain in her accordingly. Strictly charging all the Officers and Company belonging to said Ship subordinate to you to behave themselves jointly and severally in their respective Employments with all due Respect and Obedience unto you, their said Captain, and you likewise to observe and execute such Orders and Directions you shall receive from time to time from your superior officers for His Majesty's Service.

"Hereof nor you nor any one of you fail as you will answer the contrary at your peril. And for so doing this shall be your Warrant. Given under our hands and the Seal of Office of Admiralty, this Twenty-Fifth day of April, Eighteen-Oh-Three, in the Fourty-Third year of His Majesty's Reign," he concluded in a matching "quarterdeck" voice.

The ritual done, Lewrie rolled up the document and looked down at his hands in the waist, on the gangways. "Men! It seems that that Corsican tyrant . . . that ogre Napoleon Bonaparte hasn't learned his lesson yet. Like a wolf pretendin' t'be a setter, he'd *like* t'enter the house . . . *pretend* he can grin and wag his tail, and all the while just waitin' to eat up the whole house, and all of Europe, including our island. *Your* homes, *your* people, from Land's End to John O' Groats. Only problem is, nobody ever told Napoleon ye can't play-act a trusty setter if ye keep piddlin' on the carpet and shittin' in the parlour!

"We're called once again t'teach him proper manners," he told them as the laughter that his Billingsgate, not usually heard from a gentleman-captain, died away. "And if he *can't* learn t'live peaceful among the world's nations . . . then it's *our* job . . . the Royal Navy . . . this fine frigate . . . and every one of *you*, volunteer or pressed man, experienced tar or raw landsman . . . true blue hearts of oak . . . to put him down like a rabid stray, like a ravenin' wolf in the sheep fold that Napoleon *is*, and stop his business, all *French* business, for good and all!

"Before *Reliant* raises anchor and sets sail on the King's Business," he promised them in a slightly softer voice, "I, and your officers and mates, will make sure that ev'ry Man Jack of you know all you need t'know to work this ship, to sail her into any corner of the wide world over . . . as shipmates, as *men* who can boast that they're the best in the entire world . . . that they're British tars. Reliants!"

That raised a cheer, even from the dubious first draught of men from the Impress tenders and the receiving ships.

"That's all for now, Mister Westcott."

"Aye, sir. Ship's comp'ny . . . on hats, and dismiss. Carry on!" Westcott ordered.

"Ah, *those* two *are* ours, sir," Lewrie said, pointing to Desmond and Furfy, who were just gaining the deck with the first light loads of Lewrie's dunnage and the wicker cage for the cats, who were peering wide-eyed, braced on their haunches with their noses to the wicker to sniff out their new home.

"The cats, sir?" Lt. Westcott dared jape. "Or the sailors?"

"You'll find my Cox'n, Desmond, and Ordinary Seaman Furfy more use to you, Mister Westcott," Lewrie drawled back in like humour. "My cats keep me from turnin' a floggin' Tartar."

"Very good, sir," Lt. Westcott said with a grin. "I'll see to hoisting your goods aboard."

Now the ceremony of reading himself in was over, the Midshipmen yet aboard *Reliant* were circling round Hugh very *much* like a pack of the aforementioned wolves, ready to put "John New-Come" in his place at the bottom of their pecking order.

"Gentlemen," Lewrie said, going to rescue him. "Allow me to name to you my son, Hugh, who will be going aboard HMS *Pegasus* tomorrow. And you are, young sirs?"

"Uhm . . . Vincent Houghton, sir," the oldest and most senior of them quickly said. He looked to be "upwards of twenty," as the Navy required of a fellow who had done at least six years at sea and was able to stand before his first oral examinations for his Lieutenancy. "May I name to you, sir, Mister Entwhistle," a stocky lad about eighteen or so; "Mister Warburton" (that worthy was a slim fellow with dark red hair and a very fair complexion, about fifteen or sixteen, a lad with a "cheeky" expression), "and Mister Grainger, sir." The last was the youngest, about fifteen Lewrie judged, a tad shorter than the rest, and a bit chubbier. "We're two short so far, sir," Houghton said.

"All of you have sea experience?" Lewrie asked, and was happy to learn that Houghton and Entwhistle had at least six years at sea in various ships, whilst Warburton had had one three-year appointment, and Grainger the same.

"Damme," Lewrie chuckled, "someone at Admiralty's erred badly, t'place so many tarry young gentleman in the same ship, 'stead of tossin' us a pack of cods-heads. I'll be countin' on you to make sure we put to sea with a crew that knows the ropes."

"Count on us, sir!" Midshipman Houghton vowed, quickly seconded by the rest.

"Purser aboard?" Lewrie asked further. "The Marine officer?"

"Mister Cadbury, sir?" Houghton said. "He and his clerk and his Jack-in-the-Breadroom are ashore, sir. Leftenant Simcock went ashore with him, t'see to wardroom stores."

"Very well, catch up with 'em later," Lewrie decided. "Which of you have a good copperplate hand?" Two shot up their hands.

"Capital!" Lewrie cried. "I'll put you, Mister Entwhistle, and you, Mister Grainger, to copyin' out my Order Book for six Midshipmen and all officers."

Blank-faced looks from the two volunteers, faint sneers from the others, even a snicker from Warburton.

"Carry on," Lewrie told them.

"Uhm, could we look about the ship, father?" Sewallis asked.

"Mister Warburton," Lewrie said, stopping him in his tracks. "Would you mind showing my sons about the ship? All the cautions?"

"Of course, sir!"

"I'll be aft," Lewrie said, turning to go, but stopping at the foot of the larboard ladderway to the gun-deck to watch his sons get the first bit of their tour; Sewallis a head taller in his usual dark and sobre suit, his hat in his hands, to bare his darker hair, and Hugh, uniformed and kitted out in London before they had coached down, his new-styled narrow-brimmed and thimble-shaped hat still on his head, though with his mother's blonder hair tumbling in its usual unruly way over his shirt collar and his ears.

Would she *have been proud of his choice?* Lewrie wondered; *much as Caroline disliked it . . . would she have cursed me for lettin' him go to sea? Pushed* him *to it?*

"Damned demandin', what ye read," Sir Hugo commented as he came to join him. "All *my* promotions and such started out with 'To our Trusty and well beloved'—fill in the name—'Greetings' "!

"Well, ye paid enough for 'em, I should't wonder why the King *wouldn't*!" Lewrie teased.

Now there was a proper captain aboard, whose privacy and goods must be guarded, there was a Marine private in full kit outside the door to the great-cabins, right aft. He stamped, presented his musket in salute, and roared "Sah!"

"Good Christ!" Sir Hugo barked, once laying eyes on the place. It was bare, the black-and-white chequer canvas deck cover was faded and worn;

the deal-and-canvas partitions and all the inner faces of the planking above the line of empty gun-ports and the usual dark red paint below the wainscot line—everything was done in a pale blue, picked out with gilt-painted mouldings, replete with wee painted cherubs. "The last captain ship his wife with him . . . or did he run a bawdy house?"

"Re-paint . . . soonest," Lewrie vowed.

"And turn yer cats loose," Sir Hugo added, pointing with his walking-stick at a particularly large rat, with a brace of his smaller brothers, busy gnawing at what might have once been a tufted dark blue pad atop the transom settee. "Yer brothel's got rats, hee hee!"

CHAPTER THIRTY-SIX

*O*nce sending Sir Hugo, Hugh, and Sewallis ashore for a while, as Desmond and Furfy supervised a work-party in setting up his cabins to his liking, Lewrie made it a point to meet the Purser, Mr. Cadbury, and his clerk, the Bosun Mr. Sprague, and his Mate, Wheeler; their Master Gunner, who turned out to be the Prussian Johan Rahl, who had served with him long ago; the Gunner's Mate, Mr. Acres; and the Yeoman of the Powder, Kemp; Sailmaker, Mr. Yearsley and his Mate, Duncan, and all of the people who formed the Standing Officers who lived aboard while she was laid up in-ordinary, as well as those few other petty officers who had already come aboard.

Then he spent some time with his Lieutenants, discussing the ship's history, her material condition, her lacks, and how many hands were aboard; how many were rated Able, Ordinary, or Landsmen, and how many remained to be recruited . . . by fair means or foul.

"I've spoken with a printer, sir," Lt. Westcott said, "though I have not yet placed an order. Didn't know who to advert as our Captain, you see," he said with a grin. "How boastful to be."

Lt. Geoffrey Westcott was about Lewrie's height of five feet nine inches, a bit slimmer in build, and carried himself with a quick urgency. His hair was dark and cut quite short, almost as short as a fellow ashore who preferred a wig and had his scalp shorn to keep the risk of bugs down. He had a high-cheeked and slightly narrow hatchet face, which on a villain might have looked menacing. Westcott, though, seemed possessed of a merry, if slightly worldly-wise, disposition. He smiled rather a lot, sometimes only the briefest flash of a smile, with a lifting of his rather short upper lip to reveal his teeth.

"We've a partial proof, sir," Lt. Spendlove contributed, showing Lewrie a poster-sized sheet of paper, which featured VOLUNTEERS at the top, the King's royal crest and G.R. III, and a paragraph of type that called for Englishmen good and true, etc. Below that came BOLD ROYAL TARS OF OLD ENGLAND, but the rest was yet blank.

"You've chosen a 'rondy,' Mister Westcott?" Lewrie enquired.

"I have, sir. A centrally located public house, adjacent to the docks," Lt. Westcott assured him. "Though I fear there are many more ships' rendezvous in competition with us, along with the Impress Service's, which will recruit for *any* ship. I put a deposit down, but . . ."

"I'll re-pay you," Lewrie told him, liking Westcott's initiative "Well, 'faint heart ne'er won fair ladies,' and we'll not reel anyone in without proper bait. Let's go all-out and not be shy."

Together, they thrashed out the salient points; that *Reliant*, a Fifth Rate *frigate*, was *spacious*; come all loyal sea-rovers who wished *action*, speed and *dash*, and the chance of *prize-money* never to be had aboard a ship of the line! Prime rations, full issue of rum! Bounty to be paid—£20 for Able Seamen, £10 for Ordinary Seamen, £5 for Landsmen and Ship's Boys! And Death to the French!

Even in a *hot* Press, William Pitt's Quota Acts of 1795 had made the counties offer more and more to fill their required numbers, and the Navy had had to follow suit, raising the Joining Bounty from the pre-war's single Guinea, or £5 for Able Seamen, and even then, merchant service was more lucrative.

"Let's use my notoriety," Lewrie decided; which resulted in the blurb that *Reliant* was commanded by Capt. Alan "Ram-Cat" Lewrie, Black Alan the Liberator of the West Indies, Victor of Dozens of Sea Fights & Fortunate in Prize-Money! Confusion, And *Death*, to the French!

". . . True Blue Hearts of Oak, and all who seek Glory and Adventure, ask of Lieutenant G. Westcott at the *et cetera* and *et cetera*," he concluded. "Oh, might toss in Cape Saint Vincent, Camperdown, and Copenhagen, too. Should that do it, sirs?"

"Topping-well, sir, indeed," Lt. Westcott agreed. "I will seek out the printer this afternoon and have him polish it up."

"I'll go ashore with you, Mister Westcott," Lewrie announced as he got to his feet. "As you can see, I badly need new paint in this . . . *boudoir*, and you may fetch it back aboard as you return from the printers. Have Desmond supervise the painting. I'll also lodge ashore for tonight, to see my son off early tomorrow, then will be back aboard by Eight Bells of the Morning Watch."

"Very good, sir."

Their last supper together at the George, though quite tasty and filling, was not without its uneasy moments. There were many Navy men and their wives dining there, and Hugh was enthralled by the sight of them, all but preening in his Midshipman's uniform and excited about the beginning of a naval career. Sir Hugo told amusing tales about his military antics (the *clean* ones, it must be noted!) to raise Sewallis from his gloom and disappointed mood, when not discussing more practical matters. Lewrie mostly kept a sombre silence through their repast, knowing what Hugh was facing from his own experiences as a lowly Mid, and . . . fearing all that weather, the sea, combat, or stupid accidents could do to such an eager and callow thirteen-year-old. Would he lose a child as well as a wife? All of a sudden it struck him that once he saw the lad off in a boat to his new ship, it was good odds that they might not see each other ever again, and even if Hugh prospered, took to the Navy like a duck to water, grim Duty might demand three or four years' separation before *rencontre*, and what sort of stranger might his youngest son be when they did manage to re-meet? He felt every bit of his fourty years, and wondered where so much of them had gone!

"But why can't *I* fight the French?" Sewallis was asking, fetching Lewrie from his dreads. "It's so unfair that Hugh gets to go, and I can't. And I want to, so very much."

"You're eldest, Sewallis," Sir Hugo gently told him. "It's the way it is. Ancient right o' primogeniture, ye see. The way things are done in English families."

"I didn't ask to be first, it's . . . ," Sewallis protested; as much protest as he'd raise in such a distinguished supper crowd, and as much as his usual reticence allowed.

"First-born sons always inherit everything, Sewallis. The others have to make their own way," Lewrie explained. "It's your place to be the elder to Hugh and Charlotte . . . provide for them through good management of my estate, which goes to you if I fall."

"If Uncle Phineas takes our house and farm, we won't *have* an estate, would we?" Sewallis cleverly, though pettishly, pointed out.

"My investments in the Funds, my savings, and your grandfather's place, eventually, is my estate. Our estate, rather," Lewrie told him, wondering what had gotten into him. "T'do that means ye have need of more education, and business sense, so ye don't go squanderin' it all, or make foolish decisions. Don't mean ye can't have a career of your own besides those duties . . ."

"As much a duty t'yer family as Hugh's duty to his service and his ship," Sir Hugo stuck in before waving for a top-up of claret.

"Finish at your school . . . perhaps a year or so at university," Lewrie went on. Sir Hugo rolled his eyes heavenward to show what he thought of *that*, and Lewrie took a moment to shrug agreement with him. "Or ye might wish t'speak with our solicitor, Mister Mountjoy, about learnin' more about the law. Learn the cautions. After terms, there is my barrister, Mac-Dougall, who might advise ye about entering one o' the Inns of Court. Once you're of an age t'live in London on your own, mind, not before."

"Ever given thought what ye might wish t'be, lad? What career . . . a civilian career, that is . . . ye wanted t'take up?" Sir Hugo asked him.

"Well . . . I *once* thought of becoming a churchman, like our vicar at Saint George's," Sewallis hesitantly stated, "going up to Oxford or Cambridge, then taking Holy Orders, but . . ." He shrugged to silence.

That idea made Sir Hugo sit up like someone had goosed him, and blare his eyes. Lewrie was forced to squint, and fight the grimace that threatened to bloom on his phyz. Sir Hugo coughed.

"Well, and that's an honourable profession, I'm bound," Lewrie was quick to say, though shifting uneasily on his chair. "And there's many a churchman the eldest of his family, with his own income, beyond the manse, the glebe, and his share of the tithes," he pointed out.

"But, since Mother was murdered, I only want to fight and kill Frenchmen," Sewallis said with unaccustomed firmness. "I don't think I could ever take Holy Orders with that in my heart. If not the Navy, could I not go into the Army, grandfather? You once offered your influence at Horse Guards to help Hugh obtain a commission."

"Know why they call downwind a 'soldier's wind,' Sewallis? Because any fool can do it!" Hugh took that moment to interject, laughing at his own jape.

"Don't taunt your brother, young man!" Lewrie snapped. "It's not the best time—you're going, and all of us not knowing when we'll clap eyes on each other again." Hugh, though, was irrepressible, only pretending to be subdued. Turning back to Sewallis, Lewrie said, "First-born sons' lives are never intentionally placed in jeopardy, me lad. Like yer grandfather just said, your familial duty is to grow up to be the heir, and carry on the family name and properties."

"Younger sons in the Army," Sir Hugo added, "if there's a title or estate and their eldest brother passes, ye know what they must do? Resign, sell off their commissions, and go back to civilian life t'take his place, take on the late elder brother's duties to his family. Get the title, the lands and rents, and do right by his younger brothers and sisters. Seen enough of it in my time," the old rascal grumbled. "Take their seat in Lord's, or stand for Commons."

"Like Harry Embleton?" Sewallis asked. "But *he's* in the Army, and he's Sir Romney's eldest. If the King called out the Yeomanry and the militia, *he'd* get to fight the French!"

"Only if they *invade* us, Sewallis," Sir Hugo said with a smirk of disapproval for that fool Harry, and the dubious worth of militia or the Yeomanry. "They'll never be called t'go overseas to fight the French, where the French *are*. Harry's just *playin'* at soldierin'!"

"Well then, couldn't *I* join Harry's regiment? At least I could get *some* military experience!" Sewallis cajoled. "When school term is over?"

Lewrie wryly shook his head. It would be too embarrassing, and take much too long, to explain to Sewallis the enmity that Harry still held for *anyone* named Lewrie, and why, and how slim his odds were of a commission under Harry Embleton if Harry ran the selection—*and* just how badly Sewallis would be treated if he did get such a commission!

"Better ye enjoy what's left o' your youth at Dun Roman, with your grandfather, son," Lewrie gently told him. "Coach to London with him and stay a week or so, now and again."

"Stay with your sister, and yer Uncle Governour and Aunt Millicent, too," Sir Hugo was *very* quick to add, looking as if he'd bitten into a lemon at the suggestion that he give up his pleasurable activities to play "daddy" to the lad, not the avuncular, now-and-again "grandfather"! "Do a summer term at school?" he hastily suggested.

"I *know* it's the way it's done, but . . . it still seems so *unfair!*" Sewallis mournfully said in a chin-down sulk.

Him stay with Governour and Millicent? Lewrie thought in dread; *Good God, they'll turn him against me, too? Maybe he should go into one o' the services 'fore I lose all my children!*

"Uhm . . . school, father," Sewallis hesitantly said, looking up. "Head-master said to tell you that the tuition, uhm . . ."

"Thought I'd paid it," Lewrie replied after a bite of juicy roast beef and a sip of wine. "Ye took my note-of-hand with you when ye returned for Easter Term."

"Not that one," Sewallis told him. "There's the extras for equitation, the swordmaster, the dancing instructor, and all. And there *is* a summer term. Not too many students attend, and not all of the faculty are there, but . . . I suppose I *could* attend, and take only a few courses. That way, I could have long weekends to visit grandfather in London now and then, and there's an interval, round Mid-Summer Day, long enough to go home to Anglesgreen and see Charlotte and the family."

"Perhaps that might be best . . . this summer, at least," Sir Hugo said after a long, head-cocked thought. "Know how much it'd be? D'ye have a list of the extra fees? I'll foot it. My treat, hey?"

"Thank you, grandfather," Sewallis said to him with warmth. "If I must become half an . . . an orphan, then I suppose I must be about it as best I can, and gain more education . . . as you say, father . . . for fulfill-ing my lot in life."

Could I feel any lower? Lewrie wondered; *any guiltier?*

They retired fairly early, since Hugh had to rise so early the next morn-ing; Hugh and Sewallis to one bed, and Sir Hugo and Lewrie to another. And the old bastard snored and made strangling noises like a wheezing ox about to expire! Sending Hugh off to his own uncertain entry into a hard, cruel adult life, abandoning Sewallis to his mournful and shy loneliness, to be batted like a tennis ball between school, his begrudging grandfather, and his bitter kinfolk, was enough to keep Lewrie awake and tossing long into the night, even without his father's snores and the occasional fart. To recall his parting with Charlotte was even worse!

"Pah-pah, *why* must you go *away?*" she'd wept at one minute, then, "Why can't Mistress Gower and her husband and my nanny take care of me at *our* house?" the next. Followed by "*Must* I move in with Uncle Governour and Aunt Millicent?" Followed by "Will I keep my pony, my dolls, and my own bed? My puppy?" No matter how much Millicent assured her that all her things would be with her, that she could play every day with her cousins—hadn't it been grand, last summer, when she had stayed with them, after all? Hadn't they had ever so much fun? Don't you know we love you like our own?—Charlotte had been disconsolate and utterly bereft. "But that was when Ma-Ma was coming back!" she'd stubbornly objected.

Pah-pah and Ma-Ma—that was Governour's and Millicent's doing. When he and Caroline had coached away, it had been Daddy and Mummy and she had been so gay, delighted to spend her time at their estate and play to her heart's desire, visiting her grandfather's estate daily.

Changin' her into their *sort o' Miss Priss!* Lewrie fumed.

Then had come the hateful vindictive, along with a fresh flood of tears and wails. "I'd still *have* my Ma-Ma if you hadn't taken her off to France! I'd still have *my house*, the way things were, but for *you!*"

She didn't *have* to add "I *hate* you, just go *away!*" to wound him any deeper as she'd stomped her feet, ignored all his attempts to explain it was the *French* who'd taken her mother; she had shrunk from his attempt to hug her and console her, then dashed from the parlour, and the house, screaming inarticulately, with a flying banshee's wail!

Recalling that all over again made Lewrie start fully awake and up-right in bed, to scrub his face with both hands and wish for dawn, seeing again Millicent's stricken look and Governour's grim satisfaction!

Awakened at 6 A.M. to dress, scrub up, comb their hair, and (for the adults) to shave, and they were down to the dining room for breakfast, even more subdued than they had been at supper.

"Say good-byes here, Sewallis, father," Lewrie instructed. "Hugh and I will go on to the docks by ourselves, hey?"

They were English, of the country gentry, so public displays of emo-tion were not for them. Sir Hugo chucked Hugh under the chin and told him that he was proud of him and that he should be careful and follow all his orders and remember to uphold the Lewrie name and its honour. "Yer father's brought lustre to it, and ye can do no less."

"So long, Hugh," Sewallis said, his arms folded cross his chest and his chin up. "I'll write. You be sure to, too, right? Tell us of how you get along. You lucky imp."

"G'bye, Sewallis," Hugh said in return, sticking out his hand to shake. "Give my regards to the other lads at school. Put ink in the proctor's port, like we planned? And, when you go to grandfather's, make sure you see to my horse now and then. Well?"

"I've a cart for your dunnage," Lewrie said. "I'll be back in a bit. Have a bit of time before I go aboard *Reliant* and you coach back to London, and we can say *our* good-byes. Right? Ready, Hugh?"

"Aye, sir," Hugh replied, easily turning "nautical."

The carter trundled along before them as they strolled along behind, past the last of the civilian part of town to the dockyards and the warehouses, then to the docks. It was a raw day, with solid grey overcast clouds and a fitful April wind, damp and a bit chilly, strong enough to clatter halliards and blocks, and make the seabirds complain as Hugh and his father reached the stone stairs down to the boat landing.

"One for *Pegasus*!" Lewrie shouted to the bargees, selecting the nearest lug-sailed boat the size of his gig, and leaving it to its two-man crew and the carter to heave Hugh's sea-chest into it.

"Well . . . ," Hugh muttered, childishly shuffling his feet in his new pair of Hessian boots, eager to be away yet loath to say a real, nigh-permanent farewell.

"God, how I hate this, Hugh!" Lewrie spat. "I know it's what ye want, what ye were fated for, as my second son, but still . . . it hurts t'see ye off. Navy's a *damned* hard life. No matter you're in great hands with Thom Charlton, I'll worry 'bout ye every day."

"I'll be fine, father, just you see," Hugh assured him, naïve despite all the cautions Lewrie had drummed into him. "We'll put the French in their place."

"Here," Lewrie said, reaching into his boat-cloak. "Your Navy pay as a Midshipman ain't much, so you'll be needin' some extra funds. Soon as ye report to Captain Charlton, give him this t'dole out t'ye. The Midshipmen's mess'll always have need to whip round for luxuries. Just don't let the others gull ye outta your money on foolishness or gamblin'. And don't let on you're better off than ye are, or *you'll* be the one they strip, right down to your bones." He gave him a note-of-hand and a small wash-leather purse containing ten pounds of coin. "And this."

From the small of his back, hooked to his own sword belt under his uniform coat, he withdrew a Midshipman's dirk in its scabbard.

"Wondered why I didn't buy ye one in London? That's because I was havin' my old one re-gilt. Leather of the scabbard's a bit worn, but that'd happen to a new'un, too, after a few months at sea."

"Your *own* dirk?" Hugh exclaimed, turning it over in his hands, drawing it and waving it in the weak sunshine, his eyes agleam in joy.

"Take good care of it, mind," Lewrie told him, and showed him how to slip it through the white leather frog on his belt, and how to thread the clam-shell catch into the slit in the leather. "There," he said further, satisfied that it was secure. "And when you attain your Lieutenancy, my old hanger will be yours, too."

"Your Napoleon hanger?" Hugh gasped. "No, Daddy . . . sir. Not that one. I'll not wear a sword that . . . murderer touched."

"This'un, then," Lewrie offered, patting the hanger that hung at his left side. "When the time comes."

Hugh looked relieved and nodded his beaming acceptance.

"Well then . . . might not've said it often enough, but you must remember that I love you, Hugh," Lewrie told him, wishing he could put his arms round the lad, kneel down, and give him a good squeeze. "And I am so proud of you I could bust. My regards to Thomas Charlton, and my thanks for taking you into his ship. S'pose it's time, though," he said, pulling out his watch to check the time. "Might take half an hour t'reach *Pegasus* on this wind, and it's best did you report just at Eight Bells, and the change of watch."

"Good-bye, Da . . . father. Sir." Hugh manfully said, sticking out his hand for an adult shake, though his eyes had suddenly gone a bit tearful. They shook, and, to shun the grief, Lewrie pulled him in to give him that last, brief hug, after all, and thump him on his back. "Remember all the pranks were played on me when I first joined. The molasses in the hammock . . . come hear the dog-fish bark? Gather dilberries from the main-top, and for God's sake, *never* go cryin' for a Marine Private Cheeks, and *absolutely* refuse if they play 'Building a Galley'!"

"I'll remember, sir," Hugh said with a shaky laugh as he stepped back, settled the fit of his coat, and doffed his hat in a salute, which Lewrie returned in equally grave manner. "Write me, often as you can. I'll write, as well."

"Good-bye, Hugh. Make us proud."

Then Hugh was down the slippery, green-coated stairs and into his boat. She shoved off, the lugsail raised as soon as the last of her dock lines was free. Lewrie stood with his hat aloft for another long minute, and Hugh gaily waved back at him with his, 'til the boat was fully under way, already shrunk to a toy. Another minute or so and it was almost lost in the early morning boat traffic.

And that was the end of a major part of Lewrie's life, his care for his children, his role of a father. Now what he had was a ship.

And a war.

BOOK V

Let the die be cast.
Begin the war and try your mettle.
Yet my case is already won—
With so many brave around me.

GAIUS PETRONIUS,

THE ROAD TO CROTON, 268-271

CHAPTER THIRTY-SEVEN

$\mathscr{N}$ever seen the like, sir!" Lt. Westcott marvelled again as a fresh boat-load of real, actual *willing* volunteers came aboard direct from the rendez-vous tavern. "We've almost all our necessary hands rated Able, lack but a dozen Ordinary Seamen, and so awash in Landsmen and boys that the Surgeon, Mister Mainwaring, is rejecting people for piles and lack of teeth!"

"I *told* you I was notorious, Mister Westcott," Lewrie drawled as he enjoyed a morning cup of coffee on the quarterdeck. "A bit of fame . . . good or bad, deserved or otherwise . . . goes a long way. My sort, well . . . I've dined out on it for years!"

Wonder of wonders, people in Portsmouth *had* flocked to his recruit-ing "rondy." Free Black sailors from the West Indies who knew him as "Saint Alan the Liberator" (a sobriquet he detested) because he had stolen a dozen plantation slaves on Jamaica and made them free to crew HMS *Proteus* back in '97. There were Irish and West Country men who'd heard that he had a lucky *geas* upon him, good cess. The lure of prize-money and adventure had brought some eager young lads, that and the fact that frigates had more elbow-room per hand than other ships.

Will Cony had come through with his offer of local lads from Angles-green, two hay waggons of them, for a total of twenty-one. They would be Landsmen, of course, totally ignorant and unable to hand, reef, or steer, but they could learn, and they could man the guns, haul the lines, and fight. "God A'mighty, lads, but for tuppence, I'd *gladly* sail with ya all!" Will had declared when he'd come out to the ship with them, and assured Lewrie that he'd sternly told them what they'd be in for, so every Man Jack of 'em was there willingly, despite what shipboard life would be like.

The Third Lieutenant, George Merriman, had shown up, and he had proved to be no threat to Westcott's seniority; Merriman had passed his examinations bare months before the Peace of Amiens, and had lingered on half-pay as a Passed Midshipman 'til the government had decided to go back to war. His name fit him aptly, for he was a cheerful sort.

Their last two Midshipmen had reported aboard, both very young and with only a year or two at sea between them. The twelve-year-old was named Munsell, the thirteen-year-old Midshipman was the Honourable Phillip Rossyngton.

"Rossyngton," Lewrie had exclaimed at the time. "I served with a Midshipman Rossyngton in the old *Shrike* brig, the tail-end of the American Revolution. Any kin?"

"My father, sir!" Rossyngton had proudly said. "Soon as we knew who commanded *Reliant*, he said to extend to you his fondest regards. He said I would be in good hands . . . though at risk of cat scratches."

"And are you as big a tongue-in-cheek scamp as he was?" Lewrie had teased.

"But of course, sir . . . I'm a Midshipman, and allowed it!" the lad had rejoined with a laugh.

That had made him feel even more ancient; the last time he had seen Rossyngton, who'd been about seventeen or eighteen, and the lad was his second or third son?

After that, even more people from his past showed up. *Reliant*'s ship's cook, the typical one-legged, lamed gammer who had been a part of the Standing Officers whilst laid up in-ordinary, a Jack Nasty-Face whose idea of "done" was either burnt black or boiled to the bones, had finally become too feeble to serve, and pled for Discharge and a pension. To re-place him, up had popped Gideon Cooke, one of the Beauman plantation slaves Lewrie had freed on Jamaica; he'd cooked for scores of slaves, and when liberated, had taken Cooke, with an E, as his new name, and the crew of the *Proteus* frigate had sworn they'd never eat so well in any ship.

Then there was Pettus, his former cabin steward in his previous ship, HMS *Thermopylae*. He'd practically fallen into Lt. Westcott's arms outside the recruiting "rondy," so eager was he to sign aboard, explaining that he'd been Lewrie's "man" before.

"What've ye been up to since, Pettus?" Lewrie had just had to ask. "Did you ever get back together with that girl of yours, Nan?"

"Thankee for recalling, sir," Pettus had told him. "I traipsed about, doing this and that, 'til I landed a place as barman at the Black Spread Eagle. As for Nancy, though . . . time I finally discovered her where-abouts, and her employment, well . . . there was another man had her heart," Pettus had said, heaving a world-weary shrug. "She'd married and already had a babe, and . . . ye know, sir," he resignedly had related. Perking up, though, he asked, "Still have your cats, sir? Toulon and Chalky? Along with Desmond and Furfy? It'd be good to see them again, sir . . . if you'll have me as your steward, that is, but I'll gladly sign aboard for anything," he'd vowed.

"I do, and they'll all be glad t'see you again, too, Pettus," Lewrie had assured him, and put him to work straightaway.

Pettus had proved very useful, too, in discovering a cook for the great-cabins, and a lad who'd serve as the cabin servant. He knew a man who fancied himself a *chef* who'd lost his position when the chop-house he worked in burned to the ground a few weeks back, and was yet in need of a new place. Pettus was quick to vouch for Joseph Yeovill and his culinary skills; he even came with his own pots, pans, knives, and utensils, and a middling chest of spices and sauces!

And, from the intake of youngsters who would serve as servants and powder monkeys, Pettus had chosen a likely orphan with a quick wit and a very sketchy year or so of schooling, a twelve-year-old lad by name of Jessop, who, 'til he'd signed ship's articles, looked to be a half-starved street waif, puppy-grateful to be issued clean clothing, have three meals a day, and a pittance of pay, to boot.

Lastly, Lt. Westcott had presented Lewrie with a likely fellow to be his clerk. James Faulkes had been an apprentice clerk to one of Portsmouth's counting houses and had just completed his terms of indenture. Though he seemed to suffer Pettus's malady, for he'd not only been let go from his position when the previous owner died, but Faulkes had recently been disappointed in love, and, like many a heart-sick young cully, believed that the lass, whoever she was, would take pity on him and accept his suit did he run away to sea. No matter, for his handwriting was copperplate and precise, his sums always added up, and he seemed very organised.

Of course *Reliant* had to resort to the Impress Service, drawn mostly from the Quota Men, a group that most officers, most tars, looked on askance. They were the derelicts, the drunks, the chronically under-employed and desperately poor; the turfed-out farm labourers who had nothing once the crops were in for the winter; the foolish and unwary civilians who had been swept up "will-he-nill-he" from the streets, public houses, and brothels by Press Gangs eager to make their numbers whether the men they collared were sailors or not; and the petty criminals from the gaols. With them came the risk that they'd been got at by radical, Levelling troublemakers and their French Jacobin ideas, as well as the theft and pilfering that came with them. Some of them surely would be insubordinate, obstreperous "sea-lawyers," constant discipline problems, the leaders and enforcers of the sly-boot cliques that would try to dominate their decent mess-mates, prey on the others' rations, tobacco, and rum issue, their better slop-clothing and shoes, with violence or the threat of it.

Given his druthers, Lewrie would have gladly arranged a swap with the Army—his worst men for cash—and spent the proceeds on Joining Bounties or bribes to the Regulating Captain of the Impress or one of his more venal subordinates, but . . . needs must in war time.

And, as *Reliant* filled with men and boys, she filled herself to the gills with supplies. A constant stream of barges, hulks, and hoys came alongside beginning at Eight Bells and the start of the Forenoon Watch at 8 A.M. and might not cease 'til the middle of the First Dog at 5 P.M. Clean new water casks first, then thousands of gallons of water from the hoys were pumped below to fill them. Bales of slop-clothing to garb the hands; blue chequered shirts, red neckerchiefs, and white slop-trousers, cotton and wool stockings and waist-length dark blue jackets with brass buttons; bags of shoes and steel buckles; square wood trenchers or cheap china plates and bowls; bales of blankets and bed sheets, piles of thin batt-stuffed mattresses and pillows, and the canvas hammocks in which they'd be placed.

Kegs of salt-beef and salt-pork came aboard from the Victualling Board warehouses, all carefully inspected by the Purser, Mr. Cadbury, to ensure that none were spoiled, rotten, or previously condemned and the brand marks effaced. There was no guarantee, though, that the kegs actually contained eight-pound chunks of preserved meat, and not more bone and gristle than meat . . . or, folded scraps of old sailcloth masquerading as rations, dropped in to bring the keg up to the proper weight!

Cheeses, oatmeal, small beer (safer to drink than water after a couple of months in cask!), wine both red and white, better known among sailors as "Black Strap" and "Miss Taylor," respectively; vinegar and tobacco, dried raisins, currants, and plums for duffs and puddings, in the rare instances, came aboard as well. And bread! Each man aboard got a pound of it a day (though issued at fourteen ounces to the pound, else the Purser would not profit!) in the form of pre-baked biscuit, a tooth-breaker unless soaked when it was fresh, and a crumbling, dusty slab of cracker riddled by weevils after six months at sea. Salt and pepper, meat sauces, sugar, honey, and ever-desired mustard to liven the taste of the rations, and the flour for the duffs were solely in the cook's possession, though mustard pots could be purchased by each eight-man mess . . . for a fee to the Purser.

Two complete sets of sails, plus spares and acres of sailcloth for repairs, patching, or whole refashioning came to the frigate, along with tar, pitch, resin and turpentine, miles of cable and rope, from thigh-thick cables for the anchors to small-stuff twine, and enough spare yards and upper masts to totally replace any shot away in battle or lost to weather; all the sail-maker's or the bosun's vital stores, and hundreds of board-feet of lumber for at-sea repairs.

The upper masts had to be set up to Lewrie's and Lt. Westcott's standards, the miles of standing and running rigging roved, and blocks of varying purchase placed at the most efficient locations. Belaying pins in pin-rails and fife-rails had to be sent for from shore once the rigging was set up. Lewrie found that Lt. Westcott agreed with his notion that their ship would be more weatherly if the jib-boom and bow sprit were steeved at a shallower angle than the usual up-thrust boar-toothed manner, and the jibs and upper foretopmast stays'ls were made larger and deeper.

Then came the artillery. HMS *Reliant* rated twenty-eight 18-pounder great-guns, eight quarterdeck 9-pounders, two 12-pounders for chase guns, and eight 32-pounder carronades, all with the wood truck-carriages or pivotting wood recoil slides; the carriages came aboard first, the cannon second. Then came the kegs and kegs of black powder to fill the belowdecks magazine, all the gun tools to load, worm out, swab, or shift the united carriages and barrels, and a bale or two of empty cartridge bags for the Master Gunner, his Mate, and the Yeoman of the Powder to fill and stow away.

And cutlasses and boarding pikes and muskets with all their accoutrements, and clumsy and inaccurate Sea Pattern pistols to be put in the locked arms chests 'til needed for drill or combat . . . it was a never-ending series of barges, of hoisting aboard with the main-mast course yard as a crane, and human muscle power, to hoist it all from the boats over the bulwarks and gangways and down onto the deck, or into the holds just above the bilges, or onto the orlop.

And each and every bit of Admiralty's largesse, seemingly down to each pot of mustard or each shoe buckle, had to be signed for and carefully inventoried, by both Purser and Captain, the usage and depletion of which over the course of the ship's typical three-year commission was to be carefully, meticulously accounted for, as well, or the ones responsible would be at their financial peril.

Ten days it took to prepare HMS *Reliant* for sea, for journeys to any of the far corners of the world, for battle against the foe . . . and Alan Lewrie found that he revelled in it!

It was not so much that he sprang from his bed-cot each morning at the end of the Middle Watch at 4 A.M. with joy, no. It was more like being so engrossed in details, in projects, in planning and supervising the labours of stowing and arming that he had no time to brood on his children's fates, the coming loss of his rented farm and his house, or the lingering remnants of grief over Caroline's loss. He found that he could actually go an entire day without thinking of all that, so busy with making decisions that it was only in those rare hours he spent on shore purchasing things he would need three months, six months, at sea, or the evenings when he dined alone and did not invite his officers and midshipmen in a few at a time to get a better grasp of them and their personalities, that he had time, in a proper captain's solitude, for musing.

Over twenty-three years in King's Coat, he realised one evening as he sprawled on his familiar old settee, his stockinged feet rested on his low, old Hindoo brass tray-table before it, with a cat nodding on either thigh and a glass of claret in his hand; *and now, this is all I am? My* father's *house for a home, do I ever set foot ashore again? The Navy a substitute family? Just damn my eyes . . . mine arse on a band-box! All these young sprogs come aboard . . . Middies and children of Mids from long ago? Good Christ!* He supposed it was natural, and inevitable, did he live long enough. There were only so many warships and only so many officers to command them. Large as the Royal Navy had grown since 1793 and the start of the war with France, it was still a small, esoteric and arcane world of its own, and he had risen to become a somewhat senior member of that salty, tarstained clique. He *had* to stumble across former shipmates sometime.

Whether they were worth the time to know again, well . . . that was another matter.

"You ready t'go t'sea again, lads?" Lewrie whispered to Chalky and Toulon. They opened their eyes to stare at him, Chalky yawning as he stretched every muscle, front legs out straight. "By God, I think that *I* am! No more shore shite. Let's get orders and be about it."

Chalky took that comment as an invitation to stand, arch up, and clamber up his chest, ready to play.

CHAPTER THIRTY-EIGHT

*T*he next two weeks at anchor were spent at Harbour Drill, the basic training of lubbers and Johnny New-Comes in the mystifying maze of sheets, halliards, lines, and cables, of braces, jears, and lifts, clews and brails. The proper way to tie a host of knots at sea; to go aloft and lay out on a yard; to set sail, to reef in or gasket, to strike or hoist up top-masts without being injured, maimed, or killed! Older, experienced hands got the rust scaled off their skills, as well, and were urged to take "newlies" under their tutelage. Men who had never touched a firearm or held anything more dangerous than the hoe, axe, or scythe in their civilian lives learned how to wield the cutlass and boarding pike, and were made familiar with pistol and musket 'til the loading, charging, and firing process could be done with some skill and speed; dry-firing first, then live-firing at a painted target on a scrap sail held aloft by two oars in an anchored rowboat at fifty yards' range off the ship's beam—with no one aboard it, of course, during the firing, and well clear of other ships or work-boats beyond it. The ship's people practiced with the swivel guns, as well.

Then came practice on the great-guns, the quarterdeck 9-pounders and carronades, the 12-pounder chase guns, and the heavy main artillery pieces down each beam, with half the hands hauling quickly on the run-in tackles to simulate recoil, to teach the "newlies" how quickly and brutally arms and legs could be broken, feet torn off or crushed, did they not look lively and keep clear of the truck-carriages and their tackles, blocks, and ring bolts. Lewrie could not risk actually loading and firing round-shot in crowded Portsmouth Harbour, but he could spend powder in full-measure charges to get his people used to the noise and the heart-fluttering, lung-flattening power of their discharge, along with the drill that would, hopefully, result in three broadsides every two minutes.

Then, when orders came, they came in a rush. Barely after his morning shave and sponge-off, Lewrie was summoned to the deck, noting the arms of the semaphore towers in town working like demented Dervishes.

"Hardinge, sir," a Midshipman said, doffing his hat to present himself. "From the *Modeste*, sixty-four? Captain Stephen Blanding? He wishes you, and your First Officer, to attend him on board as soon as possible, sir."

"Indeed, Mister Hardinge?" Lewrie replied, deciding to put on a scowl of displeasure, hands in the small of his back. "Why the haste . . . and not a written request?" he pretended to grump.

"Haste, indeed, Captain Lewrie, sir," the young fellow assured him, chin up and proud to be his captain's emissary on a vital mission. "I am given to believe a squadron will be formed for a specific duty. And Captain Blanding wishes me to inform you that this morning, word came from Admiralty that the King has given orders to begin issuing Letters of Marque and Reprisal. If that satisfies you as to the urgency of the matter, sir."

"*That* does, Mister Hardinge," Lewrie answered, feeling a thrill of satisfaction that what all had expected had come to pass. "Mister Warburton, pass the word for Mister Westcott at once. My compliments to him, and that he is to attend me in proper order."

"Aye aye, sir!" his own Midshipman, Warburton, shot back, beaming with joy that it would be war.

"Where away, Mister Hardinge?" Lewrie asked of *Modeste*'s anchorage, after turning aside to summon his Cox'n and boat crew.

"Off the Monkton Fort, sir . . . yonder," Hardinge supplied. "She will be the two-decker flying a broad pendant with white ball, and has dark red hull stripes, sir. Can't miss her."

"Speak for yourself, young sir," Lewrie japed. "It's a bit too early for my Cox'n's eyes. Captain Blanding plannin' to breakfast us?"

"I am certain he will, sir," Midshipman Hardinge further assured him, smiling for the first time and relaxing his tense pose; he'd *not* had his head bitten off after all!

A red broad pendant with a white ball upon it denoted a senior officer who would command a small squadron, a Post-Captain who for all appearances might as well be a Commodore but lacked that rank and had to captain his own ship, without another of Post-rank to take that burden. And *Modeste,* his putative flagship, was a sixty-four gunned two-decker of the Third Rate, with a French name and of obvious French construction—a previous capture for certain. Sixty-fours were a bit too light to stand in the line-of-battle anymore, but were still useful outside European waters. Her lines, the fineness of her entry and bow, and her aft taper made her look fast for a two-decker.

I live long enough, I could do worse, when my frigate days're done, Lewrie told himself as he took the salute from *Modeste*'s Marines and side-party, then was escorted aft to Capt. Blanding's great-cabins under the poop.

"Captain Lewrie, and Lieutenant Westcott, of the *Reliant,* sir," his escorting Midshipman announced.

"Aha! Lewrie!" Captain Stephen Blanding said with a glad bark of pleasure and welcome as he came from his sideboard in the dining-coach, cup and sauncer in one hand, and the other out for a cheerful shake. "Heard of you, sir. Good things, all! Welcome aboard my wee barge. Mister Westcott, is it? Welcome aboard to you, as well!"

Blanding was a stocky fellow, no doubt strong as an ox, but giving a roly-poly, aged cherub impression, with his belly girth and his very curly long blond hair, which he still wore clubbed back into a long sailor's queue, bound with black riband. "The others say they know you well, Captain Lewrie," Blanding said, waving his tea cup and saucer hand at the other officers seated in the day-cabin. "Captain Stroud of the *Cockerel* frigate, and Captain Parham of *Pylades?*"

"Good God above, it *is* a family reunion!" Lewrie blurted out at the sight of them. William Parham had long ago been one of his Mids aboard the *Alacrity* gun ketch, a converted bomb, 'tween the wars in the Bahamas. Stroud . . . ?

"We were together in the Adriatic in Ninety-Six, sir," Captain Stroud more sobrely told him. "I was First Officer in *Myrmidon,* a—"

"Commander Fillebrowne's Sloop of War, aye!" Lewrie said, going to shake hands with him warmly, even though he barely recalled him. "I do recall," he lied. "Congratulations on your command, Captain Stroud. And *Cockerel*! My first ship in Ninety-Three, as her First Officer. A fine vessel."

Even if her old captain and all his kin aboard drove us nigh to mutiny and madness! Lewrie recalled to himself.

"And Parham! Look at how you've risen since!" Lewrie went on, greeting yet another old shipmate. "And *Pylades* . . . I'm sure you know that she was with us in the Adriatic, too, with Captain Stroud. Captain Benjamin Rodgers's old ship, and you surely recall *him* from the Bahamas, ha ha!"

"Indeed I do, sir!" Parham enthusiastically replied. "Happy to serve with you again, happy indeed. And pray do express my greetings to your good lady when next you write her, and say that I recall her kindnesses to callow young Mids in those days quite fondly."

"Ah," Lewrie said, "I . . ." He stumbled as a chill came over the cabins, with Blanding coughing into his fist and "ahemming."

"Mistress Lewrie was most foully murdered by the French last year, sir," Blanding told Parham. "By that tyrannical despot Napoleon Bonaparte's orders to murder Captain Lewrie, here, as well."

"God, I am so *sorry*, sir, I didn't . . . The news of it did not reach me 'til this very instant!" Parham stammered, blushing deeply.

"The bastard," Parham's First Officer spoke up.

"Condolences, sir," Stroud's First Lieutenant said, and Lewrie gawped to see that that worthy was Martin Hyde, yet another of his Midshipmen from HMS *Jester*.

"Hyde, by God! I've an old friend of yours as my Second Lieutenant . . . Clarence Spendlove," Lewrie informed him as they greeted each other.

"Spendlove, sir? Aye, I'd admire a chance to come aboard and renew his acquaintance before we sail," Lt. Hyde said, glowing with delight.

"Well, now I've drug you all from your breakfasts, pray allow me to provide one whilst we get further acquainted and I discover to you what this is all about," Capt. Blanding chearly offered. He introduced Parham's First Lieutenant, Bilbrey, and his own, Lt. Gilbraith, all round as they took their seats.

There were hot slices of ham—slabs, rather!—there were crisp rashers of bacon, sizzling spiced sausages, even smoked kippers. With all that came fresh eggs, scrambled or fried to individual order, shredded potato hash, and fresh loaves of bread from a shore bakery, cut two fingers thick, offered with a hunk of butter as big as a man's fist, and four different pots of jam! All sluiced down with coffee or tea, to each officer's preference!

They reminisced for a time, and it was all quite jolly, sharing memories and hi-jinks of younger days. *Modeste*'s First Lieutenant, Mr. Gilbraith, mostly followed his captain's example as a trencherman *par excellence*, chuckling over others' "war stories" now and then whilst piling it down as heartily as Captain Blanding did. Stroud, well . . . as Lewrie remembered him, he'd been a drab, much-put-upon figure who made very little impression; a *grey* sort of fellow of unremarkable expression and wit, or looks.

Two of 'em with but the one epaulet on their right shoulders, Lewrie took note as he ate; *less than Three Years' Seniority, and both Parham and Stroud commandin' Fifth Rate 32-gunners? Anyone to join us later, I wonder? Or am I t'be second in seniority, in whatever this turns out t'be?*

"All stuffed?" Captain Blanding asked at last. "Won't eat this well where we're going. Belcher, clear away, then take everyone out on deck for a spell. I'll call should I have need of you."

A bit more conversation of the idle sort, as the tablecloth and plates were cleared, and fresh pots of coffee or tea set on the sideboard for their convenience, and the steward and cabin-servants left.

"Now then!" Blanding said by way of beginning, rubbing his hands together with as much eagerness as he'd greeted his first helping of breakfast. In point of fact, Capt. Blanding put Lewrie in mind of Commodore Ayscough, with all his boisterous *bonhomie* and energetic way. Minus the haggises, boiled mutton, and bag-pipers, of course!

"The Crown's decided there's no living with the French, so we're going back to war. No secret, there. What *we're* to do is to seek out, intercept if possible in European waters, but if they slip past us, go in chase of and bring to action a French squadron preparing to sail to the Americas . . . specifically, from Bonaparte's little puppet Batavian Republic—Holland to good Christians—for New Orleans. Any of us familiar with New Orleans and Spanish Louisiana?"

"I am, sir," Lewrie piped up, wishing he could let out the buttons of his breeches after such a feast. "I was there once."

"Excellent!" Captain Blanding barked with delight. "I trust your experience in those waters will prove of eminent use in our endeavour, sir."

"Why Spanish Louisiana, sir?" Captain Parham asked, raising one hand like a dutiful student. "I'd think the French would wish to establish a stronger naval presence at Martinique, or Guadeloupe, after we handed those colonies back to them last year, before we place all their coast under blockade once more."

"Or a new squadron at Cape François, on Saint Domingue. We'd not winkle them out of there without an army," Lt. Martin Hyde added.

"Sensible conjectures, all," Captain Blanding congratulated as he stirred sugar into his fresh cup of coffee. "But the fact of the matter is, about two years ago, Napoleon made a secret treaty with the King of Spain to exchange Tuscany, or Etruria, or whichever piss-pot conquest of his in Italy, for the return of Louisiana and New Orleans. Seems the King of Spain has a new brother-in-law with nowhere to hang his crown . . . or needs a crown *and* a place to hang it suitably grand-sounding to suit his dignity. Bonaparte would get the incredibly rich trade *entrepôt* of New Orleans, and territory to the west of the United States so vast that *no one* knows how far it goes.

"Well!" Blanding hooted. "Neither Great Britain nor our republican American cousins would *ever* stand for *that*! And even the Corsican half-breed ogre could realise the fact. Yet for a time he *did* consider building an American empire, and gathered an army in Holland to go take formal possession. This whole past winter, there's been a General Victor in Holland, with an army of three or four demi-brigades, whatever the Pluperfect Hell *those* are . . . anyone?"

"My brother-in-law tells me a demi-brigade is about two thousand men, sir," Lewrie contributed. "With engineers, artificers, and a large artillery contingent to fortify New Orleans and the forts strung down the Mississippi at the major bends. That might be an army as big as *ten* thousand men. Can't cram much more than five hundred of them aboard each transport, so that'd be . . . twenty ships, plus escort?"

"Damme, that would mean at least six or eight line-of-battle ships and frigates," Capt. Parham spoke up. "Mean to say, sir . . . are *we* all that's meant to oppose them?"

"Thank the Good Lord, this Victor chap was iced in all Winter and has had foul winds all Spring, during which time the situation has changed," Captain Blanding was quick to assure them, laughing the thought away. "Even before Easter, anyone could see the war's renewal, if they paid the *slightest* bit of attention or read but one newspaper a month! We will *not* face such a large force. You see . . ." Captain Blanding got as close to the dining table as his girth would admit, hunching bear-like on his elbows as he imparted his news in a softer mutter. "There are *sources* in Paris, d'ye see what sort I mean? They tell our people who deal in such matters that

Bonaparte has given up on his dreams for an American empire and will settle for cash . . . with which to expand his army and navy, and prepare to fight us.

"The French Foreign Minister, Talleyrand, has been negotiating the *sale* of New Orleans, and all of formerly Spanish Louisiana, to the Yankee Doodles!"

Holy shit on a biscuit! Lewrie thought, stunned; *and what will Charité de Guilleri make o' that, I wonder? Hide a pistol up her bum, get to hand-kissin' range, and shoot that bastard Bonaparte? Serve her right . . . serve him right, and spare us a sea o' bloodshed!*

"So they'll *still* send a squadron to Louisiana, sir?" Parham enquired, puzzled. "And do our . . . sources say how big it is?"

"Much smaller, for certain," Captain Blanding said, leaning back and making his poor collapsible dining chair creak alarmingly. "Else, Admiralty would not be sending only four ships in pursuit of them. I expect that the French will now use the formal exchange as a pretext for despatching more warships to the West Indies, perhaps even using the suddenly neutral port of New Orleans as a shelter for frigates and privateers. If there are transports, I also expect that they will be sent into Cape François on Saint Domingue to re-enforce what's left of their army fighting the slave rebellion, poor Devils. Perhaps only one or two of those demi-brigades will sail, with a much smaller escort, which might see a single battalion to New Orleans to make the ceremony of handing the place over all elegant and shiny. Fireworks, cannonades, a saluting volley or three? A band playing 'La Marseillaise'?" he disparaged with another hearty chuckle. "Then the French warships are free to pursue a *guerre du course* against our West Indies trade."

"Excuse me, sir, but the French would find New Orleans not very useful to them, even if it were American, and neutral," Lewrie pointed out. "The city is over an hundred miles upriver from the mouth of the delta, so the best they could do would be to establish themselves at the Head of Passes and Fort Balise, where the Mississippi flows out to the Gulf through several easily blockaded passes. Fort Balise is a small, weak, and easily defeated water bastion, but once the exchange is done, it's an American fort. And I doubt our Yankee cousins would let them anchor there or supply them with goods from the city if we're now at war with France."

"You've seen this Fort Balise?" Blanding asked, intrigued.

"Aye, sir," Lewrie replied, trying as usual for the proper English "pooh-poohing" modesty but, again as usual, failing badly at it. "That, and the city of New Orleans, in fact. A job of work for some Foreign Office types, a few years ago, in *mufti*, as the Hindoos say. French Creole patriots who wanted Spain out and France back in, and turned pirate t'finance their scheme, d'ye see? That's not t'say the Creoles and the pirates and privateersmen still there might not *wish* t'help the Frogs, but I don't see it done directly from New Orleans. Covert supplyin' through the bayous to Barataria, Timbalier, or Terrebonne Bay, or further west out of Atchafalaya or the Cote Blanche Bays. But . . . those are all very shallow waters, sir, barely deep enough for local schooners or small brigs, not *corvettes* or frigates. And they are bad holding-ground in a blow, with no shelter from the barrier islands. I'd expect one stiff diplomatic note from you, sir, to the new American authorities would force 'em to kick the French out and sit on anyone who'd sell 'em supplies. If Panton, Leslie & Company still does business in New Orleans, we could send a boat to Fort Balise, and a letter upriver, and know which merchant houses are involved within a fortnight . . . then turn 'em in to the local American government."

"Internment, by God!" Lt. Gilbraith, Blanding's First Officer, perked up and spoke for the first time since "might you pass me that strawberry jam-pot, sir?" over an hour before. "Do we bottle them up and send that note, the French could not remain forever at anchor in the city or at this bloody fort where the river forks! The Americans could be convinced to enforce the three-day rule and tell the French squadron to sail or surrender their ships on parole 'til the end of the current hostilities. They come out to give us honourable battle or they strike their colours and hang out in New Orleans taverns 'til the Last Trump, and either way, we've eliminated them as a threat. Ha?"

"Germane and canny as usual, Jemmy," Captain Blanding told him, "but dash my eyes! We've orders to go looking for a fight, and I'll be *very* disappointed should it end that way. I want *powder* smoke and *close* broadsides . . . struck colours, prizes, and a slew of dead Frogs!"

To which fierce sentiment they all gave loud, hearty huzzahs.

"Pray God, then, gentlemen," Lewrie seconded. "We catch them up at sea, *before* they can take shelter in *any* French possession or get to the mouth of the Mississippi. I wager we *all* wish an ocean of Frog blood!"

And huzzahs for that, too!

"How soon might your ships be ready to sail?" Captain Blanding demanded, posing the question to each Captain and First Officer; two days more for *Pylades*, only one for *Cockerel*, this very afternoon for *Modeste*, Gilbraith was quick to announce, and a one-day delay from Lt. Westcott.

"We lack the last of wardroom provisions and live-stock, sir," West-cott said. "We could fall down to Saint Helen's Patch whilst we see to all that, if I may suggest, sir?" he said, turning to Lewrie for permission. "A long sail or row for the victuallers, Captain Blanding, but . . . ," he con-cluded with a shrug and one of his brief tooth-baring grins. Lewrie took note, for the first time, that Westcott had a pug nose, almost Irish in its short sweep.

"Chicks!" Blanding boomed aloud. "Chicks and rabbits and game hens. They take much less room in the manger, and much less feed and water than pigs, turkeys, or beef on the hoof. Mature rapidly and are pro-lific at reproduction."

"A sack of fat rats t'be let loose in the flour, sirs?" Lewrie suggested, tongue-in-cheek. "Can't forget t'feed our Midshipmen!"

"I'd imagine we've rats enough for a dozen ships by now, sir!" Captain Blanding roared with laughter, slamming a meaty palm on the table top in appreciative mirth. "Saint Helen's Patch it will be, as quick as dammit, soon as you're all back aboard your ships. I *trust* your frigates will prove fast enough to keep up with *me*, sirs! She is French, *Modeste*, and very quick for a sixty-four, or so her former captain's records tell me. She's six more feet of waterline than the usual sixty-four from our yards. Second one of the same name we've taken off the Frogs," Blanding happily im-parted with a wink. "Built at Toulon in Ninety-Seven and lost in the Med a year later. One'd think the French would see her name's bad luck—for them, at any rate—and drop it for good."

"Uhm . . . Harbour Drill, sir," Lewrie had to point out. "We've barely had a fortnight to train the landsmen and new-comes. I'd like at least an-other ten days of it before considerin' my lads ready for sea, and battle. To get the best speed from *Reliant*, from all of our ships, and safe and efficient handlin', well . . ." He trailed off as he took note of the disappointed looks round the table.

"'Growl we may, but go we must,' Lewrie," Captain Blanding said with a scowl. "Aye, we're all short of *complete* training, but . . . take a page from the French and deem our crews ready enough to *get* to sea, then work them to perfection on the voyage, what?

"To *war*, gentlemen!" Blanding bellowed in a throaty growl, with an-other slam of his palm on the table top for emphasis. "We will shift our anchorages down to Saint Helen's Patch, and pray for a fair wind, just as soon as you complete your lading. From there, we will prowl 'twixt Ushant and Scilly 'til the French come down to us, or . . . should we miss them there, we'll hare cross the Atlantic in pursuit, into the West Indies and Gulf of Mexico. Either way, I am bound to see all of them in Hell before we're done.

"Admiralty's chosen *us*, given us specific orders," Blanding said in a calmer tone, fussing a bit with his coat lapels. "Given us a grand opportunity, *and* a demanding task, to smite the Devil on his snout, right from the outset. And he is . . . Napoleon Bonaparte. If not Satan come to the world, then his dread minion, the Anti-Christ, as many people of my circle have come to suspect of late . . ."

We on a personal Crusade o' his? Lewrie asked himself, suddenly wary of such an apocalyptic outlook, . . . and the messianic zeal for such a quest Blanding might display, to their overall detriment, when they did cross hawses with the French squadron; *How 'bout we fetch back the Holy Grail, too? Or the Golden Fleece!*

". . . his captains and sailors are the Devil's disciples, and I mean to see them returned below, as *failed* imps and demons!" Captain Blanding declared with a roar, which delighted everyone at-table, with Lewrie the only leery exception, though he did throw in a wee "Huzzah!" just to be sociable.

"You've Chaplains aboard, gentlemen?" Blanding enquired. "No? Ah well, no matter, for mine shall suffice for all, does wind and sea allow his calling aboard each ship for Divine Services on Sundays. And with God with us, who can be against us, hey?"

My God, I've been got at by a Leapin' Methodist! Lewrie quailed.

CHAPTER THIRTY-NINE

*T*he Crown's issuance of Letters of Marque and Reprisal had been announced on the sixteenth of May. By the nineteenth, their little squadron
had briefly set sail and had come to new anchorages in St. Helen's Patch,
near the Isle of Wight, to await a suitable slant of wind. Thankfully, the
weather had proved perverse for several more days, giving Lewrie and his
officers, warrants, and petty officers just a bit more time to train and exercise their raw crew, with sail-hoisting, reefing and handing, and recovering the anchors and stowing the thick cables of the most importance, and
only three hours of the working days spent on the artillery or small arms.

At long last, on the morning of the twenty-third of May, 1803, the
wind came round to the Nor'east and a flurry of signal flags fluttered up
HMS *Modeste*'s halliards, so many and so quickly that Lewrie could imagine the boisterous and impatient Captain Blanding standing over his men
and patting a foot, drumming his fingers on his substantial midriff, and
clucking at the delay, human failure, and Beelzebub's minions.

"All ship's numbers, and 'To Weigh' two-blocked, sir!" Midshipman
Entwhistle cried, with a telescope pressed to one eye.

"Hands are at Stations to weigh, sir," Lt. Westcott reported.

"Very well," Lewrie replied. "Up-anchor and make sail when the Preparative is struck, Mister Westcott."

"Aye aye, sir," Lt. Westcott said, eyes glued to the wee bit of bunting aboard the flagship.

"I must own it feels rather good t'go to sea again," Lewrie idly commented, hands in the small of his back, head down, and pacing his quarter-deck. "For you, Mister Westcott?"

"Well, sir . . . considering the deprivation and discomfort we're in for, I may be of two minds," Westcott confessed with a brief grimace. "And I thank you for a last night ashore, in which I could savour the pleasures we leave behind, t'other day. Wine, women, song . . . a fine repast or two . . . women." He flashed one of those short, teeth-baring grins, which was as quickly gone.

"I trust she was handsome, sir?" Lewrie asked, lifting a brow in surprise to hear his First Officer admit he'd rantipoled. "One of them special?"

"They were, uhm . . . *both* equally fetching *and* special, sir," Lt. Westcott said with a sly smile.

Christ, am I in the presence of a master cocksman? Lewrie just had to wonder; *two in one night . . . he's* miles *ahead o' me, even on my best old days!*

"Are either of good family, then our sailing is your salvation, sir!" Lewrie barked in amusement.

"So to speak, indeed, sir," Westcott replied, chuckling.

"Preparative is *down*, sir!" Midshipman Entwhistle cried.

"Get us under way, sir," Lewrie ordered, turning sterner.

HMS *Reliant*'s departure was not *exactly* "Man-O'-War Fashion" or even "Bristol Fashion"; it was sloppy and inelegant, no matter how much time had been spent at Harbour Drill. The lighter kedge anchor had come up easily from the ooze, the slimy thigh-thick cable trotted forward in an undulating snake, but the best bower proved stubborn, and the confusion at the main capstan to wind up the messenger could have been almost laughable if it had not been a serious matter. Yards creaked up from their rests as a'cock-bill as they'd be set for a sea burial, and sail-tending lines—and braces once half the sails were unfurled—were swaying loose and free 'til the Bosun and his Mate, and the petty officer mast-captains, bellowed, roared, and rushed among the raw newlies to urge them to tail on and haul.

It did not help that much larger squadrons of Third Rate line-of-battle ships, First and Second Rate three-decked flagships leading them out, had been waiting for that shift of wind to sail and take up blockading stations off the French coast, too, each of them thinking that their orders took precedence over the others, and especially took precedence over a lowly 64 and her three frigates.

Closest I've seen to Bedlam since the last time I toured the real'un with a water squirt and a pokin' stick! Lewrie told himself as *Reliant* at last got way enough on to be steered into *Modeste*'s wake and take station in a *very* rough in-line-ahead . . . with his head swivelled like a crazed compass needle to avoid *so many* imminent collisions; *If this is the best we can do after a year idle, God help us!*

Reliant ghosted along, the second in their short column, about a cable and a half astern of *Modeste*; close enough for everyone on the quarterdeck to witness Captain Blanding as he strode from one side of his poop deck to the other, too enraged to stay on his own quarterdeck, a brass speaking-trumpet in his hand to bellow at the columns of line-of-battle ships sailing along on either beam . . . some too close for comfort, and others slipping a bit loo'rd or slanted as if to drive right through his own column.

"God *rot* you, Cummings! I *know* you can edge up more windward than *that*!" Blanding roared to larboard, then dashed to starboard and warned, "That you, Fairbairn? Haul your hellish wind a point or you'll be *aboard* me, do you *hear*, there? Haul *off*, I say, Andrew! Haul off! Oh, the Devil take it! Gilbraith? Load a gun, and we'll *hull* anyone who gets within a cable of us!"

Lewrie wrapped his arms across his chest and tried to maintain a stern, determined expression on his phyz, but began to shake with amusement, reduced to making snorting noises. "And how'd I miss makin' *his* acquaintance, all my years in the Navy?" he guffawed, turning to look at Westcott, who was also laughing as silently as he could. "We had best take a first reef in the main course, Mister Westcott. Do we run too close to his stern, he just might fire at *us*!"

Once clear of the Isle of Wight and into the Chops of the Channel, their little squadron was pressed to maintain course Sou'west as if bound for the Channel Islands. A long line of at least a dozen big two-deckers and their flagship passed down their starboard side about a mile alee, taking their own sweet time to wheel about to West-Sou'west, altering course one at a time when they reached the large, disturbed patch of sea where the lead ship had first turned.

After the last of the "liners" had made the turn, *Modeste* put up a signal for them to do the same; "Alter Course in Succession" and a second hoist indicating "Course Due West." A third signal went up another halliard, ordering a three-cable separation. Down came the Preparative, and *Modeste* came about, already making more sail. As *Reliant* reached *Modeste*'s disturbed patch, the helm was put over, and she went about, with Lt. Westcott busy instructing the hands to brace about for taking the wind on her starboard quarters. When Lewrie judged that the flagship was almost three cables distant, he called for the reef to be shaken out of the main course, and all plain sail set.

There was still another long column of ten or eleven two-deckers astern of them, looking as if they would either slice between *Cockerel* and *Pylades* or run right over Parham's frigate, but . . . they were on their way.

"Dismiss the hands from Stations, Mister Westcott, and set the larboard watch," Lewrie ordered. "If everything is squared away, all 'tiddly,' that is."

"It is, sir, right down to the hawse bucklers," Lt. Westcott informed him with a squinty look of amusement still on his face.

"My word, now that was excitin'," Lewrie said, chuckling softly. "Clumsy . . . embarrassin' . . . cunny-thumbed lubberly, but excitin'."

"So sorry, sir," Westcott said, suddenly downcast.

"Not your fault, Mister Westcott," Lewrie assured him. "With a crew as raw as ours, and with so little time allowed for workin' 'em to competence, I'm just relieved we got out without killin' anybody in the process, or bein' trampled by a two-decker. Now we're out at sea, though, we can continue drillin' 'em proper, to our *mutual* satisfaction of readiness."

"Thank you, sir," Westcott said with a nod of his head.

"Damn my eyes, it's a nice morning, ain't it?" Lewrie said as he looked up at the commissioning pendant streaming towards the bows, at the wind-ful sails and set of the yards' bracing; at the clouds and the patches of blue sky. "A merry May morning."

"Indeed, sir," Westcott agreed. "And the sea's moderate."

"We'll give the hands one hour in which to gawk and get used to her motion," Lewrie decided. "And some music'd suit. Desmond?" Capt. Lewrie called out. "Your lap-pipes and the other musicians, and give us some cheer!"

"Right away, sor!" his Cox'n shouted back.

Liam Desmond and his *uilleann* pipes, the young Marine drummer and two fifers, a couple of older hands who produced their fiddles, and one fellow with a shallow Irish drum, even the cook's assistant with a set of spoons beaten on his thigh, all joined together amidships in the waist atop a hatch grating. Farewell airs like "Portsmouth Lass" and "Over the Hills and Far Away"; spritelier tunes such as "The Parson Among the Peas" and "One Misty, Moisty Morning"; drinking songs like "I'll Fathom the Bowl" and "He That Would an Alehouse Keep"—an item mentioned in the recruiting flyers strewn about Portsmouth had promised "music and dancing nightly"—went down well with all hands, prompting some experienced tars to teach the "lubbers" how to dance a horn-pipe.

"'It was pleas-*ant* and delightful, on a midsummer's morn, when the *green* fields *and* the *mea-dows* were buried in corn . . . ,'" the sailors began to sing, bringing a touch of a smile on Lewrie's face for the first time.

"'. . . and the larks they sang melodious, and the larks *they* sang melodious, and the *larks* they sang melo-*dious, at* the dawning of the day,'" Lewrie joined in under his breath, though his right hand beat the measure in the air, feeling a swell of unwanted emotion, the sort best hidden aft and below in the great-cabins.

> *. . . said the sailor to his true love,*
> *I'm bound far away.*
> *I'm bound for the Indies,*
> *where the loud cannons roar,*
> *and I'm going to leave my Nancy . . .*

He turned away to face out-board, to larboard, pacing down to the lee rails, squinting with suddenly damp eyes. He reached into his coat for a handkerchief.

> *. . . and if ever I return again,*
> *and if ev-er I return again,*
> *and if ev-er I return again,*
> *I would ma-ake you my bride!*

"Damned nonsense," he muttered, blowing his nose, yet . . . the last verse! "'. . . oh-*oh,* no my love, farewell. Saying may I *go* along with you . . . saying *may I* go along with you . . . say-ing *may* I go *along* with *you . . . oh*-oh, no, my love . . . fare-*well.*'"

"A fresh cup of coffee, sir?" his cabin steward, Pettus, asked, arriving on the quarterdeck with Lewrie's old black-iron pot.

"Uhm? Aye, Pettus, that'd be welcome," Lewrie told him, taking one last embarrassed swipe at his face. He wandered back up the slight cant of the deck to his proper place at the windward bulwarks, his and his alone as captain. "Coffee, Mister Westcott?"

"Aye, sir, thank you," Westcott eagerly replied, accepting a cup from Pettus, but waving off goat milk or sugar, preferring it "*noir*."

"Is our wardroom musical, sir?" Lewrie asked as Desmond led the musicians into "The Jolly Thresher."

"One or two decent voices, sir, but no instrumental talents that I've been able to discover," Lt. Westcott told him. "I believe, however, that the Midshipmen's mess is where you'll find fiddlers and tooters on recorders, flutes, and such . . . perhaps a guitar?"

"And you, Mister Westcott?" Lewrie further enquired.

"I clap and beat time marvellously well, sir," Westcott said, a brief chuckle of self-deprecating humour punctuating his claim. "May I ask if *you* are musical, sir?"

"I've a penny-whistle," Lewrie allowed with a modest shrug. "An host of people have *begged* me to toss it, but . . ." He took a sip from his battered old pewter mug, chuckling himself, unable to remember if he had packed it in his sea-chests or had left it with his furnishings that had been carted over to his father's house.

No matter, for the winds seemed to increase a bit, and *Reliant* heeled loo'rd a degree or so more. Sunlight breaking through the thin clouds dappled the deck and straining sails, and glinted diamond-like on the sea before the bows. Desmond and his band were now giving the crew a rendition of a minuet, one unfamiliar to Lewrie, and its pacing seemed to synchronise with the frigate's stately motion. She rolled a bit to loo'rd, then rose up horizontal; she snuffled her bows into the sea and came gliding a bit bows-up, with the jib-boom and bow sprit an orchestra leader's baton. Even the chop of the Channel that could make a passage feel as rough as an un-sprung waggon on a rocky road felt as smooth as a chalked dance hall floor, over which *Reliant* swanned with the grace of an elegant young woman.

"Pleasant and delightful, indeed," Lewrie muttered, taking more than a little joy in the feel of a ship under him once more, savouring the sunshine, the moderate and pacific seas, the wind, and . . . the far horizon beyond the thrusting jib-boom. What lay there, well . . . that was up to Fate, but . . . didn't they say that the getting there was the most fun?

CHAPTER FORTY

*O*nce *Modeste*'s squadron was alone on the Atlantic, free and able to manoeuvre, without being flanked by those other columns of warships, Captain Blanding began to act more like a Rear-Admiral. Even as they made their way to a point mid-way 'twixt Ushant, the northwestern most tip of France, and the Scilly Isles and Land's End, he worked his four ships like one of those massive columns.

They wore in succession off the wind, they tacked in succession to windward; he signalled for them all to tack to form a line-abreast, then come about as one to form a line of battle. They sailed Nor'west to the Scillys in-line-ahead, then reversed course by wearing in succession at one instance, or wore or tacked together to re-form line on the reciprocal heading.

For the most part, Captain Blanding preferred that HMS *Reliant* be the lead ship in-column, with his flagship, HMS *Modeste*, the second, and the lighter frigates, *Cockerel* and *Pylades,* astern of him, obviously planning for the wished-for combat to come and placing the heaviest weight of metal, and the largest artillery, at the forefront where his initial broadsides would do the most damage, cause the most consternation. He would, though, alter their order to give Captains Parham and Stroud experience at leading.

He also worked the signalmen half to death. Blanding had gotten copies of Adm. Home Popham's revised signals book of 1803 for all ships and was so delighted with how many thousands of words, how many phrases and orders could be expressed by one-to-four numeral flags, that Mids and men of the Afterguards aboard all four warships could swear that the fellow had "flux of the flags" from dawn to dusk, ordering up any idle thought that rose in his head, to be transmitted to one and all!

Night signals, thank the Good Lord, were so rudimentary and simple that they were more like the inarticulate bellows of a village idiot desirous of a bowl of pudding. Lanthorn frames, false flares, all of them announced by the discharge of a cannon; several cannon for some of them, with the lanthorns hoisted aloft in the frames arranged in diamonds, squares, or other shapes. A row of three lights meant "Tack," with four guns the signal for execution, and a further gun for each point of of the compass to be crossed. Capt. Blanding was mostly mute during the night, especially when it came to manoeuvring ships in the dark . . . though he *did* issue rather a lot of invitations to supper!

The good weather on their day of departure did not last long, of course, though that did not deter the fellow from continuing their working-up in the occasional half a gale of wind, or rain, and with no consideration of the sea-state. "By Jingo, it won't be all 'cruising and claret' 'til we meet up with the Frogs, haw haw!" Blanding would declare with a fierce scowl, and a meaty palm slammed on his dining table, just before breaking out in a hearty belly-laugh.

After a fortnight of such training, with no sign of the French squadron in the offing, Blanding broke them up into pairs to scout a line from Nor'west to Sou'east, Lewrie and *Reliant* paired with one of the Fifth Rate 32s, with ten or twelve miles between them, depending on the weather and the limit of visibility, and no more than ten or twelve sea-miles between the two pairs, resulting in a scouting line fourty or fifty miles in length cross the hundred miles 'twixt Ushant and the Scillys, through which the French *must* pass—if they were indeed coming.

Except for Sundays. Then Blanding would order all ships into two short columns abreast and send his Chaplain to each ship in turn for Divine Services. Chaplain Brundish was a much younger fellow than Lewrie had expected, almost as stout as his patron, but agile and energetic. He was well read and a charming, erudite supper-table guest, as full of *bonhomie* as Blanding and, like many gentlemanly members of the Church of England, spoke glowingly of steeplechasing and the fox hunt, of how he missed his hounds and his favourite hunters. He had a wealth of *decent* amusing tales and japes, played the flute, recorder, and the violin, and was possessed of a loud, deep baritone voice. His homilies were marvels, too. Oh, he'd rail against the common sailors' sins of giving in to boredom and *ennui*, of petty theft and drunk on duty, nodding off on watch, but they were mostly short, pithy, and very nautical, full of animus against their foes, "mateyness" between their own, of upholding God, King, and Country as a moral, religious *calling*, as a Good Work that would lead them all to Salvation and the Eternal Glory . . . all of it bracketed by well-known, beloved hymns of the up-lifting, muscular sort that left even the leery men with grins on their faces, and humming the tunes as Chaplain Brundish departed in Captain Blanding's cutter to minister to the next ship and crew.

He, surprisingly for a man of the cloth, knew his way with the cutlass and small-sword, and had a keen eye with a musket.

After the third Sunday at sea, though, *Modeste* put up a signal for *Reliant* to come close alongside. With both ships loafing along under reduced sail, both rolling, heaving, and snuffling foam, about fifty yards apart, Blanding took up a speaking-trumpet and bellowed, "This is looking to be a rum go, Lewrie! The only Frogs we've seen are *prizes* took by *other* people!"

Wars could be declared, but merchantmen on-passage had no way of learning of it; warships returning from overseas or cruising on an innocent patrol beyond the reach of coastal semaphore towers could not be informed either, and the first they would know of it would be the pugnacious approach of an enemy warship or privateer with gun-ports open and artillery run out. Such surprises would happen to ships of both sides. Frustratingly, whilst their squadron had scouted round the approaches to the English Channel, other, luckier, British warships had sailed past them with French prizes in tow, or the odd enemy merchantman sent in under a prize-crew, with the Union Flag flying above the French Tricolour to mark the new possessor.

At several of their suppers aboard *Modeste*, Blanding had wrung his hands, or gnawed his napkins to nubbins, to be bound by specific orders which denied them the chance to hare off in search of prizes, too, and was forced to watch other captains send in fresh fortunes to be made in the Admiralty Prize-Courts.

"If they didn't sail before the war was declared, they may not have come out at *all*, sir!" Lewrie had shouted back to him. "This could be a wild goose chase!"

"And, did they put to sea a day or two *before*, then they are weeks ahead of us by now!" Blanding had roared back, despair in his voice. "It just ain't on, dash my eyes! We will go the West Indies and the mouth of the Mississippi, Lewrie! Our orders demand we do no less . . . whether they are really there or not! 'Bring to battle, or pursue,' we're ordered. Then pursuit it will be! Order of sailing . . . *Pylades*, your *Reliant*, then me, with *Cockerel* the hind-most! Two miles' separation 'tween ships, and shape course West-Sou'west, half West, cross the Bay of Biscay!"

"Aye aye, sir!" Lewrie had bawled back, wondering if his whisky, mustard, and store of jerked meat and sausages for the cats would last that long. More disturbingly, would he have to sift, rinse, and dry their litter for re-use, should the level of sand in the barrel run low?

"The Indies, sir?" Lt. Westcott asked after coming up to the windward side of the quarterdeck, with a brief tap of two fingers upon the brim of his hat for a salute.

"It appears so, Mister Westcott," Lewrie said with a sigh. "The hands . . . damned few of 'em have had a chance to go there. Damned few have ever been exposed to Yellow Jack and the other fevers, 'cept for some of our older hands, our Blacks, and such. We'll be arriving right at the height of summer, when it's the sickliest. If we don't have to spend *too* much time close to shore, we might escape the worst of it, but . . . perhaps our Surgeon, Mister Mainwaring, has some fresh insights about Yellow Jack and malaria?"

"A long passage to get there, sir," Westcott said, shrugging in a fatalistic way. "Do we not run across any foes on the way, at least we will have Captain Blanding's hoped-for skills imparted to them . . . before we start to lose some of them."

That made Lewrie cock a brow and peer closely. "Rather, let us hope, *must* we lose some of our people, it comes in battle, and not the fevers first, Mister Westcott," he told him.

CHAPTER FORTY-ONE

*T*hey went roughly Sou'west cross the Bay of Biscay, hundreds of miles out into the mid-Atlantic and offshore from France and the newly established British blockading squadrons, "reaching" most days on the prevailing Westerlies with the winds abeam and sails set "all to the royals" when the weather allowed, making haste. Captain Blanding let them be to bowl along like a Cambridge coach and work on their sail-tending and gunnery practice, his desire to press on over-riding his penchant for squadron manoeuvres, and unwilling to lose a single mile, a single hour, of his pursuit—whether they were chasing a Will-o'-the-Wisp or not.

They encountered only one other ship, off Cape Ferrol, the very northern-most tip of Spain, and that was another British frigate, headed home from the Far East and unaware that the war had resumed until they informed her. Then they plunged on further South, with the winds shifting 'til the latitude of Cape St. Vincent, where the first of the Nor'east Trade Winds began, and they could alter course West and ride them cross the Atlantic to the West Indies, running down a line of latitude for the most part.

It was only then that the four Ship's Surgeons held a meeting aboard *Modeste* to discuss preventatives against the Yellow Jack and malaria. It was not productive.

⚓

"They're certain that we should avoid all shore miasmas, sir," Mr. Mainwaring told Lewrie in his cabins after returning back aboard. Mainwaring was a stout fellow in his mid-thirties, so grizzled, though, that he put Lewrie in mind of a professional boxer, with massive hands and thick fingers. "The jungle, forest, marsh, and swamp night mists. We should avoid any anchorage that does not have a sea breeze to keep land winds, and the noisome mists, at bay. And, there is the *chichona* bark powder, which is efficacious at combatting either of the fevers," he explained, shifting in the collapsing chair and making it creak in an alarming way as he sipped a welcome glass of Lewrie's Rhenish.

"Once they're *caught*," Lewrie grumbled, "not before."

"The medical records show no usefulness in administering *chichona* bark tea to prevent outbreaks, sir . . . sorry."

"And the citronella I wrote them about, sir?" Lewrie asked. "My former Surgeon, Mister Durant in *Proteus*, used it in lanthorn oil and in candles, and we suffered very few cases of Yellow Jack after our initial plague. The Spanish and Portuguese colonies burn citronella candles by the *ton* in Fever Season, and *they* don't die by battalions."

"Ehm . . . the uses your former Surgeon cited, Captain sir, were accompanied by keeping their houses, their windows, shut at night, to keep out the miasmas," Mr. Mainwaring hesitantly related, with a faint scowl on his rugged face. "Secondly, the others reckoned that the Dons and the Portuguese have, after a couple of centuries, developed a toleration, and their only mortalities are *some* of the newborn and those just arrived in their colonies. And, thirdly, sir . . . it's the *cost* of it. The others are loath to purchase large quantities of what may be a folk nostrum of no use. Like all their other medicaments, it comes out of their own pockets. Out of *mine*, sir," he pointedly added.

"Humour me, Mister Mainwaring," Lewrie stubbornly told him. "Do we put in somewhere that citronella candles and oils are available, *I* will buy it . . . and *we* will employ it, even if the other ships do not. I've seen it work . . . God knows why, but it *seems* to. If anthing else, it seems to keep the hordes of mosquitoes at bay. We'll place tubs of candles round the hatchways at anchor, burn candles belowdecks instead of the issue glims after dark, do we cruise close ashore or in a lee of an island. And, for good measure, I'm certain you'll wish to get more *chichona* bark powders, do our people come down with Yellow Jack."

"Of course, sir," Mainwaring replied, though it was uncertain whether he was agreeing about the *chichona* bark powders or submitting to a captain's odd caprice; in his experience as a Ship's Surgeon, and in discussions with his fellows, Mainwaring had come to learn that Navy captains could be an eccentric lot.

Weeks later, in late June, the squadron was alee of Martinique and looking into the major naval port of Fort-de-France. Surprisingly, the windward approaches from the Atlantic, and the harbour itself, were already being watched by a slim squadron of three frigates or sloops of war, who reported that no fresh French squadron had been seen there, and what few enemy warships were present were effectively bottled up.

"Hear about Commodore Hood, sir?" the senior captain had called over to them with a speaking-trumpet. "He's already taken their island of Saint Lucia, and the port of Castries, and is now off to do the same to Tobago! Capital, what?"

Further North at Guadeloupe, and it was much the same story off the fortified lee-side harbour of Basse-Terre. Rear-Admiral Sir John Thomas Duckworth, commanding the Jamaica Station, must have had early premonitions or secret despatches alerting him to the fresh outbreak of war, for he had sent his few warships of a peace-time squadron out to sea, just like Commodore Sir Samuel Hood of the Leewards Islands Station. They were informed that some French privateers had gotten out to prey on British merchant shipping, but there were hardly any warships in Basse-Terre, and they showed no signs of sallying.

The ships watching Guadeloupe had not seen Blanding's mythical French squadron, either, and suggested that they might try further to the North, at St. Barthélemy or St. Martin . . . St. Domingue? "And the very best of luck to you at . . . whatever it is you're doing!"

"Were I a cursing man, a blasphemer, gentlemen, I'd be in full cry by now! Dash it! *Dash* it, I say!" Captain Blanding fumed as he stomped round his great-cabins, his face going plummy whilst holding yet another officers' conference aboard *Modeste*. "And why can I *not* engage in some raw Billingsgate, Brundish?" he demanded of his Chaplain, "when it would feel so *bloody* good about now?"

"Stoic acceptance of frustration and misfortune are the mark of the Christian, English gentleman, I fear, sir," Brundish calmly replied over a glass of claret. " 'Better to light a candle than to curse the darkness,' all that? Spurs the mind to finding solutions, I vow."

Blanding let out a clenched-teeth growl of displeasure.

"Best bet's Saint Domingue, sir," Lewrie pointed out, enjoying a glass himself. "Don't know much about Jacmel, on the South coast. Toussaint L'Ouverture took it and eliminated his rivals long ago, so I doubt the French ever got it back. But there's Port-au-Prince, if the Frogs got that far South, but it'd take a proper fleet and a big army t'go in there, if that's where they shelter. After that, there's Mole Saint Nicolas, up on the Western coast, then Cape François, the main port on the North. I'm *fairly* sure the French still hold those."

"By the skin of their teeth, I've heard, sir," Captain Stroud stuck in. "The fellow who took over from L'Ouverture when the French caught him and shipped him off to France, General Dessalines, has run the Frogs from the interior. Do they land troops, I'd think they'd be more than welcome at one of those two ports Captain Lewrie cites."

"Mouth of the Mississippi?" Captain Parham spoke up. "That, or French Guyana? We took it in Ninety-Eight or Ninety-Nine, I forget which, but—"

"In South-rotting-*America*, sir?" Captain Blanding squealed—or gave a fair approximation of a squeal. He rushed to pour himself more claret, not waiting for a cabin-servant.

"Failing Saint Dominguan harbours, sir, we might have to look into Spanish ports on the Gulf of Mexico, as well," Lewrie said with gruff despondency, despite how amusing Capt. Blanding's outbursts were. "Havana, on Cuba? Pensacola, Mobile in Spanish Elorida? Then there's Tampa Bay, and there's a quite good deep-water harbour just above the East end of the Florida Keys . . . Tamiami, or something like that. No proper town, garrison, or fortification like Saint Augustine on their Eastern coast, but it'd suit." Lewrie turned to poll his fellow captains. "Anyone know if Spanish Florida is part of the territory to be traded to the French . . . and sold to the Americans, along with Louisiana?"

"God rot the . . . !" Blanding snapped, even further exasperated. "Next you know, we'll be poking our noses into the Arctic! Prowling the coasts of bloody *Greenland*! By all that's holy, I—" He shut up quickly, admonished by a stern finger wagged by Chaplain Brundish. Captain Blanding sat himself down, heavily, into a stout chair.

Damme, but he's fun t'watch when he's explodin', Lewrie thought.

"There's ocean's of prize-money being reaped," Blanding mused aloud,

absently patting his curly blond locks and gazing upwards at the overhead. "As we've heard on our way up the Leewards, sirs, there is fame and
glory being won, and more to come when all the rest of the French West
Indies islands are seized, yet *we . . . we* swan about like a pack of imbeciles
let loose from Bedlam, hunting for ghosts. *Ghosts*, I say, who might *never*
have sailed! Why, by the time we've looked into all the ports we've suggested, lurked off the mouth of the Mississippi, and found *nothing*, ah . . . !
We'll be forced to turn ourselves over to Duckworth or Hood, for general
duties. Now *all* know the war's on . . . ," Blanding trailed off, and stuck
his nose into his wine glass.

It was not *exactly* the Proper Thing for a senior officer to express himself so freely, to doubt aloud. Well, Lewrie *might've*, but only in his early
days, and he'd learned better since.

Lose his broad-pendant, for starters, Lewrie thought, busying himself
with his own wine as the others shuffled their feet and got very silent and
depressed-looking; *Admiralty picked* him *for this hunt special, and what'll a
failure do to his career . . . even if the French squadron never existed, and he'll
have to report that? Not* his *fault, really, but . . . hmmm. When* did *Duckworth and Hood learn of the declaration of war? When did the Frogs?*

"Look here, sir," Lewrie said. "Assume the French sailed before us, by
a fortnight or less. Letters of Marque were issued in mid-May, and the official declaration of war came on the eighteenth. Now, did they get down-
Channel before that—by a fortnight or less!—they would've sailed in a
fog, whilst we—"

"What's the dashing *weather* to do with it, sir?" Capt. Blanding quickly
sneered back.

"Metaphorical, sir . . . a lack-of-information sort of fog. They *couldn't*
know of the state of war when they left Holland," Lewrie continued,
warming to his topic. "No one could catch them up *t'tell* them once they
were out to sea. And when they got to the West Indies, no one *here* knew
of it, either. They arrived *ahead* of the news! No idea they had to get a way
on, no need for haste, d'ye see, sir."

"Hmm, go on," Blanding urged, perking up considerably.

Aye, grasp any *straw when drownin' . . . even* mine! Lewrie told himself
with secret glee; *Poor bastard!*

"If they were as raw as the typical French sailors, who learn their trade
on-passage like they usually get sent out," Lewrie further said, "their
crossing would've been slower than ours, sir. If they'd sailed a line of lati-

tude t'pick up Dominica to fix their position—spot the mountains sixty miles out at sea, on a clear day!—let us say, *did* they carry at least a demi-brigade to Mole Saint Nicolas or Cape François—'Le Cap,' the Frogs call it—they'd have to take on water, firewood, and fresh victuals after landin' the bulk of the soldiers, and perhaps even give their sailors shore liberty, wastin' even *more* time before they went on to New Orleans for the hand-over!

"Even were they *five* weeks ahead of us before we left European waters, sir," Lewrie quickly speculated, "we might've made up a week on 'em with our fast passage, and made up another week sailin' a line of latitude *above* Dominica, and perhaps two more whilst they anchored at Cape François or Mole Saint Nicolas and . . . frittered. *Then*, if they finally heard of the declaration of war, they might dither a bit longer before heading for New Orleans, sir. After all, *their* senior officer's got strict orders t'be in New Orleans for the ceremonies . . . the same sort of firm orders as us, really, sir," Lewrie concluded, a sly-boots smile on his face. "A failure'd not do *his* career any good."

"By . . . Jove!" Blanding said at last, after munching that over in his head, his jaws actually working as if *chewing* the concept. "By *Jove* and by Jingo, Lewrie, of *course* he has strict orders! He'll not waste time on the smaller isles in the Leewards, he'll have put into Saint Domingue first, then . . ."

Blanding shot to his feet, beaming for a rare once since they'd departed their patrol of the Channel entrances. "*That's* where he'd be hiding! That's where he wishes to *run* from, soonest!"

"Sir?" Lewrie asked, puzzled. He'd thought to goad the fellow into a better mood, spur him into action and out of the slough of despond, but . . . where was his head going now?

"He fulfills his orders to go up the Mississippi to New Orleans, he'll find shelter from our ships!" Blanding explained . . . sort of, kind of. "He can't be blamed if he can't get *out* after the exchange of ownership there. And if he's less than a week ahead of us . . . I *say*! Top-ups, and I will have a glass with you all. We will crack on at once for the Anegada Passage 'twixt Anguilla and the Virgins, and then it's 'all to the royals,' stuns'ls, too, for the Old Bahama Channel and the Florida Straits. Does he flee Saint Domingue, he'll not wish to take a course south of Cuba . . . too close to Jamaica and our squadron there. Duckworth'll not have them . . . *we* will!"

Several fresh bottles of claret had been uncorked to breathe, so re-fills were quickly done. Blanding held up his glass on high. "Sirs, I give you confusion to the French!"

"*Sloth* to the French!" Captain William Parham amended. "Sloth and timidity!"

"But not *too* much timidity, Parham!" Lewrie added, "Else they never come out!"

CHAPTER FORTY-TWO

*T*hey dashed roughly Nor'west past Montserrat, Nevis, and St. Kitts, passing far alee of St. Martin, Eustatius, and almost within sight of Saba, then turned North for a time on a close reach to thread through 'twixt Anguilla and the eastern-most isle of the British Virgin Islands—Anegada, which gave name to the passage from the Caribbean to the Atlantic once more. From there, it was "wind on the starb'd quarters" again, with stuns'ls boomed out on either side of the main course and tops'l yards, the fore courses of all four warships partially reefed to take downward pressure off their bows and allow them to spear their bluff entries through the sea instead of pressing too deep and snuffling, robbing them of half a knot or more per hour. The Nor'Easterly Trade Winds were strong and steady, despite it being almost late July, never varying more than a point from Nor'east, and only fading lighter after dusk as the squadron ran down the line of the 20th Latitude, due West. There were spells of late afternoon rain squalls now and again, through which they drove onwards without reducing sail; there were grey and charcoal-dark storms on the horizon, so dense they resembled island mountains, but far away and unthreatening, though they were well into hurricane season, when any mariner in those waters continually looked over his shoulder and watched the cabinet barometer leerily.

Spanish Puerto Rico passed alee, as did the Mona Passage, their squadron plunging along at an impressive rate of knots, and HMS *Modeste* proving Captain Blanding's boast that she was very fast for a 64-gunned two-decker. Drill on the great-guns, drill with small arms and edged weapons filled both Forenoon and Day Watches, under a warm sun, white clouds, and the occasional afternoon rains that sluiced off the sweat the hands had worked up, sometimes lasting long enough for a thorough scrub-down with a stub of soap and a wash-rag.

Then came the coast of Spanish Santo Domingo, the eastern half of Hispaniola, the long northern coast looming up to larboard, forcing them to alter course a point or two . . . and Lewrie was back in his old hunting grounds in the *Proteus* frigate, and his memories of that time in Hispaniolan waters. When he had been more carefree.

"Monte Cristi . . . ten miles off the larboard beam, sir," Lieutenant Westcott said, lowering his telescope. "And Cape François about fourty miles to the West."

"The rebel slaves tried to blow us to Kingdom Come, round about here, Mister Westcott," Lewrie recalled aloud. "And the lone survivor we picked up after the last of their boats sank slit the throat of one my hands tryin' t'haul him up the battens. Fanatics, all of 'em."

Kit Cashman and his regiment ashore outside Port-au-Prince; a night in a restaurant-cum-brothel; the blind shelling they'd fired over the heads of British troops at Mole St. Nicolas; his intense dislike of Sir Hyde Parker's staff-captain at Kingston, "the wine keg," aye, and that Captain Blaylock, too. The duel he'd seconded for Kit against that Beauman "git," Ledyard, and his cousin, and how they had cheated and gotten gunned down. The Yellow Jack that had decimated *Proteus*'s crew and officers; the "theft" of Beauman slaves to replace some of them. Matching wits with Guillaume Choundas, cooperating with the American Navy, finding he had a bastard son . . .

"It'll be 'Beat to Quarters' in the next hour or so, Westcott," he said, shrugging off his memories.

"At long last, sir!" his First Officer said with eagerness.

"*If* they're here. If!" Lewrie replied, staring at the impossibly green mountains of Santo Domingo. So far, all their landfalls had been French islands; only one of them, Guadeloupe, he had been at all familair with. Here, though . . . ! Here were islands he'd known at coasting distance, every bay, fishing port, inlet, and shoal, close to an host of other places he'd known at first-hand; the Turks and Caicos isles to the North, and the Bahamas further North of them. And when he was prowling these shores, it had been Antigua, the Danish or British Virgins, Kingston, Jamaica, the coast of Cuba, Apalachicola Bay in Spanish Florida so long before . . . they all sprang to mind in a flood of remembrance, from his Midshipman days in 1780, the hired-in *Parrot* schooner, the *Desperate* Sloop and half-mad Capt. Tobias Treghues, then old HMS *Shrike* and Lieutenant Lily-crop and all his damned cats, and *his* first, the sullen William Pitt, the best mouser in the Fleet! And when he'd gone to the Far East, India and China in *Telesto* under Capt. Ayscough, he'd left Pitt with Caroline to care for him, long before their wedding in Anglesgreen when he returned in . . .

That didn't hurt, he thought; *should've, but it didn't. Callous, hard-hearted bastard! Or . . . what am I feelin'?*

Happy memories. Joyous recollections of past ships and former associates (for the most part, Treghues, Blaylock, and "the Wine Keg" excepted) and days like this in aquamarine and gin-clear waters, with the wind in his hair and the sun on his skin! In the West Indies!

Hmmpf! Wonder if I did *pack my penny-whistle in my traps?* he wondered.

"Carry on, Mister Westcott," he said, and ambled away towards the starboard bulkheads.

Just off Cape François, with *Reliant* at Quarters four hours later, they encountered two ships. One was a British brig-sloop keeping an eye on the port, to which Captain Blanding sent a blizzard of flag signals, summoning her captain aboard *Modeste*. The other vessel was an American brigantine, just clearing the harbour and offshore by at least five miles. Blanding ordered *Reliant* to close her and "speak" her. "Hermaphrodite" brigs, they called them, neither one nor t'other, with crossed yards and square sails on their fore masts, and fore-and-aft, schooner-like, on the after masts. For a bit she looked as if she might wish to run as *Reliant* bore down on her, but, working out of port against the Nor'East Trades, she was already slow through the sea, and did she haul her wind and flee Westerly, she would never work up enough speed to escape. Lewrie could understand her master's wish to get out of it . . . a call to fetch-to from a Royal Navy ship to have his papers and muster book read usually resulted in the impressment of some of the crew and a search for contraband that could result in seizure.

Lewrie turned the deck over to Lt. Westcott and was rowed over to her, instead of loftily summoning her master to come aboard his own ship.

His only escort was his boat crew, who remained in the boat as he scaled her sides.

"Alan Lewrie, Royal Navy," he began with a pleasant smile on his face, doffing his cocked hat to both flag and quarterdeck. "Morning!"

"Ansel Vincent," her master sourly announced himself, with his papers already under one arm. "The brigantine *Seneca*, outta Mystic, in Connecticut, bound home with rum, molasses, and sugar. I s'pose ye wish t'see my papers, Cap'm Lewrie? My *muster* book?" he added suspiciously, almost accusingly as he glowered in displeasure.

"The muster book's not necessary, sir," Lewrie told him. "We're fresh out from England with full crews, so far. I will look at your papers, however. You are part-owner?"

"Haw!" Captain Vincent rejoined. "I wish! She's a sweet sailer, and a fast'un. I'm hired on, with a 'lay' of the profits, for now."

"And her owners?" Lewrie asked.

"The Crowninshield brothers o' Mystic, as ye can see," Vincent said, waving at the papers in Lewrie's hands.

"Ezekiel and Gabriel Crowninshield!" Lewrie exclaimed, delighted. "I met them at Antigua in Ninety-Eight, when America and France almost went to war with each other. Two of their trading schooners had gone missing, and I helped recover them from the French. *Mohican* and . . . I forget the name of the other," he added with a shrug.

"*You* did?" Vincent barked in surprise, and doubt. "A Britisher helpin' Yankees? I thought it was *our* navy done it."

"We . . . cooperated, for a time. On the sly," Lewrie said with a grin and a wink as he handed back the ship's papers, mostly un-read. "You've been in port a while now? We're hunting for a French squadron that left Holland a bit before the war was declared. You didn't share the harbour with them, did you? They were bound for New Orleans, to be there for the official hand-over of Louisiana to the United States . . . might have landed some troops here, as well."

"We're gettin' Louisiana?" Vincent gawped. It was news to him!

"Lock, stock, and barrel, sir," Lewrie assured him, and news of that stirred *Seneca*'s small crew to glad buzzing.

"Well . . . hallelujah!" Capt. Vincent exclaimed, removing his old tricorne-style hat to scratch his head. "And . . . ye wish to stop it by takin' 'em, don't ye?" he accused a second later.

"No, sir," Lewrie told him. "The last thing the United States or Great Britain wishes is to have the French Empire in the Americas. If they have everything west of the Mississippi, how would your nation continue to grow? My country prefers the French *not* have a large army present for the ceremony of exchange, but . . . more power to you, and the best of good fortune for your acquisition.

"So . . . did a French squadron put into Cape François while you were here?" Lewrie asked again. "Or were they here and re-victualling before sailing for New Orleans? Even from here, I can spot the masts of a *number* of ships in port. I don't ask if they're ships of war. . . . They're not my pigeon at the moment."

"Aye, there's a lotta ships in port," Vincent reluctantly said. "Twodeckers and frigates and Indiaman-sized transports. Don't have all their guns, though. They come from France *en flute* without 'em or landed 'em t'buck up the defences. Gen'ral Rochambeau won't let any sail. He needs 'em all if he has to surrender to the Blacks and get as many of his people away before they all get massacred—men, women, and kids t'gether. Gen'ral Noailles over to Mole Saint Nicolas is in the same straits. Dessalines—he took over after the French captured L'Ouverture and took him away—has 'em hemmed in damned close. The Mole and 'Le Cap' here is all the French have left on the island.

"You Brits had an ounce o' Christian mercy, ye'd leave off yer hunt for that squadron an' fetch as many ships as ye can to help the French get away before the Blacks slaughter 'em all," Captain Vincent groused.

"I trust Rear-Admiral Duckworth, on Jamaica, is aware of that and will do all he can to help," Lewrie said, hoping that was so. His brief exposure to the savagery of the rebel slaves, and the atrocities the French had dealt out in reply, had been spine-chilling. He *wished* he could help, but . . .

"Believe it when I see it," Capt. Vincent drawled, though his anger was growing. "There weren't no cause for you to make war on the French again! Napoleon wanted peace! But I reckon your country just can't abide republics, where the *people* have rights and freedom, 'stead o' kings, queens, and titled fools tellin' folk what to do!"

"I'll not debate the whys, sir," Lewrie said, stiffening a bit, though striving to keep a peaceable and agreeable expression and air. "Did General Rochambeau keep the squadron from sailing? Or were they sent to Mole Saint Nicolas to help the evacuation over there? Landed fresh reenforcements . . . here or there, we were told they would. Or have they *already* sailed?"

"*Ye'll* not cotch 'em, Admir'l!" a sailor who'd been listening to the conversation hooted. "They's off an' gone! Two day ago!"

"Stop yer gob, ye . . . !" Vincent roared, rounding on the fellow, but it was too late. Pleased astonishment over the gain of Louisiana, and New Orleans, a chance to insult the despised Royal Navy and send a tyrant packing before he could press some of them were all just too tempting.

"Cap'm Decean, he's got two *big* frigates *and* a seventy-four . . . guns as big as tree trunks . . . a whole reg'ment o' soldiers!" the crew of *Seneca* jeered before their master bellowed them to truculent silence.

"I'll thankee t'git off my ship, whoever ye are," Vincent demanded. "Safer for ye . . .'less ye have *all* yer Marines at yer back."

"My regards to the Crowninshield brothers, Captain," Lewrie said as he doffed his hat to the ship's master, then to one and all as he made his way to the entry-port. "Have a good voyage."

"Oh la, maman, ce sont les Anglais!" came a child's wail of fear, drawing everyone's attention to the companionway that led below. Two children appeared briefly before being snatched away by a pale-faced woman.

"Gonna seize 'em 'cause they're French, too?" Vincent snapped.

"How many did you manage to evacuate, sir?" Lewrie asked him in a softer tone.

" 'Bout nineteen is all we've room for," Vincent told him, with real fear now that Lewrie, a dread "Brit," would do that very thing. "Daddies, wives, and kids, mostly. Some whole fam'lies, but most the kin o' men who haveta stay behind."

"Paying passengers?" Lewrie wryly asked.

"Ain't chargin' *full* rates, but . . ."

"Why, had you an *ounce* o' Christian mercy, sir, I'd expect you would make room for more . . . for *free* . . . sir," Lewrie drawled as he began to descend the battens to his waiting boat.

"They're in deep, dire trouble ashore, sir," Lewrie told Capt. Blanding after he had reported aboard *Modeste*, even as the squadron got under way Westerly for the Old Bahama Channel and Florida Straits. "Low on rations, powder, and shot, just about everything, and hangin' on by the skin o' their teeth. I gather that the Black General Dessalines has demanded their surrender already. If Duckworth is late in arriving here, if he plans to come at all, it'll be *worse* than a Red Indian massacre, sir. Might we consider offering this Rochambeau an alternative? Surrender to us instead, and escape the ex-slave's vengeance? The prize-money for so many ships, warships, and merchantmen would be astronomical . . . not to mention the 'head and gun' money on *thousands* of French soldiers," he beguiled. "It's a Christian—"

"Stay here?" Blanding countered, sounding shocked by the suggestion. "*Dash* it, Captain Lewrie, they're only two days' sail ahead of us! The French squadron's *real*, it ain't a myth! Some Admiralty clerk, some sneaking spy, didn't weave them out of moonbeams! By all that's holy, sir . . . this . . . Decean, is it? This Captain Decean has *his* orders, just as I have mine . . . his to reach New Orleans no matter what, and mine to catch them up and bring them to battle. No, sir, I will not let them get away, now we know how close we are on their tail and where they're bound. Right, Brundish?"

"Well, sir," his Chaplain said with his head cocked over to one side, "it *would* be Christian to assist the French and avoid a blood-bath, yet . . . we are at war with France."

"There you have it, Captain Lewrie," Blanding barked. "Ah ha! We've a grand battle in the offing, by Jingo! So let's be at it!"

CHAPTER FORTY-THREE

*T*he first three days of urgent pursuit were sunny and clear as they made
a rapid transit from St. Domingue West-Nor'west, crossing the Windward Passage and rushing along the northern coast of Spanish Cuba,
squeezing between that shore and the Great Bahama Bank, then up the
narrow deep-water throat of the Old Bahama Channel.

After they threaded the narrowest part 'twixt Cayo Cruz and Cayo
Lobos, though, the weather turned foul and boisterous, with fretted and
mounting seas, rain squalls, and rising winds, forcing them to reef courses,
tops'ls, t'gallants, and royals, and stow away the stuns'ls. Pressed by
winds fine on the starboard quarters, all four ships rolled and pitched and
heaved, and gun-drill or small-arms drill had to be put aside for constant
sail-tending. Rain hissed down by the bucket-fuls, seething on the upper
decks and gangways, sluicing to either beam, or fore and aft, with every
jerking motion, so much at times that it gurgled out the scuppers. No matter how snugly the deck planks were payed with sealing pitch over the
pounded-in oakum, water seeped through the gaps to drip and drizzle
belowdecks, and plop cold on hands trying to sleep in wildly swaying
hammocks at night, onto the mess tables during meals, and making everyone thoroughly miserable. To be "caught short," to stumble forrud to the
beakhead rails and the "seats of ease," resulted in a complete soaking—

from fresh-water rain, and salt water spray pitched up by the bows as they plunged and rose. No matter the watchfulness of the Midshipmen, the Master-At-Arms, and Ship's Corporals, it was dryer simply to piss in the odd corner of the mess-decks, shit in a wood bucket, and hope to pitch it overside when no one was looking. And the hands who got caught at it ended on report before "Captain's Mast."

"*Rrrow!*" Toulon complained as a dollop of water caught him on the head as he tried to eat his supper from his dish by Lewrie's place setting. "*Mrrf?*" was his mournful plaint as he looked aloft to seek the source of his annoyance.

"I trust the wardroom's dryer," Lewrie commented to his First Officer as they supped together, along with the Sailing Master, Mr. Caldwell, and Midshipmen Grainger and Munsell. "A deck above you, and I catch *all* the rain intended for you," he drolly pointed out.

"It seeps through, eventually, sir," Lt. Westcott replied with a brief, tooth-baring grin. It was well that he wore his napkin tucked into his shirt collar, for a drop of water raised a shot-splash in his pea soup, spattering the napkin, not his uniform. Grainger and Munsell thought it amusing. "We keep tarpaulins on our bedding, same as you, I fear."

"No need to dampen the tablecloth, I vow," Mr. Caldwell sniggered. "No plate'd *dare* slide tonight."

Munsell and Grainger found that funny, too.

"More sea-room," Lewrie said. "Out of the narrows of the Old Bahama Channel and into the Nicholas Channel by morning, is that your reckoning, Mister Caldwell?"

"Aye, sir . . . into deeper water," that worthy cautiously said. "Cross the Tropic of Cancer by Noon Sights, perhaps, as we enter the Florida Straits. Pray God the weather clears, for the Straits are a boisterous place of their own, quite the equal of the seas we've experienced lately."

"That won't make Captain Blanding happy," Westcott said with a smirk as he dabbed his lips with his napkin. "Even with clear skies and steady winds, we'd lose a knot per hour."

"'Make All Sail Conformable To The Weather,' hey?" Lewrie added, chuckling. That had been *Modeste*'s signal for two days.

"Per . . . perhaps the French are slowed by the same conditions, sir?" Midshipman Grainger essayed in a meek voice.

"Sailing two days before us, I doubt it, Mister Grainger," Mr. Westcott told them. "The worst they'd get, ahead of the squalls, is the gust-front wind, which will only make them faster.

"Beg your pardon, sir," Westcott said to Lewrie, "for talking 'shop' at-table."

"I've always found such constructive, Mister Westcott," Lewrie assured him. "I know no poetry to recite, 'cept for some doggerel, not fit for young ears. No high-toned books in my library t'discuss, and we're all most-like horrid at music, so . . . why not?"

"Then, sir . . . should we have stayed at Cape François and taken the French surrender?" Lt. Westcott posed, shifting in his chair and looking a bit distressed. "I *know* they're the enemy, but I'd not wish such a fate on anyone."

"We have explicit orders, Mister Westcott," Lewrie answered as he dabbed his own lips, then took a sip of wine. "It was, I imagine, a trial for this French fellow in charge of their squadron, Decean. *He* could have stayed . . . added his last battalion of troops to defend the city, and taken hundreds of civilians aboard for New Orleans. It's a French city, after all, and every refugee'd be welcome. Same as it is a trial for Captain Blanding. *Both* have explicit orders."

"And if we *had* stayed, sirs," Mr. Caldwell stuck in, "what are the chances the French *would've* surrendered to us? Their general may have thought he could hold out for months or delayed 'til he could deal with Rear-Admiral Duckworth, a man of rank suitable to his own. They're touchy, the Frogs. Too proud to admit they'd have to surrender, or accept terms, from *anybody*."

"And we'd have failed to execute our orders, to our peril, and Captain Blanding's career," Lewrie said as Pettus and his own cook, Yeovill, bustled in with large covered trays, fetching roasted quail raised from the eggs or chicklets bought in Portsmouth, potatoes and beans, and the *entrée* of salt-beef.

"Are the French really all *that* bad, sir?" Midshipman Munsell hesitantly asked. "*All* of them, that is? If their Commodore or whatever took pity on the people at Cape François, and took aboard as many refugees as he could . . . as you said, sir? Their big Indiaman might be full of women and children, 'stead of soldiers. Might we . . . uhm?"

Aye, they bloody are! Lewrie quickly, angrily thought. As for Munsell's fear . . . *We could end up killin' as many civilians as those Black rebels. No,* surely *they'd strike their colours, soon as we get to hailin' distance!*

Wouldn't that *make Blanding tear his hair out. A* bloodless *victory? Oh, the poor bastard.*

"If this Decean fellow *did* take civilians aboard, there would not be that many, Mister Munsell," Lewrie told him after a long frown and think. "Not aboard his armed ships, for certain. He'd have to work his guns, if overtaken . . . to protect the transport. He might've kept no more than two or three companies of troops. Mean t'say, how many Frogs does it take t'make a dumb-show or fire a ceremonial volley?"

"His frigates and seventy-four would most-like come about and fight us, Mister Munsell," Lt. Westcott added, "giving the Indiaman a shot at escaping to leeward. If she's swift enough, she's probably already placed ahead of their other ships, against that very chance."

"To shepherd her, sir?" Midshipman Munsell said, nodding as if he understood the concept . . . almost.

"Just as we'd shepherd a convoy of our own, aye," Lt. Westcott replied, then lowered his head to finish his cooling soup.

"Once out in the Gulf of Mexico, though . . . ," the Sailing Master said with a shrug, slurping up his last spoonful and looking eagerly in Yeovill's direction as the cook filled plates, "it's 'needle in a hay-stack' as to finding them. The surest wager would be to race on West-Nor'west on a bee-line for the Mississippi Delta. If the French didn't put into Havana and think it over first. Now they know they are at war again . . . oh, spiced rice with the quail, too? Good oh!"

"Easy to make, sir," Yeovill said as he and Pettus set plates before them. "And rice is cheap, but filling. Can do wonders with it, Mister Caldwell."

"Too close to Jamaica, and Duckworth's squadron?" Lewrie said, frowning again as his soup bowl was removed and the next course was placed before him; he drummed his fingers on the table top, pondering. "If Decean knows we're at war, and the bee-line is so obvious . . . hmm."

"Sir?" Lt. Westcott prompted.

"If he sheltered in Havana, he'd fail his orders," Lewrie said, looking up. "But if he steers closer to Pensacola or Mobile, that'd take him North of the obvious route but still get him to New Orleans, as far out of Duckworth's reach as he can get. If discovered, he has a chance t'duck into *one* of 'em, under the protection of a fort and its artillery, and send his troops *overland* through Spanish territory.

"His mission's a success even if his ships are interned!" Lewrie exclaimed, fighting the urge to rush to the chart-space to fetch dividers, compass, and ruler, and spread a chart over their supper dishes. "Were I Captain Blanding, I'd steer Nor'west t'hunt for 'em. If we had enough ships, that is. Or . . . spread out what we have to the limit of signallin' and sightin' distance, stretched as far North of the usual track, the most direct course, as we can."

"Glass of hock with the quail, sir?" Pettus suggested, hovering with a fresh bottle of white wine.

"Aye, Pettus, thankee," Lewrie agreed, tossing back the last of his claret and offering his glass to be filled. "Just a thought," he told the others with a shrug and a lifted eyebrow.

"Would the Dons *let* them march through their territory, though, sir?" Lt. Westcott wondered aloud. "From what I've read, the Spanish might as well be puppets of the French, but . . . are they that eager to become Bonaparte's active allies again? Their minister, Godoy, is a spineless wretch, ready to do whatever the French want, I've heard."

"Would it be a *hard* march, sir?" Mr. Caldwell asked. "On what sort of roads, I wonder. After all, this Captain Decean needs them to be . . . *presentable* when they reach New Orleans. Alive, too, I should imagine," he added with a laugh.

Lewrie recalled his time in West Florida, up the Apalachicola; there *were* no roads, just game trails, Indian trading paths.

"*Closer* to New Orleans, then," he announced with a sudden smile. "*Much* closer . . . almost to Lake Pontchartrain. We need a chart. . . ."

CHAPTER FORTY-FOUR

Six days out from Cape François, and the weather relented. The squadron cleared the Florida Straits and entered the Gulf of Mexico at last, with the Dry Tortugas a bit over the horizon on their starboard beams. Drill on the great-guns and small-arms practice resumed on all ships, All sails that could be bared to the winds bloomed aloft again, including stuns'ls; with them came laundry, damp and mildewed changes of slop-clothing, and bedding. While it had rained so hard, canvas sluices had thriftily been rigged, and some of the deluge had been funnelled into spare butts that the Cooper and his Mate had assembled from hoops and staves stored on the orlop, the first depleted casks and butts of the voyage hoisted out, scrubbed, and rinsed, then re-filled with fresh water and stored below once more. There was so much spare water, for once, that every hand could wash his slops "shore-fashion" instead of soaping the worst smuts, then towing them astern in net bags, hoping the churning ship's wake would get them *mostly* clean. That method engrained salt crystals in the cloth, and when worn, resulted in ugly salt-water boils which the Ship's Surgeon and his Mates spent time lancing and daubing with ointment . . . the cost of such services deducted from the sailors' pay, the same as a "mercury cure" for the venereal Pox.

Modeste signalled for live-fire exercises on the great-guns at least once a day, demanding three rounds from each gun every two minutes, and

God help the ship, and the captain, and the signals party of any ship that did not meet his standards! Captain Blanding would not veer from his urgent chase to the West-Nor'west long enough to set out old kegs for targets, then double back to fire at them in passing in-line-ahead. The rate of fire was paramount, not the proper elevating or aiming, to his mind; after all, would he not bring the French right up to close-broadsides, where proper aim did not matter?

"Fair enough, Mister Rahl," Lewrie congratulated the grizzled older Prussian. Their Master Gunner had suggested that they shift the guns as far forward in the ports as they could, fire a round from one of the forecastle chase guns, then let the individual gun-captains aim at the shot-splash as they sailed past it, and it seemed that most of the crews of the all-important 18-pounders were catching on quickly. "One more from the starboard chase gun, and we'll see how close they come with a full broadside before we cease for the morning."

"*Sehr gut, Kapitän! Sofort!*" Mr. Rahl barked, standing at the base of the starboard companionway to the waist, so stiffly at attention that he resembled one of Kaiser Friedrich the Great's grenadiers. "*Ja*, very *gut*, sir, at once!" he amended before turning to speak to Lt. Spendlove and Lt. Merriman, relaying Lewrie's orders.

"Quite the odd duck, sir," Lt. Westcott commented. "Once a soldier, forever a soldier. Crash-bang, about turn, hep hep!"

"Damned good gunner, though," Lewrie replied. "Though I don't know what he'd do if he ever ran out of wax for his mustachios. Go mad, I expect." He pulled out his pocket-watch to check the time; it lacked a quarter-hour to Seven Bells of the Forenoon, and the morning rum ration. "Last broadside, then Secure from Quarters. Can't delay the grog!"

"Aye, sir," Westcott said with a grin. "And may I say that I envy you your chair, sir?" he added tongue in cheek. "I must admit I own to a certain wish to *sit* through part of a watch, whether the Navy approves or not."

"*Sprawl*, rather, Mister Westcott," Lewrie corrected him. "Even *snooze*! I already stand accused o' bein' an idle, improper bastard, and freely confess to the charges. In my last days in the West Indies, I was even known to sprawl and tootle on my penny-whistle." The Carpenter, Mr. Mallard, and his Mate, Swift, had cobbled together a canvas-and-wood collapsible sling-chair to his directions, and it was now almost a permanent fixture on the windward side of the quarterdeck, the weather permitting. "We both know that half the captains in the Fleet are eccentric, so . . . ," he said with a shrug and a pleased grin.

"Starb'd batt'ry . . . by broadside . . . fire!" Lt. Spendlove was shout-ing.

"Stop ears!" Lewrie warned. The gun-captains properly waited for the scend of the sea, the up-roll, before jerking their lanyards to trip the flint-lock strikers. *Then* the guns exploded.

"Oh, well shot!" Westcott enthused to see the tall feathers of spray rise all round the chase gun's first fading shell-splash, close enough to satisfy even Captain Blanding's standards. "Mister Merriman, Mister Spendlove! Sponge out and secure from Quarters!"

"Signal, sir . . . our number, and it's 'Well Done,' " Midshipman War-burton reported from the taffrail flag lockers. "And, 'Secure' . . . then 'Rum,' sir. Spelled out."

"How oddly terse of him!" Lewrie said with a laugh. "Must have too much on his mind."

"God help us, sir, when he does have so much on his mind, he'll *signal* it to one and all!" Westcott snickered. " 'Flag Flux.' "

Lewrie had come to appreciate Lt. Westcott; not only was he an expe-rienced and tarry-handed officer, he was a likeable one. Firm but fair was his manner in bringing *Reliant* to nigh-perfect competence, to present the frigate on a serving-plate to her captain as a going concern. Any crew ap-preciated a Commission Sea Officer who seemingly had eyes in the back of his head, his finger on the pulse of everything yet was not a Tartar or a soured tyrant. Westcott did almost all duties with long-practised ease and a quirky grin on his face, a brow cocked in perpetual amusement over the failings of humankind, and rarely had to rage or shout, except to call from the quarterdeck to someone halfway to the foc's'le to pass an order. Where other officers might yell and fume, a stern look from Westcott was suffi-cient to let his men know he was wroth with their performance. And Westcott rarely had to bring a defaulter to Lewrie for corporal punish-ment; he was not a flogger, but for the most extreme faults.

And his personality off-duty was slyly, wryly witty and worldly, caus-ing Lewrie to imagine that they were kindred spirits, "two peas in a pod" rascals, with the same sort of tongue-in-cheek humour. Ballard, now dead and gone at Copenhagen, he'd mistakenly thought was a friend, but that had been a dutiful sham; Ralph Knolles in HMS *Jester* had been ear-nest, likeable, and immensely competent, but had never attempted to cross the line from subordinate to friend. Anthony Langlie had come as close to being a companionable confidant as any of his officers in the *Proteus* frig-ate. Then had come "Ed'rd" Urquhart in *Savage*; intensely sobre and

determined, so new to the frigate and dumped into her long-serving officers, mates, and crew which had "turned over" from *Proteus,* entire, and
they'd barely spent a year together before Lewrie had lost her to another,
before his trial. Geoffrey Westcott was as close as Lewrie had come in his
entire career at sea to finding someone he could un-bend with . . . or he
thought he could. Lewrie *liked* him! It was risky to do, lest a friendship
could be taken advantage of, detrimental to good order and discipline and
the enforced separateness required of a captain; like favouring one of his
offspring over another, it could lead to bad feelings in the wardroom.

"Permission t'pipe 'Clear Decks and Up Spirits,' sir?" Westcott asked
as Seven Bells chimed from the forecastle belfry.

"Carry on, sir."

The guns were swabbed out, tompions replaced, muzzles washed, and
the barrels and carriages bowsed below the port sills, the ports secured,
and all gun-tools returned below. The Marine drummer began to beat,
and the fifers launched into "The Bowld Soldier Boy," one of Lt. Simcock's particular favourites. The Purser, his clerk, and assistant, the
Master-At-Arms Mr. Appleby, and the Ship's Corporals, Scammell and
Keetch, escorted by Marine Sergeant Trickett and Corporals Mogridge
and Brownlie, brought up the red-and-gilt painted rum keg, raising a
chorus of Huzzahs and Hurrays from the waiting sailors.

I like that tune! Lewrie told himself; *my father and I sang it once in Hyde
Park . . . drunk as lords, most-like. Or well on the way to it. Where did I pack
my penny-whistle?*

He strolled about the quarterdeck as the ship's people queued up for
their tots. Hands in the small of his back, he studied the sails and rigging
for a way to wrench a bit more speed from her, where the winds stood off
her starboard quarters, by craning up at the commissioning pendant.
Looking ahead, then astern to the other ships, lined up with a mile between them. Hum-tootling the tune under his breath, and

> *. . . while up the street, each girl ye meet*
> *will cry! Oh, isn't he a dar-uhl-lin'*
> *my bowld soldier boy!*

Mouthing the words, almost silently.

This won't do, Lewrie thought, suddenly losing his good mood.

"Mister Warburton!" he called, heading aft. "A signal to *Modeste . . .*

'Submit,' then 'Form Line-Abreast.' After that, send 'Extend Hunt to Nor'west.' Take this down . . . 'Believe Chase Will Hug North Coast.' "

"Aye, sir," Midshipman Warburton said, scribbling it down with a pencil stub on a scrap of paper, then turning to his signalmen and the flag lockers.

Some of that only took one or two flags in the Popham Code, but the rest took a long time to spell out, letter by letter. It was nigh to Noon Sights before *Modeste* replied, and that was a laconic set of flags for "Acknowledged." After that, nothing.

And it was mid-afternoon, after Lewrie's mid-day meal, before *Modeste* sent up hoists, first a General for all ships, prefaced by one gun to get their attention.

" 'Alter Course West-Nor'west, Half North,' sir," Midshipman Mr. Entwhistle spelled out.

At least he'll compromise, halfway between, Lewrie thought.

"Then, uhm . . . ," Entwhistle continued, thumbing through his book to interpret the rest. " 'Form Line-Abreast . . . Order of Sailing . . . Northernmost Number Three.' "

"*Pylades*," Lewrie said aloud.

"Number Two, that's us, sir . . . Number Four, then One. Distance Between Ships . . . Ten Miles Day . . . Five Miles Night," Entwhistle read off haltingly. "The Preparative is up, sir."

"Very well. Mister Westcott? All Hands! Ready to haul up to windward and form line-abreast," Lewrie ordered.

At the drop of the Preparative, *Modeste* surged on West-Nor'west while *Cockerel* wheeled off to her starboard side, and *Reliant* and *Pylades* swung onto a beam reach, bound Due North, headed for the horizon. Though it was hard on Captain Blanding to change his mind or take heed of a suggestion, Lewrie was learning, he wasn't *entirely* pig-headed.

Modeste could scan the seas out to twelve miles to larboard and ahead, and have *Cockerel* ten miles North of her, looking ahead another twelve miles, as would *Reliant* ten miles North of her; lastly, *Pylades* could see twelve miles ahead and to the North, making a scouting line that could search a swath of ocean fifty-four miles across during the daylight hours.

"Signal from *Cockerel*, sir . . . a repeat from *Modeste*. For all ships, all private numbers . . . ," Midshipman Warburton puzzled out once they were ten miles North of *Cockerel*, and steady on West-Nor'west, Half North. "'Make All Sail Conformable With The Weather,' sir!"

"But of *course* he did!" Lewrie hooted. "I trust the ship is in your good hands, Mister Merriman?"

"Well, *aye*, sir!" the Third Officer answered, not knowing quite what to say to such a statement; or was it a question of his ability?

"Good," Lewrie said, plumping down into his sling-chair. "Wake me at the start of the First Dog. Here, laddies!" he beckoned, patting his chest to attract his cats, Toulon and Chalky, who had been sunning themselves atop the tarpaulin cover of the hammock nettings. Both got to their paws, stretched, yawned, then hopped down to swarm up his legs to his chest for a spell of "wubbies."

As soon as the cats tired of that, Lewrie actually pulled down his hat over his eyes, crossed his arms, sprawled out his legs, and gave the impression that he really *had* fallen into a nod.

Lt. Westcott came back to the quarterdeck after an hour or so of paper-shuffling and stopped dead at the top of the starboard companionway ladder from the waist, cocking a brow at Lt. Merriman before going to join him.

"The captain seems in rare takings, sir," Merriman whispered to the First Officer, with a boyishly shy grin. "Higher spirits than he's been."

"Is he really napping?" Westcott wondered aloud. Sure enough, Lewrie's head was over to one side, his mouth slightly open, and there came a nasally sleep sound. "Good," Lt. Westcott decided. "It's been a year since the French. . . . He's mourned enough. Dare I speak of it, mind."

"He's a ship to command, I expect that helps," Merriman opined. "And the chance for action . . . and revenge?"

"Back where he belongs, in familiar waters, to boot," Westcott added. "He might even be . . . happy. Better for us, to serve a happy captain, 'stead of a gloomer. Is that a word? Who cares?"

CHAPTER FORTY-FIVE

L ewrie cheated a bit, of course, by edging out North'rd 'til the mast-head lookouts could barely spot *Cockerel*, and covertly signalling Parham to take his *Pylades* out away from *Reliant* to the limits of her lookouts' vision as well. *Four more miles could make all the difference* was his main thought—*if* the French had shied as far away from any patrolling vessels out of Jamaica as they could.

Another day passed, full of boresome ship's routine and gunnery practice; decks were scoured, meals were served, rum was issued twice a day, hammocks and bedding came up from below at 4 A.M. for stowing in stanchions and nettings, then taken below at sundown, after the *Reliant* stood Evening Quarters. Watches were set and rotated; Noon Sights were taken and their position reckoned by the height of the sun and by the half-hour casts of the chip-log aft. With stuns'ls set, the squadron reeled off an average of nine or ten knots during the daylight hours, much less in the darkness, but still managed runs of nearly 195–215 miles from one noon to the next. And they were running out of ocean. Another day, and they would be off the approaches to Lake Borgne and the first passes through the low-lying Mississippi Delta.

Lewrie paced his quarterdeck, from taffrail flag lockers and lanthorns to the companionway ladder and back again, head down, hands in the small of his back, all his recent good humour gone; fretting he had been wrong, horribly wrong; fearing that the French had kept their two-day lead and had made good time, and were even now anchored at the Head of Passes off Fort Balise, ready to sail up the river to New Orleans . . . as safe and unassailable as babes in their mother's arms!

As he paced forrud towards the bows, the lowering sun was harsh in his eyes, still yellow, though in the next half-hour it would go red and amber as it neared the Western horizon. Already, the seas astern were beginning to be lost in dusk, and the seas ahead were a sheet of wrinkled copper fresh from the forge, with the wavetops tinged a coral red atop their fleeting blue-grey shadows.

"Lovely sunset in a bit, sir," Lt. Spendlove commented.

"Mine arse on a band-box!" Lewrie all but snarled back.

At the end of the First Dog Watch, which was due in a few minutes (dammit!), they would have to put over the helm and slink back to the South to take station five miles off *Cockerel*, shrinking the line to fifteen miles North-to-South, and the lookouts' vision shrunk down to five miles or less, depending on cloud cover or the lack of moon.

"Deck, there!" a lookout called down. "*Pylades* is haulin' her wind an' comin' down t'us! *Signallin'*!"

Lewrie looked about for one of the Midshipmen of the Watch and found Grainger first. "Aloft with you, Mister Grainger, with a glass and your signals book! Mister Rossyngton, make ready to answer with flag signals! Hop to it!"

He watched Grainger scale the windward shrouds and rat-lines to the cat-harpings, go out the futtock shrouds to the main-top, then get up the narrower top-mast shrouds to the cross-trees to join the sailor posted there as a lookout; glared, rather, urging haste before the evening got too dark to see!

"Deck, there!" the lookout bawled, relaying what Grainger told him, phrase by phrase. "Four . . . Strange . . . Ships! Night . . . Lights . . . on th' Horizon! *Chase!* In *Sight*! *Enemy In Sight!*"

"What course do they steer?" Lewrie shouted back, hands cupped either side of his mouth, in a quarterdeck, full-gale cry.

"Deck, there!" the lookout prefaced, needlessly. "Chase . . . Is Stern-On! Bound Nor'-Nor'west!"

"Chart!" Lewrie demanded, going to the binnacle cabinet and the traverse board. Lt. Spendlove spread out the chart, already pencilled with the Sailing Master's reckoning of their position at noon, hours before, and a rough Dead Reckoning track of knots logged on the course since. "The

Chandeleur Islands!" Lewrie exclaimed, poking a finger at the long, low-lying string of isles that lay almost dead on their own bows. "They're going North-about the Chandeleurs, into sheltered water! Sail down the lee side, with Breton Island to starboard, and get to Passe a La Loutre, where it'd be hellish-hard t'have at 'em!"

"Good Lord, sir . . . they just threw away their *lead* over us!" Lt. Spendlove said with a gasp. "It would have been safer to stand on direct for the East Pass, and they'd have been inside the river mouth *hours* ago! Why would they do that?"

"There's deep-enough water in the Mississippi Sound, up there," Lewrie told him, sweeping a finger along the coast East of Lake Pontchartrain and the string of barrier islands that sheltered a very small settlement named Old Biloxi—Cat, Ship, Dog, and Horn Islands. "He could anchor there, he be hard to get at, and land his troops at Biloxi or send all his boats through the Rigolets Pass, here at the Spanish fort, Coquilles, and get into Pontchartrain and down to New Orleans by the back entrance. No one could touch 'em then. Then, if he wished, he could even land his boats *here*, from Lake Borgne, and it's not fifteen miles up the Chef Menteur road to New Orleans proper!" Lewrie said, stabbing at the very beach where long ago he and an agent from Panton, Leslie & Company had explored a landing place for *British* soldiers!

"He'll use these little islands as a barrier between our ships and his, sir?" Spendlove excitedly said. "Even if he don't know there *are* British ships so close?"

"The Decean fellow on the lee side of 'em, and us, or anybody else's squadron on the windward, and it's as good as an iron shield," Lewrie spat, standing back and letting one corner of the chart roll up. "Mister Rossyngton? Signal to *Pylades* . . . 'Come Down To Me'!"

He referred to the chart once more. The Chandeleurs . . . did anyone live there? He'd never enquired. It was a bow-shaped arc of sand isles and shoals, about fourty miles end to end. Lewrie dug into the binnacle cabinet for a rusty pair of dividers, stepping off distances.

They were sixty miles or so off the Chandeleurs, the French not twelve miles Nor'west of *Pylades* when spotted, another twelve miles to the Nor'west of *Reliant,* and were fourty miles off the island chain.

Goin' almost Due North now, so they don't run aground on them in the dark, Lewrie quickly speculated; *hmm . . . twenty miles on* that *course, say, twenty-five to round the end of the last one* well *clear o' shoals? Under reduced sail, too,* feelin' *their way in the dark! Damn' slow, then . . . fourty miles*

Sou'west down the lee of the islands. They might *be clear of 'em by dawn to-morrow!*

"Landin' his toy soldiers ain't enough," Lewrie crowed, tossing the dividers back into the cabinet drawer. "He's this close t'success, he'll make for the Pass à La Loutre and get his *ships* up-river, too!"

Lt. Spendlove leaned over the chart to where Lewrie's finger rested, seaward of the passes but South of the Chandeleurs, windward of Breton Island and the Bay Ronde.

"There by first light tomorrow, Mister Spendlove," Lewrie said, feeling his excitement rising. "I think we've *got* 'em!"

"Uhm . . . beg pardon, sir, but . . . how do we inform *Modeste* and *Cockerel*?" Spendlove asked, delighted, wolfishly excited himself, but a bit mystified. "Once it's full dark, none of the night signals will be able to convey *any* sort of message."

"We go tell him, Mister Spendlove!" Lewrie crowed. "We barge up to him, invite ourselves to supper, and *tell* him! After all, where *he* is steering, the course *we* must steer to meet up with him, and a course t'place us where we need t'be, is pretty-much the same!"

CHAPTER FORTY-SIX

*D*o you imagine, sir, that the reason the French sailed North-about the islands is a result of navigational error?" Lt. Westcott mused in a low mutter as they stood by the starboard bulwarks, near the beginning of the sail-tending gangway, with their telescopes extended as dawn began to break.

"We know they're cunny-thumbed and cack-handed the first days they manage t'get out t'sea, but . . . *that* cack-handed?" Lewrie gawped.

"Thirty miles at the most off their intended landfall after the passage from Cape François . . . about thirteen hundred miles, all told, would be acceptable to most mariners, if their chronometers were out by a few seconds," Westcott speculated. "Or they ran into a contrary slant of wind for a day or so, and their Dead Reckoning was off by just a tick."

"Just so long as they manage t'find their way back *down* to us, I could give a bigger damn," Lewrie said in a soft growl, teeth bared in a whimsical smile. He lowered his glass and looked about the decks. HMS *Reliant*, all their ships, were darkened, their taffrail lanthorns extinguished, with only tiny glims burning by the sand-glasses at the forecastle belfry for a ship's boy to determine the half hours to ring the watch bells, and a hooded one in the binnacle to illuminate the compass for the helmsmen, Sailing Master, and Officer of the Watch.

They were all at Quarters, rousing the crews at the end of the Middle

Watch at 4 A.M. and omitting the deck-scrubbing with holystones or dragged "bears," or the rigging of the wash-deck pumps. Hammocks had been stowed in the stanchions down the tops of the bulwarks on either beam, rolled snug to pass through the ring measures and used as protection from small-arms fire and splinters. The hands had been fed early, then summoned to Quarters a little after 5 A.M., and the galley fires had been staunched.

There had been time for Lewrie to sponge off with a pint of water and some soap, to shave, then dress in clean underclothes, with silk shirt and stockings. In hopes of what the day would bring, he and his officers and mids were dressed in their best uniforms, with pistols in their belts and swords at their sides.

Chain slings were rigged aloft on the yards to keep them from crashing down if shot away; anti-boarding nets were laid out down both sides, ready to be hoisted; gun-port lids creaked open and softly came thumping back with the easy roll of the frigate as she crept along under "all plain sail," with the main course at two reefs, ready for hauling up clear of catching fire from the discharges of their own cannon.

And men stood swaying by their pieces, gun-tools in their hands. Powder monkeys had the first cartridges in their leather carriers as they knelt, facing the guns down the centreline. Lt. Simcock's Marines were fully kitted out in red and scarlet, white breeches and knee-high black denim spatterdashes, white cross-belts and black leather accoutrements, standing down either gangway behind the bulwarks and hammock nettings, waiting. Below, in the waist, aft in Lewrie's great-cabins, tiny red battle lanthorns glowed, guardedly out of sight from out-board, from a foe's sight. The slow-match coiled round the water tubs between those guns had not yet been lit; if the flintlock strikers failed to ignite or broke a flint or spring, the fuse could light the feather quills in the touch-holes, sparking off the fine-mealed priming powder.

"We'll be silouetted against the dawn, I suppose," Lt. Westcott said on, rocking on the balls of his booted feet.

"Good odds," Lewrie agreed, grunting. "No helpin' it. Pray the Frog lookouts are blind, or late in bein' posted aloft, 'stead of the decks. Gives us five minutes more t'close 'em?"

"They go about, we'll just chase them," Westcott said, sighing as he lifted his telescope again to peer ahead off the starboard bows.

Lewrie looked up, but could not quite see the long, lazy whipping of the commissioning pendant. The wind was scant that morning, a touch cool on the skin from the starboard quarter; they were angled enough off the winds to be able to feel the wind, for once. He turned and peered aft at *Modeste*. She was a large, dark shadow, as wide and bluff as a baleful barn, her grey, weathered sails eerily rustling to the wind's vagaries, equally dark against the pre-dawn gloom. She was only a little over a cable's distance astern, yet Lewrie had to *recall* what she looked like bows-on, with little more than the faint mustachio of foam under her forefoot, that creamed to either side of her bows, to positively mark her place.

Damme, is she . . . fuzzy? Lewrie thought, pinching the bridge of his nose and rubbing his eyes as false dawn only slightly began to grey the horizon astern, revealing charcoal-sketch impressions of the ships aft of *Reliant. Are my eyes goin'?* he wondered; *No, it's mist! Mine arse on a bandbox, of all the shitten luck!*

The false dawn sketched his own decks as he looked forward, gave slightly more detail of artillery, sailors, sails, rigging, and masts—all misted with a thin pre-dawn fog!

"Land Ho!" a lookout shouted down. "*Island* on th' *starb'd* side! *Two* point off th' *starb'd* bows! *Five* mile off!"

"The Sou'west tip of the last Chandeleur," Lewrie growled as he went to the Sailing Master's chart. "Be-fogged, though, we're closer than five miles, if he can see it. Three miles, more-like, sir?"

"It appears to be a thin fog, sir," Mr. Caldwell, the Sailing Master, cautiously pointed out, using dividers to measure possible distances, then lean closer and peer at the depth notations. "Still in deep water, sir, do we hold to this course."

"Mist or fog, however thin, though," Lt. Westcott fretted near them, fingers flexing on the hilt of his scabbarded sword. "We could miss them in it, even so, sir."

"Should've remembered," Lewrie muttered, turning away to pace to the forward edge of the quarterdeck. He chid himself for forgetting that the coasts hereabouts were so low-lying and marshy, the summers as humid as Canton, Calcutta, or the Ivory Coast of Africa, and a cooler sea air just naturally bred fogs and mists.

"Deck, there!" the lookout shouted once more, just as the first hints of true dawn and the first colours could be ascertained. "*Ships! Four* ships, hull-up . . . *fine* on th' starb'd bows!"

"Mister Grainger!" Lewrie bellowed over his shoulder as he lifted his telescope to peer out-board, a sense of relief, of success, beginning to fill him. "Hoist to *Modeste* . . . 'Enemy In Sight'!"

"Aye aye, sir!" the fifteen-year-old piped back.

Four Bells chimed from the foc's'le belfry; 6 A.M. and it was true dawn at last; close enough to the exact time for sunrise noted in the ephemeris. Grey murk retreated Westward as brightness surged up from the East. Coastal waters went from black to steely grey, then to dark blue with flecks of white. There were thin clouds and the first pale smears of blue skies. There was the mist, of course, a pearlescence to the West, closer to the shore, where it would be thicker.

"Next hoist to *Modeste*, Mister Grainger," Lewrie ordered as he returned to the helm. "Make it 'Four Ships, Fine On Starboard Bows.'"

"Aye, sir."

"Tip of the last o' the Chandeleurs here," Lewrie eagerly said, jabbing at the chart. "We're about here, and the French are . . . there! Do we bear off a point or two to larboard, and we'll have them on our starboard beams, bows-on to us, and open to rakin' fire. Or we hold t'this course, and we barge into them, bows-on to *their* larboard batteries."

"Up to *Modeste*, that," Lt. Westcott commented, shrugging.

"Aye, but I'd prefer to haul off . . . place ourselves 'twixt them and the East Pass into the river," Lewrie schemed aloud. "They'd *have* to fight through us or go about and run back the way they came, with Breton Island t'larboard, and the waters shoalin' fast, the closer to Biloxi or Lake Borgne they go. They fight us or they go aground, up yonder, and strike their colours."

"They're hull-up already?" Lt. Westcott said, looking dubious. "Surely they've spotted us, round the time we spotted them, sir."

"Aloft, there!" Lewrie shouted, cupping his hands about his mouth. "Have they turned away? And what is the order of their sailing?"

"Sailin' as *before*, sir!" the lookout replied. "Same course! A two-decker leadin' . . . then a frigate, another two-decker, and another frigate, the hind-most! Makin' *sail*, sir!"

"They've seen us, right enough," Lewrie told his officers. "On a tear t'get into the Delta, to the Head of Passes, before we can close 'em! And in the same order as they were last night, with their troop ship to leeward so they could protect her."

"She'll turn away," the Sailing Master speculated.

"She'll press on, even if the others engage us," Lewrie countered. "She's too close to the end of her passage t'do else. Mister Westcott, shake the reefs from the main course and *drive* her, hard. Helmsmen . . . helm up, and steer West, Nor'west."

Just pray Jesus that Blanding sees what I intend, and don't interfere! Lewrie thought, peeking astern in dread of anxious bunting.

"One can see them from the deck, sir!" Midshipman Grainger cried from the starboard mizen shrouds and a perch most of the way up them. Lewrie raised his telescope, focussed, then . . . *By God, there they are!* he exulted in silence. They *were* real, not Will-O'-The-Wisps, and not more than six or seven miles off.

I was right! Lewrie felt like shouting; *this Frog did hide his arse behind the Chandeleurs, or gave himself the option of landing his troops up North. Damme . . . I was* right? *What's the world comin' to?*

Inside that pearly mist, there were four complete sets of sails, rustling like spooks on the scant winds; there were darker smudges of hulls below them, and the mast-heads! They were *above* the mist and clear as day . . . now only *five* miles off, he reckoned!

"Deck, there!" a new voice called. Midshipman Rossyngton had gone aloft to join the lookouts, and it was his thin piping that they heard. "Lead two-decker stands on! The *trailing* ships haul their wind! *One* point off the starboard bows! Avast! Moving to *two* points off!"

Lewrie could see the hair-thin mast-heads pivotting, aligning themselves atop each other, as the three French warships came about to point roughly bows-on to their own line of battle.

They're lasking! Lewrie realised; *sailin' a bow-and-quarter line . . . oblique to us! Clever devil, yonder.*

The French would close them, with a frigate nearest to them and their two-decker 74 perhaps a cable further away, off the frigate's larboard quarters, and the trailing frigate even further away, off the 74's larboard quarter, like the last three fingers of Lewrie's left hand.

"Worn to larboard tack, sir?" Mr. Caldwell said, scratching his scalp with a pencil stub, up under his hat. "They'll have to come off the wind 'fore they can cross our bows and rake us."

"A clever way to close the range quickly," Lt. Westcott mused.

"No, sirs . . . not clever at *all*!" Lewrie suddenly whooped, all but startling his First Officer and Sailing Master. "A new signal for *Modeste*, Mister Grainger . . . 'Submit . . . New Course . . . West by North. Enemy Is Lasking on Larboard Tack'!"

"Aye, sir!" Grainger replied, hustling back to his duties by the flag lockers, perplexed by the term.

"He should've changed course no more than two points, in line-of-succession, not all at once," Lewrie pointed out. "*That* would've placed him cross *our* bows, but no . . . he had 'em all wheel as one and wear to larboard tack. We turn more Westerly, he'll barge up to us with all of our guns directed at the nearest frigate, and the two-decker's fire is masked . . . as is the trailin' frigate's!

"They stay as they are and think t'sail down our starboard beam for broadsides on opposin' tacks, they're stacked on top of each other, 'less the followin' ships luff up in order t'fall in trail of the lead ship!" Lewrie urgently explained, arms swinging and his hands clapping before him, almost skipping about the deck in glee.

"And, do they come back to their original course, they'll end up bows-on to our *line*, and under raking fire from all four of ours!" Lt. Westcott quickly grasped. "Just too clever by half, the poor bastard."

"Now, let's all pray Captain Blanding sees what we see," Lewrie replied, turning to peer intently at *Modeste*'s signals halliards. "The troop ship might escape us whilst we're engaged with these three, but I s'pose it can't be helped. Better for us, had *Cockerel* or *Pylades* led our line."

If Captain Blanding sent one of his lighter 32-gunned frigates off in chase that instant, from the rear of their line, it would take hours for one of them to fetch the two-decker transport into even *long* gun-range . . . perhaps only a few miles off Pass a La Loutre, or have to chase her right up to Fort Balise and the Head of Passes in what, at the moment, was still officially Spanish territory!

"Signal, sir!" Midshipman Grainger crisply reported. "'Form Line of Battle . . . Course West by North . . . With All Despatch'!"

"We've got 'em, Mister Westcott!" Lewrie exulted with a growl. "By God, we've *got* 'em!"

CHAPTER FORTY-SEVEN

*T*hey're coming back to line-ahead, sir!" Midshipman Rossyngton shouted down from the main-mast royal yard, a perch even more precarious than the cross-trees.

"Thankee, Mister Rossyngton!" Lewrie shouted back. "Now come to the deck and take your station at Quarters! Hellish-odd," he said in a much softer voice to Westcott as he lifted his glass to peer out for a sign of the foe. "They see our mast-trucks and commissioning pendants, we see theirs, and all else is damn-all squiffy."

"Aha, sir!" Lt. Westcott said, pointing with his telescope. "I can just make out the lead frigate . . . there, sir! She'll be directly bows-on to us, square on our starboard beam, does she not alter course!"

Lewrie swivelled, found a ghostly bow sprit and jib-boom, about a mile to windward; found jibs and a foretopmast stays'l, then the tan-in-white square shapes of the leading frigate's forecourse and fore topsail. "To windward of us . . . now *they're* silhouetted 'gainst the dawn, the damned fools. French!" he sniffed. "They just *can't* keep it simple. All that elegant *jeune école* bumf they came up with two wars ago, back in the Seventeen Sixties. What odds'd ye give me, Mister Westcott, do they load with star-shot and chain-shot, and try t'dismast us, as their doctrine demands?"

"I doubt they'll have *time* to turn a whole battery upon us for that practise, sir," Lt. Westcott replied. He was smiling, not one of his brief, tooth-baring flash-grins, but a gladsome, widespread mouth. "There's her main-mast, a hint of her mizen, and . . ."

Lewrie looked up at the commissioning pendant; their line was on starboard tack, with the light winds from the Nor'east by East, and the French, after their last manoeuvre into line-ahead formation, were now sailing with those winds fine on their larboard quarters.

"And there's their seventy-four, just emerging astern of her," Westcott added as the ponderous behemoth loomed up more solid from the mists, about a cable astern of the frigate.

"Stand by, Mister Spendlove!" Lewrie alerted the Second Officer, in charge of the main guns in the waist. "You will make sure that all pieces fire as they bear, and bow-rake her!"

"Not quite yet . . . not quite . . . ," Lt. Westcott was muttering to himself, flexing his knees to ride the easy scend and roll of the ship as he peered intently at the lead ship, judging the range.

"Here it comes," Lewrie said with a grunt as the Frenchman's two chase guns exploded from her forecastle at last. Those projectiles did not sound like round-shot; there was a whole, thin chorus of light shot that went soaring high above the decks; expanding bar-shot, chain-shot, and star-shot. "Should've laid a wager, Mister Westcott," he said with another pleased grunt as sails aloft were pierced, a few lines parted, and some splinters were torn from the top-masts.

"I make the range a bit over a quarter-mile, sir," Lt. Westcott informed him.

"Good enough for me, sir," Lewrie told him, then lifted a brass speaking-trumpet. "Mister Spendlove! As you bear, you may open upon her!"

"Aye aye, sir! *As* you *bear! Fire!*" Spendlove shouted.

As if paced by a metronome atop a parlour *piano forte*, the guns began to bellow, from the 12-pounder chase gun forrud, then down the long battery of fourteen 18-pounders, gushing great clouds of powder smoke and amber sparks that merged into a single thunderhead along the starboard side, then lingered and was blown back into the gunners' faces by the light winds, and only slowly thinned and trailed away to the un-engaged larboard side, blotting away their view of the foe for a long minute or so. Aft, HMS *Modeste* began her first broadside, as well, a greater, louder roaring from her heavier 18-pounders and 24-pounders, spewing out an even denser cloud of spent powder smoke.

"Deck, there!" a lookout high aloft, above the mists and powder smoke, shouted. "'Er foremast's by th' board! Sprit an' boom timbers be shot away!"

Lewrie had a dimmer view from the quarterdeck; even so, he could make out the French frigate's foremast crashing down in ruin, the light royal and t'gallant top-masts above her cross-trees collapsing zig-zag, and yards and sails swirling like a broken kite. The stouter timber of the mast above the foremast's fighting top was leaning forward like a new-felled tree, to drape over her forecastle, roundhouse, beakheads, and the shattered jib-boom and bow sprit!

"Bow-raked for certain, by God, sir!" Lt. Westcott was enthusing. *Reliant*'s guns, or *Modeste*'s heavier ones, no matter; the curved plankings of any ship's bluff bows were not as stout as a ship's sides, with their heavy, closer-spaced frames and thicker scantling. Bows, like the delicate squared-off stern transoms, could be holed, and when they were, the round-shot, all that broken lumber, and clouds of whirling, jagged wood splinters got funnelled down the length of the gun-deck, shattering deck planking, overhead beams, frame timbers, and dis-mounting massive guns, turning truck-carriages into more splinters, snapping the carline support posts . . . and slaughtering enemy sailors by the dozens!

"Lamb t'the slaughter, Mister Westcott," Lewrie growled, utterly delighted with the mental image of that murderous chaos, the terror, dismemberments, and wounds they had just inflicted yonder. "I don't see *why* their flag officer's comin' at us this way, but . . . more fool, him! Mister Spendlove . . . serve her another! *Skin* the bastards!"

If the plan had been to get up to gun-range to the British, then wear in-succession and lay the French squadron broadside-to-broadside, that hope was unravelling, fast. With her foremast gone, and all of her fore-and-aft headsails lost with it, the leading frigate was crippled in a twinkling, unable to turn quickly to parallel *Reliant*. She wallowed and sloughed, *trying* to wear about Northerly, but she'd been gut-shot from an agile gazelle to a sluggish snail, pressed on by the light winds and slow to wear across them, with her vulnerable, already ravaged bows still offered up for slaughter.

"Ready, lads . . . *as* you *bear*! Fire!" Lt. Spendlove roared.

The starboard foc's'le 12-pounder bow chaser erupted once more, followed by all the starboard beam 18-pounders, joined this time by the stubby 32-pounder carronades—the "Smashers"—and the quarterdeck 9-pounders. The range was even closer, and they *could* not miss! Over the deafening bellows of their own artillery, *Reliant*'s people could hear the parroty *Rrawks!* of solid iron shot slamming into her, a loud *Rawk-Crack*, then the screech of something substantial giving way.

The smoke slowly cleared from their second deliberately aimed broadside, revealing the French frigate's new hurts. She had managed to come about at 45-degree angles, baring her larboard side as if trying to bring her guns to bear, but . . . her main-mast had been decapitated a few feet above the fighting top, perhaps by a lucky hit from one of the 32-pounder carronades, and the press of wind had brought all above it down onto her larboard bulwarks, the cross-deck boat-tier beams, and her waist. Her reefed main course sail lay like a funeral shroud over it all. If she tried to fire back, there were good odds she'd set herself on fire from the sparks scattered among all that wreckage! Only her mizen mast still stood, flying t'gallant, tops'l, and her spanker. Now she was completely unable to manoeuvre or maintain steerage way! Her Tricolour flag was missing, yet . . . after a minute or so, someone over there took a small harbour jack Tricolour up the mizen shrouds to the fighting top, and nailed it to the mast.

"*Zut alors*, monsewer!" Lewrie cried through a speaking-trumpet to them, thumping a fist on the cap-rails. "*Mort de ma vie*, what're ye goin' t'do *now*, hey? *Sacre*-fuckin'-*bleu?*" he sneered as *Reliant* swept on past the frigate, putting her on her starboard quarters to subside slowly into the thinning mists.

Yet in those thinning mists, now they were clear of the frigate, Lewrie had a much clearer view of that hulking French 74-gunner! She had been about a cable astern of her consort when the first broadside had been fired. She had yet to be engaged.

"And what are *you* goin' t'do, sir?" Lewrie asked aloud, as if he could speak with the French senior officer aboard the 74. *Modeste* was firing as his own guns were being overhauled, swabbed out, and re-loaded. "Decide *quick*, monsewer, if ye care for yer paint-work!" he added as *Modeste*'s shot began to pummel their flagship.

The lead frigate was now an immobile hulk, unable to sail and making no discernible way except for a painfully slow wheel to the North, laying herself almost at right angles to her flagship's course as that two-decker came on under a full press of sail on the light winds and her captain suddenly faced a horrid choice: wear cross the wind and turn Northerly to avoid ramming into his crippled frigate, and continue the engagement in more traditional line-against-line, or put up his helm and pivot Sou'west to avoid "going aboard" the frigate, and meet *Modeste* starboard-to-starboard with her massive guns on opposing tacks.

"She turns to face *Modeste*, she lays herself open to a raking, sir," Lt. Westcott pointed out, shaking his head in wonder at how anyone could put himself in such a predicament.

"Not *completely* bows-on, Mister Westcott," Lewrie countered, in calmer takings. "One good, sharp broadside into *Modeste*, and he's the lighter frigates t'deal with, after."

Oh, shit, she's wheelin' t'starboard! Lewrie told himself as he saw her bows begin to swing Northerly; *she'll be blowin' us t'flinders next!*

"*If* she clears the frigate, sir," Westcott said, taking a deep breath as the two-decker barrelled down on the crippled frigate, wheeling with her helm hard down and her tall sides heeling so far over her lower gun-deck ports were only a foot or so above the sea.

"Lay us Due North, sir!" Lewrie snapped to his First Lieutenant. "Mister Spendlove! We will engage the two-decker!"

"Aye, sir!" Lt. Spendlove answered, though Lewrie was sure that he had to gulp in alarm first; in great sea battles, the fighting was left to the line-of-battle ships, and frigates stood by to aid any who needed assistance or to repeat signals down the smoky line. They most-certainly did *not* trade fire with warships that bore three or four times their weight of metal! "That'll open his gun-arcs to nigh abeam," he told Westcott.

"A collision would be nice about now," Lt. Westcott said with a hopeful note to his voice after passing orders to the helmsmen and the brace-tending hands.

"It *could* get int'restin' in a minute or two, either way, sir," Lewrie agreed. "But, does he get past the frigate, he'll use her for a shield against *Modeste*'s fire. Beats the bow-rake he'd have taken, had he swung Sutherly."

Modeste's guns were hammering the French flagship, hulling her "'twixt wind and water," and raising great bursts of paint, splinters, and engrained dirt from her sides. Heeled over as she was, some shot shattered gangway bulwarks, sending rolled up and stowed hammocks and bedding flying like disturbed nests of snakes. But some of *Modeste*'s broadside *was* striking the immoble frigate, not the two-decker as she ducked behind her consort in her frantic turn.

Come on! Ram the bitch! Lewrie prayed in silence, and it did look as if the 74's jib-boom and bow sprit would spear into the starboard mizen shrouds of the frigate, but . . . she slid on past, scraping her larboard bows down the frigate's starboard side. She lost her cat-head timber and larboard bower anchor, and visibly staggered, rolling almost upright for a moment, but . . . she sailed clear with little more damage to show for it.

"By broadside, Mister Spendlove! Open upon her!" Lewrie cried. "*Now*, while she's unable to respond!"

Reliant had come up to nearly a close reach to the North, with the wrecked frigate almost dead astern and the French two-decker only two points astern of lying abeam, and she was still turning, as if to fall in trail of *Reliant* or cut through between *Modeste* and Lewrie's vessel and re-join her fleeing transport. There was a scramble on the gun-deck to shift the aim of the artillery as far aft as possible, but if they *did* fire at such acute angles, when the guns recoiled there would be no controlling their backward lurches. Lt. Spendlove looked up at the quarterdeck with a shrug and a lifting of both arms.

Modeste, clear of the wrecked French frigate, was firing again at the two-decker. The two-decker's larboard side erupted in a reply. The range was only about a cable, and everyone on *Reliant*'s quarterdeck who could look aft let out a groan to see the avalanche of shot that struck *Modeste*'s sides, punched through her sails, and raised feathery plumes of shot-splashes all round her engaged side.

"*Cockerel* and *Pylades* are engaging the trailing Frenchman, sir!" Midshipman Grainger called forward. With no signals to send at that moment, he could use his telescope for his own amusements.

"Sorry, sir," Lt. Spendlove said from the foot of the starboard companionway ladder. "The guns won't bear unless we alter course."

"*Both* batteries, Mister Spendlove," Lewrie answered, leaning to smile at him. "If she's almost dead astern of us, we'll weave about from tack to tack, and rake her bows 'til she takes notice."

"Aye, sir!"

That'll take some of her attention from Modeste, *at any rate*, Lewrie told himself as he went back to the helm to re-join Westcott and explain what he wished.

"May I suggest we haul our wind to larboard for the first shots, sir," Lt. Westcott posed with a brief grin. "Give her the larboard guns, then come back Due North. Else, our East'rd turn would put us dead into the eye of the wind, and in irons if we're not quick about it."

"Very good, Mister Westcott, let's do it. Mister Spendlove . . . larboard battery first! We're going to haul our wind!"

"Aye, sir!"

"Two points down-helm first, Mister Westcott," Lewrie decided after a quick look-about. "Get some way on her, and some lead to windward, so we can lay Spendlove's guns dead abeam."

"Aye, sir! Stations for wear!" Westcott called out to the crew.

Reliant surged up to windward, on a close reach for a moment, with braces hauled in, the deck heeling, and the sea swashing more urgently down her flanks. The French two-decker, still duelling with *Modeste*, shifted from a point off the starboard quarter to a point off her larboard quarter.

"Now, Mister Westcott! Wear her! Stand ready on the guns, Mister Spendlove!" Lewrie snapped.

Reliant lost a lot of her gathered speed as she came about, the decks canting, the masts wheeling cross the skies, pivoting on a wide patch of disturbed, foamed water as she swung to Due West, steadying and laying herself cross the two-decker's course, two cables off . . .

"As . . . you . . . *bear*, Mister Spendlove!" Lewrie yelled.

"*As* you bear . . . *fire!*"

Hard iron round-shot caromed off the sea round the two-decker's bows, dapping from First Graze to smash into her bows. More iron hit her directly, punching holes into her lower gun-deck, ripping away her figurehead, her curving beakhead rails, and bowling down both her upper and lower gun-decks. Her jib-boom disappeared in a cloud of splinters, collapsing her inner jib and outer flying jib, and her fore top-mast stays. As *Reliant*'s shot hit her, Captain Blanding's *Modeste* delivered another broadside, lower deck first, then upper deck and all her carronades, and the French flagship was visibly staggered.

"Stay on this course 'til she's on our larboard quarters, Mister Westcott, then we'll go back on the wind," Lewrie ordered. "Just a bit longer, so our next broadside's at closer range."

"Aye, sir."

"Starboard side next, Mister Spendlove!" Lewrie called down to the waist.

"Signal, sir . . . our number!" Midshipman Grainger said from aft. " 'Engage The Enemy More Closely,' sir!"

"Very well, Mister Grainger. . . . Let's do that. Ready about!" Lewrie replied, grinning. "About . . . now, Mister Westcott!"

Reliant wheeled about to Due North once more, slowing again but placing the French warship square-on to the gun-ports of the starboard battery, with her at a 45-degree angle, a bit West of her course.

"I leave it to you, Mister Spendlove! Serve her a good'un!" he shouted down to the waist.

God, but I love this! Lewrie thought, imagining that he had wakened from a long, dull sleep; *most-like it's all I'm good for, but I* need *this! Big guns, shot, and powder stench! And killin' Frogs!*

"As you *bear . . . fire!"* Spendlove rasped hoarsely.

It would not be a proper bow-rake, but the bulk of their fire *would* slam into the two-decker's forrud larboard quarters this time, the range no more than a single cable, and closing quickly as *Reliant* crossed the Frenchman's course, almost on the ragged edge of the wind, and the Sailing Master, Lt. Westcott, the quartermasters on the wheel watching her luff *damned* close, waiting for the very last gun to fire to order the helm be put up, and haul off from North by West.

"Now, sir!" Lewrie shouted as the last gun aft in his cabins erupted. "Full and by, Due North, and let's get some space ahead of her 'fore we try that again."

"Oh, lovely!" Marine Lieutenant Simcock exulted. Until action was at "close pistol-shot" or until a boarding action was called for, he had no proper duties on the quarterdeck, and had been strolling about, a curious onlooker. *"That'll* ruin their digestion!"

HMS *Modeste* was meeting Captain Blanding's requirements for three broadsides every two minutes, still deliberate and controlled, not a ragged catch-as-catch-can cannonade resembling the firing line of a hunting party potting pheasant, when ships were so close together that gun-captains were allowed to fire at will. She was taking punishment, but she was dealing it out in spades, compared to the speed and skill of the French. *Modeste's* last broadside had struck almost in conjunction with *Reliant's* raking fire, and they had just mauled her together.

Upper bulwarks were disappearing in great clouds of shattered wood; the two-decker's mizen mast was hit below the fighting top and *leaped* skyward for an instant before crashing down over her quarterdeck and poop, falling to larboard, alee, like a titanic sweep-oar to drag into the sea. With her helm crushed under all that wreckage she began to slew downwind! The light upper masts and top-masts slashed down separately, raking away stays and main-mast yards and sails before slamming down into her waist, as well. She sagged further downwind . . .

"Wear, Mister Westcott!" Lewrie snapped, seizing the opportunity. *"Larboard* battery, Mister Spendlove, and it'll be a *proper* bow-rake this time!"

The French flagship was losing way, painfully turning alee and sagging towards *Modeste*'s waiting guns as *Reliant* came off the wind to a reciprocal course, Due South. The enemy's bows were square-on to her and the range . . . ! Slow as all the manoeuvring had made her, *Reliant* would be very close this time, no more than 150 yards under her bows for the broadside.

Ruin yer digestion, aye! Lewrie thought in murderous joy, hammering his fists on the cross-deck hammock nettings to urge his gunners to take advantage of this sudden change in fortune; *rip yer bloody guts out, more-like! Blow yer bloody* heart *out! Come on, come on!*

The last of the round-shot was being rammed home; the wads were being shoved down the muzzles; quills were inserted; flintlock strikers were cocked, and trigger lines hauled taut!

"*As you bear . . . fire!*" both Spendlove and Merriman shouted.

"I think she's *struck*, by God!" Lt. Westcott exclaimed, opinion lost in the deafening bellows of the guns. "Sir? Captain, sir?"

Ignore him! Lewrie told himself, eyes intent on the damage they were causing as each piece erupted in smoke, flames, and sparks, then leaped rearwards; *I want* gore!

Reliant sailed on past the devastation, the broadside done.

"Mister Westcott, up-helm and steer Sou'west before we tangle with *Modeste*."

Their own flagship was only a cable off their larboard beam as they swung away alee of her, scampering to avoid being trampled.

"You say something, Mister Westcott?" Lewrie asked, massaging his ringing ears as if he hadn't quite heard what he'd said.

"I think she's struck, sir. Yes! There's all her colours on the way down, sir! We've *beat* them, sir! They've *struck* to us!" Lt. Westcott came close to say, to point his arm at the foe. "Glorious!"

"Ah, well. Hmm, in that case . . . Mister Spendlove, Mister Merriman . . . stand easy!" Lewrie ordered, taking out his pocket-watch to ascertain the time, as if it was no great matter at all, although he felt sudden rage to be denied complete vengeance. He had to *play-act* a proper, phlegmatic sea captain!

"Deck, there!" a main-mast lookout shouted down. "T'other frigate's struck t' *Cockerel* an' *Pylades*!"

Fourty-five minutes! Lewrie marvelled; *not a whole hour, and it's* done? *Goddamn the cowardly . . . !*

"Secure from Quarters, sir," Lewrie told Westcott, who was congratulating the men of the Afterguard, the quarterdeck gun crews, and the helmsmen. "And ready the ship's boats to take charge of the foe. Mister Simcock? Work for your Marines, t'guard the prisoners."

"*Most* welcome, sir!" Simcock crowed back.

Lewrie went to one of the larboard quarterdeck carronades and clambered atop it to the bulwarks, then into the mizen stays and rat-lines so he could ascend a few feet above the deck to look things over with a glass. *Cockerel* and *Pylades* lay to either beam of the trailing French frigate, all three warships fetched-to, and boats already working between them; she looked mostly undamaged, with all her masts still standing and her sails whole. The first frigate was still wallowing and rocking, and Lewrie could see gushes of water jetting overside from her bilge pumps.

"Two frigates and a Seventy-Four, why, that has t'be worth at least fifty, sixty thousand pounds for the lot!" the Sailing Master was speculating aloud. "Two years' pay for every Man Jack, I wager!"

"Goddamned *sham* sailors, you bloody, cowardly . . . bastards!" Lewrie muttered under his breath. "Mine arse on a band-box, is that all the fight ye had in ye?" he said, louder. "Over four thousand or more miles we came . . . for *this*, damn yer thin French blood?"

"Sir?" Lt. Westcott asked from below him. "You said something?"

"I said the Frogs are a lot o' poltroons who don't have grit enough for a real fight, Mister Westcott," Lewrie gravelled, descending from his perch. "I s'pose we should come about and work our way under *Modeste*'s lee."

"Marvellous, sir!" Lt. Merriman was saying as he mounted to the quarterdeck. "D'ye know . . . we've but two hands wounded, none dead? One fellow was splintered in the foremast top, and one of my gunners had his ankle broken in the recoil tackle. Bloody miraculous, what?"

"Signal from the flag, sir . . . our number!" Midshipman Grainger intruded with a sharp cry. " 'General Chase' and 'Transport,' sir!"

"The Indiaman, too, hmm," Mr. Caldwell, the Sailing Master, speculated further. "That might mean another ten thousand pounds, all told. Head-and-gun money on all their soldiers, too, what?"

"She can't be more than . . . an hour ahead of us, sir," Westcott said, consulting his own timepiece. "Crack on for Pass a La Loutre, sir?"

"Aye, Mister Westcott," Lewrie agreed, pretending to perk up in false glee . . . when what he wanted to do, most *dearly* wanted to do, was send his hands back to the guns, barge up to the nearest French ship, and *finish* the job, the prize-money bedamned! "Mister Caldwell . . . the best, direct course for Pass a La Loutre, if you please. We've a ship to catch up 'fore dark."

"Aye aye, sir!" the Sailing Master responded, still rubbing his hands together as he turned to the traverse board to consult a chart.

"Three cheers, lads!" Midshipman the Honourable Entwhistle was urging down in the waist as the last cannon was secured and cleaned. "Three cheers for our good *Reliant!*"

"Three cheers for Captain Lewrie, huzzah!" Midshipman Houghton added. "It's *victory!*"

Bloody toady! Lewrie sourly thought, squirming inside to hear that burst of cheering, hooting, and clapping in his honour. Oh, he had to recognise it, standing at the forward edge of the quarterdeck, and look down into the ship's waist, where his crew capered and danced in joy of their first battle together, and their victory. He had to doff his hat to them, nod his head, yet keep a stern demeanour. That wasn't all that hard, for anger still rumbled in him for being cheated of the ocean of French gore he so heartily desired.

"Three cheers for *yourselves,* men!" he shouted as the din died down a bit. "For three rounds every two minutes, and good gunnery!"

That went down like a Christmas pudding, and pleased them right down to their toes. He envied them their jubilation.

"Now, lads . . . we've a last ship t'take, over yonder," Lewrie told them, pointing Westward with his hat. "and that'll make it a clean sweep. Are ye ready for one more?"

"Aye, sir! Aye! Let's be at 'em!" they shouted back.

"Then, let's be about it!" Lewrie shouted. "Soon as we're steady on course, we'll splice the main-brace!"

"Best course will be Sou'west by West, sir," the Sailing Master supplied as he turned away from their last cheers.

"Make it so, Mister Westcott." Lewrie ordered. "Sou'west by West, and crack on."

CHAPTER FORTY-EIGHT

*A*nd take her they did, sixteen miles from the entrance to the Mississippi, out of sight of land and any watchers from Fort Balise or the delta shoal islands. She was a converted two-decker Third Rate, sailing *en flute* with only half her lower-deck guns and none of her upper-deck artillery. Even before *Reliant* fetched up to her at Range to Random Shot, she struck her colours and reduced sail, stealing any hopes that Lewrie might have nourished that there would be more fighting. There would be no more vengeance to be exacted.

When Lewrie went aboard with his boat crew and half the Marine complement, even he could not summon up any more anger. The two-decker carried only two companies of French infantry and was not manned to the establishment, either—there were not over 120 of them, led by an older Major, who openly wept as he handed over his unit's colours and his sword. There should have been a full regiment, the Major explained through an interpreter, but sickness on-passage, sickness once they had reached Cape François, and the desperate need for defenders on St. Domingue to hold off the savage slave army had reduced their numbers.

"*Et l'embarras des réfugiés, m'sieur,*" the Major said, waving an arm about the decks, shrugging helplessly, and swiping at his eyes with a calico handkerchief.

"Yes, I see," Lewrie told him, looking past him to the hundreds of civilians aboard; older men and matrons, married couples with their children, so *many* children.

"*Tant de pauvres orphelins*," the Major added with a huge sigh and a sniffle. His captains and lieutenants standing behind him were just as morose as their commanding officer, and even the French sailors were hangdog miserable. "So many orphans, *m'sieur*," the interpreter said. "Zey 'ave nozzing left, mos' of zem. What zey 'ave to wear, everyone."

Lewrie glowered as he paced about the quarterdeck of the ship as it wallowed and rolled, fetched-to and with the way off her. There were simply too many frightened, utterly miserable faces to avoid, too many pathetic pleas in their eyes.

Damn 'em! Lewrie thought; *I should take 'em all back to Jamaica, intern 'em 'til their evacuation's arranged back to France, but . . .*

His men were busy gathering gun-tools, muskets, and short hangers and bayonets by the boat-load, disarming the soldiers and emptying the ship's arms chests to leave them nothing with which to resist or rise up in the Middle Watch once back out at sea for Kingston, and a Prize Court.

He owed these pathetic Frogs *nothing*, not after what they had done to him . . . to Caroline, yet . . .

"You send zem to ze hulks, *m'sieur?*" the interpreter wheedled as he dogged Lewrie's steps. "Turn zis ship to ze prison? Zey *perish*, *m'sieur!* You mak *retourner au* . . . send them *back*, back, *n'est-ce pas?* Back to Le Cap, ze *Noirs sauvages* will mak ze *massacre!*"

"Oh, stop yer bloody gob!" Lewrie snapped at him, going back to the entry-port to look down at his empty boats. He pursed his lips, thinking hard. He looked round, and everywhere there were French men, children, and women, all looking at him in dread, some softly weeping into their handkerchiefs; children wailed and clung to their parents' legs or skirts . . .

Lewrie went back to the interpreter, pointing him towards the two-decker's captain. "Ask him how many boats he has. Four, that all? And how many refugees per boat does he judge would be safe, given the weather and sea state? Only sixty at a time? Damn! How many of 'em are there? Over three *hundred*? *Hell* and damn!"

It would be impossible, even if the French seamen cooperated to the utmost. With his three ship's boats, and the Frenchman's, he *might* be able to land ninety or so per trip ashore, four trips in all, but he would have to close the coast to within half a mile or more, violating Spanish territory and raising one hell of a diplomatic stink. Louisiana was still Spanish; the hand-over to France had not yet happened as far as he knew. Better for him if it *had* reverted to France; then he could barge into enemy waters with impunity.

If the French sailors manning the oars refused to return for a second load, preferring to scamper and escape imprisonment, it would be over before it began.

And land them where? Lewrie paced to the shoreward bulwarks, hands in the small of his back, recalling how bleak and barren were the alluvial Mississippi Delta shoals either side of the Passes, both banks of the main river.

Might as well maroon 'em on the Chandeleurs! he scoffed; *an hundred miles down-river from New Orleans? Close to Fort Balise? Damn!*

That would do the refugees no good; Fort Balise was but lightly garrisoned, a joke on the term *fort*, and most-like the few Dons there lived hand-to-mouth already and would have no victuals to share. *And* there was the problem of a British warship in a Spanish river again.

Even if he *could* land them there, in the name of Christian charity, how long would it be before the Spanish got word upriver and sent a boat back to Fort Balise with extra food?

He turned to look North.

The squadron's *got boats!* he realised; *do we take this ship and our other prizes into the Mississippi Sound, anchor up near Old Biloxi, we could barge 'em into Lake Borgne and land 'em on that little beach I found. From there, it's only fifteen miles up the Chef Menteur road t'New Orleans! Send a letter along with 'em. . . . What's the bloody name o' that Panton, Leslie trade agent I worked with? Pollock. Gideon Pollock, aye!*

And if the squadron used all thirteen of their own ship's boats, commandeered all the undamaged French ship's boats, manned by British tars, there would be no risk of losing prisoners who could not be trusted to honour their temporary parole!

He went back to midships of the quarterdeck, to the interpreter once more. "Tell them that I mean t'get the civilians ashore, but not here. Tell the Major I must order him, his officers, and soldiers to go below. *M'sieur capitaine*, he and his officers will go aft, under guard, as well, along with his sailors. Warn them that any attempt at revolt will result in great bloodshed.

"I will *not* take them back to Saint Domingue, tell them!" Lewrie snapped, cutting off the quick objections. "The civilian refugees will be allowed to go to New Orleans . . . the short way, up yonder," he said, pointing an arm to the North. "Any resistance on the part of the crew of this ship, or the soldiers aboard, and they will *not*. *Comprendre?*"

"*M'sieur*, you swear? Zat zey will . . . ?" the interpreter pled.

"Upon my sacred honour and the honour of my country," he told him. "And I will require the same oath from every officer here. Upon their sacred, personal honour and . . . the sacred honour of France."

And pray God I don't have t'say that more'n once a century! he thought, keeping his phyz stern and immobile, though the idea of "the sacred honour of France" almost made him gag.

They swore, some reluctantly, but they swore, then dispersed to be herded below and locked away under Marine guard.

"Desmond? Row back to *Reliant* and deliver my compliments to Lieutenant Westcott, and bid him ferry over a prize-crew . . . armed to the teeth, mind. We will sail back to re-join the squadron."

"Aye, sor! Come on, Pat," his Cox'n replied.

"That Frog shit doesn't sup with us this evening, sir?" Lewrie asked as Captain Blanding hosted his captains in his poop cabins, ten days after the action, and almost to Kingston, Jamaica.

"Captain Julien Decean . . . our *worthy* French *opponent*, is under the weather, Captain Lewrie," Blanding replied with a wink as his steward indicated that supper was ready to be served. "A dyspeptic distress to his touchy digestion. Don't much care for English cooking, it would appear," Blanding added as he thumped his chair close to the table, so the napkin he tucked into his neck-stock could cover his girth. "There is also the matter that he feels we didn't quite fight fair."

"Man's an idiot, sir," Blanding's First Lieutenant, Gilbraith, commented. "The very idea that he expected to penetrate a line and separate us into defeatable pieces, ha! Ah, portable soup!"

"Well, Admiral Duncan did at Camperdown, Mister Gilbraith, and doubled on the Dutch," Lewrie pointed out as a bowl of soup was placed before him. "If he'd had equal numbers, well . . . or, was it tried in a *fleet* action, with two or three columns."

"Let us pray that their Navy is *full* of such dubious tacticians and lofty fools." Captain Parham chuckled. "Perhaps we should send him back to them, to let him try it on again?"

"As few of our Post-Captains are in French custody, it may be a *long* while before Decean is exchanged," Captain Blanding drawled as he tested how hot his soup was, blew on a spoonful, then tasted it. "We may only *hope* that men of his stripe are entrusted with the command of their ships. And that Napoleon Bonaparte continues to be as ignorant of the sea as he seems, and continues to appoint men like Decean."

"Hear, hear!" Captain Stroud of *Cockerel* heartily agreed.

"Upon my word, Captain Lewrie," Blanding went on, "but I would not have suspected you to possess a shred of charity towards the French, given your, uhm . . . dealings with the devils, but . . . I must own that it would have cut a bit rough with me to be so heartless as to doom those refugees to a Jamaican holding pen. We don't make war on helpless civilians. It just ain't Christian!"

"Hear, hear, sir!" Lt. Gilbraith seconded between quick slurps.

"A most fitting end to our endeavour, indeed," Chaplain Brundish stuck in. "It is one thing to show implacable wrath to those most deserving of it, yet quite another to extend the sweet, kind hand of mercy to those who do not. So British, so English, that it makes me swell with pride to be Church of England."

"Well said, sir!" Captain Blanding exclaimed. "A *most* fitting act to gild the laurel wreaths of our victory. For which we have Captain Lewrie to thank for the suggestion."

"Hear, hear!" Captain Stroud piped up, lifting his glass.

Toady! Lewrie sourly thought.

"Well . . . thankee for sayin' so, sir," Lewrie said, striving for proper modesty. "And for acceptin' my thoughts on what t'do with 'em all. Not *their* fault they're French . . . those refugees."

"I dare say," Chaplain Brundish said after a sip of wine and a dab at his lips with his napkin, "that news of our victory, as well as our merciful conclusion to it, will make *all* good Englishmen swell in pride, when it is made known in the papers back home."

"That, and the casualty list," Capt. Parham of *Pylades* added, looking slyly droll.

"Aye, Parham . . . not over a dozen of ours slain, not two dozen wounded," Captain Stroud proudly said, "The most *Modeste*'s, sorry to say, but then, you *did* bear the brunt of the action, sir. Most proficiently and ably. As opposed to the French losses, that is."

Blanding bowed in place, pleased as punch by the compliment.

"Aye, the Mob'll be mad for it," Lewrie commented.

It was what the Publick at home had come to expect of the Royal Navy, the impossible victory by an out-numbered, out-gunned squadron or lighter single frigate 'gainst a bigger, with a pleasing "butcher's bill" of enemy slain to report in the papers.

That they had accomplished; the leading French frigate had had over 350 men aboard—they always over-manned—and when she had struck and been boarded, nigh half of them were dead or wounded, with the rest staggering round in shock or slumped dead-drunk after breaking into the spirits stores of brandy, wine, rum, *ratafia*, or arrack. The French flagship had had over 700 in her crew, and a quarter of *them* had perished or been horribly maimed.

The trailing frigate that had struck to *Cockerel* and *Pylades* . . . well, that was another sterling example of British pluck and daring, and French timidity; though she had taken very little damage and very few casualties, her captain had seen the futility of vigourous resistance and had fired off only two or three broadsides before striking her colours and surrendering. Parham, a considerate young man towards his sailors, seemed satisfied, though Stroud, out to make a name for himself, Lewrie suspected, still seemed disappointed.

"As we lay up treasure of a temporal nature in a Prize-Court, I expect we also lay up *more* treasure with Admiralty, and the nation, for a job well done," Captain Blanding congratulated himself smugly as his soup bowl was removed and a fresh plate laid before him. "Oh, the sea-pie, good ho!"

"And treasure in Heaven, sir," Chaplain Brundish added with a deep, blessing-like nod of his head, "for the Christian mercy bestowed upon the innocent at its conclusion."

"Quite so, ha ha!" Stroud seconded.

"We may only hope that our *temporal* treasure will be paid out in honest measure, though, sirs," Lewrie said as he took a fork full of the hearty sea-pie. "There are half a dozen prize-agents at Kingston, and only one or two may be trusted not t'scalp us bald. I know of only one I ever dealt with who played me fair, and God only knows if he's still in business, after the long peace."

"Bedad, yes!" Blanding exclaimed. "Why, between the four ships we took, all of them French *National* ships, not merchantmen, there may be an hundred thousand pounds owing . . . and *none* of it due to Admiral Duckworth, haw haw!"

"Head-And-Gun Money on the two-decker transport, too," Stroud reminded them. "All those soldiers, to boot?"

"Be months before they're condemned and bought in to the Navy," Blanding cautioned. "Even so, some *small* advances may be made to us."

"Enough for a proper wine cellar, I trust," Captain Parham enthused, chuckling. "Serving with Captain Lewrie in the past, I gained an appreciation for fine wines . . . and lashings of prize-money from our previous captures. Some of the ships we took back then, their masters or captains were possessed of discerning palates, were they not, sir?"

"A few of 'em, aye, Parham," Lewrie wistfully agreed, "but some with the taste of Philistines. The piratical sorts, mostly."

"And what might you do with your spoils, Captain Lewrie? Any special wishes?" Stroud asked, *trying* to be "chummy."

"You know . . . ," Lewrie said, sitting back to ponder that query for a long moment. He took a sip of wine, then grinned. "I think I will buy a penny-whistle."

To the rest, it was a jape, an amazement.

But Lewrie really *meant* it.

EPILOGUE

...that if good men called werriours
Would take in hand for the commons succours,
To purge the Sea unto our great avayle,
And winne hem goods, and have up the sayle,
And on our enemies their lives to impart,
So that they might their prises well depart,
As reason wold, justice and equitie;
To make this land have Lordship of the Sea.

HAKLUYT'S VOYAGES

CHAPTER FORTY-NINE

Uhm . . . strictly speaking, sir," Lt. Westcott said, "the transport we took. The rest of the squadron wasn't 'In Sight' when we took her. Would she not he *our* prize, alone, sir?"

"In the spirit of amity, I allowed Captain Blanding to present her as a squadron capture, Mister Westcott," Lewrie told his First Officer. Lewrie looked over his shoulder through the opened sash-windows of *Reliant*'s transom at their prizes, now safely anchored in Kingston Harbour under guard of the Jamaica Station, with all their prisoners penned up aboard the hulks or in shore prisons, and felt a smug pride to see the French Tricolours idly flapping beneath Union Flags.

Lewrie was being his usual lazy self, stretched out on the transom settee cushions in white slop-trousers and shirt, with the sleeves rolled to his elbows, propped up on an upright timber.

"A piddlin' matter, Mister Westcott," he told his First Officer. "After the fulsome things he wrote about us to Admiralty." He shrugged and grinned, pointing to the prizes. "They'll be goin' home after the hurricane season's done. Months from now, dependin' on the ruling of the Prize Court. A man who commands one for the passage stands a good chance of promotion, once back in England. Interested, sir? Should I put your name forward, or let Rear-Admiral Sir John Duckworth reward one o' his favourites?"

"Not really, sir," Lt. Westcott replied, shaking his head as he sat in a chair near Lewrie's desk, nursing a tumbler of cool tea. "I'd prefer to remain in *Reliant*."

"Better 'the Devil you know,' Mister Westcott?" Lewrie japed.

"More like . . . liking the company I keep, sir," Westcott said, flashing one of his brief, toothy grins.

"Good, then. For my part, I'd hate to lose you," Lewrie told him, glad of that news. "Ye never can tell . . . we might get stuck into some new harum-scarum adventures. Or, like the old sayin' goes, 'His men'd follow him anywhere . . . just t'see what he'd get into next'?"

Westcott diplomatically said nothing, just laughed, then began to gather up the paperwork they had been going over, preparing to leave. "By the by, sir, the Purser and the Surgeon have found a source ashore for citronella oils and candles to combat the fevers. They're not at all expensive, in bulk, but they don't know how much to purchase and, ah . . . it would be an out-of-pocket expense, not covered by the Admiralty Board."

"I'll speak to them," Lewrie replied, though he had left things to his former Ship's Surgeon, Mr. Durant, and hadn't a clue how much it would take to fume the ship each day at anchor. He got to his feet to see Westcott to the forrud door of the great-cabins.

"Oh, your mail's on your desk, sir," Westcott reminded him.

"Thankee, Mister Westcott. Whilst you find some amusement in the town, I'll have that and my new penny-whistle to keep me amused. Good day to you, sir."

"Good day, sir," Lt. Westcott said, departing.

Once Westcott had left the great-cabins, Lewrie bade Pettus to pour him another glass of cold tea and sat at his desk to sort through his letters. They had left England in late May, and here it was late September, and this was the first correspondence the ship had gotten.

He looked through the official letters first, dealt with what few required answers or explanations, then turned to the personal mail. There was one from Hugh, aboard *Pegasus*, and he tore into it.

The lad was prospering nicely, Captain Charlton was very kind to him, and he was learning his trade among a swarm of other Midshipmen, most of whom were friendly; he had not fallen for most of their japes played on "newlies," though he had been the victim of a few new ones that Lewrie had never heard of.

Lewrie grimaced as he picked up one from his father and broke the wax seal, sure that he was now a thousand pounds richer, but a lot poorer in land or house.

My son (his father began)
*I write to inform you of the most Distressing turn of Events anene your
eldest, Sewallis.*

"Oh, Christ!" Lewrie groaned, passing a hand over his eyes; had he
not suffered enough this last year?

He did not *return to his school, though I assure you I saw him into the coach
myself. He has run away to Sea, employing his term Tuition, extra-
curricular Fees, and a sum of Money he evidently had saved up, including,
I regret to admit, ten pounds I gave him as a gift for sweets and such.*

"Mine arse on a *band-box!*" Lewrie yelped, jerking to his feet.

*After I did not receive any correspondence from him for a fortnight, he sent
me a Letter from Sheerness, just before I was going to coach to his School
to ask of him and his Health* (his father's missive continued)
     *With more Guile and Perserverance than we may have ever given the
lad credit for, he kitted himself out as a Midshipman, and has found
himself a captain willing to take him on. He boasted in his Letter that he
had employed a rough draft of one you penned when first seeking a place for
Hugh, copying it and substituting his own name, forging your Signature
as best he was able . . .*

"Holy shit on a *biscuit!*" Lewrie gawped. "Forgery *does* run in the family! Christ, the damned little *fool!*"

*. . . two, actually, one to Admiralty, and one to give to a Captain Benja-
min Rodgers, fitting out his Third Rate,* Aeneas, *for Channel Fleet. He
posted his Letter the very hour of Sailing, so I was unable to retrieve him,
and, I must confess, am loath to take the Matter to the attention of
Admiralty, or his new Captain, lest our family's good Name, and Sewallis's Repute, be tainted forever by the admission of Forgery. In short, I am
at a loss as to what to do which would not redound to our good credit.*

"Didn't know we *had* any!" Lewrie gravelled as he paced about.

For the nonce (his father went on) *I have sent the lad a note-of-hand for
fifty pounds' spending Money with which to keep himself in his Mess,*

along with a stern letter of Admonishment, but I do not know what else we may do!

"And neither do I, Goddammit!" Lewrie spat, fetching up near the open transom windows once more, his shock deflating with a long sigh of exasperation. "What got *into* him?" he muttered. "He ain't cut out for this life! He ain't tough enough t'prosper!"

"Bad news, sir?" Pettus asked as he and Jessop tidied up the great-cabins.

"Uh, no, not really," Lewrie lied. "S'prised, more-like." He looked down to the letter once more, reading . . .

It may be for the best, Alan. Sewallis has need of exposure to Life and its Harshness. In the end his Actions may make a Man of him. He is a Lewrie, and partly a Willoughby, may I so imagine. At any rate, it is his Choice, rash and foolhardy though it may be. He has made his bed; perhaps we must allow him to lie in it, and make his own Way.

But, if he's a miserable failure at it, he's ruined forever, Lewrie thought, sitting down on the transom settee again, the letter drooped from a limp hand, conjuring how crushed the gentle, scholarly, and stiffly withdrawn Sewallis would come out of it; of how jaundiced he would be against himself for his failure, or any other career open to him once sent ashore as a cack-handed, cunny-thumbed "lubber."

"Why the Hell did God ever let *me* be a father?" Lewrie whispered. "Surely, He knew I'd be so miserable at it . . . poor, wee chuck."

Still, Sewallis *was* scholarly, and learned quickly, retaining facts like a sponge. If he was reticent, he was bookish and good at mathematics, so he might turn out to be a dab-hand navigator. They'd taught him how to shoot and ride and handle a sword. If he was shy, he'd be the butt of all the japes in his mess, perhaps be bullied by the older, crueller lads, but . . . surely he'd already survived treatment like that at his schools.

It wasn't as if the lad had gone to sea with stars in his eyes, after all, and it hadn't been done on a passing whim; he'd *schemed* to get ready for it. He was *determined*.

I never knew he had the pluck*!* Lewrie realised; *I'd've expected it of* Hugh, *were he the eldest, but . . . Sewallis?*

"So be it," Lewrie muttered. "He's on his own bottom. Least he's Benjamin Rodgers for a captain, in a seventy-four."

There would be fifteen or more other Midshipmen aboard ... HMS *Aeneas*, was it? No one would expect too much, right off, of a "Johnny New-Come" in such a large mess. And if *Aeneas* was down for Channel Fleet, she'd most-like serve on the blockade of France, far out to sea with a squadron of line-of-battle ships, not close inshore with the frigates and sloops, in almost constant risk of going aground, or much in the way of fighting, either. The lad might never hear a gun fired in anger! Which fact settled Lewrie's fears, somewhat.

Now, what Anglesgreen, his neighbours, and his family and in-laws would make of it was another matter. They would naturally decide that he'd *deliberately* sent Sewallis to sea, the facts bedamned!

He looked back to his father's letter, noting that Sir Hugo had urged Sewallis to write and confess it all, to be a man about what he had done. *That'll be a wonder, when it comes, I'd wager,* Lewrie told himself with a cynical snort.

> *As for other matters* (his father continued) *your Property is still in negotiation, with Phineas Chiswick unwilling to pay more than £1,000, though I hear that he intends to garner £4,000 when he sells to the Trenchers. We hold out for £1,500.*
>
> *My pardons if the subject is still Grievous, but you mentioned one Sir Pulteney Plumb and his wife, Lady Imogene, whom you said had been of great Avail when you & your late Wife fled Paris, and France, shortly after the Services. After consulting DeBrett's, I could find no evidence that a man of that Name has ever been Knighted, nor any Plumb, for that matter.*
>
> *A fortnight ago, though, I attended a new Theatre in the Hay Market with Brigadier Heathcote, a friend at Horse Guards, and who should be the Owner, and lead Actor in the Sketches but one Pulteney Plumb, assisted by his émigré Wife, Imogene? While not a Garrick, this Plumb was quite impressive at Comic turns, but a few seconds behind a Screen where coat or wig changes transformed him to half a dozen roles & the same for his Wife! Their entire Show is a series of Entre-Acts employing Jugglers, Mimes, and scantily-clad girls as well as Song & Dance turns.*
>
> *Heathcote, of an Age with me, was All-Amort, for he remembered an Ensign Pulteney Plumb, then in his late Teens, on the Staff of "Gentleman Johnny" Burgoyne round the time of that worthy's Defeat and Surrender to the Yankee Doodles at Saratoga. Heathcote, a Lieutenant then, further recalled to me that this Plumb fellow was appointed more for his theatric Abilities than his Martial skills, Gen. Burgoyne famed for his*

own amateur Acting and Play Writing. There was some Scandal anent Plumb, who sold up his Commission before a Court-Martial could be Convened, though after 25 Yrs. the Particulars escape Heathcote's Memory. If ever back in London, you might attend, for the Girls are quite Fetching, and . . . Obliging, ha! The man must have Prospered nicely, for Plumb owns the Theatre, a Townhouse, and a retreat out in Islington as well as several other rental Lodgings, I have learned. . . .

Lewrie felt a fresh shudder of dread to think that he had put his life in the hands of a comic, quick-change *artiste*, a mountebank, and an utter fraud! It could have gone a *lot* worse!

"The Yellow Tansy, mine arse!" he gravelled, picking up another letter. "Hello! A Captain Speaks? Oh, yes," he muttered, breaking the wax seal and opening it, relieved that Speaks, whom he had replaced in command of HMS *Thermopylae*, had survived his pneumonia.

Sir,
There were four coal-burning Franklin-pattern stoves when you relieved me of Command, Stoves which I had Purchased with my own Funds for the Comfort & Health of my Officers & Men. Where the Hell are They? I am unable to contact the Purser, Mr. Pridemore, as to the Whereabouts & can discover no trace of them with shore Authorities at Chatham or Sheerness when Thermopylae *was laid up In-Ordinary.*

 They are quite Valuable. I would not like to entertain the Notion that a Post-Captain & Commission Sea Officer so Distinguished could be so remiss as to lose them, or sell them for Personal Gain, but . . . do you know their Whereabouts, I urge you to discover it to me by the next Post, else I shall press a suit in the London Court of Common Pleas to recover the Stoves, or their Value!"

"Oh, Christ," Lewrie said with a disbelieving groan. "Another bloody court appearance?" It was too silly to be countenanced. He called for his steward.

"Aye, sir?" Pettus replied.

"My shore-goin' rig," Lewrie said, shovelling that letter into a desk drawer . . . for *much* later.

"Right away, sir!"

I've earned it, I'm due it, Lewrie told himself as he rose to dress; *I'm goin' ashore, and get very, very, very bloody-drunk!*

AFTERWORD

$\mathcal{A}$fter the initial sense of relief the English people felt when told of the Peace of Amiens, they soon realised that there really was no living with an expansionist, republican France, or Napoleon and his ambitions, and that the war would re-erupt sooner or later. When it did start again, they were *mad* for it, volunteeering by the hundreds of thousands for the Army and Navy. The Addington goverment was pressured from the sidelines from the outset by Lord Grenville, Windham, the ousted William Pitt, and later by the king himself, to goad the French into taking the blame for it by the means described in this tale.

And when the Crown finally sent Napoleon an ambassador, their pick was the haughty, supercilious, top-lofty Lord Whitworth, who with his wife, the equally insulting Duchess of Dorset, could piss off just about anyone, from boot-blacks to saints, most especially the touchy Napoleon Bonaparte!

There are two very good books I can recommend to readers with a desire for more background; *Napoleon* by Vincent Cronin, a wonderful biography, and *The War of Wars* by Robert Harvey, which covers all the events of the French Revolutionary War and the Napoleonic War, from the start of the Revolution to Waterloo, providing even more insight into Napoleon's life.

It was not Napoleon's short stature that formed his psychobabble

"Napoleon Complex"; most people *were* short in those days. His insecurity came more from a lifetime of being the perennial outsider, and a poor one at that. More Italian and near-peasant Corsican than a Frenchman, even if the Buonapartes were very minor *aristos* in their provincial hometown of Bastia; jeered at for his olive complexion, his grammatical errors when speaking or writing French that wasn't pure Parisian; his simple tastes in food and wine, and his utter shyness at his schools. He *might've* only had one testicle, too, and if the provenance of the physical remains of his privates are true, he could have been cruelly teased as "Pinky-Finger the Flea F ___ er" by prostitutes he hired, or early lovers he attempted to woo.

Once in a position of power and wealth—recall he *was* Corsican, born to the *vendetta*, the "Get Even"—he trusted his (untrustworthy) kinfolk who were just like him, rather than more sophisticated and more capable people than himself.

One of the things that *really* got up Napoleon's nose were the British papers, and the caricatures of him which depicted him as an African, an Arab after his failed Egyptian Campaign, a *wee* fellow with a big nose and a yellow complexion (think Homer Simpson), and he truly didn't understand that the Crown could not censor or stifle those caricature artists, essayists, and editorialists like he could any French paper that did not please him.

Napoleon could make himself Consul for Life, crown *himself* the Emperor of the French, form a Bonaparte dynasty with his brothers and sisters to rule the rest of Europe, with all the trappings of a Roman emperor, yet never understood why the world treated him like a boorish *nouveau riche parvenu*! That rankled him!

New Orleans and the Louisiana Territory . . . Man, is Charité de Guilleri going to be mad enough to kick furniture when she learns that Napoleon will sell it all to the United States to finance his new war! Enough so to try to murder him in a future book, perhaps? Talleyrand, the French foreign minister, was negotiating with the American emissaries, Livingston and Monroe, in Paris, offering not just New Orleans but the whole kit and kaboodle" for a hundred million francs, and dealing under the table for a cut of it to support his hedonistic lifestyle. Napoleon *did* want a French Empire in North America but, with a war sure to come, saw that he could not hold it for long. "They [the American Commissioners] ask of me one town in Louisiana; but I already consider the colony as entirely lost," Napoleon wrote, according to George W. Cable in *The Creoles of Louisiana*. Congress actually debated whether to pony up all that much "whip-out," or just march down to New Orleans and take the bloody place . . . S'truth!

Cable also cites Napoleon's private conversation in the gardens of St. Cloud with M. Mirabois, one of his ministers he trusted a *lot* more than Talleyrand, even then: "Well! You have charge of the Treasury; let them pay you 100 million *francs*, pay their own claims (from the Quasi-War, US vs. France, in 1798) and take the whole country." When asked about the sentiment of the French in Louisiana, who had longed to be re-united to France, he rather coldly told Mirabois to "send your maxims to the London market." Napoleon always was a cold-blooded bastard when it came to what France thought, or to his casualty lists.

M. Laussat, a French colonial prefect, with a very small, mostly *civilian* party, reached New Orleans on March 26, 1803, to let those Creoles know they would soon become French again, and that General Victor (remember him, loafing around in Holland, waiting for a slant of wind?) would follow with a large army to secure the territory.

On November 30, 1803, the official exchange was held in the Place d'Armes before St. Louis Cathedral; cannon were fired, the flag of Spain was lowered, and the Tricolour soared aloft to the tune of "La Marseillaise"; the keys to the city of New Orleans were handed to Laussat, to the delirious joy of Louisianans.

Just twenty days later, however, on December 20, Laussat handed those same keys over to representatives of the United States, and the grand illusion was over, to Louisianans' utter consternation.

The bulk of the troops present were American; there was no Gen. Victor, no "large body of French soldiers," and the actual French contribution *might* have amounted to a Corporal's Guard. With so few weeks between exchanges, there certainly were some bemused Spanish troops loafing about to witness it all, waiting for a ship out.

Now, was that Captain Blanding's and Lewrie's handiwork? I'd certainly like to imagine that their taking of those ships off the Chandeleurs caused their absence. After all, that's what historical fiction is all about . . . ain't it?

So here's Alan Lewrie with his lifelong nemesis, that crooked Guillaume Choundas, dead as mutton, and the 1803 version of PetSmart crab food;

his house and rented land sure to be lost (hey, it happens in the best of families, don't it!) and not one, but *two,* sons in the Royal Navy! Will Sewallis prove to be good at it, or will he come a cropper and rue his forgery and his decision? Hugh is in good hands, but will *he* survive and prosper?

Lewrie has had his period of grief and mourning; the demands of his frigate, his men, and the Navy are now his life, but . . . at some point in the future, we all know the life of a monkish widower simply can't be tolerated any longer, and it's good odds he'll kick over the traces and get back to his old troubles ashore, in his idle hours.

And what about those pestiferous Franklin-pattern stoves? Will he end up in court *again?* If he can't find what Mr. Pridemore did with them, will the prize-money due for the defeated French squadron get him off the hook?

All these matters, and a few more—perhaps with some naughty bits slung in for giggles . . . will be revealed in the forthcoming installment of the Alan Lewrie naval adventures . . . or mis-adventures, so please you! My editor and I have settled on the title *The Invasion Year.* 'Til then . . . enjoy!